Heavenly Places

To Jessica, my dear and beautiful friend.

Arvil Jones, PhD.

Ernestine Smith and **Dr. Arvil Jones**

Wasteland Press
www.wastelandpress.net
Shelbyville, KY USA

Heavenly Places
by Ernestine Smith and Dr. Arvil Jones

Copyright © 2012 Ernestine Smith and Dr. Arvil Jones
ALL RIGHTS RESERVED

First Printing – October 2012
ISBN: 978-1-60047-786-7

This is a work of fiction. Names, characters, places and incidents either are the product of the author's imagination or are used fictitiously, and any resemblance to any actual persons, living or dead, events, or locales is entirely coincidental.

NO PART OF THIS BOOK MAY BE REPRODUCED IN ANY FORM, BY PHOTOCOPYING OR BY ANY ELECTRONIC OR MECHANICAL MEANS, INCLUDING INFORMATION STORAGE OR RETRIEVAL SYSTEMS, WITHOUT PERMISSION IN WRITING FROM THE COPYRIGHT OWNER/AUTHOR

Printed in the U.S.A.

0   1   2   3   4   5

Dedicated to our spouses, children and grandchildren

Introduction

Heavenly Places is a novel by Ernestine Smith and Arvil Jones, set in the 1800's in the beautiful majestic mountains of post-Civil War West Virginia. A young Baptist minister, Jeff Townsend, and his beautiful wife Becky brave the hardships and share the joys of raising a family while carrying on a thriving ministry amidst the strife and turmoil immediately following the end of the bloodiest war in American history. Confronted by nearly every conceivable obstruction and opposition from both man and nature, the two young Christians prove that faithfulness to a living God and unconditional love for each other are forces that cannot be defeated.

    The writers of this novel, while adhering to Christian principles, make no attempt to shun, deny or avoid the harsh realities of life or the stark realities of human nature. The writers show in vivid imagery that the godly are not exempt from the inward and outward struggles and temptations that are part of the human experience. There is uninhibited cruelty alongside unbridled passion. There are the utmost depths of sorrow alongside the heights of exquisite joy. There is cold-blooded murder sparked by racism alongside forgiveness, acceptance and divine grace. There is belligerent defiance of the law alongside poetic justice. There is deception and intrigue alongside a dogged determination to find the truth. There are dark historical facts alongside hopes for a brighter future. There is betrayal alongside unbreakable bonds of friendship.

    Although the novel itself is fictitious, much of the imagery and many of the experiences described are written recollections of the real life experiences of both writers. The two main characters, Jeff and Becky Townsend, exhibit an unshakable faith in the Lord Jesus Christ, and an unwavering trust in each other. Their passions, whether physical, emotional or spiritual are all very real, with no mixture of hypocrisy. There are printed sermons that are nearly verbatim replicas of messages once delivered by Dr. Jones. And there are heart-wrenching stories, the details of which were once lived and experienced in the heart and life of Ernestine Smith, who herself is a cancer survivor. In short, Heavenly Places does what its name implies – it takes you there!

Heavenly Places

The wrinkles on her forehead were not caused by age, but by the blinding sunlight as Becky looked up toward the blue sky. She wondered what her husband Jeff was doing at that very moment. He had been called to preach a revival two counties over - a good hard day's ride on horseback. Becky had stayed behind to tend the crops, but a strong storm had passed through just the night before causing a lot of damage to the young plants. She started right off replanting as much as she could 'til Jeff returned. Becky and Jeff were partners in everything they did - the farm, the marriage and the church. They loved working together. Becky's mind went back to the first time she met him at a church picnic in Tennessee. Their paths had crossed many times before, but she was too bashful to let him see her looking at him. She had admired him from a distance for so long. Then the day came when she decided she would get really brave.

"Talk to him," her sisters urged her, giving her a little shove toward him.

She walked over to where he was standing, she could feel her face growing red with embarrassment as she held out her hand, and in a voice as soft as a whisper she said,

"Hello, my name is Becky Davis, I live in Bradley County." Her heart was pounding as he held out his hand and replied.

"Hello, I'm Jeff Townsend."

Becky smiled as she remembered the feeling that she had, at just the touch of his gentle but callused hand. She didn't want to let go but she didn't want him to think she was being forward either, so she quickly dropped her hands to her side. Jeff spoke in a voice

Heavenly Places

so sweet and low as he held out his hand to her again, and trying to speak past the lump in his throat, he managed to get out the words–

"Would you like to go for a walk?"

Standing there in the plowed ground, her shoes soaking wet from walking through the water and mud, these, and hundreds of other sweet memories flooded her heart, one after another. She drifted back again to that moment that would forever remain frozen in time - the look in his eyes, the feel of his touch. Even there in the hot sun her body shivered slightly at the memory of the touch of his strong but gentle hands. He was the first young man to hold her hand in that way. It sent a shiver of pure joy and delight into her soul.

Wiping the sweat from her beautiful face, she wondered if he too still remembered that first time they had met long ago. She tried to shake off this dreadful feeling that Jeff was in trouble. Something was troubling her heart. Something was not right. She dropped to her knees in the freshly-plowed dirt, not noticing or caring that it was cold, damp and muddy from last night's storms that had ripped through the mountains, causing so much damage to the early crops for which she and Jeff had worked so hard. Once again she turned her angelic face toward Heaven with hands clasped together, pouring out her heart to God.

"Please Father, wherever my husband is, could you watch over him?" For some reason, my heart is so heavy, and you are the only one I can turn to for help and guidance. I ask you to protect him, and bring him home safe. Father, I ask this in the name of your Son Jesus, Amen."

Becky slowly arose from the damp ground, dusting the dirt from her well-worn faded blue dress. She remembered that she was wearing this very same dress when she met Jeff for the first time at the church picnic.

She had done all that she could do in the field that day, and slowly made her way back to their house. Every step of her tired feet and every beat of her heart seemed to echo.

"I love you Jeff, I love you Jeff, I love you Jeff."

In her heart she knew that God would protect him and bring him back to her safe, as he had done so many times before. She placed the old well-worn hoe in the tool shed and entered the house through the back door, which opened into their big comfortable bedroom, which immediately reminded her of the day her handsome husband had carried her in his strong arms over the threshold of the front door and into this room. Her heart began to pound with the purest joy. Their love was a love that had been blessed by Heaven, and no outside influence had ever been able to taint the purity of what she and Jeff had shared together as two Christian people, deeply in love.

She sat on the edge of the big four-poster bed momentarily, partly just to rest her weary frame for a brief moment, and partly to re-live that blessed and romantic courtship that she and Jeff had shared for almost two years. Before she could rise from the bed, another sweet scene came floating gently into her mind - that first kiss, the one that told her everything she needed to know about Jeff Townsend, without a word being spoken. She wondered if he was asleep yet, she knew he must be tired. There was something deep, within her stirred, bringing a soft smile to her lips. Somehow she knew that he was thinking of her also. That's how close their two hearts were knit together.

There were only two loves in Jeff's life now – his calling and his wife. Whenever he was not preaching or working, she was the only thing he thought of. Both his parents had died before he married Becky, and he missed them terribly, but when he was with Becky, nothing else mattered, nothing else distracted his mind from the fact that God had given her to him, to have and to hold for as long as they both should live. Not more than a few minutes after Becky rose up from the edge of the big bed, his own thoughts drifted there – to that night he had carried her in his arms into that same room. Both Becky and Jeff had vowed that they would save themselves for the one they married. They were both virgins, and they both knew it of each other without asking. They had only the purest of thoughts about each other, never hinting at anything sexual the whole two years of their courtship, because they didn't need to. It was a forgone conclusion that they would save everything intimate for their honeymoon. His mind drifted to that heavenly scene when he had put her down in front of him, and they had both just stood there in a sacred moment of mutual love.

Laying there in a small bed, in a secluded back bedroom, belonging to the pastor of the church where he was preaching, Jeff lay sleepless, every beat of his own heart whispering "Becky,

Becky." The mere thought of her brought a mixture of emotions flooding into his tired brain. It was as if some Heavenly, invisible messenger was carrying their thoughts of each other back and forth, with a smile and a kiss attached to every thought. Slowly he drifted back to that beautiful spot just over the hill from the picnic area, where alone under the shade of a massive oak tree he had kissed the most beautiful young lady his eyes had ever seen.

Although miles separated them now, Becky recalled all the sweet emotions of that first kiss, knowing even then that there would be many more just as sweet. She remembered taking his hand that day, the two of them strolling down by the most peaceful stream. That stream, the big oak tree, the spot where he first held her hand, these, and a thousand more places, had become forever etched in her memory. All of these, she called, Heavenly places. She never wanted to let go of his hand as they talked and laughed. It seemed as if they had known each other all their lives. Out of the blue, this tall, handsome, dark-haired, blue-eyed young man held her gently in his arms as their lips met. Becky felt as if she were in the most heavenly place on earth. Every passion and emotion in her soul was stirred in that moment. She never wanted to leave his warm embrace, and the strong muscular arms that held her so tenderly.

May, 1860, Bradley County, Tennessee

"Becky Davis, Jeff spoke in a broken voice, we have known each other for almost two years, and I have loved you since the moment we first met. I have prayed for God to send me the right one to spend the rest of my life with, and I know you are that one. Would you do me the honor of being my wife, would you marry me?" She wasn't shocked, for she felt the very same way, and was praying each day for this time to come. Becky shouted with delight as she threw her arms around his neck screaming,

"Yes, Yes, Yes I will marry you!"

In his imagination, Jeff vividly saw both the place and the moment. He and Becky were both young Christians at the time, and both had been brought up to respect the opposite sex. But when the two of them met that day, no words needed to be spoken, and no explanations were needed. The instantaneous bond that formed between them required only one thing - a kiss under a big oak tree. Both their hearts were pounding like drums as they drew near to each other. They each knew instinctively what the other was feeling, and only one thing mattered to either of them - to feel the other's lips pressing passionately upon their own. He closed his eyes and re-lived that kiss again.

The sweetness and passion of that first kiss was only the prelude to every kiss they shared thereafter. Each one was spontaneous, and each one only made them want another and another. Every time their eyes met, the fire burned in their breasts. Every kiss was as if it were their first, filled with as much love and passion as that first one. They never needed to say a lot of words about their love and craving for each other, because every look, every kiss said all that needed to be said.

June 8th, 1862, Bradley County, Tennessee

After the wedding she and Jeff had loaded the wagon with as much as possible. His first desire was to move out west and start a church, but the good Lord had other plans. He had been called by God to preach His Word, and nowhere in the country was that Word needed more than in the mountains of West Virginia. Coming from Tennessee was a several-day's journey in the wagon. Becky had brought as many beautiful things with her as she could, and all of them reminded her of home, but anywhere her beloved Jeff was, that was home to her. They settled in a beautiful valley at the foothills of the beautiful mountains of Preston County West Virginia, about twenty miles from Morgantown. Jeff had inherited sixty acres of land originally owned by his grandfather, who had settled in the area long before West Virginia seceded from Virginia. There he built a small, two bedroom home made from logs that he cut and hauled in by him-self. Their house had a long front porch with wide steps leading down the front. A beautiful picket fence outlined the yard. Jeff had made a swing and chairs for the front porch, so many evenings were spent there as they just sat and counted their daily blessings, enjoying each other's company. Becky had hand-made all the curtains for the windows. Over the fireplace was a picture of the young couple in their wedding clothes. Her white gown only added to the beauty of her perfectly proportioned young figure. Jeff in his black suit was so handsome, like a prince from a story book. The picture was a gift from her parents. Becky stood there and once again prayed for the safe return of her beloved husband.

Nightfall had come, and Becky couldn't shake the uneasy feeling that something was wrong. She hurried about her chores so that she would be finished before the last flicker of sunlight had faded. She rushed to the small barn that Jeff had built, just big enough for their two horses and the sweet gentle cow Daisy. She gave the black horse some straw, sat down on a small stool, and milked Daisy. The gentle old cow just stood there chewing on the straw and swishing her tail to keep annoying flies away. Becky couldn't help but smile.

When she and Jeff had left the little community in Bradley County Tennessee, they were a sight to see – with an overloaded wagon, and old Daisy plodding faithfully behind, with her bell just tinkling all the way. Becky didn't care about how they looked. At that moment she was the happiest girl in the world. She sat so proud upon that big wagon seat beside the only man that she had, and would ever love. A smack from Daisy's tail brought her back to reality. She hurried and finished with her chores in the barn, went into the house and strained the fresh milk into a jar; she placed it in the edge of the spring that Jeff had discovered flowing from the mountain's base. The water was cold as ice and clear as crystal. Jeff had made a shelf of rocks where they kept their milk and butter. About a hundred yards downstream from the spring, Jeff had dammed up a small pool, just big enough for the two of them to frolic and bathe in.

In the winter, they always bathed strictly inside the house, but from mid-spring until early fall, they bathed and swam in the little pool together.

Becky had made herself a thin bathing suit from a well-worn sheet, emblazoned with wildflowers. She would catch Jeff looking at her with a well-pleased grin as her wet and well-proportioned body shone through the bathing suit. Jeff always jumped into the water wearing a pair of faded, cut-off trousers that were nearly worn out from much wear and tear. With everything done, Becky filled the big tub with warm water and used some of her scented soap that she had brought from home. She slipped off her clothes and lay there in the water. Once again her mind went back to her precious Jeff. Her wet body shimmered in the pale light from the dancing flame of the coal oil lamp. With every stroke of the scented soap up and down her arms, and across her body, she closed her eyes, daydreaming of the many playful hours that she and Jeff had spent both in and out of that little pool of water.

Jeff had deliberately built their house deep inside the valley, well off the beaten path. The nearest neighbor was at least two miles away, across the steep mountain that separated their two properties. Their little house was virtually invisible to anyone but a hunter or trapper who might be in the vicinity. They enjoyed well-guarded privacy, surrounded by mountains and trees. The only easy access to their farm was from the southern end of the valley. At the northern end stood yet another mountain, so steep that not even a mountain goat could climb it, thus they were enclosed on three sides by mountains. When Jeff built their house, it was the only house in the valley, which, from north to south, extended more than a mile.

She lay there in the big tub, reminiscing about the times when Jeff would take her in his arms, kiss her passionately, and carry her up out of the pool and onto the faded blanket they had laid upon the grass. And when they had dried each other's bodies sufficiently, he would carry her back to the house. Their love was the kind of love that God intended for all his children, the kind that lasted a life time, each of them intent upon pleasing the other. Jeff was reminded of a passage of scripture in **Proverbs 5: 18-19 – Let thy fountain be blessed: and rejoice with the wife of thy youth. Let her be as the hind and pleasant roe; let her breasts satisfy thee at all times; and be thou ravished always with her love.**

The barking of the dog brought her back to reality. The little dog was given to them by a neighbor from far over the mountain. They named him Spot, and whenever Spot heard, saw, or smelled an intruder, he never failed to let them know. Becky climbed out of the tub and dried herself quickly, shivering from head to toe. She became excited, hoping that maybe Jeff was home! She got dressed as fast as she could, and ran to the door, hoping to see her beloved husband. What she saw were five men on horseback. Becky thought she recognized two of the men from the little church where Jeff was the pastor, but she wasn't sure. When the people learned that there was a preacher coming to the community, they got really excited, and used the one-room school for a dual purpose – a school, and a church meeting place once a month on Saturday nights.

The man in front of the group, was the spokesman for the men, he was the first to speak. With a blank expression on his face, he removed his sweaty hat, asking Becky if her husband was home. Becky didn't want to outright lie, but she got a very uneasy feeling from one of the men in the back. He was dark-skinned, and looked very much like an Indian. She noticed that he looked at her as if he was stripping her naked. She pulled her dress closer to her body as a chill crept up her spine.

"Well Sir, she replied, my husband will be home shortly." And in the same breath, she whispered a silent prayer –"God forgive me."

"May I ask what business you have with my husband?" She continued.

"Ma'am, the spokesman replied, my young'un is bent on getting married, and I would be much obliged if'n your man could do the marrying."

The man in the back chuckled as he spit tobacco juice on the ground. Becky knew she had to get these men out of there as soon as possible. She turned herself half way around as if these words were her last words to them, and took a step toward the house, saying –

"As soon as my husband gets here tonight, I will tell him, and he will let you know."

"Thank you Ma'am, the man in front replied, I will be a waitin fur him."

The man tipped his hat in a very polite way, turned his horse around and ordered the others –

"Let's go boys."

All the men nodded as they left the yard except the man in the back. He rode his horse up as close to the porch as he could, after making sure that the other's backs were turned, he looked at Becky and winked, and with a voice almost like a growl he grunted,

"I'll be back."

Becky ran back into the house and barred the door shut. She was shaking from head to toe. "Lord please, bring Jeff home soon," she pleaded.

Jeff had been gone for a week now. He usually would not leave her this long, and sometimes she would even go with him. He loved his ministry so much that she did not want to complain. She couldn't get the image of this big, rough-looking man out of her mind. She made sure all the windows were shut tight and that the extra latch on the door was fastened. Then she remembered Spot. She quickly opened the door again, and called Spot inside. She told him that he was going to sleep by the door. He looked at her with his head turned sideways.

"Poor little Spot," she thought, could he fight off a big man? Or would he even hear if someone came up on the porch?" Becky was terrified! She sat there on the floor with her hand on the little dog's head, just being thankful that she had one friend beside her. She drifted off to sleep from sheer exhaustion.

The revival had gone so well, with another soul being saved each night. The Pastor and congregation begged Jeff to stay over and preach one more time on Sunday morning. This was not the first time this had happened to Jeff, and it wouldn't be the last. Seldom had he ever been away from Becky more than six nights. He had a big decision to make and not a lot of time in which to make it. His heart yearned to see his wife so bad he could hardly look the Pastor in the eye without a tear in his own. But one thing that he and Becky had agreed upon before they married was that each of them was willing to make some major sacrifices for the sake of his spreading the Gospel. Every fiber of his being wanted to say no to the Pastor, but the Holy Spirit said otherwise. With his big heart aching to hold Becky in his arms, he said a silent prayer for her protection, and agreed to preach one more message. He knew that if he left the church right after the Sunday morning service, he could reach home sometime around midnight Sunday night. He didn't relish the idea of riding his horse alone in the dark along the narrow paths that crisscrossed the treacherous mountains and valleys of western West Virginia. Once again, his mind wandered back to his beloved Becky, and that first kiss.

The Civil War had ended only a year ago. The nation was still reeling, and struggling hard to recover from the devastation and carnage of the war itself, and the assassination of President Lincoln. Emotions and passions still ran high between Northerners and Southerners, and in spite of the fact that the issue of slavery had supposedly been settled, hardly anyone in the entire country really believed that any issue had yet been finally settled. The roads and mountain passes were often strewn with thieves, robbers, disgruntled southerners, and even former slaves who had nothing to do but rob the most vulnerable victim they could find. And then there were the ever-present rattlesnakes, copper heads, and mountain lions, all of which could spook a horse with little or no warning. Some of the narrow paths that Jeff would have to take ran along the tops of sheer cliffs, more than a thousand feet from top to bottom. If a man's horse or mule was startled suddenly, both horse and rider could quickly end up at the bottom of a steep cliff, badly wounded or dead. To be a traveling preacher required a lot of faith, nerve, and endurance, and in Jeff Townsend, God had found the right man for the job. After a sleepless night, Jeff shook hands with the Pastor of the church, agreeing to preach again. At that very moment, another man was making a decision - an evil decision that would later prove to be very costly to him.

After another sleepless night of her own, Becky finished breakfast with great anticipation. Jeff would be home today. It was Saturday, and she had so much to do to get prepared for his return. She quickly did the dishes and walked over to the door to feed Spot - poor little fella. She had forced him to sit right by the door with her all night. She gave him an extra biscuit for his night of service. She rubbed the little dog's head, talking to him as if he were human...

"Thank you boy, you're a good dog."

She looked around, still a little fearful that the dark-skinned man might return. She could still hear his gruff voice saying – **"I'll be back,"** and those piercing evil eyes that stared at her. Becky shook off the dreadful feeling, and with one final pat on Spot's head, she walked cautiously to the barn to do the morning chores.

It was a beautiful day. The sun was shining brightly and the air was crisp and clean. Becky loved their little farm. Her parents had tried to give her and Jeff some property in Tennessee, and the church there in Cleveland had offered her husband a full time job as Pastor of the community church. But Jeff declined, saying that God was calling him to the mountains of West Virginia. He believed that God had a great job for him to do - winning those mountain folks to the Lord. So far it had been wonderful, and days like today made it all worthwhile. She recalled the many sweet homecomings they had enjoyed after they had been separated for a week. They would laugh and talk far into the night. Their love for each other was a love that God alone could give.

"Good morning Daisy," Becky spoke to the cow, and what a fine day it is."

Becky finished milking and turned the horse into the corral. She gathered the eggs as she sang a sweet little tune. With all the work done up outside she began making plans for her husband's return.

She laid out a fresh dress that she only wore on special occasions, and this was special. She decorated the kitchen table with a white lace table cloth that her mother had given her. She carefully took out the golden candlesticks and two white candles from her hope chest. She had picked wildflowers from the little grove near the spring when she took the milk down this morning, placing them in the middle of the table. She carefully placed her best china, and the table was fit for a king. She prepared Jeff's favorite food - fried chicken, mashed potatoes, green beans and an apple cobbler. Becky was a good cook from having spent many hours in the kitchen with her mother, learning all of her mother's great recipes. Being the youngest of nine children, her mother was very protective of her. Evening was drawing close, and Becky knew that Jeff would be arriving at any time. He had most likely headed out at first light.

She could see him now, in the pulpit, preaching God's word. She loved to watch him preach, as his eyes lit up with a sparkle, and a smile on his face that never left during the entire service. He spoke with authority, and the people listened, hanging onto every word he said. She loved him so much that she would never complain about his traveling, despite the fact that she missed him terribly.

Becky had finished her bath, dressed up, and was waiting. She waited and waited. Finally, she had to give up, knowing that he had probably stayed over for the Sunday morning service. He often did that, so Becky just left the table as it was and changed into her night clothes. She was disappointed, but knew that this was one of those things she would have to get used to. She brought Spot in to sleep by the door again. She took down the rifle from over the mantle and checked the chamber to make sure it was loaded, just in case, and hung it back on its pegs. The rifle was used only for hunting, but Becky wasn't taking any chances after last night's scare. Her father had taught her to shoot. He believed that everyone needed to know how to shoot a gun, even a girl. Dead tired, she climbed into the big four poster bed, hugging Jeff's pillow close to her chest, smelling the sweet scent of his hair that still lingered. With a smile she drifted off to sleep.

The next day Becky did her chores, and sat down with her Bible and read the scriptures, whispering a prayer for her husband's safe return. She took a walk down by the spring and the man-made pool that Jeff had built. So many wonderful memories of this place again flooded her mind. She and Jeff hoped to have children someday. She smiled at the thought of happy little boys and girls running around on the farm. Becky knew Jeff should arrive home around midnight if he left right after the morning service. She decided to take a nap so she could be up when he got home. After a refreshing sleep Becky hurried to freshen up the house as well as her-self.

With the table still set, she lit the candles. They flooded the room with a very romantic glow. While she waited for Jeff she decided she would do some knitting.

He called himself Tom Great Bear Tillotson. Everyone who knew him just called him Tom or Tillotson. A few referred to him as T.T. Tom himself had added the Great Bear to his name, claiming that he had earned the right to call himself Great Bear for a couple reasons. He once claimed that he was a full-blooded Cherokee Indian, and that he had captured and killed the biggest black bear ever captured in West Virginia, but it was obvious from the texture of his skin that he had some Caucasian blood in his veins also. But the one thing that defined and described Tom Tillotson more than any other was the fact that he had become a renegade – he now claimed no close affinity to any race or religion. He lived by his wits and skill, killing and eating anything that was edible, and selling the hides to anyone who would buy them from him. He lived in a little one-room shack that amounted to not much more than a lean to. It kept him dry in a storm, and warm in the winter.

It was Tom who had winked at Becky, telling her that he would be back. He was indeed a fearful looking character, standing about six feet, three inches tall, and always carried his three most prized possessions with him wherever he went – a razor-sharp Bowie knife, a Colt revolver, and a long leather whip. And now he had decided that he was going to follow through with his promise to that gorgeous, dark-haired lady – Mrs. Townsend. Without a second thought, he put his wicked plan in motion, leaped into his saddle, and headed up the valley toward the Townsend place. And precisely at that moment, Jeff Townsend had mounted his own horse, leaving the little church, the whole crowd waving him farewell, and telling him to come back soon. Three more souls had been saved in the morning service, so Jeff knew that he had made the right decision. Now only one thing mattered to him – getting back to his beloved Becky as quickly as God and nature would allow. God had His hand of mercy upon Jeff Townsend, and the devil had his hand upon the mind and conscience of Tom Tillotson.

Two men who could not be more different were riding toward a single destination, each one with a totally opposite motive in mind. In a few hours, they would meet in a life-and-death struggle. With his heart pounding in rhythm to the voice of the Holy Spirit, and with a smile of great satisfaction, Jeff spurred his horse into a trot for as long the road would allow it. With any luck, he might even reach Becky and home before midnight. Jeff himself, when viewed up close, was an imposing figure of a man, standing six feet, four inches tall. He was tough as an anvil from all the hard work he had done all his life, and stood straight as a pine tree. His big hands were calloused, and skilled at many things. He had logged huge trees out of the woods, and built his own house and furniture with his bare hands and a few tools he had inherited from his father. No thought of physical violence had ever lingered long upon Jeff's heart. He had never threatened anyone with bodily harm. But he was no coward either. He had never met a man of whom he was afraid. Little did he know that his faith, courage, strength and humility were about to be tested in a way he had never suspected.

He rode steadily for about three hours, stopping only long enough to let his horse drink from a nearby stream, being ever cautious to scan his surroundings, and to look for any fresh tracks or footprints from someone who might have come this way before him. He said another prayer, and mounted up again. The sun was descending westward now, as he checked his kerosene lantern in the saddle bag to make sure that it was still intact, and had ample kerosene to get him over the narrow trails that lay ahead. In the same way that Becky's intuition, coupled with her deep concern for her husband had nagged at her insides, a similar foreboding now crept into Jeff's gut. He was not easily alarmed or distracted by much of anything, but when it came to Becky and her safety he somehow instinctively knew that her safety was being threatened. It tore at his heart like a knife that he was not there to protect her, but he tried to shake it off as just the devil fighting him in his attempt to get back to her. He knew he must keep moving toward home as quickly and as carefully as he could. He wanted to cover as many miles as possible before dark, because when it became necessary to light the little lantern, that itself only added to the danger of being spotted by some robber.

Tom Tillotson was driving his horse hard toward Jeff's home, stopping only to take another long drink from his jug of West Virginia moonshine, barely letting his horse get enough water to keep him from dehydrating. His drunken brain was obsessed with what he was intending to do to that gorgeous creature, Mrs. Townsend. The sun was setting now, quickly slipping down behind the western mountain range surrounding the vast area that would, in another four years, be called Bruceton Mills, West Virginia. Tom spurred his horse more violently up the valley. He spotted the small plume of smoke rising lazily from the chimney of Jeff's house. He grinned and grunted with an evil smile, revealing his ugly, rotten teeth. He slowed his horse to a walk, staying in the shadows so as not to be spotted by any hunter or robber that might be close by. Since he had been to the house before, he needed no light to make his final approach to the house. The three-quarter moon provided enough light for him to ease his way up close. He dismounted and tethered his horse to a low branch of a silver maple, and began his slow and stealthy approach toward the house. Spot smelled him from about fifty feet away, and began to growl, and to bark excitedly. Becky immediately dropped her knitting, expecting to hear Jeff's voice any moment. What she heard was the quick, sharp snapping of a whip, and a drunken Indian screaming out profanity. She ran to the door, picked up Spot, and began to stroke him and shush him to be quiet.

The sharp crack of the whip was getting closer and closer with each snap. She again checked the doors, making sure they were barred. The only way anyone could get into the house was through a window. Her heart started to pound uncontrollably as she tried to think of what she might have in the house that would scare whoever was out there away. She knew how to use the rifle that hung over the fireplace, and she would not hesitate to use it if it came to that, but she desperately wanted to do or say something that would persuade the man out front to abandon his cause, without having to shoot him. She heard Tom lashing his whip against the front door, and kicking it hard, and cursing, telling her that he only wanted to come in and show her what a real man could do for her. She reached for the rifle, and cocked it. If the man outside somehow managed to get that door open, she was determined to put the first shot between his eyes. But before she could raise the rifle to her shoulder, Tom came crashing through the side window, breaking the small glass panes to shivers, and landing in the middle of the floor directly behind her. Before she could spin the rifle around, his whip had lashed around her ankles, pulling her feet out from under her, sending the rifle barrel upward. The bullet went into the ceiling.

Tom Tillotson had been accused of doing this same thing to more than one woman while her husband was away, leaving the women raped and badly beaten. His reputation for deadly accuracy with all three of his weapons was well known all over the Commonwealth. More than a few men had tasted the lash of that whip, the blade of the Bowie knife, or the hot lead from Tom's revolver. He got some kind of sadistic satisfaction from leaving the marks of his whip on the bodies of the women he raped. But it was only a matter of time, and the divine justice of God, until Mr. Tillotson would meet his match for the first time. Becky was no shrinking violet by any means. She had become used to hard work and long hours on the farm, working beside Jeff in the fields. She had never been threatened or frightened by any man. She had enjoyed the love and protection of her big strong husband for so long that no thought of being harmed by an outsider had ever plagued her mind. But she was not prepared for an ungodly, drunken, man like Tom Tillotson.

She did everything in her power to fight him off, clawing, scratching and kicking as hard as she could. While Tom was so intent upon raping her, she managed to get her left arm free, sinking her fingernails, deep into the right side of his face. This, of course, only infuriated him more. He wiped the blood from his face, raising what was left of her pretty dress, and wiped his own blood along the length of her left leg. She was no match for his superior strength. He deliberately wrestled her into submission, as her own strength faded.

He had torn most of her clothes from her body, and sat atop her, grinning like the devil he was, grunting like a hog, anticipating the pleasure he was about to experience. The whole time he had been subduing Becky; Spot had been barking and nipping at his heels. It was no more than a small annoyance to him, but enough to interfere with his wicked passion. He quickly drew the pistol from its holster. A single shot silenced the little dog forever. Becky had recovered just enough strength to make one last effort to shove him off her, but to no avail. She screamed, begging him to stop. The echo of the gunshot that killed Spot had reverberated up the valley just far enough to reach the ears of Jeff Townsend. A thousand thoughts, like a flash of lightning streaked across his mind in an instant. Without hesitating to try and analyze what that echo meant, Jeff spurred his horse into a full gallop, oblivious to everything around him. He had to reach Becky at all cost. Becky struggled with the last ounce of strength in her body to free herself from Tom's weight, only to collapse hopelessly from exhaustion as he bent down toward her mouth to kiss her. His horrid breath reeked of tobacco and moonshine, sickening her. She knew then that if God did not intervene for her, she was going to be raped, and maybe even killed. Tom drew the knife from its sheath, put the sharp blade to her throat, whispering and moaning in her face...

"Listen whore, we can do this the easy way, or I can make it very uncomfortable fur ya."

In what seemed a fraction of a second, the tall form of a man in a black suit came bounding through the same window through which Tom had leaped. In the blink of an eye, his passion for Becky's body was replaced with a new passion – that of dealing with this man as he had dealt with the little dog. Jeff landed on the floor only a foot or so from Tom and Becky. Tom quickly went for his pistol again, but before he got the gun half way out of the holster, Jeff kicked it out of his hand. Still holding the knife in his left hand, Tom struck the blade swiftly toward Jeff's throat, missing by less than an inch. With the return stroke, he felt the vice-like grip of Jeff's left hand locked around his wrist. Jeff's sheer strength was crushing the bones and tendons in Tom's wrist. The knife dropped to the floor.

Tom tried desperately to rise from his knees and fight Jeff in hand to hand combat. Something inside him told him that this was life or death for him or his opponent. He swung at Jeff with all his power. Jeff blocked the blow, and with a single punch straight between Tom's eyes, the fight was over. Tom felt the hard fist like a sledge hammer slam into his face, closing both his eyes instantly. Tom reeled backward, falling to the floor like an empty corn sack, unconscious.

The shame and humiliation of what had nearly happened to her was instantly replaced with sheer joy at the sight of her valiant hero. Jeff's attention was immediately withdrawn from the unconscious form of Tom Tillotson to the half-naked, blood-spattered body of his beloved wife. She was in his arms in an instant, clinging to him, sobbing and rejoicing at the same time. She held onto Jeff as if her very life depended upon his holding her near his breast. He dropped his hands down to her hips, holding her at arm's length, inspecting her body thoroughly to see where the blood was coming from. She quickly assured him that she was not cut. He lifted her into his arms, carried her into the kitchen, and began wiping the blood from her body with a wash rag soaked in cold water. Big tears filled his eyes as he gently washed the blood away. As each swipe of the cloth removed the blood, he sighed with some relief to discover that she was not lacerated. After wrapping her in a warm blanket, he carried her back into the living room, where the half-conscious form of Tom Great Bear Tillotson lay, barely able to move, struggling to regain consciousness. Jeff laid Becky gently onto the big sofa, bent down and kissed her lips ever so gently, stepped back into the kitchen just long enough to pick up the cold bucket of water, and returned to the living room. Knowing that his Becky was safe and unhurt, he walked over to where Tom had fallen, pouring the remainder of the cold water into his face. As the shock of the cold water did its intended work, Jeff bent down and collected the knife, the pistol, and the whip from the floor, tossing them into the corner beside the fireplace.

Becky was almost fully recovered from her own shock now, and sat up, motioning for Jeff to come and sit with her. As soon as Jeff sat down, she sat in his lap like a frightened child, holding onto him with both arms locked around his neck. Tom had regained enough composure and strength to rise to his knees, glancing around him as if he hardly recognized his surroundings. His mind cleared substantially as he saw Becky in Jeff's lap, hugging and kissing him over and over. He frowned with pure hatred at the couple. Jeff eyed him cautiously, but calmly. Tom's eyes quickly glanced toward the corner where Jeff had thrown the knife, pistol and whip. He quickly dismissed the temptation to dive for his weapons. His better judgment told him that he did not want to engage this big man in another fight.

Jeff lifted Becky from his lap, walked over to Tom, grasped him by the shirt collar, and escorted him into the kitchen, shoving him down onto the big wooden chair at the head of the big oak table. Without a word being exchanged between them, Tom knew that it was Jeff who was in full control of the situation. Jeff looked through into the living room, and motioned for Becky to join him and Tom in the kitchen. Becky quickly tied a length of rope around her waist to prevent the blanket from falling off her body, and shuffled into the kitchen. No words were spoken. Jeff simply looked into her eyes, nodding toward the cook stove. She instinctively knew what Jeff meant. She began to stoke the fire in the little stove, and to prepare a hot meal for the three of them. Tom sat at the table in total silence, not believing what his eyes were seeing. Becky was looking toward him without a hint of animosity or hatred in her face. As the fire grew hotter in the stove, she shuffled into the bedroom, removed the blanket, and donned her woolen robe and slippers. She walked past Tom with a weak smile, opened the front door, and returned in two minutes with a cold jug of milk from the spring. She took a big stone cup from the cupboard, filled it to the brim with milk, and sat it down in front of Tom. She returned to the cupboard, took down some flour, and began mixing the batter for some hot biscuits.

With the biscuits in the oven, she stepped out to the smokehouse with a sharp butcher knife, cutting off enough ham to feed three people. Try as he would, Tom could not muster the courage or strength to utter a single word. He stared at the big cup of milk in front of him, glancing at Jeff as if to ask permission to take a drink of it. Jeff smiled at him, picking up his own cup of milk, lifting it toward Tom as if he were granting him permission to drink from his own cup. They both raised their cups of milk to their lips at the same time. Tom glanced from Jeff to Becky and back again, still not understanding nor believing what his eyes were seeing. When he finally realized that Jeff was not going kill him, he was forced to ask himself the question…

"What kind of people are these folks?"

He had forced his way into this home, fully intending to rape this man's wife, and perhaps even kill her. He had definitely intended to kill Jeff once the struggle ensued, and now they were both treating him as if he were a welcome guest in their home. He could contain his thoughts no longer. All he could manage to say to Jeff was…

"Mister, who are you? And why in hell did you not kill me?" Jeff responded immediately… "Watch your mouth in my house mister. The good Book says, if thine enemy hunger, feed him, if he thirst, give him drink, and you appear to fit that description to me."

Jeff's words came from his heart, with the power and permission of the Holy Spirit. Tom Tillotson had never heard such powerful and gracious words in his entire life. Suddenly, without any warning, hot tears flooded his eyes – tears that he simply could not control. The Holy Spirit was convicting him with deep conviction, breaking his hardened heart. He could not understand why he suddenly felt something within his breast that he had never felt before. Sobbing, he lowered his head to the table, begging Jeff…

"Please mister, tell me what I need to do to get rid of this terrible conviction and emptiness in my chest."

Jeff reached out and took Tom by the hand, and asked him if he had ever heard of Jesus, the Son of God. Tom replied that he had heard that name long ago from a traveling missionary, but had dismissed it as not being worthy of his attention. Jeff slowly and deliberately explained to him the love of God for all men, and the simple plan of forgiveness and salvation through faith in the shed blood of Jesus Christ.

Tom noticed that Becky herself was standing in the entrance between the two rooms, her head bowed, whispering a prayer as Jeff shared the Gospel with him. The sheer grace and power of what he was seeing, feeling and hearing overpowered Tom's spirit. He asked both Jeff and Becky if they could forgive him for what he had done. They both smiled, nodding in agreement. Without another word, Tom Great Bear Tillotson knew that it was Jesus speaking to his heart. He joined hands with Jeff and Becky, asking the Lord Jesus to come into his heart, and be his Savior.

One moment Tom Tillotson was a hell bound sinner, bent upon raping and murdering others. A few minutes later, he was a blood-bought child of God, with a heart full of love for Christ and for his fellow men. But still, he felt as if something was yet missing. He asked Jeff if there was anything else that he needed to do. Jeff told him that he needed to be baptized, and to join in fellowship with a church. Tom immediately asked if Jeff would baptize him. Jeff lit a lantern, and he and Becky, with Tom between them, walked down to the little pool. Becky held the lantern up high as Jeff and Tom waded into the cold water together. Jeff raised his right hand upward, and with a voice that sounded almost tearful, he said –

"Heavenly Father, in obedience to your command, and upon his profession of faith in Jesus Christ, I baptize this my brother, in the name of the Father, and of the Son, and of the Holy Ghost."

He then submerged Tom completely beneath the water. When he raised Tom up out of the water, Tom began bouncing up and down, clapping his hands, and praising the Lord Jesus Christ.

They walked back to the house, where Becky immediately went into the bedroom, returning with some big towels, two pair of Jeff's trousers, and two dry shirts, handing them to Tom and Jeff. Tom thanked her, went into the bedroom, dried himself off, and returned wearing Jeff's clothes. Becky hung their wet clothes in front of the fireplace to dry. Tom asked Jeff if he could have the honor of doing one more thing before he left. Jeff asked what that might be. Tom asked Jeff if had a shovel, glancing toward the lifeless body of old Spot, lying in the corner where he had shot him. Jeff nodded his approval, and again the three of them walked down the little path to a spot beneath an old oak tree. Tom dug the small grave all by himself, not allowing Jeff to help him. He picked up the little dog, placed him gently into the grave, and covered him with dirt, tears streaming from his eyes. He patted the fresh dirt with the shovel, and remarked to Jeff and Becky –

"It's the least I can do."

It was now 3:00 am Monday morning. Jeff asked Tom if he needed to borrow a lantern to make his way out of the valley. Tom assured Jeff that he could manage without a lantern. He shook hands with Jeff one last time, nodded to Becky, and walked away down the narrow path to where his horse stood, still tethered to the silver maple. Without thinking, Tom began to pet and rub the horse, speaking to him in gentler tones than he had ever been able to manage before. With a smile and a chuckle, he untied the horse, looked him in the eyes, and said –

"I love you old hoss."

He mounted up, and for the first time in his life, Tom Great Bear Tillotson whistled a tune as he rode slowly toward his own little shack, several miles from the end of the valley, stopping at regular intervals to water the horse, letting him drink as long as he wished. He didn't even think about his pistol, knife or whip, all of which he had left at Jeff's house.

Jeff quickly moved from the barn to the smokehouse, and finally to the tool shed outside, making sure that all was secure, bringing in another armload of firewood, allowing Becky enough time to slip into her most beautiful night shirt. She dabbed on just a bit of her favorite perfume – the one that Jeff was especially fond of. Jeff put the firewood in the wooden box, and barred the doors, nailing a few boards over the broken window. Becky had already swept up the glass, and pitched it into the low pit that they used for burning trash. Jeff smelled her perfume wafting gently through the house. He removed his clothes, quickly washed himself off, and walked toward the bedroom with his heart pounding wildly. He stepped into the room slowly, seeing the smiling face of his beloved Becky. She was under the blanket, and had turned down the blanket on his side too, reaching over and gently running her left hand over his side of the bed. He blew out the lamp, eased his tall frame in beside her, taking her into his grateful arms.

The life-threatening events of that long night may have affected other couples in quite a different way than they affected Jeff and Becky Townsend. In fact, those very events themselves, instead of instilling any degree of fear or doubt into their hearts and minds, hardly affected them at all. Such trauma as they had experienced might have prompted folks of lesser faith and character to sit up all night, trembling with fear and holding a loaded rifle or shotgun, but not Jeff and Becky. They went to bed that morning with as much faith in God as they had ever done before. Jeff simply believed the Scriptures to be the inspired, infallible, and inerrant word of God. They both simply believed that God Himself was overseeing, and guiding their lives toward a sure and certain destiny. Jeff had long ago given himself over to God's divine direction and authority, believing that as God's anointed servant, his own steps were ordered by the Lord.

To them, all of the events, and the circumstances surrounding those events, from beginning to end, when taken together as a whole, had somehow culminated in God being glorified, and them being blessed. As for the near-death experiences of them both, each was just another bump in the road, a minor distraction, a tiny hindrance, temporarily impeding their journey toward God's Celestial City. With all that had happened, and in spite of the emotional and physical drain of it all, they allowed themselves only one extra hour in bed. They were up at 6:00 a.m., going about the everyday chores that had to be done in order to sustain life, and maintain their home. Losing or giving up a few hours of sleep was more the rule than the exception in maintaining all that pertained to a sixty-acre, operational farm in the mountains of West Virginia. Together, side by side, they set about repairing the broken window, then milking the cow, feeding the animals, mending sagging or fallen fences that had been damaged by the storm, and re-planting or replacing the damaged plants in the garden and in the field of corn.

The food produced from the garden would be eaten, of course, and whatever was left over would be canned for the winter. The corn and hay crops would sustain the cow, the pigs, the chickens and the horses through the winter. Keeping it all hoed and healthy required nearly every hour of daylight labor that they could put in, and more often than not, a few nighttime hours also. In 1866, keeping a close watch over the fields, the crops, the animals, the buildings, and each other, meant the difference between survival and starvation. Jeff and Becky simply had the added responsibility of his being a Pastor and evangelist, a calling that often took him away from the duties and responsibilities of the farm, leaving Becky to maintain it all as best she could until Jeff returned. But neither of them ever complained - they simply claimed the unfailing promises of their God, and believed the Scripture that says…Casting all your cares upon Him, for He careth for you.

Whenever Jeff was at home, he had to accomplish everything he possibly could, to prevent Becky from being overloaded with all the hard work. There wasn't much that Becky couldn't do by herself or for herself on the farm, but there were a few things that required the strength of a pretty strong man, like birthing a calf or a foal, or chopping down a big tree and cutting it up for firewood. Once Jeff had felled a big tree, and had chopped off the limbs, Becky would join him on one end of the crosscut saw, helping him saw the wood into lengths that would fit in the stove and fireplace. Jeff did virtually all of the wood splitting. The two of them often remarked that their bodies were – tanned by the sun, and toned by the saw. And no one except the two of them had ever seen the bare flesh of those tanned and toned bodies – Tom Tillotson being the exception when he tried to rape Becky.

That extra hour of sleep Monday morning necessitated an extra hour of work that evening. The luxury of getting caught up on one's work on a farm was nonexistent. There was always something that needed attention, and Jeff always saw to it that no more work than was absolutely necessary was left undone for Becky to do on her own. He took every precaution to take as much work off her as he possibly could. Becky sometimes just jumped right in beside him, in spite of all his objections, insisting on helping him. Her motive for doing so was not only to help her husband, but to be as close to him as she possibly could, for as long as she possibly could. The two of them never attempted to make it a secret how much they desired each other. Whenever they were within arm's reach of each other, their passion shone in their faces and in their eyes. But with a lot of work to do, they would look at each other with a smile that said all that needed to be said, anticipating what awaited them each night when the work was done.

All the work that could be done that Monday had been done. They both sighed with relief, quickly stripping off their sweaty clothes, and headed for the little pool. The cold water alone seemed to remove at least some of the tiredness from their bodies, at least temporarily. They splashed water in each other's faces, playing like two children for a few minutes, laughing and rejoicing that the hard work of another day was over, and all was well. The mirth of a few minutes quickly turned into hot passion. They were in each other's arms, as another heavenly moment happened in another heavenly place, their kisses again taking them back to that spot beneath that big oak tree. He carried her out of the pool into the house, entering by the back door that opened into their big bedroom. Becky hurried to the closet, coming back with a towel. When they finished drying off, Becky leaped into Jeff's arms with her arms around his neck, her eyes saying all that needed to be said.

There was something different in their love making that night, something that had not been sensed by either of them before – something extra. They could both see it in the other's eyes, and in the way they held onto each other. It was a passion that exceeded anything they had experienced in their marriage. Without either of them saying anything, they both knew what the other was thinking and feeling. As much as they had always wanted each other as man and wife, they both now sensed that there was something else that they both wanted – they wanted a son – a God-given child that they could raise together in the fear of God. Becky wanted a son that she could mold into the image of her husband. Jeff wanted to see Becky with a child in her arms, loving and nurturing him with all the love of her great heart.

Tuesday, May 22nd, 1866, 11:09 p.m.

Love suffers long, and is kind; love does not envy; love does not vaunt itself; is not puffed up, does not behave itself unseemly, seeks not her own, is not easily provoked, thinks no evil; does not rejoice in iniquity, but rejoices in the truth; bears all things; believes all things; hopes all things; endures all things. Love never fails (I Corinthians 13:4-8a).

After Jeff had fallen asleep, Becky lay there in his arms, watching his chest rise with each breath he took. She gently swept her fingers through his black hair. Oh how she loved him! She was so thankful that she had not been harmed by that awful man the other night. She shuddered at the thought of what could have happened if Jeff had not returned home at that moment. The vision became so real in her mind she had to get out of bed. She slipped softly from under the covers so as not to awaken him, tiptoeing quietly into the big living room. Standing by the window she pulled back the white lace curtains, staring wistfully at the big beautiful moon hanging in the heavens. She prayed –

"Dear God, please take this vision away from my mind and give me peace."

She had not yet shared her feelings with her husband about it all. She felt dirty, betrayed and violated. She always wanted to be as pure as she could be for the one man that she had ever loved. This man Tom had violated all of that, even though he had only torn off her clothes. But his intentions would forever be engraved in her mind, making her feel somewhat less of a woman.

She couldn't get it out of her mind. Maybe tomorrow she could find the courage to share it with Jeff, and find peace with it. She had felt weak and tired for several days. The sordid ordeal with Tom had left her even weaker. She had something else on her mind also, and wanted it to be a joyful occasion for them both, but once again was hindered and haunted by the memory of that terrible night. She had skipped two months and was not sure, but in her heart she felt that God had finally given them a child. She was planning on telling her wonderful husband when he returned from his trip. How could she break the news to him now? Would he be happy? Tears welled up in her eyes as she began to weep. She stood there, blinded by tears of both sorrow and joy all mixed together, as every emotion she had manifested itself - Love, most of all for Jeff; Joy, that she knew she was carrying his child, their child, for which they had prayed so long, and hatred for the man that had almost destroyed it all. Becky sank to the floor, crying uncontrollably. Jeff heard her pitiful plea -

"Jeff, please come here, I need you."

In one leap Jeff was by her side, holding her and rocking her like a baby as she sobbed out all her fears and feelings there on the floor.

She told him how scared she was, how dirty she felt, and how sorry she was that all this had happened. It was clear to Jeff that she was blaming herself, at least to some degree, for what had happened to her. But if there was one thing other than their love for each other that bonded Jeff and Becky Townsend together more than any other, it was their ability to communicate, often without a word being spoken. The soft, gentle, loving look in Jeff's blue eyes, and the little smile on his face said all that Becky needed to know. She was still, and would forever be, his pure and faithful wife.

As they lay there he held her as he had never held her before. She whispered softly... "My darling, God has answered our prayers."

"Yes, I know," Jeff replied, "He protected us Becky."

"No Jeff, God has given us a child - I am going to have a child Jeff, our baby. I wanted to tell you but couldn't till now."

Needless to say, there was nothing but pure rejoicing in the Townsend house at that moment. All Becky's fears vanished. She never felt more loved in her life. They lay there and made plans for the baby till the sun came shining through the windows. But all was not over till Jeff got up and did a dance all over the house with Becky right behind him, laughing and frolicking like two children. The next day they were still bubbling over with joy, with every step they made they added a skip.

Jeff went around with his chest out, whistling a tune. Becky, of course, was overjoyed. She hoped it would be a boy just like Jeff. It was just a little frightening to think that she and Jeff would have this baby so far away from her mother, but she knew that God would be with them and bless them in every way. She was determined to be the best mother that this child could ever want, and she had no doubt that Jeff would be a proud and wonderful father. They hurried about their work. The week was swiftly passing, and Jeff had to preach at the church just two nights away, and maybe they would share their wonderful news with their neighbors.

Saturday, May 25th, 1866, 6:00 p.m.

The sheer joy of knowing that they were going to have a child filled Jeff and Becky with such pride and happiness they could hardly contain it all. Every time their eyes met, they glowed with a new radiance. As close as they had been since that first kiss, they were now even closer, a part of them both growing inside Becky's womb, uniting them in a way that only the hope of a newborn baby can unite two people. And no two people on Earth were more ready or more jubilant at the news than were Becky and Jeff Townsend. But with all the joy and jubilation that came with the news of their coming child, the labors of the farm could not be neglected, not even for a single day. Wednesday, Thursday, and Friday were filled with as much sweat and labor as every day before. But now Jeff seemed even more determined to take even more of the work upon him-self. Whenever Becky would try to pitch in and help he would pick her up in his strong arms, set her down on a stump, and tell her –

"You just sit right there my love, and watch me get it done."

And get it done he did, with a new vigor that Becky had never seen in him before. Jeff chopped twice as much wood as he had before, in about the same time as before.

Everything Jeff did, he did with a smile on his face and a song on his lips, keeping Becky as close as he could, without her getting involved in the work itself. He wouldn't even let her pick up a stick of firewood. He even tried to dissuade her from milking the cow, or collecting the eggs, but Becky drew the line there. She assured him that for now she was quite capable of doing practically everything she had always done, with only a few exceptions. Jeff would try to slip out of bed early without waking her in order to get more of the work done. Becky knew every time he slipped out, but allowed him to believe that she hadn't noticed. It made her love him even more, as she silently contemplated what a great father Jeff would be to their child, hoping and praying that this son would grow up to be the kind of man his father was.

Saturday night was called *meetin* night at the little school house, which also served as a church. All the hard labor and sweat of the rest of the week didn't seem as hard, as Saturday night approached. Jeff and Becky both looked forward to it with great anticipation. Not only was it an opportunity to share the Gospel with as many as would come, but it was also an opportunity to see, and talk with their distant neighbors and their families.

After all the chores were done, and they had taken a bath in the little pool, they went back up to the house where Becky quickly prepared a small meal for the two of them. They bowed their heads, thanking God for all their blessings. This time Jeff added another word of gratitude for the blessing of another life, a life imparted to a tiny little creature inside the womb of his beloved wife; a divine miracle wrought by the unseen hand of a loving Creator, and an everlasting responsibility for the two of them to bring him up in the fear and admonition of the One who gave him life, and to train him up in the way that he should go; a responsibility that each of them had joyfully accepted long ago when they agreed to become husband and wife. They both quickly washed the dishes, and put on their *meetin* clothes. Becky applied just a hint of her perfume, and Jeff just a dab of cologne. Jeff, with his Bible in hand, again bowed his head just before they left the house, asking God to give them travelling mercy, and the honor of His presence at the *meetin*. He quickly grabbed an extra pillow from the bed – a little extra cushioning for his beloved Becky. She smiled and thanked him, knowing that the carriage ride to the church would have been just a bit more unpleasant without the pillow.

Jeff Townsend was a man of great faith, a pretty good student of human nature, and a good discerner of character as well. He lived his life believing that when God changed a man's heart, that man received a new nature, imparted and infused into his being by the regenerative act of the Holy Spirit. He believed that when a man was born again, that his past was wiped clean, and he was new creature in Christ Jesus. Jeff didn't mull over what degree of influence that he himself had had in the lives of those he had led to Christ. He always simply gave all the glory and honor to Christ Himself for whatever change had taken place in someone's life. And now, just before leaving the house to go to meetin, he thought of Tom Tillotson, and what they had said to each other before parting ways. He walked over to the corner beside the fireplace, picking up the whip, the Colt, and the Bowie knife, carrying them in one hand, and his Bible in the other.

So many thoughts were going through Becky's mind as she sat there on the buggy seat beside Jeff, heading out for the little one-room school house, which tonight would be used as a place to worship their God. Such singing she had never heard. When the voices of those mountain folks came together they sounded like a heavenly choir. All the different voices harmonized with such sweetness and power, the hair would stand up on your head. And to top it off, her wonderful husband would deliver an anointed message from God that would cause Satan himself to tremble in fear. The road would get rough, but she and Jeff held on, admiring the beauty that God had made of this place. The tall mountains loomed high into the sky, with just a ray of sunshine beaming through the tree tops, with a touch of blue still visible here and there. The sweet fragrance of honeysuckle drifted their way as they would pass. Birds fluttered from the low bushes as the horse and buggy drew near.

Becky was so excited to see all the folks at the church, and especially her friend Sarah Puckett. Sarah had blonde hair, which she kept braided and wrapped into a circle around the base of her neck, and the most beautiful blue eyes that sparkled each time she smiled. Clark was a big tall man with the reddest hair she had ever seen. His eyes were a light shade of green. But the thing that endeared Clark to Becky was his infectious smile. When she and Jeff had first moved here, Sarah and her husband Clark and their two children were the first to make them welcome. Their children - Mollie, with blonde bouncy curls like her mother, was four. And Carter, who was blessed with his father's red hair, was six. Sarah had lost a child the first year they had moved here in the dead of winter. The baby was still-born, and she had spoken of it only a few times, always with tears in her eyes. The Pucketts lived in Monongalia County, about ten miles away. But despite the distance between the two families, they depended on each other for help whenever it was needed. They had been here long enough to know how the fierce, cold hard winters and scorching hot summers, along with all the storms, could affect the very means of living for a family.

The Pucketts were a few years older than Becky and Jeff (who were both now twenty-three,) but just enough to be able to give

Heavenly Places

them good advice. Becky couldn't wait to share her news with Sarah about the child she was carrying, and the joy she and Jeff were both feeling. The buggy jolted. Becky placed her hand on her stomach. She was just a little bit dizzy from the riding and jolting on the rough trails, and the thoughts of the baby being harmed made her just a little bit scared. She quickly looked at Jeff. He reached over as if to read her mind and gave her hand a tight squeeze.

"It's ok," Jeff assured her, quickly taking control of the buggy again.

He smiled at her and she knew all was well. They rode on in silence till they rounded the bend, and there, in a small clearing, stood the little white school building, with a sign painted over the door - **Valley Grove School**. During church service a wooden sign made from a long white board with black letters was hung on a nail over the front wall which read - **Valley Grove Baptist Church. Est. in 1816.**

On the sides of the building were long, slim wooden-framed windows. Three wooden steps led up to the front door. A black stove pipe connected to an old black pop-bellied stove stuck out from the wall to the outside. Just a tiny streak of smoke was floating lazily from the end. The evening would be cool after the sun went down, so someone had made just enough fire to keep out the dampness. As soon as the folks spotted Jeff's buggy they all came running - children, teenagers and older folks, all so glad to see each other.

"Howdy Preacher," they all said almost at once. Clark hurried to Becky's side, lifting her down from the buggy as if she were a child. She was instantly being hugged by Sarah as Mollie buried her face in her mother's shoulder.

"It is so good to see you Sarah, Becky said, giving her friend a big hug in return, we have so much to talk about."

The two women were like children, and couldn't wait to be by themselves to talk. But they had so many more folks there to speak to. Jeff took the horse and buggy to a shady area where they would be comfortable, and gave the horse some water and a small bag of feed that he had brought along. He was soon rushed off by the men folk talking about the crops, and revivals that he had been preaching. Becky could see the pleasure in his eyes as he too was enjoying the company of their neighbors.

After everyone had greeted each other they all went off in small groups, talking and laughing. Becky and Sarah both talked at once. Sarah's eyes filled with tears of joy as Becky told her about the baby she and Jeff were expecting. She grasped Becky's hand with such tenderness, "Oh Becky, I am so happy for you, now you send Jeff for me as soon as your time comes, I will be there."
Becky took great comfort and assurance from Sarah's words, because she knew that Sarah had delivered several babies since she and Clark had lived in these mountains.
Soon someone came to the door and rang the little school bell, the same bell that the teacher used to call in the students. Everyone crowded into the tight little room. The seats, which flipped down in front, only held one person, but some of the farmers had brought along some straight back chairs from their own homes for the ladies. Jeff had brought one for Becky as well. In front the men had hung lanterns to light the building, with another hanging above the door as well. On a small table in the corner was a big silver bucket of cold water from the spring. A bright shiny dipper with a long handle hung from a nail just above the bucket. Becky and Sarah sat side by side during the whole service. Clark got up and called the choir up for singing. Becky and Sarah stood straight and tall, singing at the top of their lungs. Next to hearing Jeff preach the Gospel, Becky's greatest passion was for singing. And in the same way that the whole congregation sat up and listened while Jeff preached, they also listened attentively and very appreciatively whenever Becky lifted her angelic voice to sing.

The sad and sordid reputation of Tom Great Bear Tillotson preceded him wherever he went. Whole communities warned their wives and young daughters to beware a tall, rough-looking Indian, carrying a whip slung over his shoulder, riding a black, blaze-faced horse. And even though he had been accused of more than one rape and murder, Tom had somehow managed to elude the law and justice, and had never been convicted of any crime. The few lawmen scattered throughout the area made it no secret that they themselves feared Tom Tillotson. Once he pulled his Colt from its holster, whatever or whoever was standing in front of him never lived to tell the tale. He could put out the flame of a candle with the tip of his whip, and never touch the candle itself. The hides of several species of animals hanging on the sides of his little shack were evidence enough of his skill with the Bowie knife. As long as Tom did not pose an immediate threat to human life, other men simply gave him a wide berth, and left him alone.

The singing was so beautiful that night that nearly every hand in the house was raised in praise to God. The Holy Spirit made His power and presence known throughout the house. Some of the women were up shouting, and a few of the men had big tears of joy running down their cheeks. But there was also a deep conviction in the place. As Jeff sat in the big wooden chair just to one side of the pulpit, he slowly scanned the crowd, searching their faces for signs of conviction or uneasiness. He didn't have to search very long. The congregation sensed it too, and quickly ended the singing part of the service, allowing Brother Clark to call everyone who wanted to join them in prayer up to the mourner's bench. Every member of the congregation gathered to pray for themselves, their loved ones, the nation and its leaders, and for anyone else who might be standing in the need of prayer.

With prayer being ended, Jeff stepped into the pulpit, cleared his throat, and began reading from the Book of Romans, chapter eight, verses 33 and 34:

Who shall lay anything to the charge of God's elect? It is God that justifieth. Who is he that condemneth? It is Christ that died, yea rather, that is risen again, who is even at the right hand of God, who also maketh intercession for us.

No one in the house, including Jeff, knew that there was a man standing just outside the front door of the building, on the top step, straining to hear the words of the Preacher. Tom didn't know whether to knock on the door, or to just walk in unannounced, or to turn and ride away. But he couldn't forget the words that Jeff had spoken to him before the two of them had parted company a few days ago – that he should take up fellowship with a Bible-believing church as soon as possible. The devil told him to forget about this religious stuff, and leave while he still could. But another, more powerful voice from within told him that he should stay. The powerful and anointed voice of Jeff Townsend that had so overwhelmed his spirit before once again penetrated the thick wooden door of the church, and drew him like a magnet to open the door, and step inside.

For the briefest moment, even Jeff himself did not recognize Tom. The only things that did cause him to recognize him were that Tom was wearing Jeff's old shirt and trousers that Becky had given him last Monday morning, and the slight scratch marks on his right cheek from where Becky had clawed his face. Tom was clean shaven, his hair was cut and combed, his boots were shined, and he beamed with a big toothless grin. No other souls in the house except Jeff and Becky recognized the toothless stranger as the notorious outlaw, Tom Great Bear Tillotson. As soon as Jeff had recovered from the initial shock of recognizing Tom, and seeing that Becky had recognized him also, Jeff nodded to Becky, and then to Tom, motioning with his big hand, and saying to Tom,

"Welcome stranger, come on in and find a seat."

Jeff then instructed some of the men in the rear to shake hands with the newcomer, and make him welcome. Before it was over, nearly every man in the house had made his way to where Tom was sitting, shaking hands with him, and making him feel like he was at home among them. Once again, a spirit of humility and gratitude crept into Tom's heart, and vented itself through his tear ducts.

The only times that anyone except Jeff Townsend had extended his hand to Tom Tillotson, that hand had been holding a rifle or a pistol. But now a whole community had offered their hearts and hands to him as if he were one of their own family. And the same love, forgiveness and compassion that he had felt a few days ago at the head of Jeff Townsend's table, he felt now, here among total strangers, who, in an instant, had become the closest thing he had ever known to friend and family for many years.

But the service was not over yet, and the devil had his designs. Not every man in the little building had offered Tom his hand. The one man who had not done so was Lucas Bratcher, who was himself an avid hunter and trapper, and had scoured the mountains and valleys of West Virginia for many years. He eyed the newcomer with a narrow squint, and the longer he eyed him, the more he was certain that he had seen this man before – somewhere. He began to re-cast the image in his mind – a man with longer hair, rotten teeth, a foul odor, and carrying a whip, a Colt revolver, and a Bowie knife. He glanced quickly out the side window, seeing Tom's black, blaze-faced horse tethered to a bush.

Jeff saw the look on Lucas Bratcher's face, and knew immediately that he had recognized Tom. But before Jeff could get to Lucas and stop him, Lucas shouted out…

"Hey folks, I know that man, that man is Tom Great Bear Tillotson."

Before Lucas could say more, Jeff had gotten to him, and taking him by the arm, led him to his seat in the amen corner, gently pushing him down onto the seat. Jeff didn't need to say a word to Lucas. The steely expression on his face was enough. But the damage had already been done. Nearly two-thirds of the men who had just moments before shaken hands with Tom were now scowling at him, taking their wives and daughters by the arms, ushering them toward the door. Tom's heart sank. But before a single man or woman could get out the door, Jeff placed himself between them and the door, blocking their exit, holding his Bible to his chest. With the same calm, but powerful voice that all of them had heard so many times before, Jeff assured them…

"Ain't anybody goin anywhere til I preach my sermon."

A moment of total silence ensued, but only a moment, and slowly, and somewhat grudgingly, the people began to sit down. Jeff motioned for Clark Puckett to come and take his place at the door. During his time as Pastor of the little church, Jeff had earned both the respect and love of those who listened to his preaching. His voice was authoritative, his preaching was powerful and anointed, and his manner of life – his walk, matched his talk. Just about every man in the community was older than Jeff, and he showed the utmost respect for all of them, but at the same time, he commanded their respect also. They never hesitated to call on him whenever they needed or wanted a sympathetic ear, or wise counsel. When Jeff spoke, he meant what he said, and he said what he meant, and he never sugarcoated the truth just to hold their friendship. He based his counsel and advice upon the Holy Bible, and that alone.

He walked back into the pulpit, quoted the same passage from Romans again, and then added another quote from the lips of Jesus, as recorded in John 8:7…**Let him that is without sin among you**

cast the first stone. Immediately, faces began to turn red, heads dropped, and Clark Puckett and Tom Tillotson both smiled at the same time. This was going to be a good meetin after all. Jeff summoned all the love and grace he could muster from his big heart, and began to preach to the people as if they were his own children. No lengthy sermon was needed, because the Holy Spirit had already done a mighty work upon the hearts of this crowd.

Ever since Jeff had been called to be the Pastor of the little congregation, he had a little rock, weighing about a pound, lying on the right side of the pulpit. Everyone who came into the building saw the little rock, and wondered why it was there, and why Jeff had never offered any explanation for it being there. But out of sheer respect for their Pastor, no one had ever questioned him about the rock. Jeff had been saving that rock for just such an occasion as tonight. After quoting the words of Christ, he picked up the little rock, asking Tom Tillotson to stand up. He then walked over to Lucas Bratcher, offering him the rock, asking him if he would like to throw it at Tom's head. Lucas hung his head in shame. Jeff carried the rock from pew to pew, offering it to every man and woman, asking them if they would like to throw it at Tom's head. Every time he offered the rock to someone, another face blushed with shame, and another head bowed.

Jeff stepped back into the pulpit with a big smile on his face, posing a question to the whole congregation,

"Folks, where do you all think this rock came from, and where do you think it belongs?"

Lucas Bratcher was the first to respond. He stood with his hands behind his back, and with a trembling voice replied,

"Preacher, that rock came from somewhere out there, outside our little church, and I think that's where it belongs."

Jeff nodded to Clark Puckett to stand away from the door, and handed the rock to Lucas. Lucas nodded to Jeff, took the rock to the door of the church, and threw it as far as his strength would allow.

Tom Tillotson was still standing. Jeff asked him to come forward. Tom came immediately, standing beside Jeff just in front of the mourner's bench. Jeff asked Tom to tell the congregation what had happened to him in the last few days.

Becky had always trusted Jeff's judgment both as a husband and as a Pastor, and had never questioned any decision that Jeff had made. But now, looking into the face of that same man who had just a few days before attempted to rape her, she had some misgivings about this decision. What if Tom told the whole sordid story? She swallowed hard as Tom approached the front. In her heart she knew that God had forgiven Tom, and that he had received the Lord Jesus as his Savior, and that she had forgiven him also. But still there was that mental image of what he had tried to do. Her human nature – her woman nature screamed silently as she re-lived the whole thing in a moment of time. She bowed her head, praying silently that God would somehow cause Tom to say only what needed to be said, and not to divulge the sordid details of the attempted rape. The time it took for Tom to get from his pew, to the front of the church seemed like an eternity to Becky. She just wanted it all to be over, and to be cradled in the strong arms of her husband, where so many times she had found the safety and solace she had so desperately needed.

When Tom stepped to the front, and stood directly beside Jeff, all eyes were fastened on him, and all ears were straining to hear every word. Tom had never spoken to this many people before. In fact, the only time he had seen this many people in one place was the day that President Lincoln had been assassinated, and the news had spread far and wide, and folks had gathered in both small and large groups to talk about the gruesome murder of the President, and the fallout that was certain to follow. But somehow Tom now had the courage to face this crowd with hardly a hint of trepidation. As far as he was concerned, all his sins had been forgiven, and his past was wiped away – obliterated by the shed blood of Christ Jesus, and would never be brought before him again. And with a man like Jeff Townsend standing beside him, he felt as safe and secure as a baby in its mother's arms. Tom kept his words to a minimum – he began,

"Folks, a few days ago I tried to take something from this here man, (pointing to Jeff) that didn't belong to me, an he caught me. But instead of shooting me or having me arrested, this here man told me about the Lord Jesus Christ, an how He died fur me, an how He rose again from the dead. This here man an his wife both prayed fur me an with me, an Jesus has saved my rotten soul. This man right here tuk me down to the water an baptized me that very night, an told me that I ort ta join a church, an so here I am if'n you all will have me. I done sum terrible thangs in my life, but the good Lord has tuk away of all that, an I am ready an willin ta do His will, an I thank ye all fur yore uhtenshun."

And without further ado, Jeff was the next to speak,

"Folks, you have all heard this man's confession, his testimony, and his desire. Do I hear a motion and second that we receive him into the fellowship of the Valley Grove Baptist Church?"

Lucas Bratcher was the first to raise his hand, replying,

"I make that motion Pastor."

Almost in the same instant, Bradley Sedgefield, another elder of the church, chimed in,

"I second the motion."

"All in favor, Jeff inserted…raise your right hand."

Every hand in the house shot up instantly, including Becky's. Then, very quickly, Jeff added,

"Any opposed?"

There was dead silence. Jeff smiled and asked everyone to come and extend to their newest member the right hand of fellowship, welcoming him into their midst as a full-fledged member, with all the rights and privileges that they all enjoyed as members of the Valley Grove Baptist Church.

To Jeff's own surprise, all the younger folks and children were the first to come forward, all of them at once, some gathering around Tom, shaking his hand, some hugging his neck, and others doing the same to Jeff. Becky waited till they had all returned to their seats. She bowed her own head in a silent prayer of repentance for the thoughts of her heart, and stepped in front of Tom, taking him by the right hand, placing her left hand on his shoulder, and looking him straight in the eye, whispered…

"Welcome to our little church Mr. Tillotson, and thank you."

Tom nodded and smiled, and they both knew that all was now right between them, and that no one but themselves would ever know all of what had happened that night.

Jeff quickly dismissed the service, asking Tom not to leave until everyone else had left.

"I have something for you out in the carriage." He whispered to Tom.

"Well I have something for you and Mrs. Townsend too." Tom whispered right back to Jeff.

Jeff whispered back to Tom, "Her name is Becky." They both smiled.

The three of them lingered 'til the last wagon had disappeared around the bend. Jeff ushered Tom toward the carriage, and reached under the seat, pulling out the whip, the Colt, and the Bowie knife, handing them to Tom. Tom looked at Jeff with shock, asking, "How did you know I would be here Preacher?"

"Oh, just a wild guess," Jeff replied.

"Yeah, shore," Tom answered, with a chuckle.

He then asked Jeff and Becky to come over to where his horse was tethered. He reached down in the bushes, and brought up a small basket, handing it to Becky. Becky blushed slightly, not having any idea what might be in the basket. She opened the lid slowly, and took out the cutest little puppy her eyes had ever seen. He looked just like Spot had looked when he was a pup. Jeff and Becky knew without asking that Tom had gone to some length, and perhaps to some expense, to find a puppy that so closely resembled the one that he had killed.

With all the other folks gone, and no one watching except Jeff, she handed the puppy to Jeff, and threw her arms around Tom's neck, and hugged him, as they both cried together. As they parted company, Tom just couldn't ride away without telling them,

"Folks, I ain't never met nobody like you two in my life, so I guess my old sorry life ain't been totally wasted after all, cause the good Lord, he allowed me to get to know you both."

They both just smiled at him and at each other. As Tom turned his horse to go Jeff reminded him,

"See you next month Tom, same time, same place."

Tom saluted them, and rode off into the night.

9:15 p.m.

The worship service had lasted much longer than any other they had enjoyed since Jeff had become the Pastor, which meant that they would be getting home much later also. Even though it was late spring, and the days were getting longer, the high mountains often hid most of the evening sunlight from those who traveled along the narrow paths and trails that threaded through them. Jeff stopped the carriage, and lit the two lanterns that were mounted inside metal frames that he had designed himself. Living and surviving in the mountains of West Virginia in 1866 required that a man have at least some blacksmithing skills of his own, and Jeff Townsend was a man of many talents. He fashioned the metal frames so as to keep the lanterns from swinging back and forth, and yet not obstruct the light coming from the globes.

The sun had set now, and most of the families that had been to the meeting had already reached their respective homes. A few were still struggling slowly along the rougher routes, with deep ruts, wide creeks, and thick mud to hinder their progress. About a quarter mile from the little school, the roads, trails and paths went off in several directions, each leading to the different farms scattered throughout the County. And every family, and every adolescent in each family, knew the way to each other's farms. All of them knew that at one time or another they would each have to call on one another for some form of neighborly kindness or assistance. They all helped each other whenever a need arose. When a neighbor was in need, all the other neighbors dropped whatever they were doing, and went to his neighbor's side, and stayed there till the need was taken care of.

The same trail that led to the home of Lucas Bratcher eventually dwindled to no more than a path, just wide enough for a horse and rider. But unknown to any of the families or individuals who attended the church, that same path veered off into a narrow valley no more than ten feet wide at its widest point. The mouth of the valley was overgrown with vines and bushes, virtually invisible to the casual passerby. Deep inside that narrow valley was where Tom Tillotson had chosen to live – away from peering eyes.

Jeff was opening the big gate that marked the outer limit of his own farm when he and Becky heard the sound – the same sound that Jeff had heard last week as he was nearing home – the weak but audible echo of gunfire, a single shot. Nearly every family from the church heard it also. Tom Tillotson, who had already reached his own little shack, heard it too. The sound of gunfire during the daytime usually caused no alarm at all to any family who heard it. The mountains were full of hunters whose only livelihood was hunting wild game for food, clothing, and hides to sell. No one paid much attention to the echoes that resounded through the valleys on a daily basis. But gunfire this late at night was cause for some concern. But everyone had had enough excitement for one night, and dismissed it as some young coon hunter or possum hunter who had refused to give up his quest before nightfall. Deep in his gut, Jeff felt a dark foreboding, but quickly turned his attention back to Becky and the carriage. Becky was turning her eyes from east to west, and back again, as if she were trying to pinpoint the location from where the shot had come, but knowing that it was impossible to do so.

Neither of them said a word as Jeff climbed back into the carriage, and drove the rest of the way up to the barn. He lifted Becky and the puppy down from the carriage, unhooked the carriage from the horse, and backed the carriage into the little shed he had built for it on one side of the barn. He led the horse into the barn, took of his harness, hung it up on its hooks, and closed the big barn door behind him. With Becky only slightly objecting, he lifted her into his arms, and carried her and the puppy around to the back door of the house. She held onto his neck as he held her in one arm, and unlocked the big padlock. And as he had done nearly every time that he and Becky had entered their home since the first day, he carried her inside and gently put her down in front of him, kissing her with all the passion of his soul.

Jeff took a match from the box that sat beside the lamp atop the mantle, and lit the lamp. They just stood and looked into each other's eyes for a moment, each of them searching for the hint of concern that still lingered from the sound of the gunshot. They were both trying desperately to dismiss it from their minds, but neither of them could. The vivid memory of what had happened after that gunshot he had heard last Monday morning still lurked in the back of Jeff's mind. But it was bedtime, and there was nothing that either of them could do except pray that nothing terrible had happened. Jeff made one more check of the doors and windows, placed the little puppy in his basket, and put him in the corner beside the fireplace.

In the time it took for Jeff to go from the bedroom to the living room and back, Becky had undressed, dabbing just a hint of her favorite perfume on her neck and between her breasts, and was standing beside the bed, waiting for Jeff to enter the room. Nearly two years of marriage had not lessened their desire for one another to any degree. The sight of her standing there made Jeff's heart pound harder and faster, and he could see the same passion in her eyes. Suddenly all the events of the night seemed to disappear in an instant, including the gunshot. She was in his arms, kissing him with as much passion as ever as he picked her up in his arms and lowered her softly onto the bed. He threw his hat into a corner, removed his suit coat, and kept kissing her as she unbuttoned his shirt. He flung the shirt after the hat, blew out the lamp, hurriedly took off his shoes and trousers, and lay down beside her.

Sunday, May 26th, 1866, 5:00 a.m.

The sound of cock-a-doodle-doo awakened Jeff first. He was up and had his pants on in less than a minute. He grabbed the water bucket and headed barefoot to the spring. He brought the water back to the house, poured some of it into a porcelain basin, splashed the cold water into his face, and quickly dried with a towel. He built a fire in the little cook stove, returned to the bedroom, and began kissing Becky awake. She flung her arms around his waist, pulling him onto the bed, laughing like a little girl, tickling his ribs as he pretended to be trying to get away from her. He rolled across the bed and off the other side onto the floor laughing, and trying to tell her that she needed to get up and start cooking because they had company coming today. Little did either of them know what kind of company they would be seeing, before this day would be over.

Most Sundays on the Townsend farm were spent with some of the families from the church coming to Jeff's house to spend nearly the whole day eating, singing, playing games, and listening to Jeff preach another message. The families that came were usually only the ones who lived closest to Jeff and Becky. It was called - *all day meetin, and dinner on the ground.* The men mostly pitched horse shoes. The children rode the horses, and played hide-n-seek, or tag, or whatever game they chose. The women folk prepared the food, and spread the blankets, and carried food to the others. Jeff and Becky always set a pretty large spread themselves, and looked forward to feeding and entertaining everyone who came. It was also a day when the people of the church brought extra things also. They couldn't afford to pay Jeff a salary as Pastor, so they made up for it with fruits and vegetables from their own farms. Some brought baskets of eggs. Some of the women brought cloth material for Becky to make dresses for herself, shirts for Jeff, and quilts for the bed. It was their way of showing their gratitude for all that Jeff and Becky did for all of them and their families.

Becky had cooked most of the morning, and Jeff had done all the everyday chores that had to be done outside, and was driving the horseshoe stakes into the ground when he heard the sound of fast-approaching horse hooves, and a lone rider shouting as loud as he could…

"Preacher! Preacher! Oh my God! Preacher!"

As the rider drew closer, Jeff recognized Clark Puckett. The thick lather on his horse told Jeff that he had ridden hard and fast. Clark quickly dismounted. His face was ashen white. Suddenly the echo of that shot in the night resounded in Jeff's mind. He knew something terrible had happened. Clark wasted no time with amenities. He blurted it all out in a single breath…

"Jeff, Luke Bratcher was shot and killed last night."

Jeff turned pale, and before he could speak, Clark added…

"And that ain't all Jeff, the Sedgefield family was headed up here this morning when they found Luke's body lying face down in the creek. He was shot in the back Jeff, and they found a Bowie knife just a few feet from his body. They sent their boy to fetch the Sheriff, and he's already putting out wanted posters for Tom Great Bear Tillotson, and the posters say Wanted, Dead or Alive!"

Jeff hung his head and said a quick silent prayer on behalf of Tom. He knew that there was no need to pray for Lucas Bratcher now, and as far as he knew Lucas had no family. Luke was a widower, and for some reason unknown to anyone, his wife couldn't have children. He told Clark to go on into the house while he watered his horse and let him cool down. Becky was excited to see Clark, and looked past him to ask where Sarah and the children were. Clark looked at Becky with the most pitiful look she had ever seen on his face. Clark hung his head slightly, shaking his head from side to side.

"I'm afraid Sarah and the kids won't be coming today Becky. There's been a killin. It happened last night. Luke Bratcher was shot in the back."

Jeff came in the door just in time to catch Becky in his arms as she fainted. He quickly laid her on the big couch as Clark ran to the kitchen to get the bucket of cold water and a rag.

When Becky had fully recovered, Jeff asked Clark if he would stay with Becky and watch after her 'til he could go and find Tom Tillotson before a posse did. Clark quickly agreed, and Jeff was out the door saddling his own horse. News of Lucas Bratcher's murder had already spread across five counties, and so had the news of a thousand dollar reward for Tom Great Bear Tillotson – Dead or Alive. Jeff had no idea how or where to find Tom, but Clark had told him where Luke's body had been found, and he determined to start looking right there. As it turned out, Providence was smiling on both Jeff and Tom at the same time. Tom had no idea that he was now a wanted man, and was on his way out of the little valley as Jeff rose up from the spot where Luke Bratcher's body had been found. Jeff leaped into the saddle and galloped along the narrow path 'til it looked as if it would end abruptly. As Jeff passed the mouth of the narrow valley, Tom Tillotson rode out just a few feet behind him. He saw Jeff's back, and recognized Jeff's black suit coat and hat. He wondered what Jeff was doing this far away from home on Sunday. He shouted…

"Hey Preacher, ain't you a little bit lost?"

Jeff swung his horse around and faced Tom. The first words out of Jeff's mouth were…

"Where's your Bowie knife Tom?"

Tom looked totally bewildered, but instinctively pulled back his vest and took the knife from its sheath, holding it up for Jeff to see.

"That's all I need to know," Jeff quickly nodded, and asked Tom if there was some place private and secluded where they could talk.

Tom trusted Jeff, and quickly steered his horse into the mouth of the valley, ducking under the low-hanging vines and branches, motioning for Jeff to follow him. Nothing was said until they reached the little shack that Tom called home. Once inside, Jeff quickly explained the whole situation to Tom, including the wanted posters and the reward. He also reminded Tom that he knew he was innocent, and that someone was trying to frame him, and doing a pretty darn good job of it. Tom sat silent for a few moments, then looked Jeff in the eye and asked...

"What am I going to do Jeff?"

Jeff asked him if he knew of any shortcuts off the main trails that would lead them to his farm without them being seen. Tom objected immediately...

"Yeah, Preacher, I know plenty shortcuts, but I don't aim to git you and your wife involved in this mess."

Jeff replied. "We're already involved Tom, and if I don't get you somewhere safe before the sun sets, you're a dead man. They will shoot you on sight, or hang you on the spot Tom. We have to get you to my place and hide you until I can find whoever did this, and bring him to justice."

They both agreed that there was no time to waste. Mounting up, Tom led Jeff northward, deeper into the valley, along paths that looked as if they were made by mountain goats. It was slow going for hours, but suddenly Jeff recognized the big stand of poplars that marked the outer boundary of his own farm. He nodded and smiled at Tom with both approval and gratitude. Now all they had to do was get across the open pastures without being seen. Jeff told Tom to put his whip in the saddlebag where it wouldn't be a dead giveaway.

They were just about to spur their horses when Tom reached out and stopped Jeff, sniffing the air as if he smelled something odd. Jeff smelled it too – it was the smell of burning cloth. Jeff insisted that they ignore it, reminding Tom that they needed to get to his house as soon as possible. Tom was about to agree with Jeff, but hesitated.

"Jeff, he slowly whispered, that ain't just a rag burning – it's rags and wood together."

Jeff urged Tom to let it go, and to follow him around the outer edge of the farm so that they could approach from the front and maybe not attract as much attention as they might by approaching from the back. They both knew that there might be one or more bounty hunters lurking nearby hoping to get a shot at Tom. But Tom refused to go. With what almost sounded like a pitiful plea, he assured Jeff that he had smelled that same odor before, and that he had a *gut feelin* that the two of them should find the source of that odor, and check it out.

Jeff not only wanted to get Tom to some place of relative safety, he also wanted to get back to Becky. But the life of an innocent man was in jeopardy, and he could somehow aid in preventing that man from being shot or hung, he was willing to do what he could. He knew that Becky was in good hands with Clark Puckett. What he didn't know was that Becky had already sent Clark back to his own family, assuring him that she was capable of taking care of herself until Jeff returned. Clark was reluctant to leave, but finally gave in to Becky's insistence. Immediately after Clark left, Becky fell on her knees beside the bed, praying for Jeff and Tom.

Jeff and Tom were downwind of the bonfire. The wind carried the smell and smoke straight toward them. As the scent became steadily stronger, they dismounted and tethered their horses to low branches. Tom motioned for Jeff to stay hidden behind a big beech tree as he began to climb the tree to see if he could get a better look from higher up. Nearing the top, his eyes confirmed what his gut had told him. About fifty yards ahead of them was a little group of four men gathered around the bonfire, laughing and shaking hands as if they were congratulating one another for something. Lying on the ground behind them were their robes and hoods. One of the men was holding up a robe in front of him, waving it back and forth and howling like a wolf. Tom could see that the lower half of the robe had been burnt. The man holding it threw it into the fire. Tom recognized all four of them. He could also see that one of them was wearing a leather sheath – with no knife in it. Their rifles were all leaned together against a big oak tree. He made his way down the tree as quickly and as quietly as possible and told Jeff what he had seen. When he told Jeff who the men were, Jeff didn't look all that surprised because he knew all four of them also. They both knew now what had happened to Luke Bratcher – he had been murdered by the KKK, and Tom had been neatly framed for the crime.

Tom described the men's surroundings in detail to Jeff, and offered Jeff his Colt. Jeff refused it, whispering to Tom…

"We can take them all alive Tom. I'll sneak up behind the oak and dispose of their rifles. You surprise them with your whip and knife. While you have them distracted, I'll take care of the rest."

Tom grinned knowingly, remembering that huge fist that had knocked him unconscious not long ago. Jeff came up behind them as quietly as a mouse. He peeked around the oak to make sure that Tom was in position. Jeff stepped from behind the oak as casually as if he was stepping behind his pulpit, and introduced himself...

"Howdy gentlemen, I'm Jeff Townsend."

Before he or anyone else could utter another word, Tom's whip had wrapped around the ankles of two of the men, pulling them face forward onto the ground in front of Jeff. A swift kick to the groin from Jeff's size-twelve boot instantly took all the fight out of another, and a roundhouse right knocked the last one unconscious.

Tom sliced their robes into lengths long enough to tie all their hands behind their backs, and kicked dirt into the fire to make sure it was out. He then tied all of them separately and securely to four trees about ten yards from each other. He tied a strip of their robes around their necks, their waists and their feet. Jeff found all their hoods, and placed them neatly on each of their heads, calling each of them by name as he pulled the hood down over his face. Satisfied that all the men were virtually helpless, Tom drew his Bowie knife from its sheath, placing the sharp blade underneath Herb Valentine's chin, whispering,

"Where's your Bowie knife Herb? Did ya lose it somewhere? As you can see, I still have mine." Herb cursed back at Tom...

"You go to Hell, you stinkin injun."

Tom backhanded Herb across the mouth, asking him...

"Now is that any way to talk in front of a Preacher Herb?"

Jeff told all of them...

"Now you fellas don't go nowhere till we come back with the Sheriff."

Tom thought it best if he stayed with the four men while Jeff went for the Sheriff. Jeff quickly agreed. Jeff hadn't taken two steps when Sheriff John Collins cocked his rifle, pointing it at Tom. Jeff was certain that John was about to pull the trigger. He quickly stepped between the two men. The barrel of the rifle was now pressed against Jeff's chest. The four men tied to the trees were all screaming…

"Shoot him Sheriff, shoot the sorry bastard."

Still holding the rifle to Jeff's chest, John reached behind his back, pulling out a Bowie knife, holding it up for all to see. He hadn't noticed that Tom still had his own Bowie knife in his hand. Tom quickly took charge of the situation, telling John to look at the butt of the knife that he was holding up. John turned the knife over, and there on the butt of it was carved the initials…H.V. Tom smiled at John knowingly, nodding his head…

"Now I ain't got much education Sheriff, but I do believe that them there initials stand for Herbert Valentine."

John asked which one was Herb as Jeff removed Herb's hood. John immediately noticed that Herb's knife sheath was empty. John instructed Jeff to put his hood back on his head, and to untie all of them from the trees, but to leave their hands tied. Jeff, Tom and the Sheriff helped all of them onto their horses. The whole group headed toward Jeff's farm, with John in front, the four suspects in the middle, and Jeff and Tom bringing up the rear. When they reached Jeff's farm the sun was setting. Becky was standing on the front porch, looking in every direction, praying that Jeff and Tom were still alive. As the seven men approached the gate, Jeff spurred his horse to the front and dismounted, running the rest of the way, catching Becky in his arms as she leaped and locked her arms around his neck, crying and laughing at the same time, murmuring…

"Thank you sweet Jesus!"

Jeff gave Becky a short version of what had happened, and explained to her that he and Tom would have to help the Sheriff escort these men to the county jail. John told Jeff that if he could spare him some rope, he could take all of them to jail by himself. Jeff rushed to the barn and came back with enough rope to tie all four of the men to each other, with enough left for John to lead them single file behind him. John apologized to Tom for all the trouble, and assured him that he would be taking down all the Wanted posters, and withdrawing the reward, and that he would be putting up new ones with a picture of Herbert Valentine, and a message at the bottom stating…Murderer of Lucas Bratcher Captured. Tom assured John that he would be taking down every poster that he saw too, and burning them. John asked Jeff if he could keep Tom here on the farm until he could deliver these varmints to Judge Bracken in Morgantown, and get this thing cleared up. Jeff nodded to John and smiled, saying...

"I think I can keep him busy and out of trouble for a week or so John. We'll see if he's as good with a plow as he is with a whip."

Tom gave Jeff a squint-eyed stare at the mention of a plow, but offered no objection, just being thankful that for the first time in his life he had found a true and faithful friend – one who had proven his friendship by stepping in front of a cocked rifle.

The streets of Morgantown West Virginia were lined with onlookers as Sheriff John Collins rode into town with four men in tow, each of them donned with a KKK hood. All John had to do was to whisper to a single bystander that he had caught the murderer of Lucas Bratcher, and the news spread like wildfire throughout the town. With the four men still lashed together, John pulled off their hoods in front of the whole town, beginning with Herb Valentine. Four women fainted instantly as they saw the faces of their own husbands emerge from under the hoods. Herbert Valentine was the head of City Council, and owned the local General Store, where he had often bought hides and furs from Tom Great Bear Tillotson. He had also traded Tom a new Bowie knife for ten beaver pelts. During the trade Herb had shown Tom his own Bowie knife, with his initials carved into the end.

Wesley Phelps was the local blacksmith where Tom had his horse shod more than once. Preston Jenkins was the owner of the saloon where Tom had often drunk himself into a stupor, and William Bowen owned the Morgantown Hotel where Tom had often bedded down with a local prostitute. Lucas Bratcher was killed because he was a former member of the KKK, and wanted out because he had seen too much innocent blood shed. Herb Valentine had drawn the short straw that designated him as the man to pull the trigger on Lucas.

Monday, May 27th, 1866, 2:30 p.m.

News of the capture of a murderer and his accomplices was buzzing all over Morgantown. The same news was also buzzing along the telegraph wires to every town that had a telegraph office.

Judge Elias (Eli) W. Bracken had been informed of all the details surrounding the case. Herb Valentine, Wesley Phelps, Preston Jenkins and William Bowen were in jail, awaiting the selection of a jury, and a trial. After each of them had spoken to an attorney, Judge Bracken had spoken with each of them separately in a pre-trial interview, just to see if their stories matched. None of them did. When Judge Bracken returned home at 2:30 p.m., his wife Nola met him just inside the door, holding a note, and trembling. The note was a death threat against the Judge and his wife, stating that if either of the accused men were found guilty, neither the Judge nor his wife would live to see another sunrise. And since the note was not a telegram, Judge Bracken knew immediately that someone right here in Morgantown had written the note, and had slipped it under his front door sometime between the time he had gone to the jail and 2:30 in the afternoon. That meant, of course, that the one who either wrote or delivered the note (or both) was fairly close by. He took his wife into his arms, reassuring her that he would not let anything bad happen to either of them. This was not the first death threat that he had received, and neither would it be the last. But Judge Bracken was a fearless barrister – never one to shrink from a challenge or a threat. He had been one of the most prestigious and feared prosecutors that the Commonwealth of West Virginia had ever produced. Governor Boreman himself had appointed the younger Mr. Bracken to the position of Circuit Judge, presiding over three counties, and he had since been elected to the office, and re-elected twice. He carried the reputation of being fair but firm, and he was not easily fooled by shysters or liars.

The shocking discovery that four of the more prominent citizens of Morgantown were members of the KKK, and that one of them was now accused of cold blooded murder had the whole town whispering and gossiping. A few were not surprised at all. Many more were sorely disappointed that the attempted frame up of Tom Tillotson had failed. And even though Tom had been eliminated as a suspect, there were more than a few who still wanted him dead. In fact, Tom was now more hated and despised by some than he was before the murder, and Tom knew it all too well. But Tom was now a changed man, and bore no ill will toward anyone - he determined that he was not going to live his life in fear or in hiding. He knew that if someone wanted him dead there was not much that he could do about it except to watch his back and pray, and he prayed every day.

With a little training from Jeff, Tom turned into a fairly good plowman in less than a week. He worked side by side with Jeff in the fields, and ate three hot meals a day at Jeff's table-good food like he had never tasted in his life. Both Jeff and Becky made him feel like an honored guest. He refused to sleep in the extra bedroom that Jeff and Becky offered him, making the excuse that he was going to be leaving soon, and didn't want to get spoiled by sleeping in a nice clean bed every night. He insisted that he would sleep in the barn loft. Becky insisted that he take a pillow and two blankets. Jeff even offered him the use of the big tub in which to take a bath, but again Tom refused, insisting that he would wash off in the stream. Jeff and Becky knew that Tom was just being a gentleman, and wanting them to have their privacy and they both appreciated it, and respected Tom for it.

Monday, June 3rd, 1866. Morgantown West Virginia, 9:00 a.m.

With Tom to help him, Jeff got all the morning chores done in record time, and the two of them took the early train to Morgantown. They were both key witnesses in the trial, and had to be there by order of the court. Without Tom's or Jeff's knowledge, Judge Bracken had ordered Sheriff Collins to assign two deputies to stay close to them while they were in town. He wanted to protect the two key witnesses for the prosecution as best he could. The two deputies met Jeff and Tom at the train station and escorted them quickly to the courthouse. The jury was seated, the handcuffed prisoners were seated, and the attorneys were seated. Everyone entering the courthouse was disarmed. Judge Bracken gaveled the trial to order.

Prosecutor Carson McCoy called his first witness – Tom Tillotson to the stand. The crowd immediately erupted into howls and jeers, calling Tom a murderer, a savage, and a thief. Judge Bracken immediately responded with a threat to clear the courtroom if there was another outburst. There was total silence as Tom placed his left hand on the Bible and raised his right hand to repeat the oath. Tom was asked if he knew the four defendants. He replied that he knew all four of them. He was asked to point to and name each defendant one at a time. Tom began with Herb Valentine, and pointed to and named all four of the men in the order in which they were seated. Mr. McCoy asked Tom to tell the court how he knew the defendants and in what way he was associated with them. Tom responded very calmly and deliberately, telling how he had done business with each of the men several times.

Mr. McCoy then asked Tom to relate the story of the events leading up to, and including the arrest of the four men. Again Tom described every event in vivid detail. When the prosecutor was finished questioning Tom, he gave him over to the defense attorney, Charles L. Jones, who immediately pounced upon Tom's character and reputation, asking,

"Mr. Thomas Great Bear Tillotson, have you ever murdered anyone?"

Prosecutor McCoy leaped to his feet with a loud objection.

"Mr. Tillotson is not on trial here Your Honor."

Judge Bracken sustained the objection, warning Mr. Jones to confine his questions to the case at hand, or be held in contempt. Mr. Jones tried every trick he knew to rattle Tom's nerves and cause him to bring his own credibility into question to the jury, but to no avail – Tom answered every question with perfect calm, looking Mr. Jones straight in the eye. With every answer Tom gave, Mr. Jones became a little more frustrated, and finally gave up. Judge Bracken dismissed Tom to his seat.

When the prosecutor called Jeff Townsend to the stand, several young women immediately turned their attention away from the trial itself, and toward the tall, handsome, blue-eyed stranger. When Jeff's testimony revealed that he was a minister, and married, their interest in him suddenly waned. Jeff's every answer perfectly corroborated Tom's testimony in every detail. Mr. Jones was now getting nervous, glancing at his clients and shaking his head. Sheriff Collins was called to the stand, and again, his story matched that of Jeff and Tom. Mr. Jones asked Judge Bracken if he could have a moment to confer with his clients. Judge Bracken granted his request. Mr. Jones whispered to the four men, asking them if any of them wanted to testify in his own behalf. Each of them refused, smugly affirming that none of them were going to be convicted. Mr. Jones quickly explained to them that the evidence against them was damning evidence, and that they stood hardly any chance of being acquitted. Herb Valentine leaned over to Mr. Jones and whispered...

"They can all go to Hell. Even if we are convicted, we ain't gonna be punished. We got an ace in the hole that nobody knows about."

Mr. Jones told them that he had done all he could do for them, and would have to give the case to the jury.

The backup plan that was supposed to guarantee the release of the four defendants was to have another member of the KKK to kidnap Nola Bracken during the trial, and take her to a secluded place, and to send a note to Judge Bracken to the effect that his wife would have her throat slit if either of the accused were found guilty. They made one mistake – they underestimated the intelligence of Judge Bracken, and the courage of his wife Nola. Judge Bracken was one step ahead of them from the beginning.

Melvin Jenkins, the brother of Preston Jenkins, eased up to the back door of Judge Bracken's home with a knife in one hand and a pistol in the other. To his surprise the door was unlocked. He suspected nothing. Nola Bracken was sitting at the table, sipping a cup of tea. Melvin stepped inside the house. Mrs. Bracken lowered her tea and clasped her left hand over her breast, gasping as if she were totally surprised and terrified. It was all an act. When Melvin took one more step, the butt of Deputy Sheriff Ancel Smith's rifle caught him right between the eyes, knocking him to the floor. Deputy Smith quickly tied his hands behind his back. Mrs. Bracken poured cold water in his face, reviving him. Deputy Smith shoved him out the door and helped him onto his horse. Ancel mounted his own horse, pointing his rifle toward the courthouse.

As Deputy Smith and Melvin Jenkins entered the courthouse, the foreman of the jury was standing, pronouncing...

"We find the defendants guilty as charged Your Honor."

Judge Bracken grinned approvingly as Deputy Smith ushered Melvin to the front of the courtroom, shoving the barrel of his rifle into Melvin's back. As soon as they stepped in front of Judge Bracken Mrs. Bracken walked in, taking a seat beside Jeff and Tom, smiling from ear to ear.

"Well what do we have here Deputy?" asked the Judge.

"Another low down skunk who just tried to murder your wife Sir," replied Deputy Smith.

No one in the courtroom could contain themselves any longer, they began to whisper and talk among themselves, most of them wondering what was going on. Again Judge Bracken gaveled the courtroom into silence. He began…

"Well folks, it seems we're going to have to have another trial, that is unless Mr. Jenkins here wants to say something, and save the county some much-needed time and taxes."

Melvin Jenkins glanced back to the table where his brother and the other three defendants were sitting, then to Mr. Jones, who immediately shook his head, indicating that he would not defend him.

Judge Bracken turned to Deputy Smith and asked him to tell the court what had happened. Deputy Smith addressed the jury, telling them how he had caught Mr. Jenkins in the Judge's house with a knife and pistol in his hand, attempting to abduct Mrs. Bracken. Mrs. Bracken stood up and corroborated Deputy Smith's story, and handed the note that had been slipped under her door to the foreman of the jury. The note was then passed from one juror to another 'til all twelve had read it. The foreman asked Judge Bracken exactly what Mr. Jenkins was being charged with.

Judge Bracken replied. "He is being charged with Conspiracy to commit kidnapping, and conspiracy to commit murder."

Herb Valentine and Preston Jenkins leaped to their feet screaming…

"Tell' em all to go to Hell Melvin, don't admit nary thang."

Melvin stared at his brother for a few moments, then at the other three. Tears welled up in his eyes as he again looked into the eyes of his brother, sobbing he sank to the floor.

"It has to end Preston, it has to end here and now, there's been too much killin and beatin, I can't do it no more."

He looked up at Judge Bracken, then to the jury, and blurted out the whole sordid story of the murder of Lucas Bratcher and the plan to kidnap and kill Nola Bracken if any of the accused were convicted. Judge Bracken ordered Melvin to be taken to the jail and held there until he dealt with these four varmints."

Wesley Phelps, Preston Jenkins, and William Bowen were all sentenced to ten years in the newly constructed Federal Prison in

Heavenly Places

Moundsville, West Virginia, nearly ninety miles from Morgantown. Herbert Valentine was sentenced to hang by the neck until he was dead. The hanging was set to take place on Saturday, June 8th, 1866, at noon. A crew of men was dispatched immediately to begin building the gallows. Court was dismissed, and Preston Jenkins, Wesley Phelps, and William Bowen were escorted to the train station to be taken to Moundsville West Virginia, about twelve miles south of Wheeling, where a brand new State Penitentiary was under construction. Herbert Valentine joined Melvin Jenkins in the county jail to await execution. Judge Bracken walked over to the jail and ordered Melvin Jenkins released, telling him that because of his cooperation and testimony he was cleared of all charges. He then ordered Deputy Smith to release Melvin. Melvin was overcome with joy and gratitude. As he mounted his horse and rode away Judge Bracken advised him…

"Watch your back Melvin, God be merciful to you."

The little farm and house where Melvin and his family lived was actually still owned by Melvin's brother Preston. Melvin's name was nowhere on the deed. Preston only allowed his younger brother to occupy the place because Melvin simply had no other place to live. Preston had often reminded Melvin that he was doing him a big favor by letting him live on two good acres of land with a house and barn – free of charge. But it was mutually agreed that in order for Melvin and his family to enjoy that *"gift"* Melvin had to do Preston's bidding – his *"dirty work."* What Preston had not told Melvin was that if he ever failed or refused to do his bidding, he and his family would be evicted immediately. But with Preston in the penitentiary, Melvin was sure that the little farm would now be his for as long as he lived.

Melvin rode hard and fast toward his little two-acre farm, rejoicing that he had finally done something right in his life, even if it meant losing a brother. He had been bullied and beaten by his older brother Preston for most of his life, and had never found the courage or strength to stand up to him. Now, somehow, he felt like a free man – free from the bondage of fear that had for so long rendered him less than a man, and had earned him the label of a coward. His heart pounded at the thought of seeing his beloved wife Clarissa and his little daughter Carla. He couldn't wait to tell them the news that Preston had finally gotten what was coming to him, and that he had been the one who presented the evidence that convicted him.

When he reached his little farm, Melvin was so excited to see his family he didn't even bother to unsaddle his horse. He just slapped him on the rump and turned him into the barn. He was going to come back and feed and water the horse after telling his family the good news. As he ran the last few yards to the house he yelled out...

"Clarissa, Clarissa, honey I'm back and I have some great news."

Any other time, Clarissa and Carla would have met him at the front door with a smile and a hug. But he was sure that they were busy with something and hadn't heard him ride in. He wondered why they hadn't heard him yelling. And where was Old Boss, the beagle dog that loved him so much? Something was wrong – he could feel it in his gut.

Melvin turned around and deliberately cursed himself...

"Damn it Melvin, you forgot to unsaddle Old Hacksaw again."

He wanted to get back to the barn and his horse, and the rifle that was still in its sheath. He prayed with every step that whoever was in his house hadn't hurt his wife and child. He pulled the rifle from its sheath and crept through the bushes behind the barn to get to the rear of his house. He kicked the back door open with the rifle already to his shoulder. Clarissa and Carla were both bound to their chairs facing each other, gagged with handkerchiefs. Two men wearing robes and hoods opened fire at the same time. As Melvin sank to his knees he saw the heads of his wife and daughter slump to their breasts, blood spurting from their chests. He fell dead between the two of them.

Reese Bowen, brother to William Bowen, and Orville Phelps, brother to Wesley Phelps, removed their robes and hoods, stuffed them into burlap sacks, and set the house on fire. They did the same to the barn, smokehouse and tool shed. They shook hands, congratulating one another on a job well done, and mounted their horses to ride back into Morgantown. As Reese swung his right foot over the saddle, his wire-rimmed glasses fell out of his vest pocket onto the ground without him noticing. Arriving back in Morgantown the two men split up. Reese took over the operation of the Morgantown Hotel owned by his brother William, and

Heavenly Places

Orville Phelps assumed ownership of his brother's blacksmith shop. The smoke from the burnt buildings had nearly dissipated as the train carrying Jeff and Tom rolled by the outer edge of Melvin Jenkins' farm. No one suspected what had happened there only a few hours before.

After giving his testimony at the trial, Jeff hadn't spoken a word. He had spent the whole time in silent prayer – praying for the souls of four men who could so casually commit such a heinous crime, and show no remorse whatsoever. He had prayed for Melvin Jenkins and his family. He had prayed for Becky and her safety, and he had prayed for the people of Morgantown West Virginia. Before leaving for the train station, he walked across the street to the dress shop. He had a few things he wanted to get for Becky for their anniversary. Both he and Tom sat silently the whole trip back. The silence was broken suddenly as the train whistle blew and the conductor announced to Tom and Jeff that they had arrived at their station. The two men walked silently to the livery stable where their horses had been boarded, paid the livery boy, and rode toward Jeff's farm.

As they approached the mouth of the valley, Tom reined in his horse and stopped. Jeff had gone a few yards farther and turned to face Tom. They just sat there on their horses, looking into each other's eyes, trying to figure out what the other was thinking. Jeff was the first to speak.

"Tom, you know you're welcome to come and live with me and Becky. I'll even give you a couple acres of land if you will just help me do the chores and farming. You'll get three hot meals a day, and we can build you a little house to live in if you want one."

Tom eyed Jeff for a few moments before he found the words with which to respond.

"Well, he began, I sure ain't got much back there to look farward to, but I shore don't want to be a bother to ya and Becky nur any unnecessary danger either. You folks have been the closest thang to a family I've ever had."

Jeff nodded and continued, "It's your decision Tom, I won't press you, but if you change your mind, you know the way." Jeff turned his horse and started to ride away. He hadn't gone fifty yards when he heard Tom yell.

"Well ya sure don't give a man a lot of time to make up his mind do ya Preacher?"

Jeff turned and grinned as Tom spurred his horse and caught up to him. Tom reminded Jeff that he didn't know a whole lot about building houses. Jeff nodded and laughed in agreement.

"Yeah, I know, I saw the house you built."

"Well ya plan on goin back to Morgantown for the hanging preacher?"

"No, I'm not Tom, because that's my anniversary, and I have far better things to do than to watch a man dancing from the end of a rope."

"Well do ya mind if'n I go?" asked Tom.

Jeff gave Tom that knowing glance again, and replied…

"In fact Tom, I insist that you do."

Jeff knew that Tom not only wanted to see a murderer get justice, he also wanted to give Jeff and Becky their privacy on their anniversary. He also wanted to ride back to his old shack and pick up a few of his belongings that he had left behind, one of which was a picture of his Mother. Jeff told Tom to take as long as he wanted to do whatever he had to do before coming back to the farm. They shook hands, and Tom turned his horse and rode back toward his own little valley. There were still four and one half days until the hanging.

On his way back to his place, Tom decided that he would enjoy all the free time he could before going back to Morgantown for the hanging. He also decided that he was going to get himself some false teeth when he did arrive in Morgantown. It would take almost a full day to ride the twenty-one miles into town, and another day to ride back to Jeff's farm, so that would give him three days to just enjoy life, and to reflect upon all that had happened in his life in such a short time. He removed his hat, bowed his head, and thanked the good Lord for all the good things in his life.

Tom rode for as long as he could see a ray of sunlight, and stopped near a little creek to camp for the night before riding on into town the next morning. His big black horse Promenade gave a whinny of relief when both his rider and saddle were removed from his back. Tom built a small fire, led Promenade down to the creek for a drink, brought him back and tethered him to bush, and fed him some apples from a nearby apple tree. He laid his saddle blanket on top of his saddle, and drifted off to sleep, thinking about owning his own two acres of land, and a little house of his own, and having good neighbors like Jeff and Becky Townsend.

He was up at sunrise, bathed in the creek, ate two apples, saddled Promenade, and headed for Morgantown. He decided to stop and visit Melvin Jenkins and his family before riding on into town, just to thank Melvin for doing what he did, testifying against his own brother at the trial. He veered off the main road onto the narrow trail that led to Melvin's farm, whistling as he rode. When the little farm came into view, Tom's heart felt as if it had skipped a beat at what he saw. Everything was burned to the ground. He gave a quick glance all around him to see if anyone else was around. He held Promenade to a very slow walk as he cautiously approached the outer perimeter of the farm. He decided to walk the rest of the way up to the gate. As soon as his feet touched the ground, he thought he saw a glare just a few yards ahead. It was the sun glaring off the lenses of Reese Bowen's glasses. Tom took another quick look around, pulled his Colt from its holster, and squatted down and picked up the glasses, questioning.

"Now, jest where have I seen these glasses afore?"

He quickly slipped the glasses into his saddlebag, and walked up to the path toward what used to be Melvin Jenkins home. Even the wooden fence had been set on fire. Tom thought to himself…

"Whoever did this, wanted to make dead shore that there was no evidence left behind."

He stepped into the pile of rubble, only to discover the gruesome, charred remains of three bodies – a man, a woman, and a child. The stench was sickening. Leaving the scene just as he had found it, Tom mounted his horse, and rode down the path that led from the back of Melvin's farm to the railroad. The station where he and Jeff had gotten on and off the train the day of the trial was only a quarter-mile north of Melvin's farm, and had a telegraph office. Tom spurred his horse into a gallop along the side of the railroad. Reaching the station, he ran in immediately and told the telegraph operator that he needed to send a telegram to Sheriff Collins in Morgantown. The telegram read simply –

"Murder – M. Jenkins farm - bring shovels."

Tom rode back to the farm and waited for Sheriff Collins to arrive. About two and a half hours later, Sheriff Collins and Deputy Smith arrived at the scene together. Lifting their bandanas over their mouths, the three of them took turns with the two shovels, digging three graves. Tom found enough sticks and vines with which to lash them together, and made three little crosses. All three men removed their hats as Tom prayed a short prayer. Then, just before Sheriff Collins and Deputy Smith were about to leave, Tom reached into his saddlebag and handed John the glasses he had found, pointing to the spot where he had found them. John thought to himself...

"Now just where have I seen these glasses before?"

He thanked Tom for the glasses and for helping with the burials. When the three of them rode into Morgantown, it was 6:00 p.m. Most of the shops were closed in town. The Morgantown Hotel, of course, was always open. Tom waited outside while Sheriff Collins and his deputy rode straight up to the hitching post of the Hotel and walked in, expecting to see Reese Bowen behind the desk. Instead, there was Reese's' wife, Bertha. Sheriff Collins asked where Reese might be. Mrs. Bowen appeared to be a little shocked, but told him that Reese had walked down the street to the Optometrist's office to see if he could get a new pair of glasses before the doctor closed for the day.

"I've had to do all the paperwork around here lately, she added, cause Reese went and lost his glasses, he just can't see well enough to run this hotel without'em ."

John pulled out the pair of glasses in his shirt pocket, showed them to Mrs. Bowen, and asked if they might belong to her husband. One glance at the glasses, and Mrs. Bowen replied instantly...

"Why yes, I do believe that's Reese's glasses, he had'em special made fur himself, with one lens a little stronger than the other cause one of his eyes is worse than the other. As you can see Sheriff, one lens is a little thicker than the other. Thank you so much for bringing them back to Reese. He will be much obliged."

She was about to put the glasses on the shelf behind her when Sherriff Collins stopped her, and asked for the glasses back.

"I'll be holding onto'em Ma'am," he said with a small grin.

John sent Deputy Smith to Doctor Blevins' office to see if he was still open. Reese Bowen was walking out just as Deputy Smith rode up to the front of the office. Reese was not wearing any glasses.

"How you doin Reese?" asked Deputy Smith.

"Aw, can't complain deputy, Reese replied, jest had to order me some new glasses. The doc ain't got none like I need - have to have'em special made ya know, cause I got one eye worse than the other."

Deputy Smith pulled his revolver from its holster, stuck it in Reese's stomach, and said...

"You're under arrest Mr. Bowen, for the murder of Melvin Jenkins, his wife Clarissa, and his daughter Carla, now hand me your gun belt – slowly."

Reese turned as pale as a ghost, and began shaking uncontrollably.

Deputy Smith threw Reese's gun belt over his shoulder, and marched Reese back to the hotel. Sheriff Collins and Tom met them about half way between the doctor's office and the hotel. Sheriff Collins told Deputy Smith to just take Reese on over to the jail while he and Tom went to find Judge Bracken. When Judge Bracken stepped into the cell with Reese, he sat down on the cot beside Reese.

"Reese, he began, you just don't strike me as a man that would be either brave enough or smart enough to pull off a crime like this on your own. Ya know Reese; it would really be a damn shame for you to hang for something like this all by yourself when there was someone else who masterminded this whole thing. You sure there ain't something you'd like to tell me Reese, like maybe a name?"

"Orville Phelps, Judge, Reese blurted out...it was Orville Phelps an me, he said it was all fur the false conviction of his brother, an fur the honor of the Klan, that Melvin an his family had to be punished."

Orville and his wife Caroline had just finished supper when Judge Bracken, Sheriff Collins, and Tom Tillotson rode up to his house. Tom went around to the back of the house just in case Orville tried to escape. Judge Bracken stood to one side of the front door, and Sheriff Collins stood on the other side. Reese was placed in the center, with his hands tied behind his back. John knocked on the door and quickly stepped back into position a few feet to the side of the door. Orville opened the door to see Reese standing there white as a ghost, his hands behind his back, and trembling. He knew in an instant that he was in big trouble, turning as pale as Reese. He was going to slam the door and try to make a dive for his rifle when Sheriff Collins stuck the barrel of his own rifle in his face. A quick search of the house uncovered a robe and hood tucked away in an old trunk underneath his wife's wedding gown. His hands were tied, and he and Reese were escorted back to the jail.

Becky so longed in her heart to see her folks before she was unable to travel, but due to the circumstances of the murder case and all she was unable to do that. And now she was too far along - just a few more months 'til the baby would be here. "Ah, the baby" she sighed. With a loving smile and gentle hand she felt her waist which was starting to get bigger each day it seemed. Her mind wandered back to Tennessee and her home as she sat there knitting on the baby's blanket. The yarn that her friend Sarah had given her was a beautiful baby blue with the slightest shade of pale yellow mingled through it. It would work if the baby was a girl or boy. Somehow Becky knew in her heart that it was a boy.

She missed her folks terribly. Her father, Daniel Ray Davis, was a pillow of strength and leadership in his community. He was a long time Deacon of the little Copper Springs Baptist Church in Bradley County Tennessee. Daniel Ray was a jolly fellow, standing around six feet, four inches tall. He had black hair and a full beard to match. His big bright brown eyes would light up like stars when he smiled. Becky was sure that she had inherited her own beautiful brown eyes from him. Her father always had a smile on his face. Even in the times of trouble, he'd smile and try to settle the problem. Most folks around called him the peacemaker. If there was sickness or someone's home had burned, or any kind of need in that community, Daniel would gather up the other men and give the order,

"Let's go boys, we got work to do."

They'd all set out on their horses and ride for miles, and no one left until the work was done. He was also known as the casket maker. Becky could not remember a single death in the community in which her father had not made the casket, and he never charged a penny for making them year after year. Folks tried to pay him, but he'd just smile and say...

"This is the last thing a man can do for the dead, so there will never be any charge."

The community, of course, was grateful. They'd shake his hand and that was all that was needed. Oh how she missed her father! Her mother Ellen Davis was a gentle soul - soft spoken, blue eyes and jet black hair. Becky's fondest memories were of her mother in the kitchen cooking and singing. Oh! How she loved to sing. She was well known and loved for her singing. And in the same way that Daniel was always called upon to build a casket for a departed friend or neighbor, Ellen was called upon to sing at the funerals. Her beautiful voice rang out unbroken, and unfaltering in any way. Somehow she always managed to hold up under the worst of circumstances when it came to her singing, even if she were ill herself. She too said that this was the last thing that she could do for the dead. She also helped Daniel with the casket building, especially with the silk lining and pillow covers.

When Becky told her father that she and Jeff were getting married and that they would be moving to West Virginia he had to walk out of the house. Before he reached the door she saw him wiping the tears. Her folks loved Jeff, but they were so hoping that the two would settle down in Tennessee. So when they broke the news that they would be moving everyone was sad. But a few days of planning and packing made all of them get used to the idea, even though they never accepted it. Becky's four sisters, Emma, Joy Lynn, Lizzie and Bella were excited for their younger sister. They knew they would miss her, but they too longed to see what was on the other side of those tall dark mountains. Becky had a sister, Elva, the firstborn, who had died at the age of eight from the dreaded Typhoid fever, many years ago.

Her sister Emma was married to a nice fellow named Jim Jackson. They had two children, Abby and Alexander. Becky sure did miss their sweet little voices and all the energy they displayed. They would each take her by the hand, laughing and practically dragging her outside, yelling...

"Come outside Aunt Becky, wes's play."

Becky always pretended she didn't want to go, but loved every minute of it. She hoped her baby would get to meet his cousins someday. Emma was a spitting image of her mother. She too was a singer, and loved to cook. Joy Lynn was an outdoors person. She loved following her brother's around, riding horses and gathering up the cattle when they would scatter over the mountain sides. She and Becky would hitch a horse and have him geared up and mounted as quickly as their brothers could. Lizzie and Bella were homemakers. They loved to make quilts and pretty up the house as much as possible. They would put their heads together and have some of the prettiest quilts and curtains that eyes had ever seen. The two of them had made Becky and Jeff two quilts for their wedding.

Becky knew she would treasure them always. Becky's brothers thought Jeff was the best thing since apple pie, and told him so. On some weekends they would jump on their horses and come for a long visit. They knew they were going to miss their little sister so much. The oldest, Carlton, looked like his father - same hair and eyes, but with a more serious nature. Marvin was more like his mother - soft spoken, black hair and blue eyes, but had his father's smile, just like Becky. Ross was tall and skinny as a rail, and quiet-natured, unless he was riled about something, then his voice boomed like thunder. He was always smiling, like his father - a peacemaker. Whenever Becky's folks had to be away, which was quite often, due to the fact that Becky's mother was a midwife, and was called out it seemed in the middle of the night every other night, then Ross was the one who had to watch over the other children, as well as the farm.

Becky remembered so many times when an argument would break out with her other two brothers, and Ross would get them both by the shirt collar, and with that big loud voice he firmly planted them in a chair, scowling...

"Now see here boys, we ain't gonna have none of that foolishness."

They always did whatever he said, because they knew he would tell the folks when they returned. Becky had gotten so caught up in her reminiscing that she had knitted a row so long that it appeared to go on forever. "Lordy Mercy," she laughed till the tears flowed from her eyes. Even though she had to undo it and start over, she was sure that it was God's way of making a sad situation into a joyful one. Becky put down her knitting and walked to the door. She stood there for just a moment, watching Cricket, the little dog that Tom had given them to replace Spot. She missed Spot, but she and Jeff both had grown very fond of Cricket. She stepped out onto the big long porch and sat on the steps. Cricket came bounding up and laid his head on her lap. Becky rubbed the little dog on the head.

"What you doing little buddy?" she asked as she stared out over the mountain tops, wondering how things were going with Jeff and Tom today. One of the neighboring families, Steve and Nancy Harper, was in need of help. They were both in their seventies, and poor old Steve had tried to cut himself some wood, and the axe slipped and cut his leg open, and now it appeared that he was going to be laid up for a long time. Jeff and Tom had gone over to finish the work for them. She smiled at the thought of Jeff and Tom and how close they had become during the murder trial. The incident that happened with Tom here at their house was just a dim vision now. Becky would now trust Tom with her life. He was a great example of what God could do for anyone if they would only allow Him.

After playing with Cricket for a while, Becky settled back down to her knitting. Once again her mind went back to Bradley County Tennessee. She was hoping that maybe her folks could come out to see them before the long hard winter set in. Becky wished that Jeff's parents were alive to see this child, but it would never be until they all got to Heaven. Jeff spoke about them often, but never without sadness in his eyes. She wished they could have lived to see their grandchild that she was carrying. Jeff's father, Silas Townsend, was a well-known blacksmith there in the small community of Mason County Tennessee, which joined Bradley County. Becky recalled many times when she and her father would ride for miles to get their horses shod by Mr. Townsend. She also remembered the skinny, dark-haired, blue-eyed boy who always grinned at her every time she and her father came. Mr. Townsend was a tall, slim- framed man with black hair, brown eyes, and a charming smile.

Jeff's mother Lilly was a very soft spoken lady. She too had black hair and the bluest eyes. Jeff got his beautiful blue eyes from his Mother. Jeff told Becky that his mother loved to grow flowers. Her favorites were red roses. She had them planted all along the front of their big house. It was such a tragedy when the neighbor's heard what had happen to Jeff's parents. They were on their way back from a revival in another county not too far from where they lived, riding along the narrow trail under the moon light, when suddenly a blood-curdling scream from a nearby bobcat spooked the horses. The horses had bolted, and fallen off the edge of the embankment with the buggy still attached.

Jeff's Uncle Robert and his wife Ethel Townsend were just a few yards behind. They tried frantically to save Jeff's parents, but it was too late. Jeff said it was the biggest funeral he had ever seen in Mason County. Becky had met two of Jeff's sisters at the wedding - Lora Stewart and her husband Calvin. They had five children, including a cute set of twin girls, Mary and Carry. They had long curly red hair and both chattered all the time. They had an older sister Lana, and two brothers, Clyde and Buck. Jeff's youngest sister Lila and her husband James Young had one little girl, Lora Lee, who was named after Jeff's sister Lora. Becky and Jeff were expecting Uncle Robert and Aunt Ethel sometime real soon for a visit. Jeff's uncle Robert had taken them all under his wing since their parents' accident. Becky was hoping the visit would be very soon.

Robert was a very handsome man. Becky could see her Jeff in him. Robert was always joking and making sure that he met everyone and had a good time. Jeff's aunt Ethel was kind of quiet, and serious. Becky noticed that sometimes Ethel would become a little embarrassed at her husband's jokes, but never said anything. She just enjoyed seeing her husband so happy. Becky's thoughts were interrupted by the sound of the horse's hooves.

"Oh I hope that is Jeff," she said to the little dog. She laid down her knitting and went to the door. A rider appeared from behind the trees. It was their friend Clark Puckett. As he rode up to the edge of the yard, Becky started walking down the steps.

"Clark, it's so good to see you, get down and let your horse rest and I will get you some cold water."

"Stop, Becky!" Don't come any closer." He yelled.

Clark held up his hand and motioned her to stay where she was. Becky froze in her tracks.

"I don't understand Clark, what's wrong?" Becky questioned.

"Looks like it might be bad Becky, Clark frowned... two families have Typhoid fever, and they are saying that we might just be in fur a big outbreak."

"Oh, Lord, have mercy!" Becky said with a tremble in her voice, What about Sarah and the children? Are they safe?"

"Yes so far, Clark assured her, I went to help the Williams family with a young calf and two of their children are very bad."

"What can we do to help Clark?" Becky asked with a concerned look on her face.

Clark shook his head, replying. "There's nothing anyone can do right now Becky, except pray and stay away from anyone that has been exposed. I didn't go inside the Williams' house, and left as soon as I was told, but we can't take any chances."

Clark had a very worried look on his face, which made Becky even more worried herself.

"I'm gonna stay in the barn a few days, till this has passed, don't want to take something in on Sarah and the children. Tell Jeff when he gets home, and pray for everyone."

He waved his hand and was gone.

Becky's knees grew weak with the thought of a typhoid outbreak. She sank down on the steps with her face in her hands and prayed...

"Oh God, please have mercy on us all."

She sat there for what seemed like an eternity. She must protect this baby at all cost. She was so hoping that Jeff would return soon so she could tell him. She grew tired and ordered Cricket to stay on the porch while she went inside and lay on the bed. When she awoke the house was dark. She quickly lit the lamps and was preparing supper when she heard a familiar whistle. She ran to the door just in time to see Jeff dismount and give Cricket a quick pat on the head. As he came bounding up the steps, Becky met him at the door and fell into his arms, almost whimpering...

"I am so glad you are home."

He held her at arm's length, looking in her eyes.

"Are you ok Bec? Is the baby ok?" he questioned.

Becky couldn't help but chuckle seeing her husband's face at that moment. He looked like he was scared to death.

"I am fine honey, no need to fret, and the baby is fine too. I'm just so glad that you are home. Go wash up and we will eat and I will tell you about Clark's visit today."

With a big smile on his face, knowing that she was alright he said,

"Shew, I was afraid that something was wrong, I would never forgive myself if something happen to you while I was gone. I'll be right back."

He planted a big kiss on her lips and scampered out the door to put the horse in the barn and to wash up for supper. As they sat down at the table, Jeff gave thanks for all they had. Then Becky told him about what Clark had said.

They both prayed that this would not turn out to be an epidemic of Typhoid that killed so many people. It was a dreaded disease, and never enough medicine to go around to everyone.

"I'll take Tom with me tomorrow, and we will go see some of the folks and find out what is going on and what we can do to help." Jeff quickly volunteered.

Jeff knew he and Tom could only go as far as yelling distance to the houses. He was not about to get close and carry something in on Becky and the baby. With supper over, the dishes put away, they went to the porch and sat on the swing like two lovebirds. It was such a beautiful, peaceful night. The moon was full and the sky was filled with stars. Out in the yard lighting bugs twinkled like millions of little lights floating around. They sat there, Jeff with his arm around Becky, both of them caught up in the beauty of the night and the love that they had for each other.

The next morning Jeff awoke early. Finishing his chores, he saddled his horse, reassuring Becky over and over that he would not get too close to any houses that were infected. Tom emerged from the outhouse, washed his face and hands in the creek, and mounted up. They went from farm to farm, checking on every family. Five more homes, in addition to the Williams home, were sick. The Morgan's, who lived far up into the mountains had already buried a child, and two more of their children were sick. Along the way Jeff and Tom cut firewood, fed animals, milked cows, and carried fresh water to the edge of the yards. With each house they visited they never left without saying a prayer for those people.

"We'll be back to check on you folks," Jeff yelled as he and Tom rode off.

This continued for weeks. There were simply too many deaths for funerals to be held for all of them. Most of the dead were buried immediately for fear that the disease would only spread more.

Then the worst news of all came to Becky. Her sweet mother had gotten the fever and died. Becky cried herself to sleep for weeks. She knew she would never see her mother again, and the baby would never get to know either of his grandmothers. Becky couldn't even go to the funeral for fear of catching the fever herself. She mourned each day for her mother. Many lives were lost that year in Tennessee, Kentucky and Virginia because of the typhoid fever.

The year 1866 went down in history, being remembered for several destructive things, including the invention of dynamite by Alfred Nobel, the invention of the torpedo by Robert Whitehead, both of which, of course, were supposedly designed for peaceful purposes, the many battles and deaths caused by moonshiners and revenuers killing one another, and the many deaths caused by Typhoid fever.

That year was also remembered for the many mysterious deaths of several individuals and families, and for the trials and subsequent hangings of a few members of the KKK. Many of those murders, however, were never solved. Many God-fearing, decent folks lived with the fear and suspicion that their friend, next-door-neighbor or fellow church member might be a member of the Klan. Little did they know that most of their suspicions were well justified.

Saturday, June 8th, 1866. Morgantown, West Virginia - Noon.

In 1866, a hanging – any hanging, drew its own melting pot of diverse individuals and groups. Some drove wagons or rode horses for more than fifty miles just to witness the occasion. Some, of course, were the photographers, who were paid a handsome sum for photographing the condemned criminals themselves, and anyone else who was willing to have his or her face in the same newspaper with the criminals. Others came with nothing more than the presupposition that they were about to witness American justice being carried out in its noblest form. Still others stood with heads bowed as if in deepest sorrow, praying for the souls of the condemned. And a few came for no other reason than to be able to tell their grandchildren that they had been present when a certain notorious criminal was hanged. But hangings also had their own note of solemnity. As long as the condemned man was still alive, even up to the moment just before the trap door was pulled, some folks stood yelling obscenities at him, calling for his execution, demanding justice. But the moment the body fell through that trap door, and hung there motionless and lifeless, a dark and solemn hush came over the whole crowd. A whole life had just ended in an instant. A thousand thoughts streaked across the minds of the crowd.

"What if, What if."

"What if he had made better choices? What if he had been given one more chance to do better? "Where is his soul now – in Heaven, or in Hell?"

Such was the atmosphere on June 8th, 1866, as hundreds of townspeople and total strangers gathered, lining the boardwalks of Morgantown West Virginia to witness the hanging of three men – Herbert Valentine, Reese Bowen, and Orville Phelps. Photographers gathered early, each of them trying to get his camera set up in just the right spot to get the best angle. The three men were stopped upon leaving the jail for a photograph. They were stopped again at the foot of the gallows, with some townspeople and some visitors trying to crowd in to have their picture taken with the condemned men. They were stopped again half way up the steps. They were photographed with the old padre who asked them if they had any last words.

Just before the black hood was placed over herb Valentine's head, he began to sob…

"I am so sorry fur what I have done. Lucas Bratcher never did me no harm. He has no family to whom I can apologize. Please, pray for my wretched soul, that God will forgive me for what I have done."

Tom was standing at the foot of the gallows, hearing Herb's plea. He asked Judge Bracken if he could go up and speak to the three men just for a moment. Judge Bracken replied…

"Well, it's highly unusual Tom, but I'll grant you a few moments."

Tom hurried up the steps, and stood facing the three men. The padre stepped aside, and gave Tom a nod. Tom knew he didn't have much time, so he made his testimony short and to the point. He told them how that preacher Jeff Townsend had led him to the Lord Jesus Christ. There were tears in his eyes as he told them of the terrible conviction he had felt, and how the Lord had forgiven him in an instant. The Holy Spirit did the rest. Tom asked them if they would like to pray, and ask the Lord Jesus into their hearts. They all said yes. Tom bowed his head and prayed with them, noticing that everyone on the platform had their heads bowed also, including the hangman. Three condemned men accepted Jesus Christ as their personal Savior. Three hoods were placed over their heads, and the trapdoor was sprung. Tom descended the steps, knowing now that the hand of God had been at work secretly, guiding him to attend the hanging. The crowd dispersed, the streets soon cleared, and the bodies were taken to the local undertaker's office.

The four years that Jeff had been married to Becky were the happiest and most blessed and fulfilling years of his life, and today was their fourth anniversary. He tried to simply dismiss all thoughts of the trial from his mind, and he certainly did not want to think about the hanging that was to take place today. The news of the trial, conviction and hanging of two more men beside Herb Valentine had already spread far and wide. He had done his civic duty, and justice had been served. He had far more pleasant things to think about than three men being hanged. He had a beautiful wife who was carrying his child, a thriving church, a thriving farm, good neighbors, and a God who was providing for his every need. He felt extremely blessed.

Becky had been anxiously watching for Jeff and Tom to ride into view. She was just a bit surprised and curious when she saw that Jeff was alone. Maybe Tom had decided to go his own way after all. She saw how Jeff was deliberately trying to keep something hidden from view as he dismounted his horse, and walked around to the side that she couldn't see. Jeff saw her out of the corner of his eye, trying to see what he was trying to hide. Every year on their anniversary they had both somehow managed to surprise each other with something that they both loved, and needed. Jeff unsaddled his horse, Mr. Beecher, (so named for the famous Congregationalist preacher, Henry Ward Beecher,) and turned him into the corral.

Jeff was able to hide what was in the brown paper package well enough, but the one thing he couldn't hide was the pretty hat box. He yelled to Becky from the gate, telling her that she had to close her eyes 'til he came inside. She put her hands over her eyes, giggling like a little school girl. Jeff put her gifts down on the porch and took her in his arms. She threw her arms around him, staring up into his blue eyes. He locked his arms around her waist and swung her around in a slow circle, being ever so careful not to squeeze her too tightly. She stared up into his blue eyes for a moment just before they embraced in a long passionate kiss. She whispered…

"Oh Jeff, I've missed you so bad, thank God you're back."

She glanced down at the package and the hat box, beaming with approval and anticipation. She had completely forgotten to ask about Tom and his whereabouts.

Once inside the house, she quickly removed the ribbon from the hat box first. She squealed with pure delight as she lifted a beautiful black ladies hat with a bright red silk band around it. She tried it on immediately, running to the mirror to see how it looked. It fit perfectly. She was back in his arms in an instant, kissing his cheeks and hugging him. Then she untied the string from the package, revealing a beautiful red dress that perfectly matched the red band around the hat. Jeff got another big kiss and hug. Underneath the dress, in the bottom of the package, was a roll of black cloth - enough to make another dress. Tears of joy ran down her cheeks as she again threw her arms around his neck, thanking him for the hat and the material.

Then it was Becky's turn to surprise Jeff. She hoped he would like what she had gotten him. She knew he would be the most handsome man in the valley. She had worked most of the day preparing for this special time, making his favorite foods, and setting out the beautiful dishes that her mother had given her. Tears welled up in her eyes at the thought of her sweet mother. Quickly she dried her eyes, scolding herself for crying on such a happy occasion. She put on her best dress, a pale yellow with little red

Heavenly Places

roses around the sleeves and the hem. Jeff had bought it for her birthday two years ago and she still got so much pleasure from wearing it. It brought back so many happy memories of their life together. She was so happy with her gifts and couldn't wait to show off for her husband in the new dress and beautiful hat.

She laid the hat and material aside, taking him by the hand, telling him that he had to close his eyes. He held her hand with one hand, putting his other hand over his eyes, allowing her to lead him into the bedroom.

"Alright honey, you can look now." She said stopping beside the bed.

Jeff didn't know quite what to expect. He gasped when he opened his eyes and saw a brand new black suit, complete with a new white shirt, black tie, and black hat to match. He smiled a big smile of approval and gratitude, took off his old suit coat and hat, and tried on the new ones. Becky walked around him slowly, making sure that the suit coat fit perfectly, telling him how handsome he was. Jeff removed the hat and coat, picked her up in his arms, lowered her down gently across the bed, and kissed her with all the passion in his soul. Neither of them mentioned Tom, or the trial, or the hanging. All that could wait 'til tomorrow.

After admiring their gifts Becky told him to get washed up and they would have supper. As Jeff sat down at the table he had another surprise, a small black box lying on the table beside his plate. Becky smiled as he sat there with his mouth open.

"More gifts for me! He stammered. "No sweetheart, you have given me enough."

Becky insisted that he open it immediately, he opened the box and brought out a golden pocket watch attached to a long golden chain, on the back it was engraved…To my husband Jeff, with love, your wife Becky. Tears rolled down Jeff's face as he took her in his arms and held her for the longest time. The food had gotten cold, but they didn't mind - it was the best Anniversary they could remember. All the murders, the hanging and bad things were dismissed from their minds at that time. God had blessed them so much and the only thing on their minds that night was their love for each other. And just when Becky was thinking that no woman in the world could be any happier, Jeff interrupted her thoughts with…

"Oh sweetheart, I almost forgot."

"Forgot what?" Becky questioned.

He told her to close her eyes one more time. It was hard keeping her eyes closed, not knowing what to expect next. Jeff went into the kitchen, and came back with a huge bouquet of her favorite flowers, beautiful yellow roses. Becky was totally stunned!

"How had he managed to sneak that big bouquet of roses past her without her seeing it?"

Saturday, June 23rd, 1866. Valley Grove Baptist Church. 7:00 p.m.

The Flemmins family was the first to arrive at the church that evening, with Foster Flemmins, the old patriarch of the Flemings' clan driving the lead wagon. Beside him was his wife Cleo. In the back of the wagon were Claudette Flemmins and her fiancé, Rufus Rutherford. Rufus' hands were tied to the back of the seat just behind Foster – to prevent Rufus from running away at the last minute. Claudette was in a family way – about a month, in fact. Following close behind Foster's wagon was Ralph and Hilda Rutherford, Rufus' mother and father. Five more wagons followed, loaded with family members from both families – brothers, sisters, Aunts, Uncles, and first, second, and third cousins. The wagon behind Mr. and Mrs. Rutherford was filled with members of the Flemmins clan; all seated facing the wagon behind them, with rifles and shotguns pointed in the direction of that wagon. The Rutherfords were all seated facing the wagon in front of them, with rifles and shotguns pointing at the Flemmins family. And so it was with the other three wagons – each family facing the other with their gun barrels facing the other family.

Nearly all the men and some of the women from both families were slightly intoxicated from the jugs of moonshine that lined the floors of each wagon. Most of the men and some of the women also had tobacco juice running from one corner of their mouths. The full beards of the men were streaked with stains from tobacco juice. Their clothes were stained with tobacco juice, and the teeth of those who had any teeth left were stained a dark yellow. Their clothes were ragged, covered with patches, and smelled of mildew. Not one among them had taken a bath in more than a month. The

Heavenly Places

women folk had all wanted to get cleaned up a little better before leaving for the wedding, but Foster and Ralph had both insisted...

"Thar ain't no need, an thar ain't no time fur fixin up, cause this here marryin's done been put off way too long."

After arriving at the church without anyone being killed on either side, the families arranged their wagons in a half circle around the outer edge of the school yard, and waited for the Preacher. As Jeff, Becky, and Tom drew close to the church, Tom immediately recognized Foster Flemmins, but Foster didn't recognize Tom so easily. Not only was Tom clean shaven and sporting a short haircut, he was also showing off a clean white set of false teeth. Foster, of course, was an old acquaintance of Tom's from long ago, having been Tom's exclusive supplier of moonshine. Once Foster finally recognized Tom, and saw that he was riding in the same wagon with the preacher and his wife, he shook his head in disbelief, muttering so as not to be heard by the preacher...

"Well I be danged if'n ole Tom ain't went an got religion."

Becky also recognized Foster Flemmins from the day he had come to the house and asked for Jeff. He was still wearing the same clothes he had worn more than a month ago. Jeff scanned the whole crowd slowly, as each wagon load of people jumped down from the wagons with rifles and shotguns in their hands, some of them staggering to keep their balance. Foster ordered Claudette to untie Rufus and have him help her down from the wagon. After everyone was on the ground, Foster immediately shoved Rufus to the front. He then halfheartedly gestured the barrel of his shotgun toward Jeff, spitting tobacco juice on the ground, and ordered Jeff...

"Awright preacher, it's time to git on with this marryin, and git these two hitched."

Jeff calmly walked straight up to Foster, looked him in the eye, and spoke loud enough for all to hear.

"There will be no marrying until all of you put your guns in your wagons and get sober."

Foster was about to shove the shotgun in Jeff's face when Tom and the whole congregation stepped between Jeff and Foster. Tom grabbed the barrel of the shotgun, wrestling it from Foster's hands with one swift motion. He pointed the shotgun at Foster's chest, addressing the crowd.

"If'n you all want to live to see a wedding tonight, I suggest you do as the Preacher says. There's a clear cold creek jest under the hill there, and yun's can all go down and git yourselves cleaned up and sobered up. When yun's be fit to smell, ya can come back and have your wedding, and not afore."

In Foster Flemmins' lifetime, no man had ever stood up to him that way and lived to tell about it. His huge frame and rough voice had put fear into many a man's heart, including his own family. But when it came right down to it, he was a bluffer and a coward, and both Tom and Jeff saw it in his eyes. Without a shotgun in his hands, Foster Flemmins was as tame as a lamb. Tom, still holding the shotgun against Foster's chest, and motioning with his left hand, pointed the way to the creek. To Jeff's surprise, every Rutherford and Flemmins unloaded their rifles and shotguns and laid them in their respective wagons without a word of objection, and headed single file toward the creek.

With the initial shock and excitement past, Sarah and Becky immediately hugged each other and began laughing and chattering as they hurried into the church house where they began to light the candles and to set up the special flower arrangements that each of them had brought especially for Claudette. Clark put out some extra chairs, knowing that there was not going to be nearly enough room in the house for all the people. He propped the front door open, and raised the windows so that those who could not get inside could at least see and hear through the open windows. By the time the church and been decorated, the two clans were coming up out of the creek, a little cleaner, and a little less drunk. The women and girls came up the hill first because the men and boys had gone a little further downstream to bathe. Jeff watched them from the steps of the church, smiling a little as he saw the women from the two families helping each other up the narrow path that led down to the creek.

When every seat available was taken there were still a dozen persons standing on the outside – two at each of the six windows. To everyone's amazement there was a young Rutherford boy with a Flemmins girl standing beside him. Another window had a Flemmins boy with a Rutherford girl beside him. Every window had a Flemmins and a Rutherford standing looking in, holding hands. Foster Flemmins and Ralph Rutherford got teary-eyed, but quickly wiped the tears away before either of them could see the others eyes. As Rufus came forward to take his place to the right side of the pulpit, he hesitated momentarily to ask Tom if he would be his best man. Tom quickly agreed, and joined Rufus in front of the pulpit.

As Foster and Claudette stepped over the threshold of the church, Becky and Sarah stood and sang Rock of Ages. Jeff could tell by the look on many of the faces that most of these folks had never heard a good old gospel song before. The words of the song itself, and the sweet harmony and spirit with which Becky and Sarah sang it brought tears and smiles to nearly every face in the house. A hush came over the crowd as Foster and Claudette stopped in front of the pulpit. Jeff asked…

"Who gives this woman to be wed to this man?"

Foster cleared his throat, responding with a broken voice…

"I reckon that'd be me and my missus preacher."

For the first time in twenty years Foster Flemmins managed a little half smile as he presented his daughter to the man that she loved. They joined hands, and Jeff asked the congregation to bow their heads for a word of prayer.

As Jeff was praying, some loud sniffles could be heard all over the house. Jeff prayed for the success and longevity of the marriage, but he also prayed for the salvation of every soul present that night. After pronouncing the couple man and wife, Jeff invited the whole crowd to come to his farm the next day for a time of food, fun, and fellowship. Knowing that both the Flemmins and Rutherford's had a long journey to make tonight, he gave them the option of either camping out there on the church grounds that night, or of following him and Becky back to their place and spending the night there so that all of them could be well fed and better prepared for that journey on Sunday afternoon. He also wanted the chance to preach a message to all of them. To his surprise, both families accepted the offer to follow him and Becky back to his farm. The long precession of wagons looked like a wagon train of pioneers moving north.

June 23rd Saturday night

There were five wagons of relatives, the Flemmins' wagon and the Rutherford's wagon, Becky and Jeff's buggy, and a wagon driven by Clark and Sarah with their children Mollie and Carter, who had agreed to come along so that Sarah and Becky could get busy cooking and baking for the service the next day. Tom was on horseback bringing up the rear to make sure no more fighting along the way. Becky reached over, lovingly placing her hand on Jeff's arm. In a voice soft and gentle she said….

"It was a beautiful wedding my dear, even if it was a shotgun wedding." She had to giggle. Jeff grinned…

"Yep Bec it was, even if I must say so myself." But what are we gonna do with every one? This is ok with you that I invited them all out wasn't it?"

He had a worried look in his eyes. He didn't want to put extra work on Becky right now, or to endanger her health in any way.

"Yes, we will make do some way, Sarah and I will do the cooking and you and Clark can help them all get settled in for the night, everything will be alright, you'll see."

She reached over and planted a kiss on his cheek, reassuring him.

"Ok sweet heart, let's go home."

Jeff gave the horse a little nudge to speed him up. The Clarks were the next wagon behind Jeff. Clark yelled up in a friendly manner,

"Where ya going so fast preacher?"

Jeff yelled back… "Sorry Clark, just trying to get this bunch home before the moon goes behind those clouds."

"Ok I'm right behind you, let's go." Clark yelled back.

The voices of the others could be heard laughing and talking. They were no longer feuding and fighting, no guns pointing at each other, no cussing, no whiskey bottles thrown from wagon to wagon. When that final "I do" was said at the church, they all became one family, which made Jeff and everyone else in the congregation very happy. They soon arrived at the Townsend farm. Jeff drove the buggy to the yard gate and helped Becky down and Clark did the same for Sarah and the children who had already fallen asleep. Clark and Jeff carried Mollie and Carter into the house to the spare bedroom where Becky and Sarah quickly made a bed on the floor for them. Jeff and Clark went back to the wagons where Tom had directed them into the nearby field behind the barn where they made a circle with the wagons. The women folk started preparing bedding in the wagons for the night. The men folk made a neat fire in the center of the circle of wagons and soon pots and pans were brought out and food was cooking and coffee was brewing. Those mountain folks had come prepared.

Becky had worried for nothing. The newlyweds were all hugged up in a blanket in front of the fire and all was peaceful, and even a bit romantic. Becky and Sarah stepped out onto the porch just as Jeff and Clark came back in. Tom had already left for his cabin for the night, but not before making sure that Jeff and Clark could handle things here. Jeff, Becky, Sarah and Clark all sat down and had a nice cup of coffee as they listened to the happy noise coming from behind the barn.

Foster brought out his old fiddle, Ralph cut lose with his Doghouse bass, and Claudette's cousin Chester took out his harmonica. Rufus himself climbed out from under the warm blanket with his new bride and grabbed his old Martin guitar. Cousin Pearly Mae Rutherford joined in with her banjo. Some of the prettiest music that the Townsends and Puckett's had ever heard came floating from that little field. The Flemmins and Rutherfords were singing, and some dancing, but all having a high old time. They sang **"Oh Susanna, don't you cry for me."** Then someone started singing – **"I'll fly away Oh Glory, I'll fly away"** Right after that came –**"Blue Moon of Kentucky keep on shining, shine on the one that's gone and left me blue."** Jeff, Becky, Sarah and Clark all sat quiet and still through all of these songs, but when someone started The Tennessee Waltz, they could sit still no longer. Jeff took Becky's hand, asking…

"Madam, may I have this dance?"

Jeff took Becky in his arms as they danced quietly to the song that took them both back home to Tennessee. The porch suddenly became a ballroom, as Clark gently bowed to Sarah, took her hand in his, and they floated gracefully across the porch, dancing in the wind, carefree as a bird. It was a wonderful night.

After the dance, they sat there listening far into the night as the music played, as the sounds of happiness and laughter came wafting on the evening breeze. Foster Flemmins himself came up to the porch and invited them to come down and join them in the field. Jeff and Clark accepted the invitation, but reminded Foster that it could only be for just a little while. Becky and Sarah stayed at the house with the children. Soon they were busy making pies and cakes for the next day. They worked long into the night, baking and chatting. Becky shared her sorrow over the loss of her mother with Sarah. Sarah told her it would all get easier with time, and that she too had lost her mother just before she and Clark had moved out here. Then they talked about the baby that Becky was carrying. Once again Sarah reminded Becky that she must send Jeff for her as soon as she was ready to deliver. Becky promised that she would. She was so happy to know that Sarah was there for her. She showed Sarah all the pretty clothes and the blanket that she had made for the baby. They soon finished their work and decided to go to bed. Becky was so tired she hardly remembered when Jeff came to bed.

The next morning Becky and Jeff woke up to the smell of bacon frying and coffee brewing. The folks from the field, most of them had slept in their wagons, had already been up a long time, and were getting ready for the big day ahead. Becky rolled over into Jeff's arms with a soft sigh, whispering…

"Oh honey, I don't want to get up. Do we have to?"

She was so tired from the night before. Jeff held her close for a moment, himself wishing that they could just stay here in each other's arms all day, but he knew he had a duty to these folks and to the others that would soon be arriving. He had promised God that he would take his gospel to everyone that he met, and he was hoping that today he would see some souls saved. Becky also knew that she must make herself get up. She had company to attend to as well as getting ready for the service. With one long hug and kiss they got out of bed and got dressed. As they walked into the kitchen Clark and Sarah were already up, and breakfast was ready.

"Good morning you two," they said with big smiles on their faces.

Sarah knew how tired Becky was from the night before, so she and Clark had gotten up very quietly so as to not awaken them or the children, and had prepared breakfast for them. Becky told Sarah that she shouldn't have done all that work by herself, giving her friend a big hug. After Clark got the children up they all sat down and enjoyed themselves. After breakfast was over and the dishes were all put away, Jeff and Clark, along with Mollie and Carter, went to the wagon circle to check on everyone. Jeff showed them the pool that he and Becky used for bathing. They all started getting washed up and ready for the service. Jeff whispered a prayer...

"Please Lord; let me reach them today with your word."

On the way back to the house, Mollie and Carter ran on ahead. Jeff shared his thoughts with Clark. They stopped at the barn, kneeling down together, praying that someone would accept the Lord into their life that very day.

Jeff and Becky, instead of using the pool as they always did, heated water on the stove, washing up and getting ready for the service, which was going to be held in the middle of the circle of wagons. Bales of hay were laid out for everyone to use as seats. By now other wagons were beginning to arrive. Soon the field was overrun with wagons and horses, with dozens of children running and playing, folks talking and laughing and getting acquainted with each other. Cricket suddenly became the most popular animal on the farm, as every child took turns petting him and enticing him to chase them. Tables that Jeff had made from extra lumber he had stored in the barn were covered with white sheets and table cloths. When all the food was ready and placed on the tables, Jeff walked up to the little preacher's stand that Clark had made for him and stood momentarily, looking out over the crowd. It was the largest group of people that he had ever addressed in one place. He politely asked them to bow their heads as he gave thanks for the food that they were about to receive.

Neither the Rutherfords nor the Flemmins had ever eaten such good, fresh, well-prepared food in their lives. There was fried chicken fresh from the chop block, corn on the cob, mashed potatoes, sliced tomatoes, green beans, green onions, biscuits, cornbread, pinto beans, chicken-n-dumplings, a huge pot roast, and a dozen homemade pies. Sarah and Becky received more compliments on their cooking that day than they had ever received in their lives. After everyone had eaten heartily, and all the scraps had been picked up, and all the dishes were washed and put away, Jeff announced that they were going to have a meetin out behind the house. All the men folk were asked to arrange all the chairs facing the little podium underneath the big oak tree.

When everyone was seated, Jeff asked Clark Puckett to lead in a word of prayer. As soon as Clark said Amen, the whole crowd answered with a loud "***Amen***." Jeff opened his Bible, and read from Luke 12:1…Beware the leaven of the Pharisees, which is hypocrisy. He then asked a simple question.

"How many of you folks hate hypocrisy?"

Every hand in the crowd was raised immediately. Then Jeff began his sermon…

"You know folks, in all the years that I have been a minister; I've done a lot of traveling across many counties and states. God has given me the opportunity to preach to thousands of folks, most of which were gathered together in smaller congregations than we have here today. But God has also given me the opportunity to visit the homes of many of those to whom I have preached. And as a minister of the Gospel, I have made some very interesting observations in my travels. And if you dear folks will bear with me for a few moments, I want to share with you just one of those observations. I have discovered that there is a hypocrite among us."

Every head in the crowd suddenly turned toward the person sitting next to him or her. Some fidgeted just a little in their seats. Jeff gave them just a moment to recover from the initial shock of what he had just said, and continued…

"Not only have I discovered that there is a hypocrite among us, I have discovered that there is more than one hypocrite among us."

Now even Becky, Sarah, and Clark looked a bit concerned. They had never heard Jeff preach quite like this before. The Holy Spirit was moving powerfully among the crowd as Jeff continued.

"My friends, I have discovered that there is a hypocrite in every single family – not only in our own little congregation, but in every single family that I have visited during my entire ministry."

Jeff could see that some of the faces in the crowd were turning beet-red. A few even stood up and started to leave when Jeff quickly began to explain what he meant.

"Now just calm down folks, and let me explain what I am talking about. As I have visited the homes of my own entire congregation, and the homes of so many more all over this country, I have noticed that all of them have one thing in common

– they all have a scarecrow standing in their cornfields. The hypocrite of whom I speak is not any of you – he is that scarecrow that each of you have in your fields. There he stands, dressed like a man, appearing to be a man. Some of your scarecrows are very lifelike in appearance, and some more so than others. Your scarecrow wears the outer garments of a man, the hat of a man, and some of you have added some very convincing eyes, ears, noses and mouths to your scarecrows."

Jeff could see now that the congregation was greatly relieved since he had shifted the point of his message from them to their scarecrows. Everyone was listening attentively now. Jeff smiled and went on…

"The hypocrite, like the scarecrow, is good at what he does – he pretends to be something that he is not. The scarecrow fools the crow into believing that he is the real thing, just as the hypocrite fools other men into believing that he is a Christian. The scarecrow, like the hypocrite, is incapable of changing himself. If he is not changed by another, he will forever remain what he is – a pretender. The scarecrow, like the hypocrite, is moveable – he can be re-located to another place in order to give the appearance that he is really human. The hypocrite can move from one place to another, fooling more folks for a while. But we must always remind ourselves dear friends that, no matter how lifelike the scarecrow may appear to be – he is still only a scarecrow made of straw - he is not human. And no matter how Christ like the hypocrite may appear to be, he is still a hypocrite, and not a Christian. And I have also noticed that after so long a time, even the crows discover that the scarecrow is not real, and they come and roost upon his lifeless arms made of sticks, and they peck out his eyes made of buttons. The hypocrite, like the scarecrow, can only fool folks for so long a time, until he is discovered to be what he really is. And as I close, may I add one last comment upon the similarities between the hypocrite and the scarecrow - they are both easily set on fire, and quickly consumed."

"But there is yet hope for the hypocrite, or for any other man or woman who needs and wants to be saved, no matter how far he or she has gone. The one Person who is able to change them is the Lord Jesus Christ. I say to you that if God is able to take of these stones under our feet and raise up children unto Abraham, He can change a scarecrow into a living man. And that same God is also able to change the very heart of the worst man who ever lived."

He got a resounding Amen from Tom Tillotson. If there was one thing that Jeff had learned as a Pastor and evangelist, it was to obey the leading of the Holy Spirit, and he knew that there were folks here who needed and wanted to be saved – right now. He asked the crowd to bow their heads, asking.

"Are there any here today who would like to be saved? if so would you lift your hands so I can see them."

About twenty hands went up instantly. Jeff could see the tears flowing from the eyes of men, women, boys and girls. Becky and Sarah stood and led the congregation with the hymn - Just as I am. Jeff stepped around in front of the pulpit just as Rufus and Claudette came forward, hand in hand. To everyone's surprise, Foster Flemmins came next, weeping and kneeling down on the grass. Behind Foster was his wife Cleo. Then came Ralph and Hilda Rutherford, followed by Mollie and Carter Puckett. Lewis Flemmins took Kitty Rutherford's hand, Hester Rutherford took Clyde Flemmins by the arm, Morris Flemmins followed Lou Ellen Rutherford forward, Chester Flemmins led Bonnie Rutherford, Mary Rutherford led Earl Flemmins, and Wayne Flemmins walked hand in hand with Maude Rutherford – the six couples who had stood at the windows of the church at the wedding, all came forward to receive Jesus Christ as their personal Savior. And just when Jeff thought that the invitation was over, Pearly Mae Rutherford nearly ran over the others, crying and sobbing as she hurried to the front and fell on her knees, calling on the Lord.

Twenty-one souls were saved that day, each of them making his or her personal profession of faith publicly. It was the finest soul-saving meetin that Jeff and his congregation had ever witnessed. But Jeff had also learned other lessons as a minister. He knew that whenever the Holy Spirit began to work in the hearts of folks, the devil was always lurking nearby. He was thrilled at the sight of twenty-one souls coming to Christ, but he also saw the face of one man, Homer Rutherford, near the back of the crowd, with a scowl of pure hatred. Jeff thought...

"That man has daggers in his eyes."

He especially noticed that Homer kept glancing at Tom with a squint in his eye and a frown on his face. But Jeff wouldn't allow this one man to spoil the glorious atmosphere that prevailed. He dwelt upon the precious souls that had just found perfect peace for the first time in their lives. And now he had a major task to perform- getting all of them baptized before dark. Both Clark and Tom saw the scowl on Mr. Rutherford's face also, but they too chose to ignore him. Clark asked Jeff if he would like for him to help him with the baptizing. Jeff quickly agreed, and thanked him for volunteering, because two of those Flemmins boys weighed about 250 pounds each! The scene resembled a band of pilgrims, marching toward a long-awaited destination, as the whole crowd followed Jeff and Clark down to the little pool of water, singing...***Shall we gather at the river***. Two by two, the new converts helped each other into the water, hand in hand, and were all baptized. Jeff did most of the baptizing by himself but allowed Clark to help him with the two heaviest Flemmins boys. Tom led Pearly Mae Rutherford into the pool, and stood beside her as Jeff plunged her beneath the water. She smiled at Tom and thanked him as he led her up out of the pool. The blood in Homer Rutherford's veins boiled at the sight of a half breed Indian holding hands with a white woman. He began to plot in his mind how he could "remedy" the situation. He would wait 'til he could contact his fellow clan members. Not one person in the whole Rutherford family knew that Homer was a Klansman.

It had been a long but glorious day. Everyone was well-fed and happy, but tired. Knowing that both families had a long and rough journey ahead of them, Sarah and Clark Puckett persuaded them to stop at their home and spend the night before making the rest of the journey Monday morning. They could see by the smiles that both families were well-pleased by the invitation, and thankful for such hospitality from folks they had only known for less than a day. They all said their goodbyes to Jeff, Becky and Cricket. Tom had to come up with an excuse real fast. He cleared his throat, speaking to Pearly Mae's father, Jason Rutherford, brother to Ralph...

"You know Mr. Rutherford, the road from the end of the valley here on over to the Puckett's place is awfully rough, and I'd be happy to ride along ahead of you all just in case you have any trouble."

Jason looked around at Pearly Mae, who was beaming at Tom's suggestion. He turned back to Tom and answered...

"Well I reckon it won't do no harm to have an extra man along, jest in case. Tie yer hoss to the back of the wagon son, an ya can ride with us."

Tom quickly obeyed, jumping into the back of the wagon, sitting beside Pearly Mae Rutherford. Jeff and Becky smiled approvingly as Tom and Pearly waved to them from the back of the wagon. Tom had the biggest, brightest smile on his face that either of them had seen since they had known him. Homer cringed and gritted his teeth. He threw one last hateful glance at Jeff. In that instant, something inside him trembled. He suddenly remembered every word of Jeff's sermon about the hypocrite and the scarecrow. That message haunted him with every turn of the wagon's wheels.

Saturday, July 28th, 1866. Valley Grove Baptist Church 7:00 p.m.

Jeff and Becky didn't know quite what to expect at the next church meeting, whether the crowd would be a lot larger or not. They didn't really expect all of the Flemmins' and Rutherford's to come since they lived so far away, but since they only had service once a month, Jeff was hoping that at least some of them could make it, especially the ones who played musical instruments. He dreamed of a larger choir, and maybe even a larger building – a brand new Church House that would seat a hundred or more. His dream was going to be fulfilled, but not in the manner in which he imagined it.

Homer Rutherford was a bitter man, despiteful, proud and belligerent. And if there was one thing he despised more than any other, it was religion. As soon as he had reached home that day after the big feast and church service at Jeff Townsend's farm, he immediately contacted two of his fellow clan members, describing the going's on that he had witnessed at the meeting, and being especially careful to inform them that he had seen a half-breed Indian, mixing and mingling with white folks, even holding hands with a white woman. It was enough to spur the clan into immediate action. Six men, led by Homer Rutherford himself donned their robes and hoods, built a wooden cross, and headed out toward the Valley Grove School House. They arrived more than an hour before the church folk were supposed to meet, allowing plenty of time for the building to burn to the ground before the Preacher and his half breed friend would arrive.

When Jeff, Becky and Tom rounded the bend in sight of the school house, there was no school house – it was ashes! The moment that Homer and his fellow Klansmen spotted Jeff's wagon, and knew that Jeff had also spotted them, Homer threw his torch at the foot of the cross, which broke into a blaze instantly. The seven of them turned their horses in the opposite direction and fled in a cloud of dust. Tom instinctively went for his Colt revolver, totally forgetting that he had left his gun belt at home. Jeff noticed Tom's quick motion toward his hip and the embarrassment on Tom's face when he realized that he had no pistol. In a way, Tom was glad that he had left the gun behind, because if he had brought it, there would have certainly been another senseless killing. He bowed his head, and repented for the thoughts of his heart.

Jeff and Becky walked all around the ruins of the little building with tears streaming from their faces. The building and its contents were a total loss. Jeff and Tom sifted through the ashes, hoping to find any object that may have survived the fire. To his amazement, Jeff found one old hymnbook. The cover was badly scorched, and the edges of the pages were singed, but the book itself was still intact, and every page was still there. Everything else was nothing but ashes.

The Puckett's arrived next, followed by the Sedgefield family, and five wagons filled with Flemmins' and Rutherfords. Everyone (except Homer Rutherford,) who had come to the wedding and the feast that followed had come back to the monthly meeting, and all of them had their instruments with them. Tom quickly spotted Pearly Mae, and ran to her wagon to help her down. The shock and disappointment of what they saw upon arrival showed on every face. When Jeff was satisfied that everyone who was going to be there was there, he told the crowd what had happened, and who was responsible. Jeff slowly scanned the crowd, searching for Homer. Homer was not there. His gut wrenched inside him. He asked Ralph why Homer hadn't come with them. Ralph replied that Homer had told them that he had some important business to attend to, and couldn't come. Jeff had a horrible premonition that the business of which Ralph spoke was smoldering behind him. Jeff addressed the crowd...

"Folks, what has happened here is horrible in the extreme, as you can all see. But you folks have come a long way to worship tonight, and we appreciate the effort that you all made to get here. So in spite of what the devil has accomplished here, we are not going to let him defeat us. If you folks don't mind sitting on the grass or standing, we are going to have church."

Everyone who had brought his or her instrument came forward, taking their places beside Becky and Sarah, who led them with the hymn – **"It is the voice of Jesus that I hear."** Becky and Sarah were both beaming as many of the other ladies joined in and helped them sing. They were also very thankful for the music. They actually had a church choir now – but they had no church house. This was one of those many tough times in which their faith in God was going to be severely tested. But, as Jeff had preached to his congregation so many times before –

"Faith un-tested cannot be trusted." Their faith had been tested many times, and in many ways, and God had always proven himself faithful to every promise.

Jeff preached to the crowd just as fervently and as sincerely as he had before, obeying the leading of the Holy Spirit, holding nothing back. In his message, he never mentioned the burning of the school house, or the Ku Klux Klan. He concentrated on fallen man's need of Jesus Christ and Salvation. He told of ***the fall of Adam, the call of Abraham,*** and ***the cross of Christ.***

"In the fall of Adam, he began, we see the sad and sordid consequences of sin, and the depraved nature of the first man after sin had done its evil work upon all his faculties. And by the daily witness of our own fallen nature that all of us inherited from our fallen father Adam, we know that we are lost creatures from birth, desiring to do wrong, and reluctant to do right, totally incapable of pleasing the Heavenly Father by any act of our own will. From our mother's womb, we are prone to lean toward that which is evil, and to loathe that which is good. And in this matter of human depravity, all of us stand on even ground, none of us either better or worse than his neighbor, regardless of our race, color or creed."

"But glory to God in the highest, he continued...In the eternal mind of a loving Father, there dwelt a plan for the redemption of the fallen race. By his own Sovereign will and choice, the great God of Heaven called a man named Abram, whose name He changed to Abraham. And from the loins of one man God raised up the mighty nation of Israel, so named after the grandson of Abraham. And from the loins of Israel He raised up Judah, through whom He promised a Savior would someday come. And to prove Himself faithful, he preserved the holy seed from generation to generation, until the fullness of the time had come."

Jeff then read from the Bible:

But when the fullness of time was come, God sent forth His Son, made of a woman, made under the law, to redeem them that were under the law, that we might receive the adoption of sons. And because ye are sons, God hath sent forth the Spirit of His Son into your hearts, crying Abba, Father (Galatians 4:5,6).

He asked the congregation to bow their heads and pray silently as the choir came forward to sing. As they were coming Jeff walked very slowly from one side of the crowd to the other, looking into each face, searching for any sign of conviction. He saw several men, women, boys and girls with tears running down their cheeks. He softly asked...

"Do you know for a certainty tonight that you are a son or daughter of God? Does His Holy Spirit dwell within your heart? Can you call Him your Father? Have you trusted the Person and finished work of Jesus Christ as your only hope of salvation? If not, we invite you to come now, just as you are."

Nine women and five men responded to the invitation, stepping forward immediately, and falling on their knees, asking the Lord Jesus to come into their hearts. From the Flemmins family there were Olivia, Isabella, Georgia, Alexander, Alonzo, Rachel and Matthew. The Rutherfords included Laura, Dill, Lee, Lizzie, Violet, Gracie and Josephine. In one month, the church had now more than doubled its number of members. Now all Jeff had to do was baptize these fourteen new members, and pray that God would provide them with a house of worship, and soon.

Since the two families had come so far to be at the meeting, and since God had so richly blessed the work they were doing, Jeff and Becky had decided to make the Sunday feast a monthly tradition also, giving these faithful people a place to rest after the service, and a great feast the next day before they returned to their homes deep in the mountains. But before anyone left tonight, Jeff wanted all of them to join hands in a prayer circle, to pray that God would provide them with a house of worship. No sooner had Jeff said amen than Foster Flemmins and Ralph Rutherford came to him with their hats in their hands. Foster initiated the proposal…

"Preacher, you and this little church have been mighty good to us and our families, and we'd like to show you just how much we appreciate all you've done. If you can find a place to build a new church house, we will furnish the lumber and the manpower to build it, because from what we're seeing, you're gonna have a lot of baptizing and marrying to do pretty soon."

Jeff and Becky got a little choked up at Foster's and Ralph's offer, but Jeff managed to reply…

"Well that's awful kind and generous of you fellas, and I assure you that I will be looking for a place to build that new church real soon."

They shook hands, and everybody loaded into the wagons for the trip to Jeff's farm. Without being asked or ordered, Tom tied Promenade to the back of Pearly Mae's wagon and jumped in beside her, holding her hand all the way to the farm.

Jeff knew that the County would rebuild the school house, but he also knew that when the news of what had happened reached the ears of the county officials they might not allow the church congregation to meet in the new school house anymore. He was right. The reasoning of the board of education was that if the church congregation had not been allowed to use the building, the burning would most likely not have happened in the first place. He knew that their only hope was to build a new church house, but where to build it presented a problem. To build it on his farm would make it too far for some of the folks to travel. It needed to be somewhere relatively close to all the families. He decided to place an advertisement in *The Monongalia Gazette* in Morgantown. The advertisement read – **Valley Grove Baptist Church needs approximately two acres of land within a forty-mile radius of Morgantown. Pastor Jeff Townsend.**

Heavenly Places

The more Tom Tillotson looked at the advertisement, the more he scratched his head. He had an idea. And the more he thought about it the more he was convinced that it just might work. He suddenly remembered climbing the steps to the platform of the gallows where three men were hanged. He remembered the look of sorrow and repentance on their faces as he had witnessed to them of Jesus Christ. He thought to himself…

"If the Lord can change the hearts of those men, He can change the heart of Preston Jenkins."

As far as anyone knew, Preston Jenkins was the only surviving relative of Melvin Jenkins. And just maybe Preston Jenkins was now the owner of the little farm where Melvin and his family had been murdered. And just maybe if he could get to Moundsville, and talk to Preston, he might be able to convince him to sell the land to the church. He might even be able to lead Preston to the Lord, as he had the three condemned men. It was worth a try. He asked Jeff if he could have a few days off from his job on the farm. When Jeff asked him why he needed the time off, Tom replied.

"There's something I just have to do Jeff, and it needs to be done right now, as soon as possible." Jeff chuckled and replied…

"You're gonna go and propose to the Rutherford girl ain't ya ol buddy?"

"Well, I might just do that," Tom shot back.

"Well you take all the time you need my friend," Jeff answered.

Tom shook his hand quickly and was on his horse in the blink of an eye. As Jeff watched Tom ride away in a big hurry, he smiled, shaking his head, thinking…

"Now there goes a man in love."

Tom took down a poster from the side of a barn, folded it, and put it in the inside pocket of his vest. Upon arriving at the train station, he took his horse to the livery stable. The owner of the livery stable, Seth Bromley, was an old friend of Tom's.

"So, where you headed this time Tom?" Seth asked.

Tom told Seth that he was headed for Moundsville, and might be gone for a couple days, and for him to take good care of old Promenade for him. Seth smiled with a questioning grin…

"Moundsville, I hear they just built a new prison there. Ain't that where them three convicted Klansmen was sent to?"

Tom nodded, paid Seth in advance, and bought a ticket to Moundsville. As the train rolled past the Jenkins farm, Tom bowed his head and said a prayer that God would prosper his journey.

Three hours later the train rolled into Moundsville. The new Penitentiary itself was still being designed. A smaller, temporary wooden structure had been built to house the prisoners until the much larger sandstone Gothic-style Penitentiary could be completed. Tom wasted no time getting to the warden's office. He introduced himself to the warden. The warden, George Bickford, stood up and offered Tom his hand with a big smile and congratulations. Tom asked how the warden knew him. The warden quickly explained that he had heard Tom's name mentioned nearly every day from the mouths of three of his most notorious inmates. He added that two of those inmates had made it quite clear that if they ever laid eyes on Tom Tillotson again, he would be a dead man. Tom grinned without asking which two had made that threat, replying...

"Well, warden, I've heard that wind blow before, but I'm really here to see just one of your prisoners – Preston Jenkins."

The warden looked a bit surprised, answering

"That's strange Mr. Tillotson, because Mr. Jenkins has wanted to see you too, and he's the only one of the three who doesn't want to kill you on sight."

Now it was Tom's turn to look shocked. But then he remembered the prayer he had prayed before coming to this place. Maybe the good Lord was already answering his prayer before he got here. He asked if he could talk to Preston Jenkins. After making sure that Tom wasn't carrying a weapon, the warden personally escorted Tom back to Preston Jenkins' cell. To Tom's utter surprise, Preston seemed genuinely glad to see him. Tom could see from Preston's expression that being here in this prison had softened his disposition, if only slightly. Tom asked if he could step inside the cell with Preston. The warden stared from one man to the other for a moment. He squinted at Preston and turned to Tom, saying...

"I guess you know that this is against the rules Mr. Tillotson, but I'll bend the rules just this once. I'll give you ten minutes."

Tom didn't know quite what to expect from Preston Jenkins, seeing as how his own testimony had been a key factor in Preston's conviction. But right now, Tom couldn't dwell on the past – he had to think of the church, and the families whose lives were going to be affected by what might or might not happen in the next ten minutes. He prayed silently for the guidance of the Holy Spirit. He pulled the poster from his vest pocket and showed it to Preston. Preston's eyes immediately filled with tears. The poster itself said all that needed to be said. Without Tom saying a word, Preston Jenkins took the advertisement from Tom's hand, pressing it to his own heart. His voice trembled as he began to speak...

"Tom, I know you think that I hate you, and that I want you dead, but that ain't the case at all. I've had a lot of time to take stock of my wicked life since I've been in this hell hole. I know I've done some horrible things Tom – too horrible to put into words. I had a hand in the murder of Lucas Bratcher, and now I've had my own brother and his little family murdered. I need help Tom. I need help that only God Almighty can give me. Tom, can you tell me how to find peace in my soul?"

Tom's heart leaped with gratitude to God for answering his prayer. He knew that he didn't have to say much at all, because the Holy Spirit was already working on Preston's heart. Tom simply told him how the Lord had saved his own soul. The Holy Spirit did the rest. Preston Jenkins wanted to be saved, and Jesus wanted to save him. They bowed their heads as Tom prayed with him and for him. Preston poured out his heart to God, asking for forgiveness for all his sins. Tom heard him ask the Lord Jesus to come into his heart, and be his personal Savior. When they both raised their heads, an expression of perfect peace came upon Preston Jenkins' face. For the first time in his life, he smiled a genuine smile that came from deep within, and shone through his eyes. The two men hugged each other, both of them sobbing tears of joy.

The ten minutes were nearly gone. Preston called for the warden to come back into the cell block. He showed the warden the poster that Tom had brought. He then asked the warden if he could draw up a note to the effect that he was donating two acres of land to the Valley Grove Baptist Church in Preston County West Virginia, free and clear. George Bickford smiled from ear to ear, replying...

"It just so happen's Mr. Jenkins that I am a Notary Public myself. If you will sign the note, I will notarize it, and Mr. Tillotson here can take it to the land office in Morgantown and secure the deed."

When Tom, walked out of Preston's cell, the warden asked him if he'd like to see Wesley Phelps and William Bowen also. Tom nodded yes. The moment both of them saw Tom they began to curse him. They screamed obscenities that made both Tom and the warden blush. William Bowen shouted...

"May you rot in Hell Tom Tillotson. You're the sorry bastard half breed that got our two brothers hung, you and that damned preacher. Damn you. Damn you both."

They were both reaching through the steel bars, trying to get their hands on Tom. Tom stayed just out of arm's reach. He and the warden looked sadly into each other's eyes as the warden said to Tom...

"I don't think there's anything either of us can do for these two Tom."

"I'm afraid you're right warden," Tom replied sadly.

When they returned to the warden's office, George offered Tom a seat while he drew up the paper for Preston Jenkins to sign. He allowed Tom to take the paper back to the cell for Preston's signature. He and Preston shook hands for the last time. With the paper notarized and in his vest pocket, Tom walked over to the Hotel and rented a room for the night. Next morning he was up bright and early. He took a quick bath, grabbed a bite of breakfast at the only restaurant in town, and headed for the train station, where he waited for the train headed back to Morgantown.

It was 11:00 a.m. when Tom arrived in Morgantown. He went straight to Judge Bracken's home. Both the Judge and his wife Nola came to the door. They were both surprised and pleased to see Tom. Nola went straight to the kitchen, coming back with a cup of tea for Tom. Tom wasted no time in showing Judge Bracken the note that Preston Jenkins had signed, pointing out the Notary seal. He asked Judge Bracken...

"Judge, I just came from the Moundsville Penitentiary. Preston Jenkins and warden Bickford gave me this note. I just wanted to ask you if it was legal before I try to get a deed for that property."

Judge Bracken assured Tom that the note was legal, and that he would be glad to accompany him to the land office to make sure that he got the deed.

It was 8:00 p.m. when Tom arrived at the little train station where he had left his horse the day before. It was 12:00 a.m. when he rode into Jeff's front yard. Cricket was barking as Tom knocked on the front door. Jeff opened the door with a lantern in his hand. He had a very worried look on his face. He couldn't imagine why Tom would be here at this time of the morning. He also wondered why Tom hadn't gone to his own little house at the back of the farm. Once Tom was inside, he reached inside his vest pocket, pulling out both the notarized paper and the deed to the Jenkins farm, handing them to Jeff. Becky had thrown a robe around her and joined them in the living room. Jeff had big tears in his eyes as he sat down on the sofa. He handed Becky the note and deed. He was so choked up he could hardly speak. As Becky looked over the deed slowly, her own eyes filled with tears. The three of them joined hands and did a little dance right there on the living room floor. Even Cricket got excited, jumping and barking as if he understood what had just happened.

Saturday, August 4th, 1866. The Jenkins farm 10:00 a.m.

Every able-bodied man in the congregation of the Valley Grove Baptist Church gathered on the grassy area surrounding the ruins of what used to be the home of Melvin Jenkins and his family. The congregation had now grown to about seventy souls. The wagons were loaded with lumber, bricks, nails, and saws, hammers, framing squares, levels, shovels, mattocks and rulers. The women folk had brought as much food as they could stuff into sacks, piled on top of the lumber. Jeff dismounted, addressing the whole group...

"Folks, the good Lord has blessed us with a piece of land, on which to build a new Church house. I think it would be fitting before we do anything else to bow our heads and give Him thanks for this great gift. As some of you may not know the circumstances surrounding the means by which we came by this land, let me just say that we owe a great debt of gratitude to Mr. Preston Jenkins, who is presently serving time in the Moundsville Penitentiary. Mr. Jenkins is the man who gave us this land, free and clear. We also owe a great debt of gratitude to Mr. Tom Tillotson here, who went all the way to Moundsville to visit Mr. Jenkins, led him to the Lord, and came back with this note and deed that you see in my hand."

"If you will look to your left, you will see three graves, wherein lie the bodies of three beloved children of God – Melvin Jenkins, his wife Clarissa Jenkins, and his daughter Carla Jenkins, all of whom were murdered inside the house that used to sit right here in front of us. It is my sincere hope and prayer that their innocent blood that was spilled upon this ground will be the seed from which will spring many living souls. Let us pray."

Every man, woman and child bowed their heads as Jeff began to pray...

"Our Gracious Heavenly Father, we thank you for answered prayers. And now, as we stand here on the sacred soil today, we dedicate this piece of ground to you, for your honor and glory. With faith we look to you for strength to perform the task that lies ahead of us. I thank you Lord for every precious soul that you have added to the congregation, and for everyone who has come here today to do the work that must be done. From the great work that we begin here today, we pray for a great harvest of souls. In Jesus name we pray, Amen."

The first order of business was to make three strong wooden crosses to place at the head of the three graves. Then everyone pitched in and began to clean up the ruins of the house, barn, smokehouse and tool shed. Everything was shoveled into wheelbarrows and hauled to a shallow gully near the outer perimeter of the two-acre farm. Stakes were driven, strings were stretched and tied to the stakes, and the outer perimeter of the new church house was measured and squared. The men paired up into groups of six, digging the ditches in which the foundation was to be laid. The dirt from the ditches was hauled to the gully, where it was dumped and spread over the debris from the burnt buildings. Some of the women sowed wildflower seeds all over the site. By 4:00 p.m. the foundation of the new Jenkins Memorial Baptist Church had been poured and leveled. While the work was in progress, some of the younger ones had pitched their family's tent. The women had been preparing food, and the children who were old enough to carry water brought buckets of water from the well that Melvin Jenkins himself had dug. All the families camped out on the site that night, including Jeff and Becky. They all awoke on Sunday morning to the smell of bacon frying. Sarah, Becky, Pearly Mae, Claudette, Cleo, Hilda and several other ladies were busy cooking a hearty breakfast before the Sunday morning worship service.

Sunday morning August 5th, 1866.

Homer Rutherford was a drifter - never able to settle down in one place for more than a month or two at most. During spring, summer, and early fall, he slept under the stars. In the winter he slept in any barn or shack that he could find. He mostly lived off the land, but accepted any meal or handout that any generous soul offered him. He had no interest in a family or marriage, and no definite plans for the future. But now two things beyond his control had affected Homer. Age had affected his body and joints, and a sermon from the lips of an anointed preacher had affected his spirit. Homer belonged to a Klan of men, all of whom professed to be God-fearing Christians. But these same men could take the life of anyone who disagreed with their philosophy without blinking an eye, and show absolutely no remorse for having done so. They could beat and maim men, women and children, and burn them and their property, and laugh with devilish delight while doing it.

Homer Rutherford's conscience began to bother him the day he heard Jeff Townsend preach a sermon about a hypocrite and a scarecrow, and that conscience refused to be quieted, no matter where he went, or what he did to quiet it. He had let his beard and mustache grow till he was hardly recognizable. He drank heavily, supposing that the whiskey and moonshine would erase the horrible conviction that pricked his conscience every waking moment, but to no avail. Every time he passed a cornfield, there stood a scarecrow, staring him in the face, accusing his conscience. The powerful words of the preacher kept echoing in his heart…

"The scarecrow, like the hypocrite, is incapable of changing himself. If he is not changed by another, he will forever remain what he is – a pretender. The scarecrow, like the hypocrite, is easily set on fire, and quickly consumed."

As he sat there astride his horse, staring at the lifeless scarecrow in front of him, he drew his pistol from its holster. His tormented brain told him that two shots would end all of his misery. One shot would destroy the scarecrow, the other would end his own life. He pointed the pistol at the scarecrow and pulled the trigger, expecting to receive at least some degree of relief as the chest of the scarecrow was ripped apart by the bullet. Instead he felt as if he had just killed another man. He put the gun barrel to his temple, applying just enough pressure on the trigger to pull it half way back. Tears filled his eyes. His heart pounded hard and fast. Then, without any warning, another inner voice whispered...

"Don't do it Homer."

As quick as a flash of lightning, the true meaning of that sermon suddenly dawned upon his mind. In an instant, Homer Rutherford accepted the cold hard truth that he was the hypocrite - the pretender, as devoid of life as the scarecrow that seemingly stared into his soul.

The faint echo of the shot that went through the chest of the scarecrow reached the ears of those who were awake at the construction site. Jeff and Tom looked at each other as Tom confirmed to Jeff that the shot had come from a pistol and not a rifle. That meant, of course, that whoever fired the shot couldn't be too far away. Tom asked Jeff if he wanted him to ride in the direction of the shot and investigate. Jeff told him to wait and see if any more shots were fired. If more than one more shot was fired, it might be someone is distress, needing help. They waited five minutes. No more shots were heard. Everyone soon recovered from the startling effect of the shot, and turned their attention back to the hot savory food on their plates.

As they continued to enjoy their hearty breakfast, a lone rider appeared on the same trail that had brought Tom here the day he had discovered the burned bodies of the Jenkins family. The rider reined in his horse about two hundred yards from the crowd. He sat there on his horse, motionless, taking in the scene out in front of him. As he counted the number of tents and wagons, and saw some children running and playing, his first thought was that it might be a band of new settlers migrating from Pennsylvania or Maryland. Before getting any closer he took a cartridge from his gun belt, shoving it into his revolver, replacing the one he had fired into the scarecrow.

He was still too far away for anyone to see what he was doing. He clucked to his horse, not spurring him, easing forward very slowly and cautiously. Tom left the group immediately, circling around the trees so as to come up behind the lone rider without being seen. He kept just inside the tree line that lined the narrow trail so that he could keep an eye on the horseman, but the horseman could not see him. As Homer slowly covered another hundred yards he smelled the bacon frying. The whole crowd had now spotted Homer, but he was still too far away to be recognized. All the men who had rifles in their wagons had now advanced to the front of their families, forming a line between the rider and themselves. Somehow, they all looked very familiar to Homer.

At that moment Tom stepped on a dry stick, breaking it with a loud snap. Homer jerked around instantly, only to see Tom Great Bear Tillotson with a rifle pointed at his chest. Tom demanded...

"State yur business pilgrim."

Homer recognized Tom, but Tom didn't recognize Homer. Homer now knew who the men were out there in front of him – they were his family. He didn't have any idea what they were all doing this far from home, until he turned and saw the tall form of Jeff Townsend approaching. Then it dawned on him –

"They're having church out here."

With his hands in the air, Homer replied...

"Howdy Tom, it's me, Homer Rutherford."

He looked past Jeff to the line of men standing with their rifles at the ready and shouted...

"Hey Ralph! It's me, Homer."

Ralph, Rufus, and all of Homer's kin handed their rifles to the younger boys to carry back to the wagons. The Flemmins men did the same. Homer dismounted and walked his horse the rest of the way toward the crowd with Tom and Jeff on either side.

No one knew for sure what Homer had been doing since they last saw him, and no one asked. No one suspected that their own flesh and blood was a member of the KKK. No one (except Jeff and Tom) suspected that Homer had anything to do with the burning of the school house. No one had to ask, because Homer would soon tell the whole sordid tale of his own free will. But before he could tell anything, one of the ladies had already offered him a plate of hot food, which he very gratefully accepted. Homer hadn't had a hot meal in months, and both his appearance and appetite proved it. After a good hot meal and coffee, he asked Jeff if he would come and sit with him and his kin folk. Jeff looked at his new pocket watch, informing Homer that it was almost time to start the service. Homer pleaded with Jeff to allow him to say a few words to the whole crowd before starting the worship service. When Jeff agreed, Homer stood up, asking the whole congregation to gather around closer so that all of them could hear him. With great sobs of remorse in his voice, Homer began with the day that he had heard Jeff preach that sermon about the hypocrite and the scarecrow. He told them how the hatred had boiled up inside him. He told them how that he had gone to the other six members of the Klan, and had informed them about Tom and Pearly Mae holding hands. Before he could go farther, some members of both families – the Rutherfords and the Flemmins, gasped in disbelief. Whispers began to spread through the crowd that Homer was a Klan member. One of the men started to take a rifle from one of the wagons when Jeff stepped in front of him, grabbing his arm, shaking his head, insisting...

"*No my friend, let's hear him out first.*"

Homer assured them that his story was about to get a lot worse, and that he deserved to be shot for what he had done. Jeff assured him that no one was going to shoot him. Homer confessed everything, including the burning of the school house. He told them how he had drifted from place to place, tormented by the foul deeds he had done. Then, with big tears in his eyes, he told them how that Jeff's message had convicted his soul that day, and how he had been trying to find peace, but couldn't. He told them how that just that morning he had been on the verge of taking his own life. Homer broke down completely in front of the whole crowd, crying and begging for forgiveness from all of them. All the men of the congregation, seeing the intensity and sincerity of Homer's sorrow, and remembering their own grief and conviction when they were lost sinners, began to weep with him, and to pray for him.

Jeff put his arm around Homer's shoulder, kneeling directly in front of him. He told him of the saving grace of Jesus Christ, and how that Christ had died for him on the cross, and had risen again for his justification. He asked Homer if he remembered the part of his message that day in which he had told him that the only Person who could change a man was Jesus Christ. Homer answered that he remembered it very well. Jeff continued...

"Homer, the deep sorrow that you feel in your soul right now is the sorrow for the sins you have committed – that is called repentance. And now Homer, you're half way to Heaven. All of us here have forgiven you, but now you need the forgiveness that only Christ Himself can give. Homer, the Bible says that whosoever shall call upon the name of the Lord shall be saved. If you will ask Him from your heart, He will forgive you, and come into your heart, and be your Lord and Savior."

Homer looked Jeff straight in the eye, sobbing...

"Preacher, I want Jesus in my heart more than anything else in the whole world."

The whole congregation bowed their heads and prayed with Homer as he accepted Jesus Christ as his personal Savior. Homer raised his head with a big smile of contentment and peace. A loud shout went up from the congregation. Homer wanted to be baptized immediately. The whole church followed Jeff and Homer down to the edge of Big Sandy Creek, singing "***Shall we gather at the river.***" Thus the first worship service on the site of the new Jenkins Memorial Baptist Church began. Jeff and the congregation took Homer Rutherford's salvation that day as a good omen of far greater things to come. On Monday morning, August 6th, Homer, accompanied by his brother Ralph and Tom Tillotson, turned himself in to Sheriff John Collins, confessing to him that he had burned the Valley Grove School.

John asked Homer if anyone else had been involved in the burning of the school. Homer didn't want to lie, but neither did he want to place other innocent lives in danger. He simply replied...

"John, I am the man who planned the whole thing, and I am the man who lit the torch, and that's all I have to say."

After repeating his confession in front of Judge Bracken, the Judge asked him the same question...

"Homer, did you have any help in the burning of the school? And before you answer, let me remind you that if you refuse to name any others who may or may not have been involved, they are just going to continue to do the same things Homer, and worse things too, and you know it better than anyone. Right now would be a good time to bring them to justice, and maybe save some innocent lives."

Homer looked at Tom and Ralph as if to ask for their advice. Both of them agreed with Judge Bracken. Homer nodded as Judge Bracken began to write the names of the other six men on a piece of paper. When the last name was written, he handed Sheriff Collins warrants for the arrest of all six men, all of whom lived within a five-mile radius of Morgantown. For his cooperation, Judge Bracken gave Homer a suspended sentence of two years in the County jail. Homer asked exactly what a suspended sentence meant. Judge Bracken explained that, as long as he did not commit any other crime within the space of two years, he was a free man.

"Well Homer, Ralph offered as they left Judge Bracken's office, you're a free man now. I just want you to know that if you don't have any other plans, you're welcome to come and live with me and Hilda if you want."

Homer smiled, replying...

"Well, that's mighty kind of you brother Ralph, and I may just take you up on that offer for a while anyway, till I can get back on my feet. But right now I think I'll go and camp out with the folks at the new church site, and help with the work if'n it's alright with the preacher."

Both Ralph and Tom assured him that Jeff Townsend would be glad to get all the help he could get on building the new church house.

Saturday, August 25th, 1866. Jenkins Memorial Baptist Church 7:00 p.m.

As news of the construction of the new Church began to spread, total strangers began to show up at the site with hammers and saws, volunteering to help with the work in any way they could. The Church house, complete with steeple and bell, and a detached fellowship canopy, was finished and ready for worship in less than three weeks. The new building had new pews – enough to seat 150 persons, a new pulpit, new hymn books, and two rows of pews behind the pulpit for the choir. Jeff himself had designed the metal cages for the lamps that lined each wall. The lamps were mounted just high enough to keep the children from reaching them, but low enough to be lit by an adult.

The new Church was another four miles farther away for Jeff and Becky, but four miles closer for the rest of the congregation. That meant, of course, that Jeff, Becky and Tom would have to get up and leave a little earlier than before. And now that they had their own Church building, and were not obligated to the County, Jeff and the whole congregation agreed that they should start having meetings every Sunday morning, complete with Sunday school classes for all age groups. The congregation itself had now grown to 100 souls. Every baptized member of the Church became Charter members of the new Jenkins Memorial Baptist Church. Clark and Sarah Puckett kept the Church ledger with all the names recorded, along with the date that each was saved and baptized. With all the business taken care of, Jeff asked the whole congregation to stand as he prayed a prayer of thanksgiving, dedicating the new building to the Lord. Both the pews behind the pulpit were immediately filled by anyone who could carry a tune, as Foster Flemmins with his violin, and Rufus Rutherford with his guitar queued up the old hymn *Amazing Grace*, which had already become widely known as – "*The Baptist Anthem*".

Everyone who was able to find a place to kneel or stand gathered around the long wooden altar in unified prayer for the Pastor, his wife, and the continued blessing and success of the new Church. Jeff began his first sermon in the new Church house...

"Please turn in your Bibles to First Corinthians 13:13, where we read...**And now abideth faith, hope, charity, these three; but the greatest of these is charity.**

I would like to entitle this first message in our new Church building as "*Hope is in the middle*" All of you who have been saved now know what it means to have faith in Jesus Christ. You also know what it means to have the love of Jesus Christ in your hearts. We, as ministers of the Gospel, often spend much time and energy upon these two great themes, and rightly so. But I greatly fear that in our dwelling at great length upon the doctrines of faith and love, we may have unintentionally neglected to even notice that little word between faith and charity – the word, *hope*. I, for one, refuse to believe that it is mere coincidence or accident that the term *hope* was inserted between the terms faith and charity. If you that are saved will recall your own conversion, you may recall that in the days, weeks, or months just prior to your conversion, you seemed to be without hope. And perhaps as I speak to you tonight, some of you can think of someone else who seems to be without hope. But since the blessed Savior Himself has lit the candle of hope within your own breasts, you now know that no one except the reprobate is beyond the hope of being saved."

"The hope of which I speak tonight is the only hope of its kind. It is a hope that no one except a blood-washed child of God can claim. May the Holy Spirit bear witness as I deal with this blessed term under five headings tonight. First of all, the hope that burns within the breast of the believer is a *loving hope* – a hope that is based – not upon my love for God, but upon God's love for me. My hope is inseparably connected to the love of Christ Jesus. Without His love, I would have no hope. In First John, chapter three, beginning at verse one, we read…

Behold what manner of love the Father hath bestowed upon us, that we should be called the sons of God: therefore the world knoweth us not, because it knew Him not. Beloved, now are we the sons of God, and it doth not yet appear what we shall be: but we know that when He shall appear, we shall be like Him; for we shall see Him as He is. And every man that hath this hope in him purifieth himself, even as He is pure.

And again, in Romans chapter five, verses one through five, we read:
Therefore being justified by faith, we have peace with God through our Lord Jesus Christ: By whom also we have access by faith into this grace wherein we stand, and rejoice in hope of the glory of God. And not only so, but we glory in tribulations also: knowing that tribulation worketh patience; And patience experience; and experience hope: and hope maketh not ashamed; because the love of God is shed abroad in our hearts by the Holy Ghost which is given unto us.

From these, and numerous other passages of Scripture, we can readily see that our hope and God's love are inseparable. If we profess to have a hope, then we, like the Apostles before us, must first know that Christ has loved us, and has given Himself for us. Why?

For God so loved the world, that He gave His only begotten Son, that whosoever believeth in Him should not perish, but have everlasting life (John 3:16).

Secondly, the hope that burns within our breasts is a *living hope* – it is a hope that has the promise of life attached to it. In the Gospel of John, chapter ten, verse ten, we read:

The thief cometh not, but for to steal, and to kill, and to destroy: I am come that they might have *life*, and that they might have it more abundantly.

The Christian life is not about dying, it is about living. It is about living a larger and more vibrant and abundant life than any other religious or non-religious entity can claim. No one but the child of God can have or live the kind of life that springs up within him as living waters from a living Fountain. And the *living hope* that dwells within the heart of every believer sustains him – not only in this life, but also for the life to come. It is a hope that reaches beyond this life, yea, beyond death, and beyond the grave itself. This living hope, of course, has its source in the Lord Jesus Himself, because He is our hope, and He is our life.

Thirdly, our hope is a *lifting hope*. I will be the first to admit that in my own walk with Christ, there have been times when both body and spirit were near to despair. It seemed that all hope of deliverance was gone. My prayers seemed to go unanswered. I needed someone or something to raise me up from the slough of despond. It was during those times that the very hope that burned within me became my deliverer, and I, like David could say:

I waited patiently for the Lord; and he inclined unto me, and heard my cry. He brought me up also out of a horrible pit, out of the mire clay, and set my feet upon a rock, and established my goings. And he hath put a new song in my mouth, even praise unto our God: many shall see it, and fear, and shall trust in the Lord (Psalm 40:1-3).

Yea, even while in the pit of despair, the highly favored child of God can sing with Hannah:

The Lord killeth, and maketh alive: he bringeth down to the grave, and bringeth up. He raiseth up the poor out of the dust, and lifteth up the beggar from the dunghill, to set them among princes,

and to make them inherit the throne of glory: for the pillars of the earth are the Lord's, and he hath set the world upon them (I Samuel 2:6-8).

The burning hope that throbs in the heart of each believer lifts him or her above the circumstances that surround them. While the poor, unbelieving soul writhes and thrashes in the quicksand of gloom and despair, only to sink further and further into it, the *lifting* hope that rules the heart of a Christian gives him the calm assurance that he shall not be swallowed up. Even as the whale that swallowed Jonah carried him to the darkest depths of the sea, but was compelled to vomit him out upon the dry land, so shall the child of God be brought again from the deepest abyss of hopelessness to look again toward God's holy temple.

Fourthly, the hope that lives within us is a *lively hope*, as opposed to the false and lifeless hope of the pagan, whose very expectation shall ultimately land him in Hell. His religion in which he trusts will be the vehicle in which he rides into the lake of fire. But we, like Peter anointed with the Spirit, can rejoice…

Blessed be the God and Father of our Lord Jesus Christ, which according to his abundant mercy hath begotten us again unto a lively hope by the resurrection of Jesus Christ from the dead, To an inheritance incorruptible, and undefiled, and that fadeth not away, reserved in heaven for you, Who are kept by the power of God through faith unto salvation ready to be revealed in the last time (I Peter 1:3-5).

You and I have seen this lively hope demonstrated in our midst, when the great Holy Spirit moves the hearts, the hands, and the feet of God's people to praise Him with upraised hands and dancing feet.

And finally, that loving, living, lifting, lively hope that so moves the heart to worship, is also a *lasting hope*. He who is regenerated by the Spirit is justified and sealed by the same Spirit, and will never need to be justified again. Our blessed Lord Himself has said…

My sheep hear my voice, and I know them, and they follow me: And I give unto them eternal life: and they shall never perish, neither shall any man pluck them out of my hand. My Father, which

gave them me, is greater than all: and no man is able to pluck them out of my Father's hand (John 10:27-29).

The child of God need never fear losing that which the Holy Spirit has wrought within his soul. Our Lord Jesus Christ died for us once, and has sat down on the right hand of His Father, having done all that was necessary to redeem the lost. There is nothing else that ever needs to be added to His perfect sacrifice – once for all, for it is written:

For Christ is not entered into the holy places made with hands, which are the figures of the true: but into heaven itself, now to appear in the presence of God for us: Nor yet that he should offer himself often, as the hight priest entereth into the holy place every year with blood of others: For then must he often have suffered since the foundation of the world: but now, once in the end of the world hath he appeared to put away sin by the sacrifice of himself. And as it is appointed unto men once to die, but after this the judgment: So Christ was once offered to bear the sins of many; and unto them that look for him shall he appear the second time without sin unto salvation (Hebrews 9:23-28).

It is a ***lasting hope*** in that Christ, our forerunner, has now entered the Holy of Holies by His own blood, having obtained eternal redemption for us:

Neither by the blood of goats and calves, but by his own blood he entered in once into the holy place, having obtained eternal redemption for us (Hebrews 9:12).

And in closing, lest there should be any of you who yet doubt the security of your souls, please turn to Hebrews, chapter six, beginning at verse seventeen:

Wherein God, willing more abundantly to show unto the heirs of promise the immutability of his counsel, confirmed it by and oath: That by two immutable things, in which it was impossible for God to lie, we might have a strong consolation who have fled for refuge to lay hold upon the hope set before us: Which hope we have as an anchor of the soul, both sure and steadfast, and which entereth into that within the veil; Whither the forerunner is for us entered, even Jesus, made a high priest forever after the order of Melchizedec.

Here, in these inspired verses, Paul compares our hope to an anchor. If anyone ever understood the value of an anchor, it was

Paul, who sailed in and out of many a harbor on board the great wooden ships of his day. As many of you may know, an anchor, in order to hold the ship to which it is attached, must necessarily be made of stronger material than the ship itself. The anchor must be weighty enough to prevent the ship from drifting out to sea, yet light enough to be carried on board the ship. The anchor, when lowered, is invisible to the naked eye, and yet we know that it is there without our seeing it. The anchor, if lying upon a sandy bottom, may yet allow the ship to drift, but when the anchor has attached itself to a solid rock, the shipmaster may go about his business, not having to concern himself about the safety of his ship.

And so it is with the Christian – his hope is stronger than himself, that hope being Christ Himself. The lasting hope that holds the believer securely is weighty enough to prevent him from drifting out to sea in a storm, yet light enough for him to carry in his bosom. The lasting hope of the child of God is within, invisible to the human eye, yet making its presence and power known to the one who has it. The lasting hope of the believer, like an anchor, is attached to the great Rock of Ages, immoveable, indestructible. And though the violent storms may shake the ship upward and downward and from side to side, and rip the sails from their masts, the anchor holds.

And that brings us full circle my friends, back to the beginning of this message, which I entitled...***Hope is in the middle***. More than eighteen hundred years ago, three crosses stood on the hill called Calvary. On either side there hung a thief, condemned to die for crimes of which both were guilty. But in the middle, there hung the sinless Son of God, dying for crimes that He had not committed. I say to you that there was hope for both of the thieves, but only one recognized that Hope, and called upon Him for salvation. Jesus was the Hope of the world then, and He is the Hope of the world today. And He is still in the middle, between God and man, between Heaven and Hell.

As we stand and sing a hymn of invitation, I simply must ask…

"*Where is your hope*? Have you compared the hope that you have with the hope that I have described from the inspired Scriptures, and does your hope match that hope? If not, we invite you to come, and receive that Hope now, in the Person of Jesus Christ."

As the Holy Spirit drew precious souls to Christ, the whole congregation bowed their heads, praying fervently for their loved ones to be saved. Strangers who had come to work on the new building came forward – some to receive Jesus as their personal Savior, and others to become members of the new Church. Some came forward just to re-dedicate their lives to the service of God. Ten souls were saved that evening, and were scheduled to be baptized next Sunday in Big Sandy Creek.

Saturday, August, 25th, 1866. Jenkins Memorial Baptist Church.

As horrible as the Civil War itself had been, what followed the war was not a pretty sight either. Living conditions were horrible in the extreme, especially for black freedmen and their families. The national economy was in shambles. The Southern landscape was littered with the ruins of blackened structures that used to be homes. Thousands of freed black individuals and families fled North via the Undergound Railroad. Many wandered from place to place, seeking refuge and sustenance anywhere they could find it. The radical Republican Congress had placed the South under military rule. Carpetbaggers and scalawags (scallywags) occupied the state houses, raising taxes and looting the state treasuries. Blacks were now armed with the right to vote, but were struggling to claim those rights. Ex-Confederate soldiers returned to a land that was desolate. In an attempt to regain at least some control, and to restore some semblance of order to their disrupted society, southerners began to form secret organizations – the Pale Faces, the Sons of Midnight, and the Knights of the White Camelia, whose objective was to terrorize and intimidate blacks and unionists. These organizations, of course, were the forerunners of what later became known as the Ku Klux Klan, whose first grand wizard was the former Confederate General, Nathan Bedford Forrest.

In 1866, 2,773 freedmen lived in West Virginia. One of those freedmen, Buford R. Williams, along with his wife Mattie and their twin daughters, Greta and Gloria, found his way to Preston County West Virginia, looking for a new life in a new place. All his worldly goods, which amounted to a few blacksmithing tools, were in the back of a rickety wagon, pulled by a team of starving mules. They had eaten their last piece of dry bread, and had given the last piece of beef jerky to the girls. Buford had no idea where he was, or where he was going. In fact, both he and Mattie had agreed before leaving Morgantown that they would cast themselves and their children upon the mercy of the good Lord above, and simply trust Him to guide them to wherever they needed to be.

Where they needed to be on Saturday evening, August 25th, was in the yard of the Jenkins Memorial Baptist Church. Jeff and Becky were standing just outside the front door, shaking hands with the departing crowd, when someone spotted the old wagon rolling slowly onto the Church property. There was just enough daylight left for everyone to notice that the man and woman on the seat of the wagon were black. Everyone stood silently as the wagon drew closer and then stopped about forty yards away from the crowd. Jeff, with his Bible in his hand, walked toward the wagon. Approaching the wagon, he could quickly see that the mules pulling the wagon, and the family in the wagon were starving. His heart broke at the haggard look on Buford Williams' face. Jeff introduced himself, extending his hand, first to Buford, then to Mattie. Then he noticed the two little girls in the back of the wagon. They were so thin!

Without another word to Buford, Jeff yelled back to the crowd, asking if anyone had anything to eat in their wagons. Several families responded immediately that they had brought bread, cheese, and some fruit. Jeff took the mules by their bridles, leading them toward the Church house. When they reached the crowd, five families gathered around the wagon, reaching armloads of food up to Buford and his family. Some of the men who had brought straw for their own horses shared it with Buford's mules. Becky started to draw a fresh bucket of water from the well when Tom stopped her, drawing it himself. Buford eyed Tom quizzically. He had never seen a half breed mixing and mingling so casually among white folks. And he most certainly had never seen a half breed extend such friendship and charity to a black man.

The Williams family ate as if they hadn't had a meal in days. Jeff unhitched the mules and led them down to the Big Sandy

Creek for water. Buford Williams and his family didn't know quite how to react to such genuine Christian charity from a bunch of white folks. As they ate, they just looked gratefully at Jeff and the crowd, nodding their heads as if that was the only way they knew to say thank you. After they had eaten all they could hold, Jeff handed Clark his Bible and helped Mrs. Williams down from the wagon. Clark handed the Bible to Becky and lifted Greta and Gloria off the back of the wagon. The sun was setting now, so Jeff asked Foster to go back into the Church house and light the lamps.

Neither Buford nor any of his family had spoken a word since their arrival at the Church. Jeff asked them to come into the Church house. At first Buford objected, shaking his head, but saying nothing. Jeff assured him that it was alright for them to come inside. Buford looked at his wife Mattie as if asking her advice. Mattie just stared at him with a blank stare. They both stared down at their dirty ragged clothes, then back to Jeff. Jeff smiled knowingly, taking Buford by the hand, assuring him...

"It's alright Sir, you and your family are welcome here. Come in and rest. May I ask your name?" Buford removed his floppy hat, replying...

"I's be Buford R. Williams mister, and this here is my missus Mattie, and them two be the young'uns Greta an Gloria, we's been runnin from sum white men fur fo days now, seems we's lost our way. But we sho is grateful fur da food and kindness."

Jeff told the congregation that they should all go to their homes. Some wanted to stay behind, but Jeff insisted that he and Becky would be fine. Clark Puckett refused to leave Jeff and Becky alone. He lingered outside with Sarah and the children. As the crowd left, Jeff escorted Buford and his family into the Church. He and Becky listened as Buford began telling them how he and his family had come to be there. His voice trembled slightly as he began...

"A group dat calls demselves "The Sons of Midnight" come's a ridin onto our little place on da outskirts of Morgantown fo days ago. They's catches me working in da field, an's they's went an beats up my Mattie somethin awful afore I could git ta her. Da holds a knife to her throat, telling me dat if'n we's didn't get out'a Morgan County da would cut our throats. One of them went to firing his pistol betwixt my feet, while's the rest of them sets fire ta my house and barn. They kilt our cow and our hog, tuk what few chickens we's had fur themselves. They's told me they's would give us ten minutes ta hitch up da mules an leave, and that if'n we looked back da would shoot us. I's drove da team as hard as I's could gittin away."

Jeff and Becky both had tears in their eyes as Buford told his story. Mattie sat silently, as if she were still in a state of shock. The two girls sat quietly with their heads down, staring at the floor. Jeff asked Buford if he had any family anywhere near. Buford assured him that he had no family except Mattie and the two girls. Buford thanked Jeff again for all the food and kindness, and was about to get up and leave when Jeff stopped him.

"Where will you go Mr. Williams?" He asked.

"We's don't rightly know Preacher, Buford replied, guess we's be trying to find some mo black folks somewhere's, we be's praying hard dat their hearts be as big as yurs."

Jeff was about to say something when Clark knocked on the wooden door frame, apologizing to Jeff and Buford for interrupting their conversation. Jeff asked him if everything was alright outside. Clark assured him that everything was fine, but that he needed to ask the stranger a question. Jeff introduced Buford and his family to Clark. Clark spoke to Buford first...

"Mr. Williams, I couldn't help but notice that you have some blacksmithing tools in the back of your wagon. Are you a blacksmith by trade?" Buford answered.

"Yes siree, I sho is a blacksmith, or I's *wuz* a blacksmith, til bout a month ago when these white men come's to my shop an they's told me dat Morgantown West Virginia didn't need no nigger blacksmith. They went an tore my shop to pieces, they's tuk most of my tools, and threatened our lives ifn'n I continued to work in Morgantown. I's bought that shop fair an square at a Sheriff's auction. They done went and told me dat the man who used to own it wus in prison, an his brother wus hanged fur murder. I paid all my life's savings fo dat shop, an now it's all gone cept'in for the few tools I managed ta put into this here wagon four days ago."

Clark and Jeff looked at each other as if they both had the same idea at the same moment. Clark offered Buford a proposition...

Heavenly Places

"Mr. Williams, just about all of us have to go all the way to Morgantown whenever we need some major blacksmithing done, and as you know, it's about twenty miles away fur most of us. We shore could use a good blacksmith right here in Preston County."

Buford glanced from Clark to Jeff stammering…

"Mister, I sho do appreciate yun's thinking of me and my family so kindly, but I ain't got me no land, no shop, and a mighty few tools left. I's don't sees no way in da world I's could start a blacksmith shop."

Clark answered, "Mr. Williams, I live less than six miles from here, and I have more land than I will ever need. If you would agree to become the new blacksmith for Preston County, I will give you as much land as you need, and the logs to build your family a home and a blacksmith shop, and I do believe that we can find both the material and the manpower to do both."

Tears welled up in both Buford's and Mattie's eyes. Mattie hadn't spoken a word until now. Her voice trembled as she threw her arms around Buford's neck…

"Lawdy, Lawdy Buford, the good Lawd sho has gone an answered our prayers!"

Buford was still somewhat in shock at the genuine love and kindness these white folks were showing to him and his family. No one had ever shown this kind of generosity and sincerity to him since he was born, especially not any white folks. As Buford shook hands with Jeff and Clark, they could see that he was all choked up with gratitude, and could hardly speak.

Jeff asked, "Do you mind if I ask you a personal question about your religion?"

Before he could say anything else, Buford and Mattie both chimed in…

"We's sho don't mind preacher."

Buford looked Jeff in the eye, professing…

"Brother Townsend, we's been saved an dipped in de wautuh fo many years now, but seems like we's jest ain't welcome in any church we's been to."

Jeff assured him that he and his family would be welcomed with open arms at the Jenkins Memorial Baptist Church. Buford nodded his approval, replying…

"Well, we's sho be seeing y'all come next Sunday."

Jeff, Becky, Clark and Sarah hugged the whole family, reminding them to bring Greta and Gloria to Sunday school. Buford thanked them again for all their kindness. Clark helped him hitch the mules to the wagon, and they were on their way to the Puckett farm, where they would live with Clark and Sarah Puckett. During the next two months, every man and woman who could spare a little time and material pitched in and helped the Williams family build a new log house, and a brand new blacksmith shop.

Saturday, September 15th 1866 The Townsend farm.
    Becky and Jeff's wedding was an event to be remembered, but nothing that Becky had ever seen could compare to the wedding of Tom Tillotson and Pearly Mae Rutherford. Such a sight had never before been seen in Preston County West Virginia. Pearly Mae Rutherford was an outstanding human being, and as pure as the driven snow, a woman who, by her own choice, had catered to her family and many others since she was a very young girl. At age thirty-eight she still, from the kindness of her heart, always put others before herself. Her deep generosity was now paying off. For all the many good deeds, all the kindness, the babies she had delivered, the sick folks she had tended to, and for all the times she had spent away from home to help someone - for all those situations, there was now a person, or a family, that wanted to pitch in and help with the wedding, and Becky and Sarah denied no one the pleasure of doing just that.
    Some folks questioned why she was marrying Tom Tillotson, who had the reputation of being the most ruthless, hell-raising, heartless man around. Those were the ones who could not let go of the past, the ones that did not know the God that Tom now served. Some were angry that a half Indian was marrying a white woman. The news had reached Morgantown, and folks who did not know either Tom or Pearly Mae were gossiping. But now that six more members of the KKK had been caught and brought to justice, Jeff didn't worry too much about the safety of his friends. He thought to himself...

"It's just a lot of poor lost people who don't understand that God loves us all the same. Perhaps someday they'll come to know the Lord."

Yes, Tom Tillotson was a vicious, mean and destructive man just a short time ago, a man that would shoot a person down, or cut a man or woman's throat at the drop of a hat. But God had saved his wretched soul, and changed him from a cruel and hateful man into a humble and forgiving man. The people in the Church, many who had once been a lot like Tom himself, had been changed, and knew what the mighty hand of God could do for anyone who wished to change and was willing to change. Tom himself admitted that he was not deserving of such a great woman as Pearly Mae, but was sure that God had given her to him. The old Tom was dead, the new Tom was very much alive, and the union that was taking place was blessed by God Himself. It was plain to see that the dark-skinned, dark-haired man had captured Pearly Mae's heart. Whenever she was with Tom, her eyes sparkled, like the stars on a clear cloudless night.

Becky and Sarah were overwhelmed by all the help, so they met at the new Church, assigning every volunteer a certain job to do. Claudette, who had wanted a big wedding for herself and Rufus was Pearly Mae's maid of honor, she was very happy and excited for Pearly Mae. Now she could be a part of one of the finest weddings she would ever see. Tom wanted Jeff to be the best man, but since he was the minister, it was not proper for him to do both parts, so Tom called on Rufus, and it was settled. Mollie Puckett was the flower girl, and a beautiful one at that. Carter Puckett was the ring bearer. The surprise of all surprises was that Clark Puckett had been learning to play the violin, and had volunteered to play a special tune as Pearly Mae marched down the aisle - a special tune which he refused to tell anyone.

"I ain't tellin nary soul til the hitching," he declared, with a big jolly laugh that everyone had grown to love. Sarah herself was surprised, but pleased to learn that he had taken a liking to the violin. Becky and Sarah were also planning a special song for Pearly Mae.

Tom drove Becky and his sweet Pearl into Morgantown to pick out all the material and other items that were needed for the occasion. Sarah and the other women folk were making the wedding gown as well as the other dresses that were needed. All the preparation started taking place one week prior to the wedding, which was going to take place on the Townsend farm just a short distance from Tom's new cabin, where he and Pearly Mae would be living. Becky was so excited to be going to Morgantown. She needed some things for the baby as well as some items for the house. She was most excited to be helping pick out the things that Pearly Mae needed for her wedding. Tom pulled the buggy over at the General store, jumping down from the buggy and gently helping the two women down. Planting a quick kiss on Pearly Mae's lips, he informed them that he would be "jest round the corner" if they needed him. He was going to take the horse and buggy to the livery stable…

"fur a new pair of shoes," he whispered mysteriously, looking at Becky with a nod and a grin.

Tom had told Jeff that he was buying his sweet Pearl a special gift while he was in town. Becky knew he was headed toward a jewelry store to purchase a fancy ring for sweet Pearl. Becky and Pearly Mae had so much fun buying things for the wedding. After shopping at the General store Tom treated them to lunch at the Virginia Stone Café - a dainty little place with red and white checked table clothes and curtains to match. They were having such a good time, they didn't want the day to end, but Becky knew they must be getting back soon. She was getting very tired, and her feet were swollen from walking so much. She was now carrying extra weight. It seemed the baby was growing every day. Just a few more months, and she and Jeff would, hopefully, have a bouncing baby boy.

On the ride home Becky and Pearlie May double checked the list of items they had bought in town, matching the names of those to whom the items were to be taken. The material from which all the dresses were to be made, was going to Sarah and the ladies at the church. Hilda was making the wedding cake. Tom, Jeff and Rufus were riding back into Morgantown later that week to pick up their suits. The flower arrangements were being made by Becky, Claudette and Cleo. The excitement of the day kept Becky awake far into the night, her mind spinning like a wagon wheel. Tom was camping out in the Townsend barn at night so that Pearlie May could prepare their cabin for the honeymoon. Finally, after much preparation, the big day arrived.

Becky awoke early, laying out her dress that she had made from the material that Jeff had bought her for their anniversary - a beautiful black-pleated dress, trimmed in yellow lace around the puffy sleeves and at the bottom. She laid out the black hat, replacing the red ribbon with a yellow one. Jeff's suit was placed on the bed beside her dress. She quickly made breakfast before he returned from the barn where he was doing all the chores and waking Tom. She took a quick look out the window as Jeff and Tom made their way toward the house. Sitting down at the table, they all bowed their heads as Jeff asked the blessing on the food and the wedding that was going to take place.

"Are you nervous my friend?" Jeff asked with a big smile as he passed the platter of fried bacon and eggs.

"I am scared to death," Tom replied, as he took the platter. I just hope I can be the man that sweet Pearl deserves. I'm the luckiest man alive. God's blessed me so much since I have met you two good people."

Tom's eyes filled with tears. Jeff reached over, patting his friend on the shoulder, replying…

"Tom, God put us all together as a family, and we are so proud of that."

The rest of the meal was in silence. Emotions were running high.

Folks started pouring in around noon. The place was decorated in no time. White daisies lined the rails of the steps where Pearly Mae would walk down and into the yard, toward the big oak tree, where stood a beautiful arch that Ralph and Rufus had built, covered with pink sweet pea vine. Chairs had been brought from the new church and set up in sections of two, with a path in the middle for the bride to walk through. Jeff had closed the barn door so that Cricket would not interrupt the wedding. Becky and Sarah seated everyone, placing the wedding party where they needed to be. Jeff, Tom and Rufus stood on the left side of the arch, so handsome in their fancy suits. Becky noticed Rufus fidgeting…

"Ain't never wore no fancy duds like this afore," he complained.

"You'll be fine," she assured him, as she pinned a yellow rose to his, Tom's, and Jeff's jackets. Far to the left were the musicians - Ralph on his fiddle, with Foster on the mandolin. A couple more men had pitched in with a bass and guitar.

Clark playing the violin was a pleasant surprise to everyone. They were all seated in a small half circle. Becky and Sarah stood nearby so they could be heard when they sang. Clark stood first, playing the beautiful wedding song - "*There is love,*" which was the signal for Claudette, the maid of honor, to walk down the steps and take her place on the right side of the arch. She was so beautiful in her long dress - a pale purple that blended perfectly with her bouquet of purple cone flowers mixed with yellow lilies. Then Carter, dressed in a black suit, carrying the rings on a silk pillow that Hilda and Sarah had made. Then Mollie, all dressed in pink, with her blonde curly hair piled high on her head, walked down the path, dropping petals from the white daisies, leading the way for Pearly Mae.

Everyone gasped at the sheer radiance of the bride. She was a beautiful sight. The bride's long, white satin gown trailed behind her, with a veil that slightly covered her face. She walked with such grace, carrying in her arms a large bouquet of Calliopsis mixed with white yarrow, with a yellow ribbon tied in a beautiful bow around the long stems. Tom had a look of great pride on his face as he watched her on the arm of her brother, Homer Rutherford. They stopped in front of the arch as Tom stepped forward, standing just in front of her.

Jeff asked, "Who gives this woman to be wed to this man?"

Homer proudly announced… "I do."

Tom took Pearly Mae's hand as Becky and Sarah stepped forward and sang…*There is Love.*

There is love
He is now to be among you, at the calling of your hearts
Rest assured this troubadour is acting on his part
The union of your spirits, here has caused him to remain
For whenever two or more of you are gathered in his name
There is love, there is love.

Jeff began… "Let us pray."

"Our gracious Heavenly Father, we thank you for your divine providence in bringing this man and this woman together. We thank you for saving their souls, and for making them our dear and close friends. And now Father, we humbly ask that you bless this union as only you can do, In Jesus name, Amen."

"Would you face each other please? Pearly Mae Rutherford, if you of your own free will intend to spend the rest of your life as the wife of Tom Tillotson, would you take his hand and look into his eyes. Do you promise in the sight of God and these witnesses to take this man to be your lawfully wedded husband, to have and to hold from this day forward; forsaking all others, and keeping yourself for him alone; Do you vow that there is no other man in your past, present, or foreseeable future who can have your love and affection; Do you promise to love, honor, and obey him in all things according to the Holy Scriptures; Do you promise to cleave unto him in sickness and in health, for richer or for poorer, for better or for worse, for as long as you both shall live?"

Pearly Mae looked straight into Tom's eyes, replying…

"I do."

Jeff asked for the ring from Carter Puckett, holding it up so that everyone could see it. Then, looking at Pearly Mae, he recited the meaning and symbolism of the wedding ring…

"Since ancient times the ring has been a symbol of eternity itself, being circular in shape, having no beginning and no end. The ring has been used by kings and emperors as a signet with which to seal documents and covenants between men and nations. Such rings were most often made of purest gold, symbolizing both the value and purity of the agreement that was to be sealed. But the value and symbolism of the wedding ring transcends that of the ring of a king or emperor, because the agreements and covenants sealed by the ring of a king or emperor may be broken or nullified by mortal men, whereas the covenant into which the two of you are about to enter cannot be broken nor nullified by men or angels."

"The wedding ring is also a visible token of the promises that the two of you are making to each other here today. When you are bodily absent from each other, this ring says to the rest of the world – hands off! This man is taken. He belongs to Pearly Mae. Would you place the ring on Tom's hand, and repeat after me – with this ring, I thee wed."

Pearly Mae eased the ring onto Tom's finger, repeating after Jeff…

"With this ring, I thee wed."

After listening to Jeff say the same vows that he had recited to Pearly Mae, Tom slipped the ring onto her finger, repeating after Jeff…

"With this ring, I thee wed."

Jeff continued, "Having witnessed your exchange of sacred vows and rings to each other, by the power vested in me by Almighty God and the Commonwealth of West Virginia, I pronounce you man and wife. Tom, you may kiss your bride."

Tom and Pearly Mae embraced in a passionate kiss, as tears of joy ran down the cheeks of family members, as shouts of praise went up from the crowd. Jeff pronounced loudly…

"Ladies and gentlemen, may I present to you Mr. and Mrs. Thomas Avery Tillotson."

Clark gently raised the violin to his chin, as Becky and Sarah fulfilled Tom's request for a song, "*just for my sweet Pearl.*"

The Sweetest Flower of them all
By George Cooper, 1840

Tis down beside the river, that sings a merry tune
I love to wander ever, neath skies of blushing June
For there I often meet her, the girl I love so well
The sweetest rose that ever grows
Her name is "my sweet Pearl"
All among the blossoms, on a happy summer day
List'ning to the robins, all alone we stray
All among the Lilly bells, and daisies bright and small
There I meet my sweet Pearl
She's the sweetest flow'r of all.

Immediately after the ceremony food was served, and the fellowship began. Tom made a speech, thanking everyone for all they had done.

"Sweet Pearl and me will furever be obliged to all of yun's," he said, waving his hand toward the whole crowd.

The music began, with everyone choosing a partner, and dancing away the evening. When Cricket was finally released from the barn, the children immediately began chasing him all over the farm. Later that evening, everyone said goodbye to Tom and Pearly Mae, as they rode toward their little cabin that was now their home. The festivities continued into the late hours of the night. It was a happy group of people that loaded their wagons, and turned their horses toward home.

December 21st 1866, The Townsend farm.

Jeff was growing colder by the moment. He was chilled to the bone. He rushed about, finishing up his chores, feeding the horses and milking the cow, making sure that all was secure inside the barn. His face was numb from the cold wind that was blowing, despite the fact that he had on a hat, and a scarf pulled around his mouth and neck. The frozen ground crunched under his boots as he went from stall to stall. He had the feeling that a snowstorm was brewing. He could just feel a difference in the air. He and Becky had been out here in this country long enough to know that the winters were uncertain, harsh, and bitter cold, with snow lasting from October to well up into March, and sometimes April. The summers were either scorching hot with months of no rain, or so much rain that the crops would drown. He gave Daisy and the horses an extra helping of feed, just in case the snow came and he couldn't reach the barn before noon, which had happened so many times before.

"Oh shoot!" he said out loud. He remembered, he had promised Becky that he would find a nice tree for Christmas, and if he didn't do that soon he might not be able to, if the dark rolling clouds in the sky were any indication of what was about to come.

He walked to the chip yard where he chopped some firewood. The cold wind nearly snapped off his big black hat. He quickly pulled it down farther over his ears. The dark clouds were forming shadows over the mountain tops.

"Hey there Preacher" - a voice could barely be heard over the wind and Jeff's muffled ears. It was Tom riding into the barnyard.

"I promised my sweet Pearl a tree from the mountains. Miss Becky got one yet?" Tom asked.

As he dismounted, he and Jeff shook hands. The two men had now become best of friends, and relied on each other for so many things.

"Good to see you my friend, Jeff replied. I promised Becky a tree, and was just thinking about getting one before this storm comes in. Ya think we can make it before dark Tom?"

Jeff looked at Tom with a grin, already knowing what Tom's answer would be.

"Shore, Tom answered, us git going. Jest maybe this storm will hold off, but looks mean out here, betcha we'll have snow fore morning."

Tom offered to saddle up Jeff's horse while he went into the house to tell Becky. Grabbing the pail of milk and basket of eggs, Jeff headed inside. Becky had been busy all day making candies and other good things for Christmas before the baby came, which could be any day. The house smelled so good. She had been so busy making all Jeff's favorite things that she had forgotten that...

"Yes, the baby could be here anytime!"

She was hoping it would arrive on Christmas Day. What a blessing that would be. She had Jeff's gift made - a beautiful blue scarf she had knitted and just finished this afternoon. Since she was unable to travel to the nearest town, due to her condition, she had Tom to pick out a handsome pair of black boots with the initials J.T. on the strap that buckled around the top. She was sure he would like them. Jeff stood in the doorway as he looked at his beautiful wife standing at the stove, stirring a hot kettle of homemade soup. What a sight! And how blessed they had been! And now any day a son or daughter would be arriving. He noticed her swollen ankles. He knew she must be tired.

"Bec, why don't you rest for a spell?" You need to get off your feet a bit." Tom and I are going up on the ridge to cut a couple of trees for you and Pearly Mae. When I get back I'll help you decorate it."

Becky was so excited that she said she would get right to making the popcorn strings now that the soup was finished.

"Promise me that you will rest first." Jeff pleaded.

"I've never felt better in my life sweetheart," she assured him, as she threw her arms around his neck.

"I love you my sweet husband, now go fetch me a tree."

"I love you too my sweet wife and I'll be going." Jeff replied, they both laughed.

Heavenly Places

Becky promised she would rest for a while, but only if he promised to be careful. Jeff bundled up with an extra blanket thrown across his shoulders.

"I'll be back soon. Now you get some rest," he insisted as he kissed her goodbye.

He hurried to the barn where Tom was waiting with his horse. The two men rode off toward the high ridge above the Townsend farm. The farther they rode the colder it became. They hadn't gone a hundred yards when large snowflakes started falling. They found and cut down the trees they wanted. After tying the trees to a rope to be pulled behind the horses they headed back down the mountain. The snow was blowing into their faces, making it nearly impossible for them or the horses to see the trail. The wind was whistling so loud there was no need to talk, because they couldn't hear each other. They rode close together so as not to get separated.

They parted ways as they reached the bottom of the ridge. The wagon trail that led from Tom's cabin to Jeff's house was more visible now. They waved goodbye and hurried on to their destination. Becky did as she had promised, and rested for a while. Then she got busy making popcorn strings for the tree. She cut out strips of colorful paper, and with paste she had made from a mixture of flour and water, she pasted them together, making a beautiful chain that would wrap completely around the tree. Becky especially loved Christmas time. She was beginning to get worried about Jeff and Tom. They had been gone a long time now. She walked out onto the porch, a little surprised to see that everything was already covered with snow. It was coming down so hard that she could barely see the barn.

Cricket was running in circles, chasing the big snowflakes. Becky laughed at the little dog. She wrapped her shawl closer around her, shielding off the cold wind. Maybe Jeff was right, maybe she had over worked herself. She was very tired. She felt a sudden sharp pain in her lower back. She knew that the baby could arrive any time, and Sarah had told her what to expect, but she was sure that the pain was just from being on her feet too long. How she wished that she could have her mother here, her heart ached at the thought of her beautiful mother, she missed her so much. With one last look to see if she could see Jeff she went back into the house, laid down across the bed, and fell asleep. Soon she was awakened by Jeff's voice.

"Bec, where are you honey? Are you alright?"

Jeff entered the bedroom door with worried look on his face. He rushed to her side, sitting down gently on the bed, whispering…

"You look tired sweetheart, go back to sleep, and I will bring in the tree."

"No honey, I just rested for a while, my back was hurting, but I feel much better now."

Becky sat up, laying her head on Jeff's shoulder.

"Bec, are you sure you are alright, do you think it's time for the baby?" Jeff was worried.

"No honey, just a back ache from standing so long. Let's have supper, and then we will decorate the tree."

Becky managed a weak smile. She too was just a little bit worried that this baby might arrive with just her and Jeff here. The snow had gotten way too high for Sarah to make it to the house. After they had eaten, Becky was so tired that it didn't take much encouragement from Jeff for her to go on to bed and let the tree trimming wait. Climbing into their big comfortable bed, she was asleep instantly. Jeff watched the storm outside as it grew worse. There was no way he could get to the Puckett farm in this snow. He fell down on his knees beside the fireplace and had a long talk with God. Before he arose he had his answer. Less than a mile away was his best friend Tom and his wonderful wife Pearly Mae, who had delivered more babies than the number of years that she had lived. Out of his concern for Becky and the baby he had overlooked the fact that a wonderful mid-wife was now living on his own farm.

"Thank you Lord," Jeff smiled, looking upward.

Now he had peace in his heart to know that help was close by. He stirred up the fire, stacked on more wood, lay down with Becky, and was soon fast asleep.

December 22nd 1866.

As if a miracle had taken place, Becky awoke the next morning full of energy and excitement. She shook Jeff awake.

"Wake up sweetheart, we have so much to do, we gotta decorate the tree. Oh Jeff, just look at the snow, come on get up."

Becky was dancing around the room, running from the window to the bed to give Jeff a big hug and kiss. Jeff laughed at the sight of his beautiful wife acting and looking like an excited child. He loved to see her so happy. She loved the snow, and often, in the winters, they would spend hours on the mountain behind their house, sliding and playing like children. But this was their first big snow, and Becky was in no condition to be sliding down a mountain side, but the memories of winters past still excited her. After breakfast she did the dishes while Jeff made his way to the barn in snow up to his knees. After his chores were finished he and Becky decorated the tree while singing Christmas carols. The day was soon gone. The snow kept falling.

December 23rd, 1866.

Knowing that Becky could have her baby any day now, Pearly Mae and Tom came to check on her every day. Since Jeff and Tom had built the little two-bedroom cabin, they had worn a clear path between their two cabins. They were always busy doing something on their farms – tending to the livestock, milking cows, sawing and splitting firewood, or repairing their barns, tool sheds and smokehouses. Jeff and Tom had become a team now. Cutting firewood had become a lot easier and faster since Tom had been around. He was much stronger than Becky, and could pull his end of the big crosscut saw much longer than she could. He and Jeff spent a lot of time during the fall and winter months doing just that – sawing and splitting firewood for both homes. Tom wanted Jeff to spend as much time close to Becky as he could, so today he let them spend the whole day inside the house while he split firewood. About every two hours Pearly Mae came out onto the porch and called him to the house for coffee and a snack. Pearly Mae wouldn't allow Becky to do anything strenuous. She did all the cooking, cleaning, washing and ironing for Becky. After a hard day's work and a good hot supper, she and Tom had prayer with Jeff and Becky, and returned to their little cabin.

December 24th, 1866, Christmas Eve.

At the break of dawn Becky was still as excited as ever. They were both like children, trying to guess what their gifts were, with Becky pleading...

"Please, please tell me." Jeff only smiled, teasing her...

"You'll see them soon enough sweetheart."

Becky and Jeff had always exchanged gifts on Christmas morning, but since Becky felt so good Jeff gave in to her pleading to open their gifts a little early. After supper was over, and with the snow still falling outside, they both knelt hand in hand. There in the peaceful atmosphere of their Christian home they humbly thanked God for all everything He had given them the past year. They gave thanks for the many souls that had been saved and added to their church, for their friends and family, and for the new life that would soon be entering their lives. With thankful hearts they said amen and got up from the floor where they were kneeling. Becky felt another sharp pain in her lower back as she got up. She didn't mention it to Jeff. She didn't want to spoil his evening. She wanted to give Jeff his Christmas gifts. Jeff's new blue scarf brought out the blue in his eyes and made him more handsome than ever. He loved his boots and the initials that were engraved on the strap.

"No one can steal my boots," he laughed, giving Becky a big kiss. Thank you sweetheart, you sure know how to make your man happy."

Jeff went into the bedroom and brought out Becky's gifts. He always had to hide them because she would poke little holes in the paper till she could see what was inside. Jeff loved that about her. She was still so full of that *"little girl"* excitement at her age, and he hoped she would stay that way as long as they lived. Jeff had put a great deal of thought into what he was going to give Becky for Christmas this year, more so than any other year they had been married. With a child coming into their lives, he wanted this year's gifts to be extra special. He had worked hard all summer and fall, saving every penny he could save just to be able to give his wife something that the two of them and their firstborn child could treasure for as long as they lived. He wanted it to be something that would be of far greater value than anything he had ever given her before. He asked her to sit on the sofa. Then he explained...

Heavenly Places

"I want you to close your eyes now, and promise not to peek till I tell you to look. I'm gonna open this one for you, so don't open your eyes till I tell you."

Becky shivered with excitement as she heard him tearing off the paper. Jeff deliberately took his time just to make her wait a few more seconds. She kept coaxing him...

"Come on now, don't take all day, I want to see what it is, hurry, please!"

"Hold out both hands sweetheart, this one is a little heavy, maybe I should just lay it on your lap," Jeff teased her.

She smelled the brand new leather as soon as Jeff un-wrapped it, but kept her eyes closed like she promised. Jeff started to tell her to open her eyes, but before he could say two words, her eyes were already open. Becky gasped with surprise and joy as she gazed at the big, brand new Family Bible. It had the names – Jeff and Becky Townsend engraved in gold on the cover. Tears of joy filled her eyes as she opened the cover. The first page had a beautiful flowered border, and blank spaces for their names, their birthdays, their wedding date, and ten blank spaces for the names and birthdates of their children. On the same page were blank spaces for the death dates of the first generation father and mother who first owned the Bible.

Seldom during their marriage had Jeff ever seen Becky totally speechless, but this was one of those rare occasions. For a few minutes they just looked into each other's eyes, smiling that smile that both of them had come to recognize as a silent but sublime expression of their love for each other. When Becky had gained enough composure to speak, she laid the big Bible on the table in front of her, throwing her arms around Jeff's neck, blubbering through her joy...

"Oh Jeff, you couldn't have given me anything more precious than that. How did you know that was what I wanted this year?"

"Oh, just a wild guess," Jeff answered. I've gotten to know you pretty good Mrs. Townsend," he added.

Becky loved the Bible so much that she had completely forgotten that Jeff always got her more than one gift at Christmas time, on her birthday, and on their anniversary. Jeff hesitated a moment, looking into her eyes with that questioning grin, as if to say...

"What? Were you expecting something else?"

He could read her facial expressions like a book. He knew she was expecting more than one gift. He turned and picked up the big Family Bible again. As he handed it to her he whispered...

"This year is very special to both of us Becky, and I've known for a long time that you've wanted a Family Bible for our home, and so have I. You know we've been saving every penny we could just to be able to buy everything the baby will need, and this Bible is all that I could afford this year, so I decided to give you a gift within a gift. Open it to the twenty third Psalms."

Now it was Becky's turn to gaze into Jeff's eyes, searching for the unspoken words behind his little grin. She knew every word of Psalms 23 by heart, and couldn't imagine why he wanted her to turn to it. Still searching Jeff's face, she slowly and cautiously opened the Bible to Psalms 23, not knowing what to expect. One of the many little joys that the two of them had shared since they had been married was the element of surprise. On every special occasion, like birthdays, or their anniversary, or Christmas, they would both begin questioning the other a few days beforehand, begging to know what their gifts were, but still managing to surprise each other every time. Jeff had surprised her a few times before, and she had the feeling that this was going to be another one of those times. When she found the place, expecting to see the words of Psalms 23, she gasped. There was a sheet of paper with something written on it. She immediately recognized Jeff's handwriting. It was a poem, written by Jeff himself.

Her heart almost skipped a beat as she looked from the poem to Jeff, and back to the poem again. In all the years she had known him, he had never written a poem, or even a letter. The only thing Jeff had ever written was the big poster, advertising the Churches need for a piece of land. She started getting all choked up again. Jeff was gazing into her beautiful face, half afraid that she might not like the poem, but still wanting her to read it, because it had come from the depths of his heart. She blushed as she began to read silently.

The first few lines brought tears of joy to Becky's eyes. She asked Jeff for a handkerchief to wipe the tears from her cheeks. With each few lines she read she glanced up at Jeff, smiling with joy and approval. The poem began...

Heavenly Places

To My Beautiful Wife
Since you already know that
I'm not very good at poetry and such,
Just allow me to tell you in my own quaint way
Just why I love you so much;
It goes without saying you're very beautiful
in every way a woman can be,
But when I look at you there is so much more than beauty
and grace that I see;
You were loving and radiant the day we first met,
and even more so today,
And what your sweet loving smile does to me,
I can't find the words to say;
If I had searched the whole world over,
I know I could never find,
A woman more loving and caring and gentle,
and gracious and cheerful and kind;
For four sweet years, some smiles and some tears,
you're always my very best friend,
And no matter what happens I know you're the one
on whom I can always depend;
You've given me courage in the hardest of times,
when it seemed that all was lost,
And you've given your all for me every day,
while never counting the cost;
You've been by my side for better or worse,
forever faithful and true,
And when I can't count on anyone else,
I can always count on you;
Oh yes, we've had our share of troubles,
and trials and stormy weather,
But I've always known that I'm never alone,
for we've faced them all together;
I'm a better man because you are my wife,
and yes, you bring out my best,
And I often stop to wonder how one man could be so blessed;
And beside all this you've giving me a child
for us both to adore,
How gracious God has been to me!

> What man could ask for more?
> And although I cherish your beauty and grace,
> and all the little things that you do,
> The greatest reason I love you so much,
> is just because you're you!
> With all my love, now and forever,
> Your loving Husband, Jeff.

The look on Becky's face said all that needed to be said. She was so overjoyed all she could do was hold the poem to her breast with a big beaming smile. After a few moments she finally managed to get out a few words…

"Jeff, these are the sweetest words I've ever read. I love you so much. I will cherish these gifts for as long as I live. I am so blessed to have you as my husband."

Jeff breathed a sigh of relief. He was so afraid that his words were unworthy of such a beautiful and godly woman. But now that he knew that Becky was pleased with both gifts, he asked her to close her eyes again, taking the poem from her hand, saying…

"I'm so glad you like it Becky, and I have just one more little gift for you."

He reached under the table and pulled out a beautiful picture frame that he had made himself, hand-carved from a piece of black walnut. The glass was a gift from Tom and Pearly Mae. The poem fit perfectly into the frame. Jeff set the poem on the table in front of Becky, and told her to open her eyes. Becky screamed with pure delight at the sight of the beautiful picture frame. She gave Jeff a big hug and kiss, holding the poem and frame to her breast. She stood up and looked at Jeff with a big smile, saying…

"I know just the place for this."

She walked over to the fireplace, and gently placed the poem on the mantle, right next to their wedding picture.

As Becky turned from the fireplace to face Jeff, she suddenly grabbed her stomach, sinking down onto the nearest chair. She was very flushed, and she knew it was time for Jeff to get Pearly Mae. They both knew that the weather was too bad to go for Sarah. Jeff could see the pain in her face as she told him that it was time for the baby to come. He kissed her on the forehead, promising he would be right back. Becky told him she would be fine till he returned. Jeff quickly put a bridle on Mr. Beecher. There was no time to strap on the saddle. He leaped onto the horses back, and prayed all the way to Tom and Pearly Mae's cabin. They were up, and it didn't take them long to get ready. Tom told Jeff to get on back to Becky and that he would bring sweet Pearl right there as fast as they could get there. Jeff rode as fast as he could in the deep snow. Becky was moaning in pain when he returned. In less than five minutes Tom and Pearly Mae arrived. Pearly Mae rushed around getting fresh sheets and blankets for the baby. She made Tom and Jeff wait in the front room.

The two men prayed for the three in the other room. It was a quick birth with no complications. Watching Jeff pacing the floor so nervously, made Tom nervous. Soon the sweet cry of a baby was heard. Tears came to the two men's eyes as they hugged each other. Pearly Mae came to the door with a big smile on her face. She proudly announced…

"Preacher, come meet yer son, he's purty as a picture, and Miss Becky is jist fine."

Jeff and Tom walked into the room, where Becky was propped up on pillows, holding a beautiful baby boy.

"Meet Samuel Jeffery Townsend," she announced with a beaming smile.

Jeff was so proud as he looked into the face of his son for the first time. He had black hair and blue eyes, perfect skin, and ten fingers and toes. For a few minutes all he could do was stand there and smile. Finally he leaned over the bed, giving Becky a kiss and kissing the baby on the cheek. Tears filled his eyes as he silently thanked God. Tom broke the silence, clearing his throat, trying desperately to hold back his own tears, saying to Jeff…

"Congratulations Preacher, he shore is a fine'un, and my sweet Pearl done herself a good job getting him here."

Tom put his arm around Pearly Mae, kissing her on the cheek. Pearly Mae blushed. Jeff gave Pearly a big strong hug, thanking her for what she had done. They all looked at the clock. It was 12:30 a.m. Little Samuel had arrived just in time to be the best Christmas gift of all. No one was in a hurry to leave, so Jeff made another pot of coffee. The four of them enjoyed each other's company right there in the bedroom with little Samuel lying in his mother's arms.

The news traveled fast, and despite the snow some of the people from the church who lived close enough dropped by with gifts, food and good wishes for the Townsend family. Sarah was just too far away to get there. The roads were too dangerous for wagons, so Tom had ridden horseback to nearly every home in the county, checking on each family to see how they had fared through the big snowfall, and to tell them the good news about the birth of little Samuel Townsend. As he was leaving the Puckett farm, Sarah yelled...

"Tell Becky I will be there as soon as this snow melts."

She didn't send him back empty handed either. She had made Samuel a beautiful yellow quilt with white doves all over. She knew that yellow was Becky's favorite color. Mollie had made him a corncob doll, and Carter, with a little help from Clark, had carved him a horse out of a piece of cedar wood. The gifts were precious to Becky. She knew Samuel would cherish them forever when he got older. Pearly Mae and Tom checked on Becky and little Samuel every day, keeping the house work done up, and cooking supper, taking all the work they could from Becky and Jeff. Sometimes they all enjoyed the cold winter evenings together, studying the Bible, sometimes playing a game of Fox and Geese, but mostly talking and laughing and enjoying each other's company and spoiling little Samuel. Becky and Jeff both agreed that Tom and Pearly Mae were to be Samuel's God parents. Tom and Pearl agreed, but insisted that they be called Uncle Tom and Aunt Pearl. So from that day forward, those were their official titles – Uncle Tom, and Aunt Pearl.

Wednesday, March, 27, 1867

Becky was doing dishes in the kitchen when she heard the sound of horse hooves. A rider was coming in fast. She looked out the window past the big oak tree that had just started budding. There was Rufus, Claudette's husband from the mountains. Rufus didn't bother to stop and open the gate. Approaching the gate at full speed, horse and rider went airborne, the horse's hind hooves barely clearing the gate. With one jump he was down from his horse, leaping onto the porch and pounding at the door, screaming...

"Miss Becky, Miss Becky!"

Heavenly Places

Becky took a quick look at little Samuel Jeffery lying peacefully in his cradle by the fireplace. She ran to the door. Rufus was so excited he could hardly speak, each word stumbling over the other. He and his horse were soaked with sweat from the long hard ride. Becky spoke calmly, "Rufus calm down and tell me what's wrong, are Claudette and the baby alright?"

She motioned for him to sit down at the table in the kitchen, but he kept rambling on.

"Miss Becky you gotta come, it's Claudette, she's right nigh bout her time an she ain't a want'en no one but you and Miss Sarah. Can you come, please Miss Becky, you gotta come."

He was talking so fast he was nearly losing his breath.

"Alright Rufus, you go and tell Miss Sarah, and I will get prepared, and we will be right there."

She held Rufus by the shoulders, gently guiding him out through the door as she talked.

"Tell me how Claudette is doing. Is she in pain yet? Who is with her?"

Rufus began telling her that Claudette was in pain in her lower back and would have nobody but Becky and Sarah, Aunt Pearly Mae was with her and that she was well overdue, and that he was scared to death for her. Becky assured him that everything would be fine and that they had plenty of time, and for him to just "go fetch Miss Sarah." She finally got him ushered out the door and on his way to get Sarah. Becky knew that this day was coming, that she and Sarah would be the ones to go to Claudette.

Since the wedding, Claudette had adopted Becky and Sarah as her family. She counted on them for everything. Becky was well-prepared as far as baby Samuel was concerned. She had prepared bottles for him to use while she was gone. She had been breast-feeding him up until now, but now the baby bottle had been invented. Sarah had carried one over from South Carolina when she had moved here, and now she had passed it on to Becky. The plan was for Jeff to keep the baby till Becky returned. Samuel was a healthy and happy baby, nearly four month's old now. He was the pride and joy of the Townsend home. Jeff came in from the barn after seeing Rufus go charging around the edge of the yard, headed for the Clark's place.

"Where is Rufus going in such a hurry?" He asked.

"He says it's time for the baby to come. Sarah and I have to go up there. Will you be alright with Samuel? I have everything made for him to eat while I am gone." Jeff replied...

"Of course I will be fine. You must go. I'll hitch up the horse for you while you finish getting ready."

"Thank you my darling, you are so good to keep the baby and all, I am sure that Claudette and Rufus will be forever thankful to you."

Becky placed a swift kiss on his cheek. Jeff smiled. He knew Becky was doing exactly what she enjoyed doing - helping others, and he certainly didn't mind spending time with his son that he loved more than life itself. There wasn't much to do around the farm at this time of year. It was still a month too early to plant anything, so being with little Samuel would be a pleasure. He knew they would both miss having Becky there with them, but maybe she wouldn't be gone too long. Jeff saddled up the horse for Becky, putting an extra blanket in the saddle bag for the ride up the mountain. They had decided that it would be much easier to take the horses than to try taking a buggy or wagon. The narrow trails could get slippery at this time of year. The higher they traveled up the mountains, the greater the probability of the ground being frozen. The ground itself could break off on the edges, causing a wagon or buggy to roll over a mountainside.

Both Becky and Sarah were good riders, and were much safer this way. Becky was busy in the house packing the things they would need for the delivery of the baby, and some extra clothes for a couple of days. She had left Jeff with the baby before just to visit Sarah or to attend a quilting at the church, but never with the expectation of being gone more than a night or two. She knew he would be fine. Tom would be there with him for Bible study. Since he was showing interest in learning, Jeff had been teaching him how to read and understand the scriptures. She prepared everything that Jeff would need while she was gone, along with everything that she and Sarah would need to take with them on their trip up the mountain. She had made Claudette's baby a beautiful quilt made of soft cotton material from all the extra quilt pieces that she had not used for her own quilts. She was ready when Jeff came in. He had brought her horse around to the porch. Becky showed him everything that he would need, giving him a long goodbye kiss.

She did the same for little Samuel, bending down and kissing him softly on the forehead.

"I love you my darling," she whispered, throwing her arms around Jeff's neck with a tight squeeze and kiss on the lips. She waved goodbye just as Sarah was riding into the yard. Jeff walked to the porch and had prayer with them before they headed out.

Rufus had gone on ahead to let Claudette know that she and Sarah were on their way. They hit the trail. Sarah had been to the homes of the folks in the mountains before, but this was a first for Becky. Sarah assured Becky that she knew how to take different routes through the mountains that would get them there sooner, but that there would be places where the horses would have to walk single file. And sure enough, as they began climbing higher, the trail became so treacherous that there was barely room for the horse's hooves to stand on the cliffs. Becky looked down, watching rocks and dirt roll down the steep embankments to the bottom. She prayed with every step, as she followed close to Sarah. After making it up the steep part, they rode through thick underbrush, where they had to lie down close to the horses backs in order to prevent the big branches from knocking them off their horses.

"Lordy Mercy" Becky sighed, if Jeff could see this!"

She chuckled at the thought of what he would do. Jeff was very protective of Becky. She still remembered the word's that he had promised her father.

"Mr. Davis, I will protect your daughter with my life. Nothing will ever harm her as long as I live."

She remembered the two of them shaking hands on it, as her father replied…

"Son, I am going to trust you with one of the most precious things in my life, and I believe you mean just what you say." Jeff had been true to his word.

Sarah looked back, noticing that Becky wasn't concentrating on the narrow trail. She yelled at her, quickly arousing her out of her daydream.

"Hey Becky, we are getting ready to go through a small settlement, so just ride straight, and don't be staring, ok?"

"Why?" Becky yelled back.

"Well, let's just say it's a working place," Sarah laughed out loud. "Come on chicken, you'll see, just let me do the talking."

She wheeled her horse around as they rode from under the trees into a clearing, where Becky saw several large dogs tied to trees, with heavy long chains around their necks. They were barking and jumping at the two women, causing the horses to be nervous. There were three small run-down cabins built alongside the base of a very large cave. Smoke ascended from under the big arched rocks which were tall enough to walk under. Two tall burly men carrying two fancy Volition repeating rifles walked from behind one of the cabins. They were dirty, with beards hanging to their belt lines.

"Who goes there?" One of them asked in a deep gruff voice, spitting tobacco on the ground and slightly raising his gun.

"Now just hold on here General. It's just me and the preacher's wife Becky Townsend, we be heading up to the Rutherford's place to attend to Claudette. It's her time, and we just need to get there fast and need to pass through your land."

General Horton was a bootlegger. That was plain to Becky now. The smell of moonshine whiskey was so strong Becky figured it could be smelled for miles if the wind was just right. She was a little bit nervous, because the two men appeared to be rough characters. But she soon realized that they were protecting what was theirs. General Horton waved them on through, telling them to be careful, and to watch out for the mountain lions. Becky couldn't help but notice the evil grin behind that statement. She whispered a prayer of gratitude as they left the clearing, proceeding cautiously along the trail again.

When they stopped for a short break to let the horses rest Sarah explained to her that General Horton and the other man, his uncle Burley Crawford, were the main sources of moonshine around these hills, and no one had ever shut them down. They didn't even try to hide it from the law. Everyone, including the law, was afraid to mess with them. The law had bragged too many times that they were going to put General Horton and Mr. Crawford out of business. But after finding too many dead bodies at the bottom of the mountain, appearing to have been eaten by wild animals, everyone decided to leave the two men alone. The Rutherford's and Flemings' had gotten permission from General

Horton and Burley Crawford for Sarah and some others to cross their land safely. Until they had gotten saved at the Valley Grove Baptist Church, the Rutherford's and Flemings' had been some of the General's best customers. The General and Burley were just two more poor souls that Becky would add to her prayer list.

After a much needed rest for both them and the horses, Becky and Sarah mounted up again, riding single file up the mountain. The fog was thick at times from the colder air as they climbed higher. Becky couldn't help noticing all the beauty of the hills. Little patches of dandelions had started to bloom. Red berries were shining on the teaberry plants close to the ground. Green holly trees still held tightly to their leaves. A few Redbud trees had budded out just enough to have a pink tint of color on their branches. A bright blue butterfly fluttered across their path. Rabbits and squirrels scampered from behind rocks and trees.

"Oh, my!" what peace and beauty," Becky thought as she and Sarah rode quietly along.

It seemed that they had ridden for hours. Then, suddenly, out of the blue, there on the trail right in front of them sat Rufus on horseback.

"Been waitin fur yun's," he said, with a big grin on his face.

"The house is jest up round that bend through that patch of woods yonder. Claudette and Aunt Pearly Mae are waitin fur us. She shore will be glad to see yun's."

Becky was glad the journey was coming to an end. She would be glad to get off the horse and rest for a while.

"Lead the way Rufus, we're right behind you," Sarah said as they caught up to him.

With the trail leveled out, it didn't take long for them to reach the small cabin where Claudette and Rufus lived. It was situated in a little grassy lot, with a clear stream of water running close by the end of the lean-to that Rufus had attached to the back of the house. Claudette loved pretty things, and for her to be so young, Becky was pleasantly surprised to see such a clean, pretty little place so far back in the woods. Outside was a flower garden, with rose bushes and Tiger Lilies. A couple of roses were showing signs of getting ready to bloom. Beautiful bird boxes that Rufus had made were hanging from low tree branches. He pointed out that Claudette loved to feed the birds and watch them play. A wooden sign that Claudette herself had carved hung over the door. It read - "Home Sweet Home."

A big yellow calico cat welcomed them on the porch, rubbing herself against Becky's dress tail. She reached down and rubbed him on the back. Rufus politely introduced them to Claudette's cat, Tabby. The inside of the house was just as pleasant as the outside. A neat fireplace was burning, with just enough fire to keep out the dampness. Claudette was lying in a big feather bed covered with a beautiful hand-crafted quilt. Two straight-back rockers sat on either side of the fireplace. Claudette held out her arms to Becky and Sarah.

"I am so beholden to yun's. I have been scared that the baby would get here afore yun's made it."

She was almost in tears. After giving Claudette a hug, and assuring her that everything was going to be alright, Sarah told her she was going to examine her to see just how soon the baby would be here. She quickly ushered Rufus out of the room, telling him to keep busy outside. Aunt Pearlie Mae Tillotson came from the kitchen wiping her hands on her apron.

She and Tom had gotten married on the Townsend farm, and now lived there, not far from Becky and Jeff, in a small cabin that Jeff and Tom had built, just big enough for the two of them. Tom had stayed behind while Pearlie Mae had been tending to Claudette. She was planning on staying as long as she was needed, but she sure missed Tom.

"My, my, she said, it is so good that yun's made it, this here poor child has been in a frenzy all day fur fear that she would have this baby alone."

Aunt Pearly Mae was a pretty woman, plain, with jet-black hair, brown eyes, and a beautiful smile. (She had delivered Samuel and Becky and Jeff would be grateful to her forever). Tom called her his "*sweet Pearl*." She offered Becky and Sarah something to eat right away, but Sarah told her she needed to check on Claudette again. Becky assisted Sarah with the exam. She told Claudette that everything was fine, and that she needed to rest so she would have strength to push when the baby was ready to be delivered, which would be tonight. Claudette promised that she would try to sleep for a while now that they were there. Becky noticed a worried look on Sarah's face as they walked out onto the porch to wash up in a basin of water that Rufus had brought up from the clear little stream.

"What's wrong Sarah, I know that look?" Becky questioned.

"Well, Sarah answered, I think the baby might be in distress, it's in a Breech position, and it will take both of us to turn it, Claudette will be in a lot of pain, the baby and Claudette could both be in grave danger."

"What do we do then? Just tell me what I need to do Sarah, and I will do my best," Becky said. Sarah reached out and took Becky's hand, almost crying.

"Right now, all we can do is pray and hope that God hears us." She said in a trembling voice.

They bowed their heads, praying that God would protect this young mother and child.

After washing up they walked back into the house, tiptoeing by the sleeping Claudette.

Walking into the kitchen they saw that Aunt Pearly Mae had made them a bowl of hot potato soup with hot corn bread and fresh butter. Becky had to admit that she was tired and hungry from the trip. Aunt Pearly Mae asked about Jeff and the baby, Mollie, Carter and Clark. She said that Tom had been up to visit, and had just left yesterday, and that she was really missing him, but that her duty was to her niece right now, and that Tom understood. Aunt Pearly Mae could have easily delivered this baby, but Claudette insisted that Rufus fetch Becky and Sarah to help. Becky and Sarah decided that after helping with the dishes they were going to get some sleep till they were needed. Pearly Mae would not hear of them helping with the dishes. She insisted that they both lie down in her bedroom and to stay in there just as long as they needed to. Both Becky and Sarah were too tired to object. They gave her a hug and carried their bags to the neat little bedroom. Rufus had fed and watered their horses and put them up for the night, so they had nothing to worry about there. They changed into clean clothes and lay across the bed. Soon they were both fast asleep, but not for long. Claudette woke them up screaming with pain. Rufus was pounding at the door with a loud whisper,

"Miss Becky, Miss Sarah, Claudette be needing yun's now."

Becky and Sarah jumped up fully dressed, running into the room where Claudette was lying, tears pouring from her eyes, her face flushed with extreme pain. The two ran to her side as Becky asked Rufus to please leave the room. Aunt Pearly Mae had been sitting with Claudette while Becky and Sarah had slept.

"What can I do fur yun's?" She wanted to know.

Sarah gave the instructions...

"Please boil some water and put out some clean white sheets for us Pearly Mae, and we will need your help, we will have a baby soon."

But then the pain grew worse. Pearly Mae pulled the two women aside and told them that she just knew that something was wrong, she had seen the signs too many times, and she felt that Claudette could lose this baby if the situation didn't change. Becky and Sarah agreed with her. Claudette's screams could be heard far out into the yard where Rufus leaned against the cabin. He started walking back and forth in the yard, from the barn to the porch, and back through the yard.

By orders from Claudette, he was not to bother any of their relatives till the baby arrived. She was a very private person, and only wanted Sarah, Becky and her Aunt Pearly Mae to be with her during the birth of the baby. Sarah and Becky both examined Claudette, agreeing that the baby had to be turned in order to have a normal safe birth. The pain was horrible for Claudette, but what had to be done must be done now.

Thursday, March 28th 1867.

It was midnight when Becky walked out onto the porch to talk with the Lord. After a hard night they were all worn out. Claudette had been in hard labor for nearly nine hours. It was time to turn this baby and try to save its life as well as Claudette's. On the porch, Becky fell down on her knees, pleading with God to please save this baby and mother, and to give her and Sarah the knowledge that they needed to deliver this child. Lifting her head and rising to her feet she was so surprised to see a small crowd at the edge of the yard, all of them kneeling and crying out to God. There were the Grandmother's, hand in hand, and the Grandfathers with booming voices, pleading for their grandchild and granddaughter. There were the Rutherford's and the Flemings - grown men, with tears streaming down their faces, every one crying out to God. Becky wiped the tears from her own face, and with a ***"Thank You God,"*** she walked back into the house to help Sarah and Aunt Pearly Mae. They worked with Claudette, encouraging her to help them. Becky quickly examined Claudette and found that the baby's head was exactly where it should be. She knew in her heart that God had answered their prayers and done this great miracle! With a beaming smile she nodded to Sarah and Pearly Mae. Then turning to Claudette she explained to the frightened young woman what she needed to do to help them.

"Sweetheart, you need to push like we showed you, and we will have a baby in just a short while." Becky wiped the sweet tender face with a soft warm cloth. Aunt Pearly Mae was holding Claudette's hand, as she prayed silently.

And a short while it was - a beautiful little girl soon lay in Claudette's arms. All the pain was forgotten, all the fear was gone. After quickly cleaning up the baby and placing her in a nice white gown and blanket, Becky walked to the porch once again - this time to meet the whole clan at the steps, led by Rufus. They had heard the baby's cry. All faces turned to Becky with concern. Becky's smile assured them that all was well.

"It's a girl," she yelled so that all could hear.

She was almost knocked down by Rufus who could stand it no longer. He went rushing past her like a streak of lightning. A cheer went up from the front yard. They hugged, danced and cried. Sarah came out for some fresh air. Everyone wanted to see the new arrival, but Sarah told them to let Claudette rest till around noon, then they could all see the newest member of the Rutherford family. They gave no argument, all of them agreeing to come back at noon. They slowly left the yard, all of them talking excitedly.

Aunt Pearly Mae brought fresh hot coffee to Becky and Sarah, as the three of them sat and talked for a long time, discussing the night's event and what they had learned from this hard birth. Soon a nice hot breakfast was served. Becky and Sarah had to pry Rufus away from his wife's bedside long enough to do his chores and to eat breakfast. Claudette ate a few bites, but couldn't keep her eyes off her beautiful little girl. Rufus was all settled back in by her side when they called Sarah and Becky in.

"We have come to an agreement on what we will be calling her," Rufus beamed.

"Tell'em honey" He whispered, as he took Claudette by the hand.

"This be Miss Rebekah Sarah Rutherford." Claudette proudly announced, smiling from ear to ear.

Becky and Sarah could not hold back the tears any longer. Filled with joy, exhaustion and thankfulness, they wept, giving Claudette a big hug, telling her how proud they were to have such a beautiful namesake. And beautiful she was, with a thick head of black hair, blue eyes, chubby little cheeks, and perfect hands and feet. God had blessed this union for sure.

The morning fog was lifting as the sun slowly melted it away. The house was all in order for the big family to arrive, and just as they were told, at noon they were all there with great anticipation. They were allowed to see the baby, two at a time - Grandmother's first. Cleo and Hilda couldn't hold back their tears when they saw their grandchild. They each held her and kissed her, examining her from head to toe. Then the two Grandfathers came in. Becky had never seen such a sight. Ralph and Foster melted, as their big, rugged callused hands held their grandchild with such tenderness and love.

"She shore is a fine un," Ralph said.

"She shore is," Foster agreed, sniffling, pretending to cough.

But he wasn't fooling anyone in the room. After every family member had seen the new baby they wandered out onto the porch and into the yard so that Claudette could rest. Becky heard them talking about having a celebration right there in the front yard if it was alright with Rufus and Claudette - to have a little **"shin-dig"** as they called it. Rufus agreed that it would be fine by him. They insisted that Becky and Sarah stay another night, and head back down the mountain early in the morning. They both agreed, and although they missed their families, this miracle of life was well worth celebrating. They both got washed up and put on clean clothes before the others came back. A window was slightly raised so that Claudette could hear the music, and there was plenty of it. Rufus sat up handmade benches that he and two of his cousins, Andrew and Lee, had quickly thrown together.

All that didn't have a bench just sat on the ground, even though it was still cool from the March weather. Becky and Sarah sat on the edge of the porch with their legs hanging over the sides.

The music began - no big hollering and whooping, just sweet, soft harmony that would put your soul to rest. Rufus stood up and got everyone's attention, announcing,

"This is fur my gals inside that house yonder." He motioned with his hands.

His powerful voice sweetly formed the words,

"You are my sunshine, my only sunshine, you make me happy when skies are gray, you'll never know dear, how much I love you, Please don't take my sunshine away."

Once again Foster started sniffling and coughing. They played and sang till it was nearly dark. Everyone had a great time. The family members left a few at a time, all waving goodbye with hugs and kisses and handshakes all around. They all thanked Sarah and Becky for what they had done.

"See yun's at church," they all yelled, and they were gone.

After making sure that Claudette and the baby were alright, Becky and Sarah said good night to Aunt Pearly Mae and Rufus, and headed off to bed. They knew they needed to get an early start the next day. Becky got up during the night and checked on the new mother and baby. All was well. They were sleeping like angels.

Friday, March 29th 1867.

The air was cool as the two mounted their horses after saying goodbye to Claudette, the baby, Aunt Pearly Mae, and Rufus. They were taking the wagon trail back down the mountain. Becky was glad that she didn't have to travel back by General Horton's moonshine still. They left the little cabin and headed east toward the Flemings farm, about one mile away. As they approached, Cleo came out of the house smiling, with a basket filled with biscuits and fried apples.

"Jist a little sumthin to tide yun's over," she said.

Claudette's younger sister Elva came running from behind the house and stood shyly, holding onto Cleo's dress. They had two twin boys - Curt and Burt, but they were nowhere to be seen. Becky and Sarah talked for just a minute, thanking her for the wonderful food then they rode on, waving at Foster who was cutting firewood in the barn yard.

"Be cureful," he yelled, waving back.

They rode in silence for the longest time. Becky's mind was on Jeff and little Samuel, and she was sure that Sarah was thinking about Clark and the children. Just around the bend, about one half mile was the Rutherford place - a tall two-story cabin perched on the mountain side. Becky could see where Rufus got his handiwork from. Ralph had made a floor from rocks that covered the path that lead to the long front porch, with a set of steps leading up to the front door, and a beautiful banister on each side, with a welcome sign hanging in the yard. Hilda came to the steps and waved at them as they passed.

"Thank yun's fur ever thang," she said with a smile.

Rufus was their only son now. His little brother Jake had died from Typhoid fever just two years ago. Ralph was nowhere in sight. They passed by several houses on the way down the mountain. They were acquainted with some of the folks who lived on the mountain, but some they didn't know at all. As they approached the houses folks would come out and speak, or ask about Claudette and the baby. Some places were quiet, with no one around. Some of the children ran alongside the horses for a short distance. Once they met two strange men on horseback. Becky grew nervous as the men drew closer, but the two men just tipped their hats and rode on by. She and Sarah spurred their horses into a gallop for as long as the trail would allow it.

Soon the Townsend farm came in sight, and what a beautiful sight it was to Becky. She waved goodbye to Sarah, telling her that she would see her soon. As she rode into the yard Jeff was standing on the porch with little Samuel in his arms. She jumped from her horse and ran up the steps, throwing her arms around both of them. She gazed into his blue eyes, whispering…

"I am so glad to be home."

After a long kiss, they walked into the house, where she played with Samuel 'til he fell asleep. As little Samuel slept, Becky sat down beside Jeff on the big sofa. She laid her head upon his chest as he put his arm around her shoulder. She felt safe, and loved, and comfortable. Jeff listened quietly as she began to share the most memorable moments of her great adventure.

April, 1867, the Townsend farm.

During the course of their own lives, Jeff and Becky Townsend had been a positive and powerful influence upon the lives of a multitude of people, including individuals, families, and entire communities. One of the many character traits that everyone admired and respected about Jeff and Becky was the fact that their character, their personalities, their beliefs and convictions never changed. The character that you saw on Sunday was the same character that you saw on Monday, and every other day of the week. Folks knew that they could confide in both Jeff and Becky, and whatever passed between them never went any farther. Jeff and Becky could be trusted completely. These were the meditations that were going through Tom Tillotson's mind as he and Pearly Mae worked side by side with Jeff and Becky on their sixty-acre farm.

Since Tom and Pearl had gotten married, Pearl had fixed the little two-bedroom cabin up really nice. She had borrowed some decorating ideas from Becky. Now that little Samuel had come into their lives, Becky had to spend most of her time tending to the house and the baby. Tom and Jeff worked side by side doing practically all of the farm work now. Jeff helped Tom with his little farm, and Tom worked with Jeff on his farm. They were like two brothers, doing everything together. They had built Tom's house near the Northern boundary of Jeff's farm, in the shade of the big grove of poplars.

If ever there was a man who was thankful for his blessings, it was Tom Tillotson. Each time he thought about how gracious and merciful God had been to him, he bowed his head and thanked the Lord. If a year ago anyone had told him that a year later he would be married to a lovely Christian woman, and be going to Church every Sunday, and would own his own little house and farm, he would have laughed in their face. His heart stirred each time he thought about how far the Lord had brought him in such a short time. Every morning now, at the breakfast table, he and Pearl bowed their heads and thanked God for the food on the table. Each evening at supper they did the same thing, and each night before bedtime they knelt together hand in hand, thanking God for every blessing, but as happy as Tom was to be married to sweet Pearl, and as grateful as he was for everything that God, and Jeff and Becky Townsend had done for him, there was still something missing in Tom's life. There was uneasiness in his spirit that wouldn't go away. Deep inside him was an insatiable desire to tell the whole world what Jesus Christ had done for him. Sometimes he felt an irresistible urge to just stop whatever he was doing and shout it out loud to the world that Jesus saves.

It had been close to a year now since he had first met Jeff and Becky. The bittersweet memory of their first encounter, and the circumstances surrounding that encounter, caused Tom to chuckle just a little. His heart swelled with pure gratitude for the grace and mercy that the good Lord had shown him since that fateful day. He had met a lot of men in his thirty nine years, but never one quite like preacher Jeff Townsend. He had noticed that both Jeff and Becky were always more concerned about the lives and wellbeing of other folks, than they were about their own. They spent their time and energy, doing anything they could, to improve the lives of others, asking nothing in return. Their faith in Jesus Christ was genuine, and it showed in their everyday lives. Whenever Jeff was not working hard on the farm or preaching at the Church, he was teaching Tom to read and understand the Bible. Two verses in particular kept gnawing at Tom's insides. He couldn't get them out of his head. It seemed that every time he opened his Bible, there were those two verses, staring him in the face. The verses were in Matthew 4:19-20.

And he saith unto them, Follow me, and I will make you fishers of men. And they straightway left their nets, and followed him.

When he lay down at night to sleep, or when he sat down at the table to eat, those verses rang in his head. There were times when he listened to Jeff preach that he could hardly sit still. It seemed he could anticipate Jeff's next words before he spoke them. He kept recalling that day that he had climbed the steps of the gallows, where he had led three condemned men to Christ. Then his mind drifted to the Moundsville Penitentiary, where he had led Preston Jenkins to the Lord. That had now become the greatest desire of his heart - to lead others to Jesus Christ.

Tom and Pearl were helping Jeff and Becky plant their potatoes. Jeff always waited for the new moon in April to plant his potatoes – a tradition he had learned from his father Silas. With little Samuel lying in a covered basket beside her, Becky sat in a big comfortable chair that Jeff had built for her, peeling the seed potatoes, while Pearly Mae quartered them, pitching them into a big bucket. Tom carried the bucket of seed potatoes to the potato patch. Jeff scattered fertilizer into the plowed rows. Tom followed Jeff with the bucket of seed potatoes, dropping them about eighteen inches apart. After all the potatoes were in the furrows, both Tom and Jeff covered them with their hoes. Jeff started at one end of a furrow and Tom at the other end, and they would meet in the middle. Jeff kept noticing that Tom was unusually quiet today. He hadn't said ten words since they began planting early that morning. When they got to the last furrow, and met in the middle, Jeff couldn't help but notice that Tom's cheeks were wet. At first he thought Tom was sweating. But it wasn't hot enough for either of them to be sweating. Jeff looked a little closer, noticing that tears were streaming from Tom's eyes.

"Tom, he asked, is something wrong brother?"

Tom couldn't hold it in any longer. He dropped his hoe in the dirt and began sobbing,

"Jeff, I've put this off as long as I can. The good Lord has called me to preach His Word!"

Jeff threw his hoe into the air with a shout.

"Well glory hallelujah! Bless the name of the Lord!" He grabbed Tom in a big bear hug.

Becky and Pearly Mae heard the two of them shouting praises to God in the middle of the potato patch, and hugging each other. Their curiosity got the best of them. Becky lifted little Samuel out of his basket as she and Pearl went running to meet Jeff and Tom. Jeff still had his arm around Tom's shoulder as the two of them ran toward Becky and Pearl. As the four of them met, Pearly demanded, "What in tarnation is going on with yun's? We thought yun's had found a pot of gold ur sumthing."

Jeff explained, "No Pearly, we found something far more precious than a pot of gold – we found us another Preacher!"

Pearly Mae's heart leaped for joy. Becky handed Samuel to Jeff, throwing her arms around Tom's neck, and hugging him. Then Pearly Mae wrapped her arms around Tom, holding him tightly. "I jest knew it Tom, she said, I jest know'de there wus something going on in that big heart of yurs."

Jeff told Tom to be ready to announce his calling to the Church the following Sunday morning, and to be ready to preach his first message at the Jenkins Memorial Baptist Church.

Sunday, April 7th, 1867 The Tillotson home.

Jeff and Becky, along with Tom and Pearl, all had to get up at least an hour earlier now on Sunday mornings because the new Church was about five miles farther away than the Valley Grove Baptist Church had been. That meant, of course, that the new Church was five miles closer for nearly everyone else. Tom had slept very little Saturday night, knowing that tomorrow he was going to be delivering his first sermon. He had studied his Bible for about an hour, and had prayed five times during the night, asking God to give him the vey message that needed to be heard. No one in the whole Church except Jeff, Becky and Pearl knew that he was going to be preaching today. He was a bit nervous. He was awake again long before dawn. He got up, and softly tiptoed barefoot into the living room, lit the lamp over the fireplace, turning the wick down low so that the light wouldn't awaken Pearly, and sat on the sofa. Slowly he began to reflect upon all that had happened in the past year. As he looked around the living room itself, with all of its beautiful homemade wooden furniture that he and Jeff had built together, the big comfortable rocking chair where Pearly Mae often sat an knitted, the big fireplace that kept them warm in the winter, the picture of their wedding over the mantle, the big oak coffee table, and the beautiful curtains that Pearly Mae and Becky had made for the windows, he thought to himself, "My, my, how blessed I am!"

He wondered if Becky had ever said anything to Pearly about the circumstances under which they had first met. He wondered if Pearly had ever asked. He wondered if she would ever ask him about it. He wondered if he should tell her without her asking. A thousand maybes crept into his mind as he sat there And now he was about to go and preach a sermon in front of a woman he had once tried to rape, and her husband who had knocked him unconscious with a single blow, and then had led him to the Lord Jesus Christ. He wondered how the people of the Church would receive and react to a half breed preacher. He thought, "There's no way I can do this." No sooner had the thought crossed his mind than he felt the gentle moving of the Holy Spirit in his heart, and that still small voice whispering.

"You are absolutely right Tom, you can't do it, but I can do it through you." A smile of sweet contentment came across his face.

He was about to get up and put on a pot of coffee when Pearly Mae walked into the living room, dressed in her beautiful blue cotton robe. The Grandfather clock chimed and bonged four times. She smiled her gentle, loving smile.

"Sweetheart, are you alright?" she ask.

Tom answered her with a long passionate kiss.

"Yeah sweet Pearl, I'm fine, just thinking about the meetin today, and the old devil's been fightin me tooth and toenail."

Pearl chuckled and gave him another quick kiss on the cheek, adding, "Well, that means yu're doing something right honey. If'n that old rascal ain't fighting ya, then yu'de shore have sumthing to worry bout. Yu're going ta be fine Tom, jest obey the Lord, and trust Him with the consequences. Now let's git sum breakfast cooking."

As they walked hand in hand toward the kitchen, Pearl stopped and looked into Tom's eyes, asking, "If it ain't asking too much Preacher, could ya tell yur loving wife what yu're gonna be preaching bout this morning, or do ya know that yet?"

Tom smiled and answered, "If the good Lord don't change my mind between now and Church time, I'm gonna be preaching from Hebrews, chapter three, verse one."

Wherefore holy brethren, partakers of the heavenly calling, consider the Apostle and High Priest of our profession, Christ Jesus.

Pearly Mae gave him a nod of approval and kissed his cheek, commenting…

"Sounds like a great sermon coming to me. Ya know I'll be there praying fur ya Tom, and so's will Jeff and Becky. I know the good Lord is going to use ya fur His glory."

Tom was about to pour the water into the coffee pot when he suddenly stopped and asked Pearly Mae to sit down at the kitchen table.

"Honey, he began, before I can go and preach today, I think there's something you should know bout my past. I really wanted ta tell ya afore we married, but couldn't find the courage. It's about how I came ta know Jeff and Becky bout a year ago."

Pearly cupped both his hands in hers, looking into his eyes with all the love of her soul.

"Tom, she said softly, I know more bout yur past than ya think I do. I know ya had a bad reputation, and I know ya did some terrible things in yur life. But I married ya anyway, cause I fell in love with the man that ya are now, not with the man ya wuz then, cause that man is dead and buried. I too have a past Tom, and it wasn't purty either. But we are both saved now, and our past has been wiped clean as a slate. I don't need or want ta know anything bout what you did back then."

Tom drew her to his chest with a big sigh of relief.

April 7th, 1867. Jenkins Memorial Baptist Church

It was easy to see that both Jeff and Tom were a bit nervous about this morning's worship service, and both of them for the same reason. How would the congregation respond to a half breed preaching the Word of God? Tom was having second thoughts about the whole thing again. As they drove their wagons onto the Church yard, Tom asked Jeff for a few minutes of his time. Jeff could see that Tom was very shaky. Tom spoke, searching for the right words to say.

"Jeff, maybe this morning I should just announce my calling, and leave it at that, and see how these folks take it, and let them get used to the idea for a while before I preach my first sermon. I don't want to cause you and Becky no problems with the Church. You know you're taking a big risk of losing some of your members if you let me preach toady don't you?"

Jeff put his hand on Tom's shoulder, replying, "Tom, I know you're nervous about this, and I understand. If you want to hold off on preaching your first message, that is fine with me, but I promise you brother, it won't be any easier a month from now. The sooner you get that first message off your heart, the better my friend. But I will honor and respect whatever decision you make, just let me know what you want to do before 11:00 o'clock." "As for anyone leaving because of the color of your skin – if that's their only reason for leaving, then they need to leave anyway." Tom nodded in agreement. They shook hands and helped Becky and Pearly Mae down from the wagon.

It is said that bad news travels fast, but, thanks to the grace of God, there are some occasions when good news travels just as quickly. The news about a new and thriving Baptist Church had spread far and wide. Pastor Jeff Townsend had a good report wherever he went. His name and reputation as a Preacher of the

Gospel was often mentioned along with such names as D.L. Moody, Ira Sankey, and C.H. Spurgeon. What was called the Third Great Awakening was still sweeping the nation. The temporary lull in the spiritual movement caused by the Civil War had now passed, and the spiritual movement had regained some strength. The war itself had produced a great deal of spiritual revival and conversions in the South, especially among General Lee's army. Several new *"movements"* had now gained national recognition also, including the Pentecostal and holiness movements. Many notable black preachers, Pastors and Evangelists arose during this period also, though most black ministers preached almost exclusively to other blacks. A half breed Indian preacher was virtually unheard of. Knowing all of this, Tom Great Bear Tillotson had some cause for anxiety about preaching to an almost all-white congregation. The only black family in the Jenkins Memorial Baptist Church was the Williams family – Buford, Mattie, and their twin daughters Greta and Gloria. Tom was the one and only member of the congregation who had Native American blood in his veins.

What Tom didn't know was that while he had been up at 4:00 a.m., praying and meditating, and worrying about what might happen today, Jeff and Becky Townsend had been on their knees at the same hour, asking God to give Tom courage, strength, and the power of the Holy Spirit to preach the Gospel. If there was one thing more than any other that stood out in the life and ministry of Jeff Townsend, it was the fact that he was a man of faith – he simply trusted God to work all things according to His own will. He somehow knew that God was going to use Tom Tillotson for His glory, and for the salvation of souls. He and Becky knew from experience and from the Scriptures that God always honors the smallest faith, that He also honors the faithful preaching of His Word, regardless of the color of the skin of the man from whose mouth it comes.

For the first time since the new Church had been built, toady it was filled to full-capacity. There was not an empty pew to be found. Clark and Buford immediately began to set out the extra chairs. When the last two chairs were placed beside the last two pews, Clark saw two strange men standing on either side of the doorway. He had never seen them before. They were shabbily dressed, but decent enough. They were General Horton and Burley

Crawford. The choir assembled behind the pulpit in their choir pews. Clark and Foster both stood with their violins and began playing **Precious Memories**. After prayer and the morning offering, Jeff stepped behind the pulpit. After welcoming all the new visitors to the Church, he proudly announced, "Folks, we have a very pleasant surprise for you all this morning. The good Lord has called one of the men of our Church to preach His Word."

Immediately there was a stirring among the crowd. Nearly every head in the house instantly turned toward Clark Puckett. Jeff noticed Clark shaking his head, as if to assure the congregation that it was not him. Jeff hesitated for just a moment, and then continued, "The man of whom I speak is a close friend of mine, and has demonstrated to me his fervent desire to lead souls to the Lord Jesus Christ. This morning he will be preaching his first message in your presence. I ask that you give him the same respect and attention that you have shown to me since I have been your Pastor. And so, without further ado, may I introduce to you Mr. Tom Tillotson."

To Jeff's and Tom's surprise, total silence pervaded the house. Tom rose slowly from the front pew. As he glanced quickly behind him, he saw the heads of every member of the Church bowed. They were praying for him. As he approached the pulpit, Jeff whispered to him, "When you're done preaching Tom, just go ahead and give the invitation." Jeff shook hands with him and stepped down, taking his seat beside Becky and Pearly Mae. Tom cleared his throat and laid his Bible on the pulpit. He thanked Jeff for allowing him to preach. He opened his Bible to **Hebrews 3:1**, asking the congregation to do the same. In that moment, the Holy Spirit took over. Not one person had left the church house. Every eye was now trained upon him. With a voice loud and clear, he began the message by reading the passage…

Wherefore holy brethren, partakers of the heavenly calling, consider the Apostle and high priest of our profession, Christ Jesus.

"If yun's will notice, the text says that we ought to *consider* the Lord Jesus Christ, and that we should consider Him in a particular office – the office of the high priest. If yun's will bear with me fur a few minutes, I'd like to give ya four reasons why that everyone should *consider* the Lord Jesus Christ. But first, I must say that, in the text, the word *consider* does not mean to simply give Him a passive thought, and then furgit about Him. The term, consider, as used here, means to give Him our utmost consideration, to look at Him with the most serious and sincere consideration that ur hearts can give Him. First of all then, we ought ta consider Him simply because the Bible says so. If there wuz no other reasons to consider him that would be enough. If the Bible says it, then it is imperative that we do it. Fur instance, the Bible says…Honor thy father and thy mother, that thy days may be prolonged upon the earth. Why, then, should we honor our father and mother? It is because the Bible says so. If we will simply do what the Bible teaches, we will be happier people, and we shall not be found in error. If, therefore, the Bible says that we are to consider the Lord Jesus Christ, we should give Him our utmost attention.

Secondly, we should consider Him because of who He is. According to the Scriptures, Jesus Christ is not only the Son of God - He is also God the Son, the second person of the blessed Trinity. In the first chapter of the Gospel of John we are told who Jesus is, for it is written:

In the beginning was the Word, and the Word was with God, and the Word was God. The same was in the beginning with God. All things were made by Him, and without Him was not anything made that was made. In Him was life; and the life was the light of men. And the light shineth in darkness; and the darkness comprehended it not. There was a man sent from God whose name was John. The same came for a witness, to bear witness of the Light that all men through him might believe. He was not that Light, but was sent to bear witness of that Light. That was the true Light, which lighteth every man that cometh into the world. He was in the world, and the world was made by him, and the world knew him not. He came unto his own, and his own received him not. But as many as received him, to them gave he power to become the sons of God, even to them that believe on his name. Which were born, not of blood, nor of the will of the flesh, nor of the will of man, but of God. And the Word was made flesh, and dwelt among us, (and we beheld his glory, the glory as of the only begotten of the Father,) full of grace and truth.

From this, and countless other passages of Scripture, it is evident that our Lord Jesus Christ is none other than the Creator of all things, meaning that He is God. And if He is God, then I ask…should we not consider Him with the utmost consideration?"

"Thirdly, we should consider Him because of what He can do fur us. If yun's will turn in your Bibles to Psalms 103, beginning at verse one, we read:

Bless the Lord, O my soul: and all that is within me bless his holy name. Bless the Lord, O my soul, and forget not all his benefits: Who forgiveth all thine iniquities:

"May I hesitate right there, and say that the very first thing that Jesus Christ wants ta do fur you is ta forgive you of all of your sins. In fact, that is the first thing that He does for every lost sinner – He forgives their sins. Forgiveness is the first act of God's redeeming grace upon the heart. About a year ago, I was a lost, hell-bound sinner, with no hope of Heaven. I thought within myself that forgiveness was *the last thing* that I could ever expect from God, but bless his holy name, it was *the first thing* He did for me. If you will remember the poor paralyzed man who was carried by four of his friends up ta the roof of Peter's house, and was let down in front of Jesus – the first thing that Jesus said to him **Man, thy sins are forgiven thee.** No one but Jesus knew that forgiveness was the first thing that the man needed. Everyone else thought that he needed to be healed of his palsy first, but Jesus knew that the real problem was sin, and that sin had to be dealt with first. And so it is with all of us today. We need to have our sins washed away by the blood of Jesus Christ."

"Yun's ought to consider Him because the Bible says so. Yun's ought to consider Him because of who He is. Yun's ought to consider Him because of what He can do fur you, and lastly, ya ought ta consider Him because you are going to face Him someday. I say to yun's that there are three things that every man, woman and child who has ever lived will all do someday, whether you want to or not. Yun's will *stand before* Jesus Christ, you will *bow before* Jesus Christ, and ya will *confess* that He is Lord. It is not a matter of *if* you will do these things - it is only a matter of *when*. In the great Book of Revelation, chapter twenty, beginning at verse eleven, we read:"

And I saw a great white throne, and him that sat on it, from whose face the earth and the heaven fled away; and there was found

no place for them. And I saw the dead, small and great, stand before God: and the books were opened: and another book was opened, which is the book of life; and the dead were judged out of those things which were written in the books, according to their works. And the sea gave up the dead which were in it; and death and hell delivered up the dead which were in them: and they were judged every man according to their works. And death and hell were cast into the lake of fire. This is the second death. And whosoever was not found written in the book of life was cast into the lake of fire.

"My dear friends, the time ta consider Him is now, and the time ta confess Him as Lord is now, for if ya wait until that day of the great and final judgment, it will be too late. Ya must confess him in this life if ya want to be saved in the life to come. Our good Pastor has asked me to extend an invitation to any and all who would like to consider the Lord Jesus Christ as your own personal Savior. As the choir comes with a hymn of invitation, we'd like to give ya that opportunity right now. Would ya bow yur heads and close your eyes fur a moment please? Is there anyone here, who by an uplifted hand, would signify that ya are a lost sinner?"

As the choir sang ***Just as I am***, Tom counted twenty hands that went up. He also noticed General Horton and Burley Crawford still standing in the back, their faces white as chalk. The Holy Spirit was drawing souls so powerfully. After one verse of the hymn, Greta and Gloria Williams were the first to step out into the aisle and come forward. Mattie and Buford both shouted at the same time, with their hands raised in praise to God, they came and knelt at the altar with their two daughters. They were quickly followed by another two sisters, Olivia and Laura Sedgefield, followed by Rachel Rutherford, Matthew Flemmins, Dill Flemmins, Lee Rutherford, Alexander and Alonzo Flemmins, Lizzie and Josephine Rutherford, and Georgia, Violet, and Gracie Flemmins.

Jeff had joined Tom in front of the pulpit now, with Jeff on one side of the church, and Tom on the other, pleading for others to come. General Horton and Burley Crawford were both trembling now, with tears running down their cheeks. But they wouldn't budge. Tom extended the invitation for two more verses, and gave the service back to Jeff. Fifteen souls were saved that morning. When the last person, (Josephine Rutherford,) had made a public profession of faith in Jesus Christ, and all fifteen had been accepted as candidates for baptism, Jeff again stepped behind the pulpit and announced, "Well folks, as you can see, God Himself has given us the evidence of His calling and approval of our dear brother Tom Tillotson. It now behooves us a Church to grant him license to preach wherever the Lord may send him. And after he has given full proof of his ministry to others outside of his home church, we will then set a date for his ordination. We invite all of you to come back next Sunday, and bring someone with you. And don't forget that we will also have another baptizing next Sunday. God bless you all."

Buford Williams, the only black man in the Church, was still standing with his wife Mattie and two daughters, hugging them and being hugged in return when Jeff asked him to dismiss the service in a word of prayer.

Nearly every person in the Church hugged Tom Tillotson and Pearly Mae, shaking hands with them. As Tom stepped outside the Church, General Horton and Burley Crawford were standing just outside the door. They immediately recognized Becky and Sarah, who were right behind Tom and Pearl, and now they knew who Jeff Townsend was too. They removed their hats and nodded to Becky and Sarah. General Horton held out his hand to Tom. His voice trembled slightly as he managed to get out a few words.

"Tom, I shore never thought I'd live ta see the day that you would be behind a pulpit preaching. We wuz expecting ta hear this Townsend fella everybody's talking bout, but dang it boy, you done a mighty fine job."

Tom shook hands with both General and Burley, and then formally introduced them to Jeff.

"We're glad you came to be with us, Jeff said, and we want you to come back every chance you get." Tom quickly added, "Yeah boys, come back next Sunday and you can hear some good preaching from Brother Townsend here."

"Well, General Horton replied, we might jest do that Tom. We ain't been ta church in a long time ya know; guess it's bout time we got started. If the good Lord can change a man like Great Bear Tillotson, there may be sum hope fur an old rascal like myself."

Spring of 1870 Bruceton Mills, WV

They arrived in the town of Bruceton Mills on a beautiful sunny afternoon, driving a fancy, white horse-drawn carriage, with a silver top and black leather seats, front and back. The new arrivals were Dr. Joseph Parks, MD, and his lovely wife Carolyn. They had just arrived from New York. The local folks immediately began to wonder why a fancy New York doctor would come so far to practice medicine in the mountains of West Virginia. Becky and Jeff were among the ones that felt that way. Jeff felt that since he was the closest minister that he and Becky should be there to welcome the newcomers. A sizeable crowd had gathered around the post office where Dr. Parks and his wife had stopped to let the postmaster know their new address. Upon seeing the color or Dr. Parks' skin, many among the welcoming committee instantly showed their disapproval. Jeff had announced to his church that a doctor was arriving soon, and the news had traveled quickly. Most of the people in Preston County were well-satisfied with Becky, Sarah and Pearly Mae taking care of their minor medical needs and baby delivering.

Many that were gathered there was overheard saying, *"They ain't no need fur a doctor."* Jeff, Becky, and a few others were overjoyed to have a real doctor to see to the needs of the people. They couldn't imagine what would happen if a real crisis hit the families here. Voices were heard grumbling about the couple's fancy appearance. Others were overheard making remarks about their color. "Just who do they think they be?" a deep male voice muttered. "Ain't no use fur no more black folks around these here parts, we oughta run'um out jest like they come in." Becky looked around quickly, just in time to see General Horton and his uncle Burley Crawford, the moonshiners from the mountains. She shivered to think that trouble could possibly be brewing up again.

Her attention was drawn back to the couple in the carriage. Dr. Parks was a tall, thin dark skinned man, darker than any other black folks that the folks in Preston County had ever seen. He was wearing a black tailored suit and top hat. His wife Carolyn was a beautiful lady, very dark in color as well, with a beautiful, unblemished complexion. She was wearing a beautiful blue dress, with a hat to match, and beautiful bracelets and strands of shiny pearls around her neck, with earrings to match.

The couple was the second Negro family to settle in this area. They appeared a bit nervous as they descended from the carriage. Jeff shook hands with Dr. Parks, saying, "Welcome to Bruceton Mills Dr. Parks, I'm Jeff Townsend, the community Pastor. This is my beautiful wife Becky. We hope you like it here, and look forward to seeing you and your lovely wife in church Sunday." Doctor Parks extended his hand to Jeff without a smile or any kind of emotion. He introduced his wife. "This is my wife Carolyn. We would be grateful if someone could point us to the nearest café. It's been a long trip, and my wife is hungry and needs to rest."

Jeff told him he would be glad to take him to the café, and that he was welcome in their home anytime. Still with no emotion Doctor Parks thanked them, tipping his hat to Becky, replying, "Maybe soon."

Dr. Parks and his wife had bought the big house on the outskirts of town. The big two-story mansion was built in 1853, seven years before the outbreak of the Civil War, by a very wealthy landowner who had lived there a very short time. His wife and child had died from Typhoid fever. He just couldn't deal with his grief, so he boarded up the windows and doors, closed up the place, and moved away. The stately mansion was situated atop a low, round-topped hill, overlooking the town of Bruceton Mills. Before moving from New York, Dr. Parks had wired telegrams to local construction companies, asking for bids to restore the mansion to its original condition. He set up his small clinic in the basement of the big house, which had an entrance from the outside, with steps leading down to the door. Over the door was a sign which read, **Dr. Joseph Parks Medical Clinic**. Becky and Sarah had often talked about the house and what it must look like inside.

Jeff escorted the couple to the café called Mama's Place, the finest café in town, while Becky and Samuel (now three years old,) and baby Ollie who was six months old, made a visit to the General store for some much needed sugar, flour and corn meal for home. After shopping, they met Jeff, and started the drive home.

"What do you think about the new Doctor and his wife?" Becky asked.

"They seem to be very nice people," Jeff replied. "I just hope the folks around these parts will accept them and make them welcome."

Heavenly Places

Becky had a bad feeling about the whole situation, especially since the doctor was black. They were both troubled by some of the remarks they had overheard today. They both silently prayed a special prayer for the doctor and his wife. Jeff told Becky that he had invited them to dinner after the services on Sunday and that they had agreed to come. Becky's mind started turning immediately, thinking about what she would cook for her guests.

Samuel was fast asleep in her arms. He was such a beautiful child, full of energy, and just as full of questions. Every trip they made to Church, or anywhere else, he would point to nearly every object he saw, asking, "Papa, what is dat?" Or "Momma, what is dis?" Becky and Jeff delighted in every move and every word he said. They knelt beside the bed with him every night as he said his prayers. In that sweet, little-boy voice he would say, "Yord, bwess Momma, and Papa, and Yord, take care of uncle Tom and aunt Pearwie Mae, and bwess my wittle sista and thank you for Jesus, amen."

Becky smiled as she kissed his forehead. Baby Ollie was also asleep in her carriage, which was secured tightly in the back seat of the buggy. She had her daddy's black hair and her mother's brown eyes. In the evenings when all the work was done and supper was ended, she and Jeff loved to place the two of them on the circular rug in front of the fireplace and just watch them – Samuel clapping his hands and laughing, as if he was trying to teach little Ollie to do the same. They still remembered how Samuel had laughed uncontrollably the first time little Ollie responded, clapping her hands and giggling at him.

Several neighbors dropped by that week to discuss the new doctor. Jeff encouraged them to give him a chance, and to not be so quick to judge. Some seemed to take his advice, but others made it perfectly clear that they did not approve of the new doctor. The week seemed to go by so fast. Becky had cleaned and prepared the house for company. She made cakes and pies and brought out her special dishes that her mother had given her. All was ready as they headed out for the church that Sunday morning. Samuel was sitting between his parents, watching every move that was made on their way to church. He kept his eyes on the horses in front of the buggy. He usually rode with Uncle Tom and Aunt Pearly Mae. Baby Ollie was on her Momma's lap.

A big crowd was gathered in the yard of the church, children running to and fro, laughing and chasing each other. Sarah met them with outstretched arms, waiting to lift Samuel down from the buggy, as Claudette grabbed baby Ollie. Once Becky and Jeff arrived at Church, they hardly got to hold either of their children. They were passed from one to another, and they didn't seem to mind. Becky was so glad to see that the Williams family was there; hoping that maybe Dr. Parks and his wife wouldn't feel so singled out with another black family present. Jeff helped Becky down from the buggy and hitched the horses up to a tree where they would be in the shade. Becky and Sarah walked on into the church house, greeting folks as they walked. The church bell was soon sounded for all to come in. Becky hadn't seen the doctor arrive yet. "Maybe he has changed his mind," Sarah whispered.

The church service began. The choir was singing "**When the Saints go marching in**" when the Doctor and his wife arrived. Jeff stood up and greeted them with a handshake, seating them near the front. Clark quickly handed them a Hymn book. Dr. Parks was dressed in a fancy navy blue suit and white tie, with a solid gold tie clasp. A bright gold chain, attached to a gold-plated pocket watch hung from his blue vest. His wife Carolyn was beautiful in her white dress with a long-sleeved purple jacket. She was wearing a genuine pearl necklace with pearl ear rings to match, all of which beautifully contrasted with her flawless complexion. As the two of them walked gracefully toward their pew, some of the folks who were already seated commented that the two of them appeared almost noble. They certainly stood out among the country folks in their plain clothes. Most of the men wore bibbed overalls and checked shirts. The women wore cotton dresses, and bonnets of all different colors. Some were dressed a bit fancier than others, with a store-bought dress and hat to match, but not one person there was dirty or ragged-looking.

Becky was wearing the beautiful red dress and black hat with red trim that Jeff had bought her for their anniversary. Jeff always wore a suit when he was delivering God's Word. Becky made sure that her husband was one of the best-dressed men around. Clark stood and welcomed everyone, extending a special welcome to the visitors. He asked everyone to stand and fellowship with each other while the next song was being sung. The music was especially good today. Rufus played the guitar, with Ralph on the mandolin, Clark on the violin, and Foster playing the big standup bass. Someone commented that the choir sang with such beautiful harmony they almost made their own music. In fact, they actually sang some of slower hymns without any music. They just considered the music and the musicians as added blessings. Becky started the old song - ***When the roll is called up yonder I'll be there***. She noticed the good doctor and his wife both singing along in harmony. Most all the people went to the new couple, shaking their hands, welcoming them to the church. But some didn't. Jeff prayed, "Lord please let me give a message to these people today, one that will soften these stony cold hearts."

Becky shook hands with them and welcomed them to the church. She noticed a soft twinkle in Carolyn Parks' eyes as she gently took one of Samuels's hands in her own. Her first words to Becky were…"You have such beautiful children Mrs. Townsend." Becky was immediately endeared to Mrs. Parks. Her voice was very soft, sincere, and articulate. Becky thanked her with a big smile. "Oh please, call me Becky," she said.

Mrs. Parks kept her eyes on Samuel and Ollie for the remainder of the service. After service was over and all the goodbyes were said Jeff instructed Doctor Parks to follow him to the farm. "You'll have to tell me everything," Sarah whispered as she hugged Becky while giving Samuel and Ollie a big kiss on the cheek. Mollie had to have a hug from Samuel and the baby as well. "I will, I promise," Becky whispered back to her.

The gentle rocking of the slow-moving wagon ride toward home had put both Samuel and the baby to sleep. Jeff carried Samuel into the house and laid him in his bed, partially closing the door so that Samuel could be heard if he should wake up. Becky lowered Ollie gently into her crib. Both Dr. Parks and his wife were very impressed with the Townsend home.

"You have a beautiful place here Madam," Dr. Parks commented.

Satisfied that her dinner had been a success, Becky invited her guests out onto the front porch to relax and talk. After asking Becky's permission, Doctor Parks lit up his pipe. Becky remembered her father smoking a pipe after he ate. He said it was relaxing. Jeff asked the Parks why they had chosen West Virginia as a place to settle. Dr. Parks replied that his father was a missionary, and that he himself wanted to be a missionary, but didn't want to take his wife so far from her people. He wanted to help those that were less fortunate than him. He felt that his love for medicine was a gift from God, and he wanted to use that gift to help those that were unable to help themselves. Jeff, sounding somewhat apologetic, told him that his pay for his services would most likely be very poor - maybe a chicken, eggs, plenty of good canned vegetables, and maybe a small amount of cash sometimes. Doctor Parks immediately assured Jeff that he neither needed nor wanted any money for his services, explaining that his father had been a very rich man, and had left all his inheritance to him, and that he simply wanted to be the best doctor possible to the folks here in Preston County, and he felt that it was a blessing just to be able to do so. Jeff told him that he would have to win some of them over, due to the way they had been raised, and him being black and all. Dr. Parks smiled for the first time.

"It is nothing new to us to meet folks that don't accept us, but in the end they always do. It's just one of the many challenges we face wherever we go." He assured Jeff.

He reached out and took his wife's hand. "As long as my sweet misses is happy, so will I be."

Jeff felt a strong bond begin to form in his heart for these people. He felt that they were good moral people, just working their way through life like everyone else. He vowed silently that he would do all in his power to see that the folks around here accepted these good people.

Samuel soon awoke, and Becky excused herself so she could feed him his dinner.

"Oh please, may I?" Mrs. Parks asked.

"Yes you may," Becky quickly agreed. As the two went into the kitchen Carolyn insisted that Becky call her by her first name. Becky could see the joy in her eyes as she fed Samuel.

"Do you have children Carolyn?" she asked.

"No, Carolyn answered with a deep sadness, Joseph and I have tried, but I have not been able to carry a child full term. I have lost two babies, and we have decided to wait. We would like to adopt later, after we are settled here for a while." Becky nodded sympathetically.

Little Ollie awoke next, so Becky left Carolyn feeding Samuel while she changed Ollie and fed her a bottle. As she came back into the kitchen, she could see that Samuel had really taken a liking to Carolyn. She invited Carolyn to the church on Wednesday night, where the women were all meeting to work on their quilts for the winter. Becky was making Pearly Mae a quilt for her baby. Becky was a bit concerned for Pearly Mae to be having a baby at her age. Maybe she could get her to see Dr. Parks just in case there were complications. Carolyn said she would think about coming and might just do so. The Parks thanked the Townsends for the good dinner and company, insisting that they must be on their way back home before dark. Dr. Parks shook hands with Jeff and Becky, handing little Samuel a crisp five-dollar bill, cautioning him, "Now you save that for your schooling young man."

Samuel, looking grateful but confused, asked, "Momma, what's schooling?" They all laughed at the little fellow.

Becky explained to him that school was a place that he would go when he got older so that he could learn to read and write. "Oh tay," he mumbled, and dashed off to find Cricket. Carolyn hugged Becky and kissed baby Ollie. "Such a sweet baby," she said. Becky saw the longing in Carolyn's eyes, and prayed silently that God would give her a child of her own.

After the couple left, Jeff and Becky went for a walk with the children down by the pool and into the meadow. Flowers were starting to bloom, and the grass was getting green. Samuel took Jeff's hand, pulling him toward the path that led to Tom and Pearly Mae's house. "Uncle Tom's house papa, pwease, can we go," he pleaded. "Ok son, if momma wants to go we will," Jeff quickly gave in. Samuel ran over to his mother, gazing up into her eyes, tugging on her dress, pleading, "Can we pwease go see Uncle Tom and Aunt Pweary Mae Momma, pwease?" Becky smiled and conceded as quickly as Jeff had.

They continued on down the path that led to Tom and Pearly Mae's cabin, pushing baby Ollie in a buggy that Jeff had made. The two couples visited often, and Samuel spent many hours at Tom and Pearly Mae's, even spending the night occasionally. Pearly Mae met them at the gate with her arms open, with a big hug for Samuel and a kiss for Ollie. Tom and Jeff wandered out to the barn while the two women sat on the porch with a cold glass of peppermint tea. Samuel was running all over the barnyard trying to catch one of the goats that Tom had bought. Tom broke the silence with a question, "Jeff, you think we're gonna have trouble with some of the folks over this new doc that's come into town?" Jeff stared off into the distance for a moment as if searching for a fitting answer to Tom's question. "Well Tom, he finally responded, I don't really know, but we had better be prepared, just in case. I think we can both agree that much prayer is needed for all our people at this time. We are doing so well in our church right now that the devil has to try to come in some way."

"Yep," Tom replied. Then quickly changing the subject, he asked, "Hey, when we gonna take us a hunting trip?" "Hmm, Jeff grinned, funny that you should ask that Tom, because I've been hankering to go hunting for a while, maybe real soon, if things stay quiet around here." As they continued walking and talking they caught a glimpse of Samuel, who had now given up on catching a goat, and was now chasing the chickens around the barn yard.

Strangely enough, back at the house Becky and Pearly Mae were talking about the same thing – their men going on a hunting trip. Jeff had been hinting to Becky that, since Tom and Pearly Mae had become their neighbors, the farming had gotten a lot easier, they now had just a little more leisure time than before. Becky had learned to read him like a book; she knew what his next words were going to be before he said them. Jeff hadn't been hunting for quite a while. As a matter of fact, he hadn't been hunting or fishing since the birth of baby Ollie, six months ago. Becky had never relished the idea of Jeff going hunting by himself, especially since the murders of Lucas Bratcher and the Jenkins family. She was worried that the Klan might show its ugly head again now that another black family had arrived. Pearly Mae voiced the same concern. She was somewhat afraid to be alone anymore for fear that since Tom was half Indian, a preacher, and married to a white woman; the Klan might come to their house. Becky reminded her that if they would simply be faithful to God, pray fervently, and trust Him, He would protect her and Tom.

The visit was way too short for Samuel. He didn't want to leave. Tom promised him that he would come by and get him in a few days, and he could spend the night with them. That day came sooner than anyone anticipated. Baby Ollie got very sick, unable to sleep, waking up holding her right ear and screaming in pain, refusing to eat or drink. Becky and Jeff decided that this would be a good time for Samuel to spend a few nights with Tom and Pearly Mae. The baby grew worse, with a fever at night, still refusing to eat. She was getting weaker as time went by. Becky suggested that they take her into town to see Dr. Parks. Jeff immediately agreed. They stopped at Tom's to let them know where they were going.

Arriving at Dr. Park's house, Carolyn met them at the buggy, asking what was wrong. When they told her they needed to see the doctor, she immediately escorted them down to his office. Being the wife of a doctor for several years, she recognized quickly that the little girl was very ill. Becky could see the deep concern in her eyes.

Dr. Parks was sitting at his desk when they came in. With one look at the baby he immediately told Becky to lay Ollie on the exam table and remove the blanket from around her. Carolyn assisted her husband in the exam. Dr. Parks used his stethoscope to listen to her heart and her breathing. He then inserted a small metal cone into her ear canal while Carolyn held a lamp as close to the larger end of the cone as she could in order to allow him to see as far into the baby's ear as possible. She then held the light just above the baby's mouth while Dr. Parks looked into her throat.

"I see," he mumbled to himself, all the while asking Becky questions about how the baby had been acting for the last few days. Baby Ollie was still as a mouse during the exam despite the fact that she had a fever of 102. Dr. Parks finished his exam.

"She has an inner ear infection," he explained, causing her throat to swell from the drainage, which explains why she is not eating or drinking. Her throat is sore and hurts her when she swallows. I will give her some liquid medicine to be given three times a day. She should feel better by tomorrow evening."

Becky and Jeff thanked the doctor, offering to pay him, but he refused. His voice quivered slightly as he looked into Becky's face, replying, "You folks showed me and the misses a great welcome the first time we saw you, you opened your home and your hearts to us, and shared your food. We don't usually receive that kind of Christian greeting the first time white folks meet us. We are so grateful. Just take this medicine and that pretty young lady will be better in no time." As they were leaving, Jeff shook his hand, saying, "Hope to see you folks in church again real soon."

Just like the doctor had predicted, Ollie was as chipper as she could be the next evening, and actually took her bottle. It is so strange sometimes how news, both good and bad, spreads so quickly. The news that Reverend Townsend and his wife had come to see the new black doctor on a professional basis had already spread all over the little community of Bruceton Mills. This, of course, was good advertisement for Dr. Parks and his practice. Slowly, others began drifting in to see the new doctor each day. But there were still many more that refused to use the doctor's service, no matter how sick they become.

The next week, after their visit to Dr. Parks, all was well in the Townsend home. Ollie was completely well, and playful as ever. On Wednesday night Pearly Mae and Becky set out to go to the church, where the ladies met to work on their quilts.

"Let's stop by and see if Carolyn wants to go," Becky suggested. They pulled the buggy in front of the house and stopped. Becky was climbing down from the buggy when she hesitated.

"*Shh,*" she whispered. The prettiest sound was flowing through the front windows of the old mansion. Becky motioned for Pearly Mae to come along. They walked up the steps and onto the porch. Looking through the window, they saw Carolyn Parks playing a piano and singing. It was a beautiful melody. Becky had only seen one other piano at a church in her home state of Tennessee. Carolyn looked up and saw them and stopped playing.

"Oh no, don't stop, they pleaded. That is the most beautiful sound. Maybe we can get one for the church someday." Carolyn thanked them, telling them that she had been playing since she was a small girl.

She accepted their invitation and went to the quilting; she seemed to have a good time. Most of the women warmed up to her rather quickly. She and Mattie Williams became close friends. Mattie quickly noticed how Mrs. Parks seemed so drawn to her twin girls, Greta and Gloria. As soon as Becky got home she told Jeff about Carolyn playing a piano. Hearing the excitement in Becky's voice, and seeing the look on her face when she talked about the piano and the beautiful music, Jeff knew that sooner or later, the Church would have one. Two weeks later, a brand new piano was hauled into the church, donated by Dr. and Mrs. Parks. Every service thereafter, Carolyn Parks was up front, playing for the choir, while her husband, beaming with pride, listened from the front pew. Becky, Sarah and Carolyn had now formed a trio. Nearly everyone in the Church requested them to sing every time the Church met to worship. News of the sweet harmony with which they sang soon reached every Church in the state. Whenever Jeff was called upon to come and preach in revival meetings, he was also asked to bring the three ladies with him.

April 1st, 1870. Bruceton Mills, West Virginia

The town of Bruceton Mills West Virginia, settled along Big Sandy Creek, was so named by an early settler, John M. Hoffman, who named the community for his stepfather, George Bruce, who claimed to be a direct descendant of Robert the Bruce, King of Scotland. Among the many things that drew settlers to the area surrounding Bruceton Mills was its sheer natural beauty and grandeur. It was often said of the state of West Virginia – *"**where the mountains touch the sky**."* Another powerful attraction to the area was its abundance of fish and wildlife. With the ending of the Civil War in 1865, and new inventions being patented all over the world, including new and better tools and methods of railroad construction, and especially the use of dynamite for blasting large sections of rock, areas that were formerly isolated and hardly accessible were now much easier to reach. Folks from some of the larger industrial towns and cities began to filter into more rural areas, wanting to escape the noisy hustle-and-bustle of crowded streets, and to enjoy the serenity of clear-flowing rivers and streams, and the beauty of majestic mountains and forests.

Some folks came to the mountains of West Virginia for the beauty and serenity, some came for the privacy, and some for jobs in the coal mines. Others came to escape the long arm of the law, while several came for the hunting experience. In the midst of all the beauty, grandeur and majesty, however, there were also those who came, and stayed, for no other reason than to advance and enforce their own ideals and agendas upon others.

In 1870, the KKK was quickly losing popularity in West Virginia. Their presence would virtually disappear from the state in another year, to re-appear again nearly a half century later. But they were still around, and active in 1870, and still made their power and presence known from time to time. One of their devious tactics was to lay low for extended periods of time, allowing public sentiments to wane. But once they decided that a certain individual or group had violated their own perverted beliefs or practices, that individual or group was marked for destruction. Jeff Townsend, Tom Tillotson, and Clark Puckett were three of those individuals. Jeff was singled out because he allowed blacks in his Church, and because he had allowed a black doctor to touch his white daughter. Tom Tillotson was hated because he was a half breed, a married to a white woman. Both Jeff and Tom were also targeted because of their testimony against members of the Klan, testimony that led to the execution of three, and the imprisonment of three more. Clark Puckett was marked for death because he had befriended a black family, and had allowed them to live in his house.

Jeff and Tom had decided that the time for a good hunting trip was now; they knew just the place to go - a vast area of thick forest just west of Bruceton Mills. The area would later become known as Cooper's Rock State Forest, a 12,747 acre state forest in Monongalia and Preston Counties. In 1870, the forest teemed with an abundance of nearly every species of wild game native to North America. It also teemed with a few dangerous species, like mountain lions and black bears. The mountains were steep, the valleys were deep, and the dangers were many. Unless a man was very familiar with the area, he could get lost quickly. If a man ventured too far into the woods alone, and was injured or bitten by a timber rattler, his chances of survival were very slim. Tom Great Bear Tillotson knew those woods like the back of his hand. He knew every river and stream, and the length, breadth and depth of each of them. Some of the narrow trails that snaked through the forest had been blazed by Tom himself.

Jeff felt safe in inviting Rufus Rutherford and Clark Puckett along with Tom and himself on the hunting trip. The plan was for them to meet at the Bruceton Mills post office early on Friday morning, and to hunt all day, then camp out in the woods Friday night, and return home Saturday morning with a wagon load of pheasant, turkey, and anything else that might fly or walk into their gun sights. On Friday, April 1st, the four of them met at the post

Heavenly Places

office as planned. Rufus came with Clark, Sarah and their two children in his wagon. Tom was with Jeff in his wagon. Jeff left his horses and wagon with Dr. Parks, who made them promise him a couple fat pheasants for taking care of their animals. Sarah, Mollie and Carter took Clark's wagon up the valley toward Jeff's farm. Just before the four men tramped into the woods, Tom laid down a few ground rules to them.

"Since we're gonna be hunting pheasant and turkey fellas, I know we have to be pretty quiet out there. Just remember, don't any of us get separated more than thirty feet from each other. I prefer that we stay in sight of each other at all times. As long as we can see each other, we know we're all going in the same direction. But if you do get outa sight from the other three, don't hesitate to holler, so we'll at least know that you're within earshot, and that you're alright. In these woods, we ain't the only hunters. Whatever we kill, we must immediately gut it, bury the innards and blood. A bear can smell blood a mile away, and we don't want to become the hunted instead of the hunters."

Little did he know, that three of them, were already being hunted even before they left Bruceton Mills. Twenty minutes after the four men entered the forest, two other men followed, each armed with a Volition Repeating Rifle, and a white sheet and hood stuffed inside a burlap sack. Less than twenty minutes into the hunt, Clark had bagged a big tom turkey, while Jeff, Tom and Rufus all three had a pheasant apiece. Jeff laughed as he held up his pheasant.

"Well, boys, he chuckled, if we don't git nuthin else, we've got our supper."

"You mean we've got doctor Parks' supper, Rufus chimed in. If we don't get any more pheasants, we're gonna be eating roast turkey for supper."

The four of them didn't know it, but with each shot they fired from their shotguns, they were giving their would-be killers an audible signal as to their location. Their stalkers were simply waiting for them to stop and make camp. Their campfire would provide enough light for the killers to come well within rifle range without being seen or heard.

Before dusk each man had as much game as he could carry swinging from his belt by a rope. Tom led them over a high ridge and down the other side to a swift-running stream. They reached the bottom of the steep ridge just as the sun sank behind the western mountains. They made camp about twenty feet from the stream. Each of them laid their game in a single pile, and began gathering large rocks from the edge of the stream, placing them in a circle in which to build their campfire. The only sounds were the crackle of the fire, the crickets, and an occasional whip-poor-will. Tom soaked Clark's turkey in the stream, plucked his feathers, and skewered him on a sharp stick. He laid the skewered turkey between two forked sticks on either side of the fire, and began turning the turkey slowly over the fire. The other three smiled their approval, knowing that Tom had done this before. When Tom was satisfied that the turkey was fully roasted, he took his Bowie knife from its sheath and began to carve the turkey, handing a leg to Jeff, another leg to Clark, and slicing two hefty slices of breast for Rufus and himself. When the four of them were full, about all that was left of the turkey was its bones.

Clark and Rufus stood up at the same time, intending to walk upstream to answer nature's call. Two shots rang out simultaneously from the top of the ridge behind them. Clark and Rufus sank to their knees at the same time, falling forward on their faces at the edge of the stream. The next two shots came within a second, one bullet missing Jeff's head by less than an inch. At the sound of the first two shots from the rifles, Tom had rolled to his right, whipping out his Colt, fanning the hammer with his left hand, firing all six shots in the direction of the attackers, as another bullet smacked into the fire, scattering it in every direction. Their white sheets and hoods made the ambushers an easy target for an expert marksman. All six bullets from Tom's Colt found their intended mark. Two seconds after Clark and Rufus sank to their knees; the two men at the top of the ridge fell forward also, tumbling down the steep hill. One of them rolled onto the fire. Jeff quickly lifted his dead body from the fire as his white sheet blazed. Jeff tore the burning sheet from his body, throwing it toward the stream. When Tom was certain that the other man was dead also, he and Jeff immediately turned their attention to Clark and Rufus.

Both men had been shot in the back, but both were still alive. Blood was gushing from their backs with each heartbeat. They had fallen so close to each other that their blood mingled on the ground where they fell. As Jeff knelt beside Clark, and Tom knelt beside Rufus, they immediately felt the two men's blood soaking into their trousers. They were both lying in pools of their own blood. There was only one hope for either of them – Dr. Parks. Jeff insisted that Tom go for Dr. Parks since he knew the terrain better than himself. Tom quickly lit a torch from the fire that remained and ran as fast at the torch and the terrain would allow. Within an hour he was pounding on the door of Dr. Parks' house. "Grab your bag doctor," he panted, Clark and Rufus have been shot in the back." That's all Dr. Parks needed to hear. As he raised his suspenders to his shoulders, Carolyn handed him his doctor's satchel and a lantern, and he and Tom were gone. Carolyn threw on her robe, hitched up the doctor's buggy, and was on her way to Jeff's house. Tom didn't know whether to run fast or take it easy on the doctor. He got his answer when Dr. Parks passed him just before they entered the woods. He glanced back at Tom, who was now trying to keep up, yelling, "Now that you know that I ain't no turtle Mr. Tillotson, would you mind taking the lead now?" Tom grinned as Dr. Parks stepped aside to allow him to lead the way.

Jeff inspected the bullet wounds as best he could. He knew he couldn't move either of them for fear of injuring them even worse. He folded two blankets, making pillows for each of them. He raised their heads as gently as possible, placing the folded blankets under their heads. He then covered them with the other two blankets they had brought. He tore the sheets from the bodies of the two dead men, using them to absorb as much blood as they could absorb, and applying pressure to their bullet wounds. He could tell from Clark's breathing that he was fading fast. Barely able to speak above a whisper, Clark insisted that he attend to Rufus, and not to worry about him. The bullet that went into Clark's back had severed his spine. He had no feeling at all in his legs. The bullet that was in Rufus' back missed his spine by a fraction of an inch. Jeff kept the folded sheets applied to their backs, turning the sheets over once the blood had soaked half way through them. He sobbed and prayed at the same time.

In less than an hour, Dr. Parks and Tom arrived, both of them panting for breath. Both the sheets that Jeff had been applying to the men's backs were now soaked through, dripping with blood. Rufus was screaming with pain. Clark was dying. Dr. Parks knelt beside Clark first, as Clark, with his last ounce of strength and his last few breaths, managed to reach out his left hand and place it on the back of Rufus' head, and he was gone. Dr. Parks felt for a pulse, but found none. He shook his head, instructing Tom and Jeff to lift Clark's body away from Rufus so that he could have better access to Rufus' back. Inspecting the wound and listening to Rufus' breathing for a moment, he opened his satchel, taking out a bottle of chloroform, a bottle of alcohol, and a scalpel. "Are you able to move your legs at all Sir?" he asked Rufus. Rufus responded by bending his left knee slightly. Dr. Parks then knew that the bullet hadn't paralyzed him. "I'm going to have to put you to sleep Mr. Rutherford," he exclaimed.

    Dr. Parks ask Jeff and Tom if either of them had brought a clean handkerchief. Neither of them had. Tom pulled the hood from the head of one of the dead men, handing it to Dr. Parks. As Dr. Parks soaked the hood in chloroform to place over Rufus' mouth, Tom and Jeff stared into the chalky face of General Horton. Jeff removed the hood from the other dead man. It was Burley Crawford. As Rufus lost consciousness, Dr. Parks looked over at the two dead men. Each of them had three bullet holes in the center of his chest. He turned back to Rufus, praying, "Dear God, help me to save this one." He instructed Tom to come near, and to be ready to apply more chloroform if Rufus began to moan or scream again. He sterilized his scalpel and hemostat with the alcohol. Jeff held the lantern over his head as he began to cut the bullet out of Rufus' back. The bullet was so close to the spine that he was afraid of cutting a nerve that might permanently paralyze Rufus. But he had no choice – the bullet had to come out. He made several quick cuts with the scalpel, inserting his finger after each cut, trying to find the bullet. After three tries, he found the bullet, deep inside Rufus' back. Gently inserting the curved hemostat into the opening, and locking onto the bullet, he gently wiggled the bullet out of Rufus' back.

    Getting the bullet out was only half the battle. Now they had to get Rufus out of the woods without doing any more damage. Dr. Parks used every bandage in his satchel to place over the wound. Now he needed something to tie around Rufus to hold the bandages in place. Jeff and Tom removed their shirts, cutting them into strips and tying them together. Dr. Parks tied the shirts tightly around Rufus body.

"Is he gonna make it doc?" Tom asked.

"If we can get him to my clinic without killing him, I think he stands a good chance," Dr. Parks replied.

Tom found two young saplings about three inches in diameter. He cut them down with his Bowie knife. Jeff gathered several armloads of green grapevines. Working together, they interwove the vines between the two poles, tying the ends around the poles so that the weight of Rufus' body itself would tighten the vines against the poles. Half an hour later, they had a sledge just wide enough to hold Rufus securely in the middle. Dr. Parks watched in admiration as the two preachers worked together so frantically to get the sledge built. They asked Dr. Parks to lie down on it to test it before attempting to haul Rufus out of the woods on it. Dr. Parks agreed. They bounced the sledge up and down a few times with Dr. Parks in it. It held his weight easily.

They agreed that Tom should stay behind with the dead bodies. Jeff and Dr. Parks would carry Rufus to Bruceton Mills. Dr. Parks hung his lantern on one side of the sledge, just behind where his hand would be. Jeff hung another lantern on the opposite side in the rear of the sledge. They gently laid Rufus onto the sledge, lifted in unison, and walked in step with each other, slowly and carefully. Stopping only twice for short breaks, it took them three hours to cover the eight miles. They walked out of the woods carrying Rufus between them at daybreak on Saturday morning.

Samuel was so excited he kept running from the kitchen where Becky was baking cookies to the front porch, then out into the yard to the gate, then back in again.

"Shucks Mama, when are they coming? When Mama?" Becky laughed.

"Sammie you must be patient. Wearing out the screen door won't bring them here any faster. Come have some cookies and milk and maybe by then they will be here" Becky poured Samuel a glass of cold milk from the jar she had brought up from the spring. Ollie was still asleep, although Becky didn't know how, because Samuel had been running in and out the door, slamming it back together with a loud bang. Sarah, Mollie and Carter were coming to spend the night. That was why Samuel was so excited. He just couldn't be still from all the excitement of having the Puckett children to play with. Becky herself was looking forward to spending time with her friend Sarah. They had so much to catch up on. Samuel overstuffed his mouth with cookies, and then overflowed it with milk, which ended up on his shirt.

"Samuel Jeffery Townsend, slow down. Don't cram your mouth so full, Becky raised her voice to him, you are going to get choked to death!"

"Yes Mama," Samuel mumbled. Then they heard the sound of a wagon.

"They's here Mama!" Samuel was up and out the door before Becky could say scat. She took off her apron and looked in on Ollie who was sound asleep in her bed. Becky went outside to meet her company. Sarah and the children pulled up at the gate and jumped down from the wagon. Becky gave the kids a big hug as Sarah hugged Samuel. "Carter, would you please take the horses out behind the barn and turn them loose in the pasture?" Sarah asked. "Yes momma. Come on Samuel, you can go too," Carter offered. Samuel looked at Becky for approval. "Go," she waved at him.

The two boys climbed onto the wagon and headed toward the barn. Sarah and Becky hugged each other, each one taking a bag that Sarah had brought. They walked hand in hand into the house with Mollie behind them. Becky told Mollie that Ollie would be up soon, and they could play with their dolls. Ollie was soon up, and the two girls were busy playing with their dolls, pretending to be mommies. Sarah and Becky adjourned to the porch with a cold glass of tea, watching the boys romp around the barn yard, shooting and banging, pretending to be cowboys and Indians, with Cricket running around like a wild dog. With supper over and the children bathed and fast asleep in bed, the two women wandered back to the porch. Pearly Mae came up and sat with them for a while.

They talked about the men hunting, about the new doctor, and the fact that school would be starting soon. Their conversation went far into the night. Pearly Mae finally excused herself, telling the other two that she had better get home and get into bed, because it wouldn't be long before Tom would be home, and hungry as a bear. They all laughed and said good night. Becky lay there after saying a prayer for the safety of all the men. She felt so uneasy, and couldn't understand why. She knew that Jeff used every precaution when he went hunting, and they had gone so many times before, and always came home safe. But over the years Becky had grown accustomed to listening to the little voice inside her head that told her that something was not quite right. That voice was now keeping her awake. Exhausted, she fell asleep, only to be awakened by a pounding on the door, and Cricket barking every breath. She bolted upright with her heart pounding. The banging on the door continued. Becky jumped up and threw her robe around her shoulders. Looking out the window she saw a horse and buggy in front of the gate. It was barely dawn, but the horse and buggy were visible enough for her to recognize it as Dr. Parks' rig. She rushed to the door, almost running over Sarah, who had also been awakened by the pounding on the door. Becky opened the door to find Carolyn Parks standing there in her robe.

"Carolyn, what in the world is wrong?" Becky inquired.

"Becky, you and Sarah need to come with me to the house, there has been a hunting accident," Carolyn's voice trembled. Becky and Sarah both grabbed their chests with a loud gasp. "Oh my God," Sarah and Becky both cried at the same time, Sarah asking if Clark had been hurt, and Becky asking if Jeff had been hurt. Carolyn quickly explained, "I don't know all the details. Tom came for Joseph and told me to come and get you and Sarah." Becky asked Carolyn to go fetch Pearly Mae while she and Sarah got dressed. Without a moment's hesitation, Carolyn rushed off to get Pearly Mae to come and stay with the children while they went into town. Becky and Sarah were both praying that their husbands were alright. Becky knew now why she couldn't sleep, and why her mind was so uneasy. "Oh Lord, please let my Jeff be alright?" She prayed. She couldn't imagine what kind of accident might have happened. *Had one of the men fallen over a cliff*, or, God forbid, *had one of them been shot*? Becky couldn't bear to think of something like that.

Carolyn Parks, on her way to get Pearly Mae, didn't know what to do. She knew that Clark and Rufus had been shot, and that's all that Tom had said. She didn't know how bad things were, and she didn't cherish the idea of having to be the one to bring such bad news to her new friends. She prayed in desperation, asking God to give her wisdom in how to break the bad news to Sarah. Knowing that all of them would know the truth before the day was over, she decided that she would wait till they reached the house, and then tell them that Clark and Rufus had been shot.

Pearly Mae was up when she arrived. It was now daylight. Pearly dressed quickly, meeting Carolyn at the door. Carolyn quickly explained the situation, assuring Pearly that Tom was alright. Pearly joined her in the buggy, and they headed back to the Townsend home to find Becky and Sarah waiting by the gate. Quick orders were given concerning the children. Becky thanked her for being such a good neighbor, assuring her that they would be back as soon as they could. Pearly Mae gave her a quick hug, hurrying her off, insisting, "Go Becky, and don't worry about anything here. I will take good care of the children, and I won't be telling them nary thang bout the accident."

Carolyn slapped the reins hard across the horse's backs. Sarah and Becky held on tight as the buggy cleared the gate in a cloud of dust, with Cricket barking and trying to give chase. By the time they got back to Dr. Parks' house, a crowd had gathered at the post office, waiting for it to open. A couple was sitting on Dr. Parks' porch waiting to see him. Carolyn told them to come back later because the doctor was off on a short trip, and would return soon. The three women went inside where Carolyn changed into a dress. Becky and Sarah pleaded with her, "Carolyn, you must have heard Tom say more, did you hear a name, or who it was that got shot, and how bad, please Carolyn, if you know anything please tell us." She told them that Tom did say that Rufus and Clark had been shot, but that's all she had heard. Hearing the news that Clark had been shot, Sarah sank to her knees, pale, clutching her chest, gasping for breath. Carolyn pumped cold water onto a white rag, holding it to Sarah's forehead while Becky put her arm around her, crying with her. Sarah sobbed, praying and trembling for ten minutes until she regained enough composure to speak again.

Taking Sarah's arms around their own shoulders, Becky and Carolyn managed to lift her to her feet, and carry her to the big leather sofa. As they laid her on the sofa Carolyn tried to offer her a ray of hope. "Sarah, she whispered, honey we don't know how bad it is yet, and maybe, just maybe it isn't as bad as we think. Let's pray and hope for the best until they get here."

Sarah sobbed and nodded in agreement. Becky stepped out to the front porch and looked over the crowd, recognizing a friend of Rufus's from the mountain - Ernest Walsh. She walked toward the post office, yelling, "Ernest, could you come here?" Ernest came trotting over toward Becky. "Yes ma'am, Miss Becky, what can I do fer ye?" Becky quickly explained about the accident, asking him if he would ride up into the mountain and fetch Claudette. She knew that Claudette needed to be here when they brought Rufus out of the woods. Ernest assured her, "I shore will, be right back with Miss Claudette afore ye know it Miss Becky." Before Becky had time to thank him, he was gone. All she saw was the dust behind the wagon.

Most of the people at the post office were from the church. Becky walked over and told them that there had been an accident and that some of them should go to the church and ring the bell. Ringing the Church bell at any time other than meeting time was a signal to let everyone know that something bad had happened, and for all who would to meet at the church and begin praying for the situation, whatever it might be. Without any hesitation or questions they all went straight to the church. Becky turned to walk back to Dr. Parks' house when she saw Dr. Parks and Jeff coming out of the woods. Her heart almost stopped at the sight of her husband. She knew the person on the man-made stretcher was Rufus. She assumed that Clark and Tom must be right behind them. She ran toward the three as fast as she could run. As she approached them she noticed that Jeff and Dr. Parks had dried blood on their hands and clothes. She turned pale, crying, "Jeff, honey I am so glad you are safe. Are you sure you are alright?" Jeff assured her that he was alright as they carried Rufus down the steps into the Clinic.

Rufus was as white as the bed in which they laid him. Once they had gotten him into the bed, Jeff turned to Becky. They held each other so tightly as though they would never let each other go ever again. Jeff whispered, "Sweetheart, let's go outside for a moment." Jeff told Dr. Parks that he would be just outside the door. Dr. Parks nodded as Carolyn brought him wet cloths with which to wipe the blood from his hands. He immediately turned his full attention to Rufus, listening to his heartbeat and lungs, and feeling his pulse. Outside, Jeff told Becky that Clark was dead, and that Tom was alright, and that General Horton and his uncle Burley were both dead. Becky broke down, sobbing her heart out. Her thoughts went to her friend, dear sweet Clark Puckett. How would she and Jeff ever be able to tell Sarah? And there were Mollie and Carter. She held onto Jeff as he told her the whole story - how General Horton and his uncle Burley were members of the KKK, and had been targeting Tom, Clark and himself, just waiting for the right time and opportunity to kill them.

Becky finally stopped crying, and tried to dry her eyes before they went in to tell Sarah. Carolyn had seen them standing outside talking. Jeff motioned for her to come out. She met them at the door with some fresh water in a basin and clean rags. She also handed Jeff one of Dr. Parks' clean shirts. She went straight to the clinic, leaving Sarah in the house. And although she had known all along that Clark had been shot, but not that he had died, she felt that that kind of news was best delivered to her by her two best friends – Becky and Jeff. Jeff and Becky walked inside the sitting room. Sarah jumped up and threw her arms around Jeff. "I am so glad you are alright Pastor." Looking past Jeff she asked, "Where is Clark?"

As Jeff held both Sarah's hands in his, she saw the horrifying truth in his eyes before he said a word. Her knees buckled again. Jeff caught her in his arms, carrying her to the sofa and kneeling down beside her. Sarah turned pale as a ghost as her eyes filled with tears. She looked at Jeff with a pleading look in her eyes. "No, No, No," she whimpered. In a broken voice Jeff told her, "Sarah, there was a shooting. Rufus and Clark were shot in the back, and Clark didn't make it." Sarah's whimpers became screams. She slid from the sofa onto the floor where she sat on her knees, her hands covering her face, screaming and crying with every breath. All that Becky and Jeff could do was to cry with her. Becky knelt on the floor with her arms around her friend, holding her like a child, as they rocked back and forth. Dr. Parks heard the screams and came in with some medicine. He said it would help calm Sarah down a little. Becky managed to get her to take it after she had cried her heart out. Sarah had so many questions, and Jeff answered them as best that he could. It was painful reliving it each time he had to tell it.

By now word of the shooting had gotten to the new Sherriff of Preston County, Clarence Murphy. He showed up at the doctor's house to talk to Jeff and Dr. Parks. After being filled in on the identities of the killers and the details of the killings, he got his deputies and a few volunteers together. Ten men headed up the mountain to help bring the dead men back down. Claudette arrived with her father Foster Flemmins. She jumped down from the wagon before it stopped, nearly falling. Becky met her at the door, escorting her down to the clinic. She took one look at Rufus' seemingly lifeless form, and fell across his chest in tears. Dr. Parks gently took her by the shoulders lifting her up, explaining to her that Rufus was in a deep sleep so that his body would heal. He told her that Rufus would have to lie very still for quite a long time, and that he would have to have special care if he were to recover. Dr. Parks invited Claudette to stay there with Rufus at their house until he could be moved. With tears still flowing, Claudette threw her arms around Dr. Parks.

"I shore do thank you doctor, I ain't never going to furget what ye did fur my Rufus. And we both will be furever beholding to ye." Dr. Parks assured her that he needed no thanks, and that he was just thankful that he was there for Rufus. He looked at Jeff with a big smile, adding, "Pastor Townsend, this is why I left New York and settled here, God is so good to his people."

Jeff went to the church where most everyone was gathered. When he told the people what had happened, all the men removed their hats, bowing their heads, crying for the loss of a good man, praying for his wife and family, and for Rufus and Claudette. Some offered to take Sarah and her children into their home. Jeff informed everyone that Clark's body was to be laid out at the Church, and the burial was to be near the church where Melvin Jenkins and his family were buried. The plot would later become known as The Jenkins Memorial Cemetery.

Jeff and Becky took Sarah to their house. Jeff sat with Mollie and Carter on the big sofa, explaining to them how their father had died. He told them of Clark's bravery and self-sacrifice, how he had refused medical treatment, so that Rufus would stand a better chance of living. Jeff explained to the two children that their father was now with Jesus in Heaven, and that they would see him again someday. As Jeff spoke softly, Mollie sobbed, burying her face in her mother's lap. Carter got up and ran out of the house and into the barn. Jeff allowed the little boy a few moments to himself, and then followed him. Carter, trying to be brave, couldn't hold his tears any longer. He fell into Jeff's arms, crying with no shame. After Carter had regained a bit of composure, Jeff explained, "Carter, my friend, you are going to be the man around your home now, and you will have to be strong for your mother and sister. I know your father would be very proud of you. I promise you Carter, if you ever need me, day or night, I will be there for you and your family."

Tom waited patiently for someone to come. The lifeless body of his friend Clark Puckett lay there covered with a blanket that Pearly Mae had packed for Tom. The blanket itself was soaked with Clark's blood. The bodies of the two murderers lay just down the hill from Clark. They too were lying in pools of their own blood. Tom had lived a rough and rugged life, but he had never been put in a situation quite like this. Since he had been saved, he had avoided trouble whenever possible, walking away from several fights. This was one time he could not walk away. His heart ached for his friend Clark and his family. He wondered if the two men that he had killed were now in Hell. Neither of them had given any evidence of having accepted Christ. He thought to himself, surely no child of God could commit the hideous crime that they had committed. Tom heard the horses coming. Sheriff Clarence Murphy and his deputies approached the gory scene cautiously. Sheriff Murphy dismounted first, walking over and lifting the blanket that covered Clark Puckett's body. Walking down to the other two, he saw the emblem of the KKK on the small patches of sheets that Dr. Parks had deliberately preserved. General Horton and Burley Crawford were known far and wide as the meanest men around. It was a known fact that they had the biggest moonshine still in the state. Everyone who knew them feared them, including the law. That was until Sheriff Clarence Murphy came along. He feared no one.

Before the shooting, he had laid plans to go in and break up the still, and to either arrest or kill General Horton and Burley Crawford. Tom Tillotson had saved him the unsavory job of killing them. Now all he had to do was bury them. He barked orders to his men to carry the bodies back to the site of the moonshine still, and bury them, and to split up the still and burn the cabins. While Tom had waited for the Sheriff, he had built another sledge on which to carry Clark's body out of the woods. Sheriff Murphy had brought two strong ropes. He and Tom tied the ropes to either side of the sledge, tying the other ends around the sheriff's saddle horn. Sheriff Murphy led his horse as Tom walked silently behind. It was late afternoon when they arrived in Bruceton Mills at the office of the coroner, Wilburn Hensley.

Tuesday, April 5th, 1870. Jenkins Memorial Baptist Church

 The day of the funeral was the saddest day that the people of Jenkins Memorial Baptist church had experienced. They had lost a friend, a brother, a Deacon, a father and a husband. Clark Puckett would not be soon forgotten. Sarah had insisted that Becky, Carolyn and Dr, Parks sing Clark's favorite song - **The Old Rugged Cross**. Becky knew it would be heart-wrenching for all three of them, but they all agreed to sing it. Jeff was dreading his part as well. He and Clark were very close friends. As they loaded into the wagon with Sarah, Mollie and Carter, Jeff asked them to pause till he had a word of prayer with them. Pearly Mae agreed to keep Samuel and Ollie at home. Becky was grateful. She didn't want to expose them to such sadness.

 When they reached the church every pew was filled. Extra chairs had to be set at the ends of every pew. Scores of beautiful flower arrangements were spread across the front of the church. Jeff and Becky had to hold Sarah up as she attempted to walk to the front, where the front pew had been reserved for the family. She wept openly as she mourned for her husband. Tom stood and thanked everyone for coming and showing their respect for such a fine man. After a short prayer, he called Becky, Carolyn and Dr. Parks to the front to sing. After the song, Jeff stood to deliver the first eulogy in the Jenkins Memorial Baptist Church, a eulogy for a dear and faithful friend.

 He read from Proverbs 18:24 – **A man that hath friends must show himself friendly: and there is a friend that sticketh closer than a brother.**

 "Clark Erskine Puckett, age 49, the son of the late Erskine R. and Elizabeth Ann Dawson-Puckett, was born on March 31st, 1821 in Raleigh, North Carolina, and departed this life on April 1st, 1870 in the woods of Preston County West Virginia. On June 10th, 1851, he was united in marriage to Sarah Renee Clemson, and to this union was born two children - Carter Otis Puckett, and Mollie Renee Puckett. Survivors include his wife Sarah Renee Puckett, one son - Carter Otis Puckett, and one daughter - Mollie Renee Puckett. He was preceded in death by two brothers, Orville and Clifton Puckett. He was a Deacon of the former Valley Grove Baptist Church, and the new Jenkins Memorial Baptist Church. Brother Puckett also leaves a host of friends and neighbors who mourn his passing."

After the reading of the obituary, the Church choir, led by Becky, Carolyn and Dr. Parks sang, **Amazing Grace**. Jeff again stepped to the lectern. He began,

"Having read to you the Scripture – a man that hath friends must show himself friendly, let me say first of all that I was proud to call Clark Puckett my friend. He was a *dear* friend, one who had a way endearing himself to virtually everyone he met. His character and personality drew others to him, both the young and the old. He exemplified the life of his Lord, in that he valued the lives of others more than his own, and demonstrated that fact more than once, but especially on the night that he died, refusing to let anyone help him while another friend lay wounded and bleeding beside him. He took in a persecuted family of a different race, feeding them from his table, letting them sleep in his bed until he could help build them a home of their own, and giving them the land on which to build it.

Clark was a *dutiful* friend. Never once did he shift his responsibilities to someone else. He recognized and shouldered his responsibilities to his God, to his family, to his country and to his Church. He was always the first to volunteer for some task that others were reluctant to accept. He was a dutiful husband to his wife, a dutiful father to his children, and a dutiful servant to his Church and community. Clark Puckett was a *determined* friend. When he saw a wrong, he determined to make it right, never counting the cost to himself. When he accepted an assignment, he saw it through to the end, notwithstanding the resistance or ridicule that he received from others. Clark was also a *deliberate* friend, one who possessed the God-given gift of recognizing the difference between right and wrong, light and darkness, truth and falsehood. Clark deliberately chose to associate himself with those who love the Lord Jesus Christ. He deliberately avoided and shunned anything and everything that might bring reproach to the name and cause of Christ and Christianity. Clark was also a ***discerning*** friend, one who could sense the needs of those less fortunate than himself, a friend who didn't have to be told that someone in the church or community needed help. He felt the pain of others in his own heart. And finally, Clark Puckett was a ***delightful*** friend, one whose smile made him a pleasure to be with in any and all circumstances. He could see the brighter side of the darkest scene. When one of his friends was discouraged, Clark would not rest nor leave that friend until he had given that friend a ray of hope. Our friend is now in Heaven, where he enjoys the company of others like himself. He now delights in the glory, the presence, and the joys of his best friend, Jesus Christ. We miss him terribly already, and we will miss him every day until we meet him again in the realm of eternal glory. As we mourn his passing, let us also celebrate and emulate his life."

The dark brown casket was carried from the Church to the little cemetery by Buford Williams, Dr. Joseph Parks, Tom Tillotson, Homer Rutherford, former Sheriff John Collins, and Judge Elias Bracken.

Standing at the graveside of one of the dearest friends they had ever known, both Tom and Jeff knew that the bullet that had killed Clark, and the one that had nearly killed Rufus were only warnings. General Horton and Burley Crawford were seasoned hunters, and expert marksmen – they never missed what they intended to kill. Had it not been for Tom's quickness and accuracy with his Colt, and the surgical skill of Dr. Joseph Parks, there would have been four funerals today. The plan was to kill Jeff, Tom and Clark at the first available opportunity. Rufus had simply been in the wrong place at the wrong time. But now that he had survived, both he and the black doctor who saved his life, and their families, were fair game. The Klan knew that Jeff and a few of his friends from the Church took a hunting trip together every year on April 1st, unless that day happened to fall on Sunday, in which case the trip was taken one day before or one day after April 1st. The attempt to kill Rufus was a warning message to Jeff and Tom that anyone and everyone they loved was now a target. As Jeff said one last prayer at the graveside, he and Tom and Dr. Parks looked at each other with that knowing glance, as if to say, "We're next."

As folks slowly left the little cemetery, Judge Bracken and Sheriff John Collins, who had now become the new Sheriff of Morgan County, deliberately lingered behind in order to say a few words to Jeff, Tom and Dr. Parks. Judge Bracken shook hands with Dr. Parks first, congratulating him for his bravery, his skill, and for his genuine care for his fellowman.

"I've been hearing a lot about you Dr. Parks, he began. I'm sorry we had to meet under such unfortunate circumstances, but I just wanted to say that it's an honor and a privilege to have a man of your caliber in our midst. If you ever get the hankering to move to the big city again, Morgantown could sure use a man like you."

Dr. Parks grinned, glancing toward Jeff and Tom, placing his arms around their shoulders, replying, "That's mighty gracious of you Sir, but right now I am right where the good Lord wants me to be."

Sheriff Collins shook hands with Dr. Parks, commenting, "Well, I'll say one thing for you doctor, you're in pretty good company with these two." Dr. Parks nodded in agreement, answering, "Yes Sir, I am. I choose the company I keep very carefully, and these two ain't bad - for a white man and a half breed." All of them chuckled a little at Dr. Parks' last comment, as Judge Bracken and Sheriff Collins headed back to Morgantown.

Tuesday, April 12th, 1870. Bruceton Mills, the home of Dr. Joseph Parks.

With the ongoing care of Dr. Parks, the good cooking of Mrs. Parks, and the love of his wife Claudette, Rufus' condition improved daily. He had now been under the doctor's care for almost two weeks. The most difficult things for Dr. Parks were keeping the wound free of infection, and keeping Rufus' fever down. Dr. Parks would not allow him to go home until he was satisfied that there was no more infection in Rufus' body. After Rufus had gone two full days without any rise in temperature, Dr. Parks agreed that he was strong enough to return home.

The news about the shooting, and the ensuing events, had now spread to neighboring counties, and as far away as Pennsylvania, Maryland and Virginia. Most folks around Bruceton Mills had now accepted Dr. and Mrs. Parks as their friends and neighbors. Some never would. But one thing was certain - Dr. Parks had earned the love and respect of all those who could see past the color of his skin. Dr. and Mrs. Parks were both highly educated and articulate. Not only had Dr. Parks studied medicine, he had also studied human nature and human behavior. He was nobody's fool. He and his wife had suffered persecution because of the color of their skin since the day they were born. But neither of them had ever retaliated against their persecutors. They refused to sacrifice their dignity and integrity by stooping to the level of the ignorant. And unlike so many others, they refused to cower in their home at the threat of persecution, or even death. They lived their lives to the fullest every day, believing that the great God of Heaven had a plan for their lives, and that they were fulfilling that plan by simply trusting Him, and doing what they both knew was the right thing to do.

The only times Dr. Parks accepted any pay for his services were when patients absolutely insisted that he take something. Whatever money he received, he spent on medicines, equipment and bandages. When the community learned that Dr. Parks was especially fond of roast pheasant, he began to receive more pheasant than Carolyn could cook. Others paid the doctor with fruits and vegetables, some with chickens, and still others with pies and cakes. Hester Rutherford-Flemmins, Pearly Mae's sister, who had married Clyde Flemmins, painted a beautiful portrait of Dr. and Mrs. Parks as payment for his having saved her right hand from having to be amputated, after being bitten by a copperhead. Citizens of Bruceton Mills who had never been treated by Dr. Parks now came with welcoming gifts, thanking him for saving the life of Rufus Rutherford.

Knowing that their homes might be burned by some Klansman, or that their very lives might be in jeopardy at every turn, Tom, Jeff, Dr. Parks and Rufus continued to live their lives as they had always lived them – one day at a time. Jeff continued to Pastor the Church, and to preach revivals. Tom filled in for Jeff at the Church whenever he was away. Dr. Parks kept treating everyone who came to him, and Rufus continued working at the saw mill, as the Klan slowly faded into obscurity.

The Jenkins Memorial Baptist Church had now grown to full capacity. The crowd had become so large that the extra chairs that had been set out for Clark's funeral were left in place to accommodate everyone. The three most powerful attractions to the Church were the anointed preaching, the soul-stirring singing, and the fact that everyone was welcome, regardless of their race or politics. There was talk of having to build a bigger sanctuary. Jeff kept an eye open for any new talent or gift that might manifest itself among the congregation. He soon discovered one of those gifts in Dr. Joseph Parks. Along with his many other talents, Dr. Parks was a serious student of the Scriptures. He had read through the Bible several times, and Jeff was very impressed with his knowledge and understanding of the major doctrines of the Christian faith. And along with his vast knowledge and understanding, he also had a big heart. He reminded Jeff a great deal of his dear departed friend Clark Puckett – always concerned for the welfare of others more than himself, always reaching out to those less fortunate, and asking nothing in return.

Being the conscientious and caring Pastor that he was, Jeff took note of the character and deeds of those around him, especially those who wished to be teachers or officers of the Church. He knew who could be trusted, and who couldn't. He had now decided that it was time to ordain Tom Tillotson. And since Clark had died, he now needed another Deacon. Who better than Dr. Parks to fill that position? And so, on Sunday, April 17th, after the morning service, he approached Tom and Dr. Parks with his decision and proposition, asking Dr. Parks if he would consider becoming a Deacon of the Church. Dr. Parks was a little hesitant, not because he didn't feel qualified, but because he loved Jeff and the Church, and didn't want to stir up any trouble. Jeff assured him that he was prepared for any trouble that might arise, and that he would take full responsibility for any repercussions that might follow his announcement that he intended to ordain Dr. Parks as the first black deacon of the Church. Dr. Parks shook Jeff's hand, accepting his offer, replying, "It's your funeral Pastor."

The following Sunday, April 24th, Jeff announced to the Church that he intended to set aside Dr. Joseph Parks as a candidate for the office of Deacon, and that he also intended to ordain Tom Tillotson to the Gospel ministry. After making the announcement, he hesitated momentarily, looking out over the crowd to see what kind of reaction would follow. He heard only a few low murmurings, noticing four young men whom he had never seen in Church before getting up and leaving hastily. Jeff asked if there were any objections to either of these men being ordained to their respective offices. There were no objections. "Since there are no objections, Jeff added, we will set a tentative date of Sunday, August 28th, for the ordination." On their way out of the Church, nearly every member shook hands with Tom and Pearly Mae, and with Dr. and Mrs. Parks, congratulating Tom and Dr. Parks, as Pearly Mae and Carolyn stood proudly beside their husbands.

Sunday, August 28th, 1870. Jenkins Memorial Baptist Church

Like any other news that in any way, or to any degree, transcends or goes beyond what the general public considers to be normal, the news that a black man was going to be ordained as a Deacon, and a half breed was going to be ordained as a Baptist minister certainly qualified. Reporters hurried to get the news, newspapers hurried to print it, and gossipers hurried to spread and expand it. Jeff Townsend took it all in stride, undaunted by the publicity seekers and rumor mongers. His concern was to spread the Gospel, and to have the most qualified men he could find helping him do it. He found those men in Tom Tillotson and Dr. Joseph Parks. With every message he delivered, Tom Tillotson, with the anointing of the Holy Spirit, had made full proof of his ministry, winning souls on a weekly basis, either at his home Church, in a revival meeting, or on the streets of whatever city or town where he happened to be. Dr. Joseph Parks had made full proof of his love and dedication to God and his fellow man by the daily self-denying acts of kindness he showed to others. Having left a lucrative practice in New York City to come to an obscure little town in the hills of West Virginia, he had endeared himself to all who needed his services. But none of that was in the headlines.

The headlines read...*Local minister dubbed "nigger lover!"* The article beneath the headline read – **"A local minister, Rev. Jeffrey Townsend, Senior Pastor of the Jenkins Memorial Baptist Church, located in Preston County, seems intent upon stirring up the discontent of the local populace through a determined effort to breach all local and national tradition. It is alleged that Reverend Townsend allows and even encourages interracial marriage in his Church. According to some sources, Reverend Townsend, along with others of his congregation, harbored former slaves in their homes,** eating from the same dishes, and sleeping in the same beds with them. Reliable sources indicate that as a direct result of Reverend Townsend's beliefs and actions, at least three local businessmen from Morgantown were hanged in 1866, and another three are now serving time in the Moundsville Penitentiary.

Apparently Reverend Townsend and some of the members of his congregation have become insensitive to the sight of blood. As recently as April of this year, a local farmer and dedicated father and husband, Clark E. Puckett, as a direct result of his relationship to Reverend Townsend, lost his life in the woods just outside Bruceton Mills. It is further alleged that another close friend of Reverend Townsend, one Rufus Rutherford, lay near death for two weeks in the basement of a certain Negro doctor, Dr. Joseph Parks. We are happy to report that, unlike the unfortunate Mr. Puckett, Mr. Rutherford survived the horrifying ordeal of being shot in the back – a direct result of his relationship to Reverend Townsend. And as if all of this was not enough to satisfy Reverend Townsend's taste for bloodshed, he now insists upon ordaining the Negro doctor as a deacon of his Church. As citizens concerned for the safety and well being of our families and our neighbors families, we simply must ask Reverend Townsend – Why?

As the congregation began to gather at the Church, they were met by three reporters from three different newspapers, each of them with pad and pencil in their hands, and each asking questions at the same time. No sooner had Jeff lifted Becky and the children down from the buggy than a reporter was in his face, demanding, "Is it true Reverend Townsend, what the papers are saying, that you intend to ordain a Negro and a half breed today?" Jeff hurried Becky and the children into the Church house. "We, as a Church, are ordaining two good men today, one to the Gospel ministry, and another to the office of Deacon. You are welcome to come inside and worship with us Sir, and to witness the proceedings if you wish. That is all that I have to say for now. I have a sermon to deliver."

A more pleasant surprise awaited Jeff and Becky when they stepped inside the Church house. Standing near the front of the church, and being welcomed by Sarah Puckett, was Becky's father, Daniel Ray Davis. He had deliberately come unannounced in order to surprise his daughter, and to see his grandchildren.

As Tom and Pearly Mae, Rufus and Claudette, along with Dr. and Mrs. Parks arrived, all three reporters immediately came to each of them, notepads in hand, asking, "Gentlemen, do you realize that there is a great controversy surrounding the beliefs and practices of Reverend Townsend? Is he not your Pastor? And do either of you understand that by submitting to the religious dictates of Reverend Townsend; you are placing your own lives and the lives of others in grave danger?" Tom and Rufus glanced at Dr. Parks as if to say, "You tell him Dr. Parks."

Dr. Parks addressed the reporters, "Sirs, first of all, my dear Mother taught me to always ask, and answer one question at a time. To answer your first question, regarding the beliefs and practices of Pastor Townsend, I must answer you with another question. Have you not in your lifetime found any other person or cause for which you were willing to die? And before you answer, dear Sirs, may I add that if you have never found anything for which you are willing to die, then you have never lived. Won't you please join us in our worship service?"

The reporters were awestruck by the very appearance of both Dr. Parks and his lovely wife, and even more so by the articulate manner in which Dr. Parks spoke – his deep bass voice, the grace and sincerity of his demeanor, and the fact that he looked them straight in the eye. Without ever having met Dr. Parks before, in a matter of a minute, they realized that they were in the presence of a man who was not only their equal, but also a man of superior intellect, intelligence and integrity. For the first time in their careers, the reporters found themselves speechless. As Dr. and Mrs. Parks and Tom and Pearly Mae hesitated momentarily, waiting for a response from either of the reporters, the reporters glanced at each other, hoping that one of them could find a proper response to Dr. Parks' invitation. One of them finally broke the silence, suggesting, "It is Sunday, and we have nothing else to do fellas, so maybe we can get some more information for our stories if we go inside?"

The newsmen put their pads and pencils in the pockets of their suit coats, and followed Dr. Parks inside, where they were immediately welcomed by members of the Church. Tom invited them to sit wherever they could find a seat. The only available seats were the extra chairs at the ends of the pews. Once seated, the men were immediately impressed with the ambience of the sanctuary and the friendliness of the people. There was something different about this place – something they had never felt before. They had no idea how many families were present, but the manner in which everyone interacted with each other gave the impression that all these people were just one big family.

When everyone was seated, Jeff stepped to the podium, welcoming everyone to the service. Buford Williams came forward and led the congregation in prayer, reminding them of the special business at hand today – the ordination. As Buford sat down he nodded to Carolyn Parks at the piano. Carolyn nodded to the choir as she began playing **Blessed Assurance**. As the sweet strains of the hymn floated melodically throughout the sanctuary, it suddenly dawned upon the minds of the three newsmen that they were indeed in a sacred place. The Holy Spirit was present and powerful. These folks were singing from their hearts, and something, or someone, was helping them. A certain warmth and serenity that they had never known touched their souls. Suddenly, getting a news story didn't matter anymore. They glanced toward each other with an expression that said, "It's good to be here."

Having forgotten that they had come here to get a scoop, the three reporters listened intently as Jeff called the Church to order for a special event. Pastors and Deacons from other Baptist Churches from as far away as Morgantown had been asked to come and participate in the ordination service. As they watched the authoritative and methodical manner in which Jeff conducted the proceedings, they slowly gained a new respect for him. The same warmth and serenity with which the choir had sung now manifested itself in the voice of Pastor Jeff Townsend. They noted the humility in Jeff, as he asked each Pastor and Deacon to assist in the ordination process. They had come expecting to see and hear a demanding and domineering preacher. What they found was a humble servant to whom others responded easily.

As Tom and Dr. Parks were seated in front of the pulpit in the two big chairs that usually sat behind the pulpit, reserved for other Pastors or dignitaries, the reporters became more deeply impressed, as they listened to the questions put to the two men, and the answers that each of them gave. They were awed by the depth of knowledge and understanding exhibited by both men concerning the great doctrines of Justification, Sanctification, Redemption, Regeneration, Propitiation, Substitution, Repentance, Faith and Resurrection. They had come expecting to meet two relatively ignorant backwoodsmen who knew very little about anything spiritual. What they found were two men of great faith, dedication and understanding, who were well-prepared to fulfill the offices to which they were called.

After being thoroughly interrogated by the presbytery and other visiting ministers, Jeff asked for a motion and second that both men be declared sound in the faith. Upon receiving the motion and second, and a unanimous affirmative vote of the presbytery, Tom and Dr. Parks carried the big chairs behind the pulpit and took their places on the altar, kneeling beside each other, as members of the presbytery came around one by one, each of them laying his hands on the heads of Tom and Dr. Parks, praying for each of them individually. After every member of the presbytery had prayed, Jeff himself came and laid hands on Tom and Dr. Parks, praying the final prayer or ordination. Tom and Dr. Parks then took their places on the front pew, directly in front of the pulpit. The reporters had never seen anything like this in their lives. They sat spellbound as Jeff opened his Bible and began to preach the charge to the two men.

To the great surprise and delight of the three newsmen and the crowd, Jeff kept his message short and sweet. He spoke of only three things – *availability*, *responsibility* and *accountability*. "If we are to be faithful, functional and fruitful servants of Christ, we must make ourselves *available* to Him whenever He calls upon us. We cannot be an absentee minister. If we wish to be counted worthy of our vocation, we must accept *responsibility*. We are *responsible* for spreading the Gospel to every creature under Heaven. We are responsible to the black man, the white man, the Indian, the Chinese, the slave and the free man. And whatever we choose to do or not do with the God-given gifts and talents that He has delivered to us, we must never forget that we are *accountable* to Him who gave them to us."

As soon as the ordination service was finished, Mr. Davis came to Jeff before anyone else could get to him. After commending Jeff on a job well done, he began, "Jeff, as you know, I attend the Copper Springs Baptist Church in Cleveland

Tennessee, and we are in dire need of a good Pastor. One of the reasons I came today was to ask you and Becky if you would be interested in coming down and meeting our folks, and maybe preaching for us a couple weekends. Our congregation is large enough to pay you a full-time salary, and furnish you and Becky a nice parsonage to boot." Jeff smiled at his father-in-law, answering immediately, "Mr. Davis, I certainly appreciate your kind offer, and I'm honored that you would ask me, but the good Lord just ain't through with us here yet. But I can highly recommend a good man to you." Mr. Davis asked, "Oh, and who might this man be Jeff?" "He's the man we just ordained Sir – Tom Tillotson. I've known a lot of preachers in my time, and I don't know of any man better qualified than Tom. I'm sure he would be happy to come down and preach for you folks anytime." "Well if you recommend him Jeff, that's good enough for me. We will be in touch with the two of you very soon."

October 31st, 1870. Bruceton Mills, WV, the home of Dr. Joseph Parks, 11:00 p.m.

With Buford R. Williams now gone, Morgantown found itself in dire need of a blacksmith. Buford had taken the deed to the property with him when he was run out of town four years ago. City Council conveniently nullified the deed on record, creating a new one, with the town named as owner. Even more convenient was the fact that Wesley Phelps and his brother Orville (before Wesley was imprisoned and Orville was hanged) passed on their blacksmithing skills to Orville's two sons, Jason and Elick. A bit of political maneuvering resulted in the two young men being awarded a lifetime lease to the blacksmith shop for the payment of one dollar per month. With William Bowen in the Moundsville Penitentiary, and his brother Reese having been hanged, the Morgantown Hotel became the property of Reese Bowen's two sons, Joshua and Gideon Bowen. Certain folks around town never let the four young men forget that their fathers were hanged, and their uncles imprisoned, as a result of the testimony of two men – a certain Reverend Townsend, and a certain half breed preacher called Tom Great Bear Tilloston.

Perhaps it could be attributed to the grace of God, or to a mixture of God's grace and their Mother's gentleness, that none of these four young men inherited the deep hatred that burned in the hearts of their fathers and uncles. Another factor could have been that the powerful influences of their fathers and uncles ended early in their lives, before they became teenagers. With neither their uncles or fathers around to sow the bitter seeds of hatred and prejudice in their hearts, the sweeter and more gracious seeds of kindness sown by their Mothers were allowed to take root. But now they were teenagers, in their late teens, making major decisions and choices of their own, choices that would affect them for the rest of their lives. One of those choices was to leave Morgantown West Virginia, and to seek their fortunes elsewhere. Twenty-one miles away lay the little town of Bruceton Mills. When they left Morgantown, they left it all – the town, the hotel and the blacksmith shop. When they came to Bruceton Mills, they came with the clothes on their backs, the skills their fathers had taught them, and about one thousand dollars apiece in their saddle bags.

Although their Mothers had barely begun to teach the boys what they should not do – *hate*, they had failed to teach them what they should do – *love*. Neither of the four boys was a killer. They simply didn't have the heart for it. But unfortunately, neither of them possessed a genuine love for their fellow man either, especially not for those of a different race. While it could not be said that any of them bore any outright hatred for blacks, neither could it be said that they bore any love for them. Somewhere between the dark and bitter hatred that their fathers had tried to instill in them, and the gentler humanity of their Mothers, the four simply bore a solid dislike for anyone of a different color or philosophy. And once in a while, that dislike raised its ugly head in the form of mischief.

The front of Dr. Parks' mansion faced east. From his front porch he could see nearly the whole town of Bruceton Mills. East of Bruceton Mills, and west of Dr. Parks' home, were thick forests, laced with small streams and wider creeks, an ideal spot for four young men to hunt, fish and enjoy life to the fullest. Pooling their resources, the young men bought two acres of forested land from Dr. Parks' nearest western neighbor – Cyrus Akers. The two acres lay about three hundred yards from Dr. Parks' back porch. They quickly threw up a log cabin just large enough to accommodate their sleeping and eating requirements. Acquiring food was never a problem – they simply hunted and fished in the spring, summer and fall, then hunted and trapped in the winter. Acquiring moonshine was never a problem either, and the four of them drank their share of it on a regular basis.

Hunting, fishing and trapping certainly had their own rewards, but before long, these activities were not enough. Boredom crept into their young and restless souls. And it was Halloween night! After a few long drinks from the jug, Jason and Elick suggested to Joshua and Gideon that they should have some fun tonight. And what better way to have a barrel of laughs than to scare the pants off the black doctor and his wife! They would cut armholes in four sheets, eye and mouth holes in four makeshift hoods tied loosely around their necks, and burn a cross in the doctor's back yard. With a few slugs of moonshine in their stomachs, it seemed like the perfectly-planned harmless prank. But in the same way that their uncles had underestimated the intelligence of Judge Eli Bracken, and the courage of his wife Nola, they had underestimated the intelligence of Dr. Joseph Parks, and the courage of his wife Carolyn.

No one but Dr. Parks and his wife knew that they kept a loaded double-barrel shotgun inside a wooden cabinet just to the right side of the back door. The cabinet door had no lock, providing quick and easy access to the shotgun. The shotgun had never been fired, but it had been pointed in the faces of a few folks who had tried to intimidate them from time to time. The sight of a double-barrel shotgun with the hammers pulled back is usually enough to dissuade any would-be troublemaker from his purpose. But a shotgun – even a double-barrel shotgun, is only as effective as the person who uses it. Some folks have only one use for a shotgun – to kill or maim something or someone. Dr. and Mrs. Parks never killed anything or anyone with theirs. But four young men were about to learn just how effective a few well-placed buck shot can be as a deterrent to mischief.

They moved as quietly as their inebriated condition would allow, which wasn't very quiet, because Carolyn Parks heard them coming a hundred yards away. They were actually trying to be quieter, but the moonshine had loosened their tongues as well as their legs. They were staggering and laughing as they came toward the house, stumbling over their own sheets. Dr. Parks was downstairs in his clinic. Carolyn decided to handle the situation herself. She took the shotgun from the cabinet and slipped out the back door. She could see the four young men, but they couldn't see her. She crept over into the trees on the north side of the back yard and kept in the shadows, slowly advancing toward the four men as they came as close as they dared to the house, which was about eighty yards away. One of them fumbled in his pocket for a match with which to light the torch, with which to ignite the cross. The instant the cross began to blaze, all four of them began yelling insults toward Dr. Parks' home, and running the other way, back toward the woods. Carolyn raised the shotgun to her shoulder and began counting – one, two, three, four, five, six, seven, eight, and pulled both triggers. She heard all four of them screaming, and saw them jumping up and down, grabbing their buttocks as they continued to run.

She knocked the burning cross over with the butt of the shotgun, scooping up handfuls of dirt, throwing them onto the cross, extinguishing the fire. She threw the cross into the stream, threw the shotgun over her shoulder, and grinned all the way back to the house. Dr. Parks was standing on the back porch when Carolyn walked up the steps and onto the porch with the barrel of the shotgun still over her right shoulder. He lowered his reading glasses, looking Carolyn in the eyes, asking, "You been out hunting sweetheart?" "Nah, she replied, just some ornery varmints I scared away. I don't think they'll be back anytime soon."

Thursday, Sept. 1st, 1870. Dr. Joseph Parks' Clinic, 7:30 a.m.
Carolyn Parks was washing the breakfast dishes when she heard the loud rapid knocking at the front door. Opening the door, she saw four young, handsome, well-dressed gentlemen asking to see Dr. Parks. Gideon Bowen stammered, "Ma'am, we need to see the doc as soon as possible, it's an emergency ma'am, is there any way we can see him right now?" Carolyn couldn't help but notice that all of them kept reaching around and pulling their trousers outward, away from the buttocks. She grinned as she opened the door wide open for them, inviting them into the house.

"May I ask, what is the nature of your problem young man? I will need to give Dr. Parks a little information before sending four patients to him at once."

"Ma'am, Joshua cut in, we need to see Dr. Parks really bad, all four of us, 'cause we had a bad hunting accident last night, and we all got buckshot in us, and it shore hurts real bad."

Carolyn escorted them to the door of the clinic. Tapping lightly on the door, she called to Dr. Parks. "Sweetheart, you have four patients waiting to see you." Dr. Parks ushered the four into his clinic. "What may I do for you gentlemen?" Joshua Bowen quivered as he tried to explain. "Well, Sir, we wuz huntin, and Jason here let his shotgun go off accidentally, and us three caught it in the rear. We got buckshot in our backsides doc, all four of us." Dr. Parks grinned as he remembered what Carolyn had said last night on the back porch. He questioned Joshua, "And I suppose that after accidentally shooting the three of you in the backside, Jason here felt so bad he turned and shot himself in the backside also."

All four of the young men dropped their eyes, knowing that Dr. Parks did not believe a word of their story. He asked them to remove their trousers and lie on the bed one at a time. When Dr. Parks had sterilized the affected areas and his instruments, he began picking the buckshot from Elick's bottom, quietly singing, "One little, two little, three little Indians," as he dropped each buckshot into an empty bucket. The other three watched in agony as they heard each buck shot plink into the bucket, and Elick screaming as each buck shot was removed.

Two weeks before Thanksgiving there was the biggest snow that Preston County had ever seen. Becky was cooking food for Jeff to take over to Tom and Pearly Mae's. Pearly was way overdue to have her baby. Doctor Parks had her on complete bed rest. Her blood pressure was far too high, and she was swollen in her feet and legs so bad that she could hardly walk. Becky and Jeff took turns going over each evening so that Tom could feed his animals and get his chores done up. They all knew that if Pearly Mae was left alone she would get up and try to do the cooking and cleaning, even though Tom was a good house keeper - "*But not much on the cooking,*" Pearly Mae would say with a sweet little grin.

Becky walked to the window where she could hear the laughter of Samuel, Ollie and Jeff. They were sliding off the hill behind the house. Becky had made them bundle up before going out. Early in the fall Jeff had made two wooden sleds with runners on the bottom. "We'll need them when the snow comes," he told Samuel and Ollie.

Samuel couldn't wait till it snowed so they could -"twy it out," he said with a big smile on his face. She watched as they came sliding down the hill, with Jeff holding Ollie in front and Samuel on the back with his arms wrapped around his father's waist, yelling, "Go faster papa, go faster." All the while Ollie was laughing and squealing at the top of her lungs. As the sled came to a smooth stop at the bottom of the slope, Samuel tumbled off, getting up and dusting the snow off his clothes, begging, "Again papa, wet's do it again?" Little Ollie clapped her hands in delight, looking up into Jeff's face with that cute little smile, which he could never deny. "Alright, just one more time," he conceded. They headed back up the hill with Jeff pulling the sled, Ollie behind him, and Samuel pushing from the back. Becky smiled, knowing that one more time really meant many more times. She had promised them she would ride with them tomorrow.

Becky was really worried about her friend Pearly Mae. She was forty- two years old, and this was her first baby. Doctor Parks had expressed his concern to Carolyn and Becky one day at the office, telling them, "I am quite concerned for Pearly Mae, she seems to be having several health issues at this time and that certainly is not good for her or the baby." The fact that she was well overdue was one concern, but Dr. Parks was even more concerned by the fact that the baby had a very weak heartbeat, and neither did he like the fact that Pearly's blood pressure was staying so high. He went out to their house every day just to check on Pearly Mae.

Becky said a prayer for her as she continued to pack their food for Jeff to take over as soon as he finished his chores. She hurried and placed their own supper on the table as she heard them stomping the snow from their feet. Jeff helped Samuel and Ollie take off their snow covered coats, hoods, gloves and boots. The children came running into the kitchen, yelling…"Mama, Mama, we had so much fun!" Their cheeks were rosy red from the cold. Becky told them to have Papa help them wash up so they could eat before the food got cold. As the family sat down at the table, Samuel asked, "Can I bwess da food papa?" Jeff smiled his approval, "Yes son that would be good." They all bowed their heads as they joined hands. Samuel began, "Ward, pwese bwess, dis food dat Mama made, an give us more snow so's we can swide agin, Amen."

Becky couldn't contain her laughter. She had to get up from the table and run into the bedroom and bury her face in the pillow and laugh till she cried. She thought, "Such an innocent prayer."

After regaining her composure she went back to the table just in time to see Jeff's shoulders shaking from holding in his own laughter. Samuel and Ollie were still eating, paying no attention to the laughter. They were so tired from the sledding that soon after they ate they were both sound asleep. Jeff did his chores and headed out for Tom's place. Becky sat down in her rocker by the good warm fire with her Bible, and read till Jeff returned. She made them some coffee and a piece of apple pie, as Jeff joined her by the fire.

Jeff told her how Pearly Mae was doing and that she and Tom said to thank her for the good food. "Tom is really worried about Pearl, he added. He was crying while I was there, and said he just didn't know if he could live if anything happened to Pearl or the baby. He and I have prayer with her before I left." Jeff reached over and pulled Becky onto his lap and kissed her. "I love you Bec," he said with a tearful voice. She knew what he was thinking, "What if it was Becky?" Becky sat there with her arms around his neck. "I love you too Jeff, you are such a wonderful husband." They sat there in total silence, holding each other in one of those tender moments that seemed to last forever.

The next morning right after breakfast and morning chores, it was more sledding. And yes, Samuel's prayer had been answered – there was more snow. This time Becky went out with them. She and Ollie took one sled and Jeff and Samuel the other. They raced down the hill side by side, with Samuel and Ollie laughing with sheer delight as Cricket ran behind them barking. The fun for the children, of course, was the sledding itself. The fun for Jeff and

Becky was hearing the children's laughter, and seeing the beaming smiles on their faces.

While Becky made supper, she kept the two of them busy with a writing tablet. She asked Jeff if she could take supper to Tom and Pearl, so she could visit with Pearly Mae. Jeff hitched up the horse for her. She left early so she could get back before dark. Jeff said he would feed the children and put them to bed. She put on plenty of clothes and headed out. The snow was up to the horse's knees, but thankfully the path that led from one house to the other was clear of rocks. Her horse had traveled to Tom's and Pearly Mae's so many times he could go blindfolded.

Becky looked at the tall pine trees covered with snow. Their lower branches were bent nearly to the ground from the heavy snow, as if in prayer for her friend. She reached the cabin with no problems. Tom met her at the gate and helped her down. He ushered her into the house then led her horse into the barn. Becky thanked him, telling him that she would sit with Pearly Mae while he did his chores. As she entered the living room, the soft glow of the lamps and the warm fire were a welcome exchange from the bitter cold outside. She placed the food in the warmer on the stove. Pearly Mae lay there in the nice big four- poster bed with beautiful hand-stitched quilts.

In one corner of the big room was a wooden cradle that Tom had made for the baby, all made up with pretty quilts and blankets. Pearly Mae held out her arms to Becky. As they hugged each other Becky noticed that Pearly Mae's face was flushed, as if she had a fever. She offered to bring her a plate of food. Pearly Mae motioned for Becky to pull up a chair beside the bed.

Pearly said "No honey, jist come sit with me a spell so's we can talk."

Becky noticed that her voice was unusually weak. She drew her chair close to the bedside.

"How are you feeling Pearly Mae?" Becky inquired.

"I've been having a terrible lot of pain in my back Becky, sometime's it's so hard to breath." Becky could see the pain and worry on her face. Pearly Mae reached over and took Becky's hand. "Miss Becky, I would be much obliged if'n you would promise me something." Becky was caught by surprise, and couldn't say a word. "Promise me something," Pearly Mae insisted, shaking Becky's hands to get her attention. "Anything Pearly Mae," Becky looked at her with a tearful look on her face. Pearly Mae, still holding Becky's hands, whimpered lowly, "Ya got to promise me if'n anything should happen to me that you and Mr. Jeff will help my Tom raise this baby in a Christian way. Now promise me Miss Becky." Becky nodded, promising, "You know we would Pearly, but everything's gonna be alright." Trying hard not to cry, Becky knew she had a tremble in her voice, and she didn't want to upset Pearly Mae. She tried so hard to turn Pearly Mae's attention to something else, but it didn't work. Pearly Mae began telling the story about the time that she first told Tom about this precious baby.

"Me and my Tom wuz on our way home from church, riding right behind you and Mr. Jeff. Member Miss Becky? She smiled as her mind went back to that night. "I told my Tom that I wuz keeping a secret from him, and he said, "A secret my sweet Pearl?" I told him I had kept it for about two months, and he stuttered…"Tuh, tuh, two months?" She continued talking as though no one was in the room. She was remembering it just as it happened. "Yes darling, two months." Tom swallowed hard, pulling back on the reins with a loud whoa! "Are you saying what I think you are saying sweet Pearl?" he stammered. "Yes my love, you gonna be a papa!" Tom leaped from the wagon to the ground, yelling at Jeff and Becky out in front of them. Becky smiled as Pearly talked. She did remember. She and Jeff looked back and saw Tom running toward them with a lantern in his hand, jumping and yelling,

"Hey Preacher, hey preacher, hold up. I got sum great news."

Pearly Mae was sitting on the wagon seat bent over with laughter at her Tom acting any such way. Jeff turned and jokingly replied, "Let me guess -your horse got saved!"

Tom almost doubled over with laughter, holding his stomach. "No Jeff, he laughed, looking back at Pearly Mae. But I am so happy right now I think I could convert him. It's better news than that Jeff. My sweet Pearl is gonna have a baby! I'm gonna be a papa Jeff. Can you believe that? I'm gonna be a papa!"

Pearly Mae had stopped laughing at Tom long enough to pull the wagon on up directly behind Jeff and Becky. When she stopped, Jeff and Becky were already on the ground, ready to give her a hug and to congratulate her and Tom. It was one of those unforgettable moments of joy that they would someday share with their grandchildren - a starry night in Preston County West Virginia, when two preachers and their wives danced with joy at the news of the coming birth of another precious child. When she finished telling her story she seemed much more relaxed.

"Now Miss Becky, I shore would be obliged if'n I could have sum of that food," she said with a smile. Becky quickly walked to the stove and dipped Pearly Mae a good helping of food onto a plate, pouring her a big glass of cold milk, all the while trying to keep her tears from showing. She loved Pearly Mae so much, and hurt so bad to see her in this condition. Soon Tom came in from the barn. He quickly washed up and had supper. They both thanked Becky, remarking that they could not make it without the help that she and Jeff had given them. Becky hugged them both, telling them that she must be going while it was still light outside.

Tom went to the barn and brought Becky's horse right up to the front steps, lifting her gently into the saddle, cautioning her, "Thanks again neighbor, ya take care riding home." "Now promise you will come and tell us when it is time," Becky insisted firmly.

Tom promised her that he would. Becky headed for home with a worried mind and prayerful heart. She arrived home, putting the horse in his stall, giving him an extra helping of feed. "Thank you old fella," she said as she rubbed him on the head.

Before she went into the house she fell down on her knees in the straw, bursting into tears of sorrow, her very heart seemed to be hurting, there in the darkness, , she begged for her friend.

"Dear Lord, please, I am begging you to let Pearly Mae have this child, and live to raise it. Dear God she has been so faithful to help others, so if you would, please help her now." Give her strength to bring this baby into the world, please give her courage to know that she can do this, I ask all of this in Jesus name, Amen."

Becky remained there on the pile of straw for a while, sobbing as though it were her own child she was pleading for. She didn't want to go into the house and let Jeff see her crying, so she stayed out for a while, just sitting there in the silence. The only sounds she heard were her own breathing and the horse chewing his feed.

Suddenly the sweet smell of the hay reminded her of her home in Tennessee, where she had spent so many hours with her brothers and sisters, romping and playing in the straw when they were supposed to be doing their chores. She would give anything to be able to talk with her mother right now. Finally she had pulled herself together enough to go on into the house, hoping that Jeff wouldn't notice that she had been bawling her eyes out. The children were asleep. Jeff handed her a steaming hot cup of coffee. She sipped the coffee slowly as she expressed her concern for Pearly Mae, telling Jeff about the promise that she had made, tears coming to her eyes. Jeff held her in his arms, brushing her tears away. Once again, the two of them knelt in prayer for their friends.

With Thanksgiving only two days away Becky began her cooking. Cakes and pies had to be baked, and Jeff decided it was time to hunt down a big turkey.

"Kin I go Papa? Pwese?" Samuel pleaded. Jeff glanced at Becky as if asking her permission. They agreed that maybe he was old enough to go with his papa on a short hunting trip. Jeff had already spotted some turkeys just up on the ridge behind the barn, so it wouldn't be too long of a trip for Samuel. He told Becky that they would go there first, and if he had to go farther, he would bring Samuel back home and go himself. She made sure that they both had on plenty of warm clothing. Samuel was so proud and excited to be going on his first hunting trip with his father he hardly knew what to do. He just danced around and around, singing.

"Dowing huntin wit my papa, dowing huntin wit my papa." As the two of them stepped outside the door, Ollie tried her best to crowd herself between them. Becky picked her up in her arms and held her tight.

"You can help Mama make a cake sweet baby," she told Ollie. Immediately She climbed up into a chair, clapping her hands, letting Becky know that she was ready to help cook.

Luck was with Jeff and Samuel. They returned in less than an hour with the biggest turkey that Becky had ever seen, with Jeff in front, dragging Samuel, the sled, and the turkey behind him. After cleaning the turkey, Jeff placed it on a shelf he had built on the porch, high up, almost against the ceiling, to keep wild animals from reaching it.

The next day was filled with more baking and preparation for Thanksgiving dinner. Dr. and Mrs. Parks, along with Sarah and the children were coming if the snow was not too deep. They had all agreed that after having Thanksgiving dinner together, they would take food to Tom and Pearly Mae, and spend the rest of the day with them. Samuel and Ollie were too excited to sleep, so Jeff sat by their bed and told them the story of the Pilgrims and the Indians, and how Thanksgiving came about. After dozens of questions, they were fast asleep.

The next day Dr. Parks and Carolyn arrived early so that Carolyn could help Becky with last minute cooking. Even though the snow was still pretty deep, Sarah and the Children soon arrived. Sarah appeared more rested now, and some of the sadness had left her eyes. She had a look of contentment.

"I'll be needing to talk to ye sometime soon, just whenever ya have time," she whispered to Becky, as she removed her snow-covered coat.

"Yes, you remind me after we get the cooking done. We haven't talked in so long. I have missed you my friend," Becky replied. Sarah smiled and gave Becky a big hug. The children had grown too. Becky hadn't seen them much since their father's death.

The dinner was soon ready, and everyone gathered around the table. Becky had laid out her mother's beautiful dishes, and the white table cloth. In the center of the table, was the big turkey that Jeff and Samuel so proudly announced that they had killed. The table was set to perfection, and the food was prepared by the loving hands of three close friends, Becky, Carolyn and Sarah. With Jeff seated at one end of the table and Dr. Parks on the other, they all joined hands, as Jeff humbly gave thanks for the food, and for this special day.

"Dear Lord, he began, we come to you today to thank you for this food, and for the loved ones who have prepared it. Thank you for the friends and family gathered around this table, and for another year that you have given us. I pray that you will always find us faithful in doing your work. It is in your Son's name that we ask all these things, Amen."

"Amen," everyone resounded. When everyone had eaten to the full, the conversation began, with each person telling everyone else all the blessings for which he or she was so thankful. It seemed the time went by all too soon. The kitchen was cleaned up by the women, as Jeff and Dr. Parks hitched up the wagon for them all to ride over to Tom's and Pearly Mae's place. Packing up the food, they loaded up, bundled in plenty warm clothing and a big blanket for the children. It was about a twenty-minute ride to Tom's place.

Tom met them at the gate with a big smile. Since his sweet Pearl had been shut in, Tom himself had not seen anyone except Jeff, Becky and Dr. Parks. The two men jumped down from the wagon greeting Tom with a hand shake. They helped everyone down from the wagon. "Sweet Pearl is shore gonna be happy seeing you young'uns today," Tom said, as he ruffled Samuels hair with his big hand. Samuel loved his Uncle Tom.

Inside the door they all removed their coats and snow covered boots. All the children went straight to Pearly Mae, giving her a big hug. She was overjoyed to see them. Tears came to her eyes as she hugged Mollie and Carter. She knew how they must be missing Clark on this special day. After all the hugging was over, Dr. Parks immediately turned his attention on his patient.

"How are you feeling Mrs. Miss Pearl?" he asked politely.

"Been feelin poorly fur nigh on ta two days now," she answered weakly, still managing a smile.

"Well, if you don't mind Pearly, after you eat your food, I'd like to do an exam." Pearly agreed.

After saying the blessing, Tom sat at the table, enjoying his food, while Jeff and Dr. Parks sat with him enjoying a fresh cup of coffee. The children were being entertained by playing Fox and Geese on the floor by the fireplace. Becky, Carolyn and Sarah gathered around Pearly Mae's bedside as she ate her dinner. She had eaten only a few bites, when she handed her plate to Becky, holding her stomach as if she were in great pain.

"I am so obliged to yun's fur this good food, but my stomach jest won't let me eat." She said.

Becky then took the plate and placed it in the warmer on the stove.

"Maybe you can eat later," Becky told her, fluffing up her pillow.

She noticed that Pearly Mae looked so tired and dark under her eyes. Becky was worried. They spent several hours enjoying each other's company. Pearly Mae whispered to Becky that she didn't feel right, that something was wrong. She was very pale, and sweating cold drops of sweat. Becky called for Dr. Parks. He quickly ordered everyone out of the room except Becky, who Pearly Mae was holding onto with all her might. After doing the exam, Dr. Parks saw that her blood pressure had dropped, and the baby's heart rate was too high. It was obvious that the baby was in distress, and both their lives were in danger.

Dr. Parks knew he had to do something, and quickly, or he would lose the baby and Pearly Mae. He called Tom into the room, quickly explaining that he needed to do a Caesarean Section, (a very delicate and dangerous operation). He explained to Tom that he had assisted in a couple of these operations in the big hospital in New York. He would have to cut Pearly Mae's abdomen open, and would have only seconds to get the baby out. Tom was terrified, but trusted his friend to do the right thing. Dr. Parks called for Becky, Sarah and Carolyn to assist him.

Jeff took Tom and the children to the barn so that they could not see what was going on in the little cabin. The children were not aware of what was happening. In the barn they entertained themselves with the animals. Jeff tried to keep Tom as calm as possible. They prayed and talked about the new life that was coming into the world. Inside the cabin Dr. Parks and the women worked frantically to save two precious lives.

Dr. Parks instructed each of them on what they needed to do, and the procedure began, and was quickly over. A big healthy baby was being cleaned up by Sarah, while Becky and Carolyn assisted Dr. Parks in sewing up Pearly Mae's incision. He used sterile silver wire, which would remain there until Pearly Mae was well-healed. Then the wire would be removed. Pearly Mae had been put to sleep with Chloroform, and after Dr. Parks was finished, she began to awaken. As soon as she was alert enough, they let her see her beautiful son. She announced to them in a sluggish voice.

"We's be calling him Thomas Clark Tillotson." Sarah's eyes filled with tears, honored that they would include her dead husband's name in the name of their firstborn son. Tom and the others were called back into the house. There were no dry eyes as they watched Tom, one of the biggest men in the valley, fall on his knees beside his wife's bedside, sobbing like a baby when he saw his son and his sweet Pearl. He looked up toward Heaven, weeping.

"Lord, I know I ain't worthy to be so blessed, but I shore do thank you." He held his son with such tenderness, kissing sweet Pearl with all the love in his soul.

Dr. Parks visited each day. Becky, Sarah and Carolyn took turns staying with Pearly Mae, tending to the baby, and doing whatever needed to be done for her to recover. After several weeks, Pearly Mae was soon back on her feet, taking care of her little man, Thomas Clark, and her big man, Thomas Avery.

Fall—Aug--Sept 1873

The beautiful spring turned into hot summer, and all too soon, summer gave way to a colorful fall, and the thing that Samuel had been looking forward to - school, would be starting in a few days.. Samuel was now six, and would be attending Bruceton Elementary School. Becky's heart skipped a beat at the very thought of her little Samuel going to school. Claudette's beautiful daughter Becky Sarah would be going to school as well. Samuel could not stop talking about that. He loved Becky Sarah, and couldn't wait to get to church on Sunday to see her.

"Momma, when do we go to school, when do we go momma?" Samuel questioned.

"It will be soon, just a few more days, my sweet boy." Becky laughed, giving him a big hug.

She hoped he would be this excited after school did start. The community was getting a new teacher, a Miss Rachel Fowler, from Morgantown. Becky prayed that she would be the teacher that the children needed. She had bought Samuel new clothes from the General store as well as a book satchel, and a new silver lunch bucket. Becky wanted Samuel to have whatever he needed for school, and she and Jeff had saved extra money from the sale of crops this year. They had been fortunate to have extra corn and hay to sell to the new feed store in Bruceton Mills.

The community had met to discuss hiring a new teacher since the former teacher had retired. Miss Fowler had come highly recommended, and when the folks in Bruceton Mills met her, they all fell in love with her. She was twenty-six years old, and a Christian. Her father was a minister at the First Methodist church of Morgantown. She had followed in her mother's footsteps, her mother being a teacher in Morgantown High School. Rachel was a beautiful young woman with dark brown hair and brown eyes. She was very excited to get started with the children in the one-room school of Bruceton Mills school district. Becky, Jeff, Dr. Parks, Carolyn and all the folks in the community were all in favor of hiring Rachel. When the school was built, a two room cabin had also been built as an added incentive to attract, and keep the best teacher's, since most of them were from another community.

Becky, Carolyn and Pearly Mae had pitched in and cleaned up the cabin for her before she arrived. Becky made new curtains for the windows. The big round rug in front of the fireplace was taken out on warm days and aired out. Jeff and Tom had cut enough wood to last her all winter. The place was ready. The week before school started the teacher arrived to get acquainted with all the parents and children. They were all gathering on Wednesday evening at the school to meet the new teacher. Becky and Carolyn were delegated to greet her on Monday when she arrived in town. She would be riding in on the mail wagon.

"Oh, I am so excited," Becky smiled, as she squeezed Carolyn's arm.

"Me too, Carolyn replied, you'd think we were going to school ourselves." They both giggled.

"Mail wagon's a comin," someone yelled from down the street.

Both Becky and Carolyn stood in awe at the first glimpse of the beautiful young lady. After being lifted down by the driver, she walked so gracefully. Her long brown hair hung loosely around her shoulders and face. Her dark brown eyes sparkled as she took a quick look around the town. She was wearing a bright green dress, trimmed in brown around the hem and the puffy sleeves. A matching bonnet hung down her back. Becky and Carolyn approached the mail wagon, extending their hands to her with a warm welcome. Rachel had the most beautiful smile that Becky had ever seen. After they introduced themselves, the driver cordially offered to take her on to the school house at the edge of town.

Becky and Carolyn told her they would meet her there, and help her with her belongings. They were so excited about having a new teacher they nearly ran down the street to the little white school building. With the driver and welcoming committee helping, it didn't take long to get her luggage and some boxes into the little cabin. Rachel curtsied to the driver as he left, thanking him for his kindness. The driver tipped his hat to her, telling her that he hoped he would see her next week when he came back by again. It was easy to see that Rachel and the driver were more than casual acquaintances. He delivered the mail from Morgantown to Bruceton Mills once a week. He had introduced himself as Harvey McAllister, originally from Kentucky, but now living in Morgantown.

Rachel informed them that she and Harvey had been seeing each other for about a year, and planned to be married after the school year was finished, that they were planning to stay on here if she was rehired. After Harvey left, the three women unpacked Rachel's belongings, taking her to the nearest café for lunch. Getting acquainted with Rachel was so easy. Becky and Carolyn felt as if they had known her all their lives. Becky told Rachel all about Samuel, how that he already knew his letters and some of his numbers. Rachel nodded her approval, replying, "It's good that you have given him a good head start."

She seemed eager to start her work there. Both Becky and Carolyn invited her to their homes for dinner, as soon as she was settled in. Carolyn pointed out the window, showing her the big mansion where she and Dr. Parks lived. Rachel smiled her approval, accepting both invitations. After dinner they all parted company, promising they would see each other Wednesday night at the school.

That night Becky told Jeff and Samuel all about the new teacher. Ollie, who was now three, was listening intently, clapping her hands, chanting, "I go kool momma, I go kool." "Only three more years, sweet pea," Jeff smiled, as he kissed her on the cheek. Becky was sure that she was expecting another child, but wanted to wait a bit longer before she told Jeff. The time just wasn't right with school starting and all.

Wednesday night the school house was packed as Jeff got up and spoke to the people, and introduced Rachel. She seemed very comfortable with everyone. She remembered that at her last teaching job she had felt so shy and uneasy, as the townspeople grilled her about every aspect of her professional and personal life. These folks were different. They accepted her at face value. She spoke with such a gentle voice that everyone fell in love with her right away. Samuel hung onto every word she said, his big eyes blinking only when he had to.

On the way home he suddenly commented, "Momma, I love Miss Rachel."

"Good Samuel, you will be a very smart boy when you grow up," she replied.

Samuel piped up from the back seat of the buggy.

"Yeah and I'sa just might marry Miss Rachel. She is purty."

"Son I think we might need to wait on that for a few years," Jeff chuckled. Becky choked back her laughter. That child could come up with the funniest things to say.

The night before school started Samuel was unable to fall sleep. He was far too excited to settle down. Both Jeff and Becky tried to calm him down. Even little Ollie rubbed him on the head, muttering, "Oh tay bubby, is oh tay." Becky sang softly to him as she gently rubbed his forehead. Finally he couldn't fight it any longer, and fell asleep, but was right back up at six o'clock ready to go to school. Becky made him biscuits, eggs and fried apples. She packed his lunch in his silver lunch pail while he double checked his book satchel. Ollie came through the house rubbing her eyes with her blond hair tied in knots. While Ollie ate, Becky quickly made herself presentable to take Samuel to school. She could hardly hold back the tears just to think that her baby boy was going to school. Just knowing her family was growing up so quickly, made her happy and sad at the same time. It seemed like only yesterday that she and Jeff had met, and now their first child was going to school! She heard Jeff come into the kitchen. He was talking to Samuel and Ollie. The sounds of their happy voices made her happy. She finished getting dressed, went back into the kitchen, asked Samuel if he was ready, and said goodbye to Jeff and Ollie, giving them a kiss. Samuel quickly gave his little sister a kiss on the cheek as he proudly picked up his book satchel and lunch pail. Jeff noticed Becky's eyes welling up with tears. He pulled her gently into his arms, whispering in her ear, "He will be fine he's just going to school, not to his wedding." Becky had to smile at that. "I know you are right." She replied.

She gave Jeff a tight hug, telling him she would see him later, and for him to please put Ollie's hair in braids. Ollie had the most unruly, but beautiful hair she had ever seen. Jeff had hitched up the buggy and had it waiting at the gate. Becky seated Samuel on the front with her, and they headed out toward the school. Samuel talked all the way. When they arrived there were others already there, including Claudette and Rufus with Becky Sarah. The little girl spotted Samuel, and made a dash toward the buggy, scaring the horse. As the horse's hooves pawed the air, Becky pulled back on the reins as tight as she could. Fortunately, Rufus had already grabbed Becky Sarah out of harm's way with one hand, and took the horse's bridle in his other hand. Becky's heart was pounding out of her chest to think that a near tragedy had happened on the first day of school. Rufus was stroking the horse, speaking calmly to him, quieting him down. Breathing a deep sigh of relief, Becky jumped down and hugged Becky Sarah with all her might, almost crying. "Oh, thank God you are alright."

Claudette came over, hugging Becky, assuring her, "Miss Becky that wuz not yur fault. My little misses' jest gets excited when she sees her Samuel."

Rufus lifted Samuel down then took the horse and buggy and tied them to a tree in the shade. Becky and Claudette took the children into the school house. Miss Rachel stood at the door, greeting all her students and their parents.

"Good morning everyone," she said with a smile.

Inside they found seats for Samuel and Becky Sarah, side by side. The seats were designed to serve a dual purpose – as a seat for one student, and a desk for the student behind that student. They were seats with desks attached to the backs. Each desk had a small compartment for the student's books and writing tablets. On top of the desk was a small round hole to hold their pencils. The teacher's desk sat up front. Across the wall, directly behind the teacher, was a long blackboard, complete with chalk and two erasers. A small table sat in the back corner, with a shiny silver bucket filled with fresh cold water and a long silver-handled dipper hanging from the wall just above the table. At the back of the room, behind all the seats, was a big, black pot-bellied stove, and a wood-box filled to capacity. Becky and Claudette stayed with their children till everyone else had arrived. Then they reluctantly said their goodbyes.

Another thing that made the Bruceton Mills Elementary school an attraction to prospective teachers was the fact that a reputable doctor lived so close to the school. Every parent knew that if their child should become ill while at school, they would be promptly treated by Dr. Parks. In fact, Carolyn Parks had volunteered to periodically check on the students, just to be sure that no one was sick. Becky, Claudette and Rufus went to the little café for a cup of coffee before they headed back home. Each day after that first one seemed a little happier than the day before for Samuel. He loved both the school and the teacher, and never missed a day. After teaching for only a month, Miss Fowler informed Becky and Claudette that Samuel and Becky Sarah were both outstanding students and were a pleasure to have in her class. The community was well pleased with Rachel Fowler, assuring her that she could remain in the Bruceton Mills School district for as long as she wished. After seeing that Samuel was happy in school, and that all was settled down in the Townsend home, Becky decided it was time for her to tell Jeff that she was expecting another child. Jeff, of course, was overjoyed, and immediately started making plans for an additional room. Samuel was big enough now that he no longer wanted to share a room with his little sister. He was delighted to learn that he would be able to have his own room.

Spring of 1810, Knox County Kentucky

Three year old Mary McAllister awoke the morning of her third birthday lying in her little bed, fully expecting to have mama come in any minute and pick her up and carry her into the kitchen for breakfast. She waited a bit longer, but mama didn't come. She waited a few more minutes, but mama still didn't come. Mary eased out of bed in her cotton night shirt and started to go into the living room. Her mama and papa were lying on the living room floor, blood gushing from their heads. With her dying breath, Mary's mother screamed her daughter's name – Mary! Mary! Before Mary could even start to cry, the big hand of a Cherokee Indian was cupped over her mouth, preventing her from screaming.

It was the last time she would ever see her parents. She was taken to an Indian village deep in the woods, where she became the daughter of the Indian brave who had killed her parents and had stolen her. He named her Ahyoka, which means *"she brought happiness."*

The little white girl did indeed bring much happiness to the Cherokee tribe, who now had become her family. In spite of the fact that she was white, she was accepted by all the Cherokee children, and played with them as if they were her own flesh and blood and they with her. She was taught the language and ways of the Cherokee. She was also taught never to trust the white man. Her Cherokee father, Great Elk, reminded her often that he had done her a great favor in rescuing her from the evil whites.

In the spring of 1824, on her seventeenth birthday, she was married to Small Deer, the son of Great Elk, the brave who had stolen her. Nine months later she lost her first child – a son that was stillborn. Her husband and the whole tribe now looked upon her differently. In their thinking, not only was she inferior to them because of being white, but she was also inferior to the Cherokee women in the tribe, none of whom had ever lost a child. There must be something evil within her if she cannot deliver a living child. She was looked upon with suspicion. The tribal elders wanted to banish her from the tribe. But Small Deer loved her, and pleaded that she be given another chance to bear a living son for him. In the fall of 1827, another son was stillborn. There was nothing that could be done now to persuade the tribal elders to allow Ahyoka to remain. Small Deer himself now had deep suspicions that his wife might be possessed by evil spirits. He asked the elders to have the Cherokee medicine man perform a Cherokee exorcism upon her. Ahyoka refused to submit to the ritual.

Her refusal to submit to the ritual infuriated the Chief and the tribal elders. They believed that her refusal itself was further evidence that she was indeed possessed by an evil spirit. She must be banished from the tribe forever. Small Deer's love for Ahyoka was stronger than his family ties. He told his father, "If she is banished, I am banished with her." With a deep sadness, Great Elk informed the tribal elders of his son's choice. Both Small Deer and Ahyoka were immediately driven from the village by every member of the tribe, who chased them, throwing sticks and rocks at them as they ran. Their only possessions were his bow, a few arrows, two small pieces of flint, and a hunting knife.

His choice to remain with his wife and to abandon his own people was the highest insult that a Cherokee could inflict upon his people. Choosing to live with a white woman who could not bear living children, over his own flesh and blood was an unforgiveable sin. Driving him from the village was only a prelude to something worse to follow. They were simply giving him a head start, a running chance to escape with his life until they could hunt him down and kill him, and both Small Deer and Ahyoka knew it. It was now midday, and they were given until tomorrow's sunrise to get as far away from the village as they could get. Then a hunting party would be sent after them. They were literally running for their lives. Banishment from the tribe also meant that even if they somehow managed to elude their pursuers, and survive, they were never to come near the village again for the rest of their lives. If either of them were ever seen near the village, they would be killed.

They ran as fast and as far as Ahyoka's legs would allow her to run. She fell to the ground in sheer exhaustion. She could go no farther. Small Deer knew that if they could make it to the Great Waters, and somehow get across, they stood a good chance of escaping. He allowed Ahyoka to rest while he gathered berries and roots for them to eat. With less than two hours of daylight left, they ran toward the southeast, stopping to rest only when Ahyoka could run no farther. They swam across the Cumberland River just before dark. Feeling safer on the other side of the river, and knowing that they could not go any farther in the dark, they lay down and slept till dawn. Waking at dawn, they ran for an hour and rested, eating whatever they could find that was edible, and running again till they were both near exhaustion. In the evening of the second day after they were driven from the village, they crossed Black Mountain into Virginia.

Since the day that she had been taken from her home in Kentucky, one horrible memory had haunted Mary every single day – the voice of her dying Mother screaming out her name. She couldn't remember much more than that, but once in a while, images of her Mother holding her in her arms flashed into her mind. She knew two things. She knew that she was white, and that her real name was Mary. She had lived as an Indian for fourteen years, and had learned their ways and customs, but she always knew, somehow, that she was not one of them. And now that she had been rejected and driven from them, she remembered the words of her father-in-law, Great Elk, **"Never trust the white man."** She looked at her own skin, and at the skin of her husband, and began to weep. In her broken and confused heart she asked silently, "Who can be trusted?"

Her marriage to Small Deer was an arranged marriage, forced upon her by the tribal elders. In her heart she had never felt any emotional or physical attraction to her husband at all. She obeyed him because she was taught to obey him. She gave herself to him because she was taught that she was inferior to him, and that being inferior to him, she was to submit to his superior will and wants, but something inside her erupted every time he touched her. In obedience to his will, she gave him everything he wanted – except her heart. She was not in love with him, and both of them knew it.

Sitting alone under the shade of a huge beech tree, waiting for Small Deer to return with something to eat, and feeling the last warm breezes of early fall against her skin, she removed her deer skin dress and moccasins and stepped into the cool stream. The cold water flowing over her body seemed to momentarily wash away all the horrible memories of her past as she laughed and splashed the cold water over herself, oblivious to the fact that Small Deer had returned with a large pheasant. He stood silently, watching her beautifully tanned body glisten in the sunlight. She was so beautiful. His desire for her body flamed in his heart. Quickly removing his vest and loincloth, he ran into the stream. She stood motionless as he took her into his arms, kissing her neck and stroking her body. He picked her up in his arms, carrying her out of the water, and laying her down upon the moss beneath the beech tree.

They survived the winter in a cave, eating whatever Small Deer could kill with his bow or his knife. Fortunately, his hunting skill had provided them with enough deer and bear skins to keep them warm. In March of 1828, it was plain to the eye that Ahyoka was with child. She had known since November, but was afraid to tell her husband. The possibility that she might lose another child was almost more than she could bear. She had decided to wait until he could see for himself that she was with child, and see what his reaction would be. The first time Small Deer began to notice her belly getting larger, he eyed her with a look of disdain. She could feel his contempt for her in his voice, and could see it in his eyes. She was now six months in the family way, living in a cave, with a man whose love for her had now turned to hate.

She wrapped herself in her deer skin blanket, easing herself close to the fire, and pretended to be asleep. Small Deer wrapped himself in his bear skin blanket, curling up on the opposite side of the fire. He also pretended to be asleep. He watched Ahyoka cautiously, and waited for the dawn. When he was satisfied that she was fast asleep, he slipped silently out of the cave. She wept silently as she heard him pick up his bow and arrows. Without so much as a backward glance, he vanished into the woods, headed northwest, toward Kentucky. Alone, and with no food or any means of obtaining any except with her bare hands, she left the cave at daybreak. A tiny plume of smoke ascended from what was left of the fire. She knew that Small Deer would try to make it back to his family and plead for his life. She had no idea where she would go, but her instinct told her to go in the opposite direction from which he had gone. Her instinct was correct.

Lieutenant Avery Thomas Tillotson, with a small detachment of soldiers from Rose Hill Virginia, was dispatched on a hunting expedition to find meat for the handful of militiamen stationed there. Ahyoka heard the reports of their rifles. As far as she was concerned, she had nothing to lose. She deliberately walked in the direction of the rifle shots. She would commit her life and the life of her unborn child into the hands of the Great Spirit, come what may. She didn't see the rattlesnake coiled less than four feet in front of her. With her next step she saw the white man, with his rifle pointed in her direction. The words, *"Never trust the white man,"* echoed in her mind. She was dressed like an Indian. "Would the white man kill her?" She asked herself. "Don't move," Lieutenant Tillotson ordered. She froze instantly. He slowly and quietly handed his rifle to the soldier behind him, easing his long black whip from his shoulder.

"So this is the way of the white man." She thought.

The rattler began rattling and hissing. Lieutenant Tillotson's whip snapped off the head of the rattler with deadly accuracy. Ahyoka fainted. She woke up in the arms of a tall handsome soldier with light brown hair, brown eyes, and a gentle smile. He was wiping her face with a yellow scarf soaked in cold water.

"Ma'am, you are safe now," he assured her.

Although she didn't understand his words, she understood the sincerity and kindness in his voice. She felt no fear at all. "What is your name?" he inquired.

She shook her head, saying nothing. He pointed to himself, saying, "I am Avery Tillotson." She now understood that he was telling her his name. She placed her hand upon her breast, replying, "Ahyoka." Lieutenant Tillotson quickly turned to Sergeant Raines, who had learned the Cherokee language. Sergeant Raines came forward, kneeling beside Lieutenant Tillotson. Speaking in Cherokee, he asked if she had a Christian name. Tears filled her eyes as her mind raced back to that morning long ago. Through her tears and whimpering she managed to reply, "Mary," "Mary." With Sergeant Raines interpreting his words, Lieutenant Tillotson told her that they needed to get her to a place of warmth and safety. She nodded in agreement, answering, "Yes." Lieutenant Tillotson helped her into the saddle, and climbed up behind her, taking the reins in one hand while wrapping his other arm around her to hold her steady in the saddle. The detachment made its way slowly back to the fort, which was little more than a two-story log fortress, manned by a few militiamen who guarded the town against raiding Indians.

Small Deer knew what the consequences would be if he were to be spotted by anyone from his tribe. But if he could somehow slip into the village undetected, and without the white woman, maybe he or his father Great Elk could persuade the elders to spare his life. He walked for four days, mulling over his options. The spirits were tearing at his heart. Should he turn back and take his chances on surviving alone, or should he take his chances that the Cherokee would accept him back into their midst? Standing on the bank of the river, he slung his bow around to his back, and dove into the river, swimming to the other side. Reaching the muddy bank, he reached for some small bushes by which to pull himself up onto the dry ground. Reaching the top of the bank, he pulled himself forward on his belly. As he started to get up, an arrow pierced his heart. He fell backward, tumbling down the muddy bank into the river.

In less than two months Mary had learned to speak English well enough to be understood. With Sergeant Raines helping her, she had told Lieutenant Tillotson and commanding officer Captain Daniel Smith as much about herself as she could remember, including her losing two children, and being driven from the Indian village, and being abandoned by her husband. She no longer wanted to be called Ahyoka. She wanted to be called Mary. As Mary related her story, Captain Smith listened intently, glancing from her to Lieutenant Tillotson. When Mary had finished her story, Captain Smith told her and Lieutenant Tillotson that he remembered a story of a little girl named Mary McAllister, who had been stolen from her murdered parents by a band of Indians about fifteen years ago in Kentucky. Putting the pieces of Mary's story and the story of the little girl together, there was little doubt that Ahyoka was indeed Mary McAllister. Upon hearing the words of Captain Smith, the horrifying image of the morning of her third birthday again flashed into her mind. Knowing now who she was, and where she came from, she asked the Captain what had happened to her parents. He told her that to the best of his knowledge her parents were buried just outside the little town of Barbourville, in Knox County Kentucky, about fifty miles from Rose Hill Virginia.

Mary was nineteen years old, and seven months with her third child, having lost the first two. Among the little group of military men, she was treated with the utmost respect. She had become like a sister to all of them. She insisted upon earning her keep. The men tried to dissuade her from working so hard in her condition, but she insisted that she was quite capable of carrying her own weight. She had watched them polish their boots with dubbin, a mixture of beeswax and lampblack. While they were asleep she would steal their boots, polish them, and place them back by their beds. Waking up the next morning, every soldier had clean shiny boots. She was up before dawn every morning cooking breakfast for them, and bringing it to the table. Everyone began to notice that Lieutenant Tillotson always got larger servings than the rest of them. They also noticed that Lieutenant Tillotson spent every spare moment either helping Mary do chores, or taking her for long walks. The inevitable happened – they fell deeply in love.

On the evening of Saturday, May 17th, 1828, Lieutenant Tillotson looked into Mary's eyes, took her into his arms, and kissed her passionately. On Saturday, June 7th, he asked her to be his wife. On Saturday morning, June 28th, her son was born, and was very much alive, and perfect. She named him Thomas. On Tuesday, July 1st, Lieutenant Tillotson and Mary McAllister became man and wife, with Captain Daniel Smith performing the ceremony. Lieutenant Tillotson not only took Mary to be his wife, he also took Thomas to be his son. He loved him like a son, and raised him like a son. He and Mary agreed to call their son Thomas Avery Tillotson.

Being the son of an Army Officer had its advantages, but it also had some disadvantages. Lieutenant Tillotson and Mary did their best to give their son a good education and a Christian home. The family, however, was often uprooted, due to Lieutenant Tillotson being transferred to various outposts of the still relatively young frontier. It seemed that each time they got settled in and accustomed to life in one place, he was transferred to another, and the whole family had to re-adjust to new surroundings. Lieutenant Tillotson tried to spend as much time with Tom as he could, but being an Officer in the U.S. Army required a lot of time and energy, and he was now up for promotion to the rank of Captain.

Mary was very understanding, and quietly accepted the fact that being married to an Officer not only imposed stringent requirements upon her husband, but also upon her and their son. Far too often, she had to be both mother and father to Tom. As Tom grew older, he became fascinated with the military way of life. His young mind was enamored by the precision with which the soldiers walked, how they saluted, and how they meticulously cleaned and maintained their weapons. When Captain Tillotson decided that Tom was old enough to accept some responsibility, he began to train him in the proper use of all kinds of weapons. It was obvious that he was training Tom to be a soldier. Mary didn't like the idea at all. She wanted Tom to grow up to be anything but a soldier. But being around soldiers on a daily basis was bound to have an effect on him, and she knew it. Tom could sense the tension between his mother and father. Sometimes at night when they thought he was asleep, he heard them arguing about how he was being raised.

Whenever Tom could sneak away from Mary, he spent every spare moment practicing with rifles, pistols, and knives. And when he wasn't practicing with the weapons, he was cleaning them. And when he wasn't using or cleaning weapons, he was riding horses. But the one thing that got and kept his attention the most was his father's black leather whip. No one was as accurate with a whip as Captain Tillotson, but at the tender age of ten, Tom was almost as proficient with the whip as his father. Another thing that greatly troubled Mary was the fact that Tom also had a fascination with pistols. When he wasn't playing with his father's whip, he was practicing the quick draw with his pistol.

Being the son of an Army Captain was one thing, but being half Indian was another. Wherever Tom and his family went, there were always some folks who noticed nothing else except the fact that Tom's skin was darker than theirs. Tom often had to endure the taunting and racial slurs of other children and adults. On his tenth birthday, Mary told him the story of his real father, Small Deer. And to make matters worse, Captain Tillotson was transferred in 1838 to Fort Cass Tennessee, where the last of the Cherokee were being deported west along what was to become known in American History as "***the trail of tears***". It was a time when force won over decency and power won over justice. Tom, standing beside his father, watched, as many of the men, women and children whose bodies had been emaciated by disease and starvation trudged toward an uncertain destiny. Nearly one third of the 4,000 deaths of the Cherokee were attributed to the conditions under which they lived in the concentration camps, otherwise known as removal forts. Captain Tillotson stared down into the tear-filled eyes of his adopted son. He saw the hurt in his son's eyes. But there was something else there also – a certain loss of respect for the half of him that was white, and a deep sympathy for the Cherokee, many of whom would not live to see another day. He saw the glances of the young Cherokee boys as they passed by, knowing that they saw the color of his skin. Tom knew that the only reason that he himself was not being deported was the fact that he was standing beside a white man, wearing a blue uniform.

Tom's young inquisitive mind could not rest without asking his father and mother why the Cherokee were being forcibly driven from their land. He reminded them of what he had read in school about *"all men being created equal"* and how that *"all men are endowed by their Creator with certain unalienable rights, including life, liberty, and the pursuit of happiness."* Mary deflected the question to her husband. The only answer that Captain Tillotson gave his son was, "Someday son, when you're older, you'll understand."

Cleveland Tennessee, 1846

With the removal of the Cherokee Nation to Oklahoma, the removal forts were no longer needed, and neither were the soldiers who manned them. Some of the camps lingered for a while, but slowly, one by one, they either disappeared or became historical landmarks. Sergeant Raines, who could speak three languages, was also a fine artist. When he received his orders, he informed Captain Tillotson that he would be moving to Georgia. Captain Tillotson asked him if he would paint a portrait of Mary before he left. In 1846, Captain Tillotson decided that it was time to retire from military life. He bought an acre of land in Cleveland Tennessee, not far from Fort Cass, and built a small two-bedroom house. With all the coaxing and training that he had done, Tom could not be persuaded to become a soldier. Tom was now eighteen, and had plans of his own.

Tom loved both his parents, but was being constantly pulled in two directions by them. His father wanted him to be a soldier, while his mother urged him to continue his education, and to pursue any career he chose, except becoming a soldier. Tom decided that he would do neither. There were two things that had been tearing at his insides – the image of the Cherokee being mistreated by the white man, and the story of his Cherokee father deserting him and his mother. He kept asking himself which was worse – being half white, or being half Indian.

Tom knew that sooner or later he would have to come to terms with who he was. He would have to choose one of two ways – the way of the white man, or the way of the Cherokee. But for now, he would choose neither. On the night of June 29th, 1846, the day after his eighteenth birthday, Tom slipped quietly out of bed, got dressed, and rode away from Cleveland Tennessee, taking only two things with him – his father's whip, and his mother's portrait. He rode slowly toward the northeast, into the deep and dark forests of a land that would someday become known as West Virginia.

Becky was overjoyed when she left Dr. Parks' office that day. He had informed her that, while checking for the baby's heartbeat, he had heard two heartbeats.

"Becky, he said, I am pretty sure that there are two babies in there, but we will keep a close watch, and I want you back in here next week, is that clear?"

"Yes, Dr. Parks, she replied, but may I tell Jeff that there is a possibility that we will have twins?" Dr. Parks gave her that solemn expression of his, replying, "Well, I'd rather you keep this to yourself till next week, then we will know for sure, and then you can tell him."

Becky agreed. She left the office ecstatic at the news that she and Jeff were having twins. She was meeting Sarah at Mama's café for dinner, remembering that Sarah had told her that she had some rather important news to share with her today. Samuel and Ollie were in school, and Jeff was working in the fields at home. As Becky crossed the street, she noticed that the town was unusually busy today. Wagons and horses were crowding the busy streets. She spotted Sarah sitting at a table in the back of the Café. Sarah waved her hand, motioning her to come and sit with her. After greeting each other with a hug, the two women sat down and ordered their food. Becky couldn't wait to share her news with Sarah.

"So what is the big secret that you wanted to talk to me about?" Becky asked with a smile.

Sarah reached across the table, grasping Becky's hands in hers. She hardly knew where to begin, "You know how much I loved my dear Clark." She stated.

"Huh…yeah," Becky replied, as if she understood that it was a rhetorical question.

"And you know that I would never hurt you." Sarah continued. "I cannot live alone Becky. It has been so hard since Clark passed on, and I will never find another man like him, but I have found someone." Sarah eyes sparkled at the mention of that *someone*.

Becky was so excited and happy for her friend she couldn't stand it any longer.

"Oh, please Sarah, tell me who." "Do I know him?" "And when is the wedding?"

Sarah couldn't bear to think that she might hurt Becky. She loved her as if she was her own. She began in the only way that she knew how.

"Becky dear, It is your father, Daniel," Sarah whispered in a soft kind voice.

Becky quickly jerked her hands from Sarah's hands!

"What!" Becky almost shouted. Suddenly she became very quiet, searching for words to say, but all she could hear was the echo of Sarah's voice, "Becky it's your father."

She couldn't imagine her father with anyone but her beautiful mother! This couldn't be true. She quickly excused herself, almost running from the Café with tear's streaming down her face. She ran straight to the Parks' house. Carolyn came to the door and found Becky sitting in a chair with her face in her hands, crying like a baby. Carolyn's heart was pounding out of her chest as she tried to get Becky calmed down enough to tell her why she was crying.

"Becky, please, what is wrong?" Carolyn begged. She helped Becky into the house and gave her a cold glass of water. Becky blurted out the whole story of her father and her best friend. She told Carolyn that she knew her father would eventually marry someone, but she never dreamed it would be Sarah. Not that she minded, because she loved Sarah, but right now she would have to let it soak in. She felt so ashamed that she had been so weak, and had walked out on Sarah. Carolyn told her that what she did was normal, that she knew Sarah well enough to know that she too would understand. After they talked for a few minutes Becky calmed down. She was actually happy for her father and Sarah, but admitted that she was too ashamed to go find Sarah and tell her so.

"Well, you won't have to Becky, because Sarah is walking up on the porch right now."

Becky wiped her eyes and sat there, waiting for Sarah to come in. As Sarah walked into the room Becky ran to meet her, throwing her arms around her, apologizing.

"I am so ashamed. I acted like a baby. Please forgive me Sarah." Becky pleaded.

With tear-filled eyes Sarah embraced her friend, laughing and crying at the same time, replying, "Mrs. Becky Townsend, I will soon be ye step mama, now jest what'de ye think o' that?"

She hoped Becky would feel better now that she had gotten over the initial shock.

"I think I like that, Mama Sarah." Becky replied with a big smile

By now Carolyn had joined in the laughter and the crying. They all sat down and listened to Sarah's wedding plans. Sarah and Becky's father were going to be married in Cleveland Tennessee. They wanted Jeff to do the ceremony. Sarah had sold the farm to the Williams family. Mr. Williams, of course, had already set up his blacksmith shop there on the farm. Sarah let them in on another secret. She made them swear that they would not tell anyone - not even Jeff or Dr. Parks. After they swore that they would not tell, she told them that, upon Jeff's own recommendation, Becky's father had asked Tom to move to Tennessee, and be the Pastor of their church, and Tom had said yes. That meant that Tom, Pearly Mae and little Thomas Clark would be leaving. Tom was going to wait for the right time, and talk to Jeff about it. It was hard to take in all the news that Becky had heard that day. So many things were changing so quickly. When she lay down that night, she wanted desperately to tell Jeff about the twins, and about Tom leaving, but she had made a promise, so she had to keep it. Jeff assured her that it didn't surprise him that Sarah and Daniel Ray had been courting. He had noticed the way they looked at each other at the ordination. He was very happy for them.

The week seemed to drag by till Becky went back to Dr. Parks' office. After the exam he smiled that big smile that told her everything she wanted to know.

"Now you can break the news to Jeff that there are indeed two babies in there!"

Becky gave him a big hug, and out the door she ran, climbing into the buggy. She rushed home, driving into the barnyard in a cloud of dust. Jeff came running from the field.

"Bec, what in the blue blazes is wrong?" She jumped into his arms.

"There's two Jeff - two babies!" Jeff swung her around and around a few times, and then put her down, holding her by the shoulders. "Two, Becky - two babies! Oh, I have to get busy building another room."

They laughed and cried and danced around the same way they had done the day they knew that Samuel and Ollie were coming into the world, rejoicing, and thanking God for all the blessings that He had given their little family.

Becky was excited as well as nervous about going back to her childhood home in Tennessee. She had only been back a few times since her mother passed away. Now she was going back to attend her Father's wedding. She still remembered the day that Sarah had told her that she had met someone, and that it was her father. Becky had gotten used to the idea now, but she was sure that when it came to the wedding itself, it would still be very hard. Jeff loaded all the clothes that they would need into the wagon. Samuel and Ollie were excited to be going to grand papa's house. After a lot of begging from Claudette and Rufus, Jeff and Becky finally agreed to let Claudette babysit the twins, Elick and Erica. So Claudette, Rufus and Becky Sarah were staying at the Townsend farm with the twins till Becky, Jeff, Samuel and Ollie returned, on Sunday. Rufus would drive them to the train station, and return to help Claudette with the children and the chores.

It was a tearful goodbye that Friday morning as they pulled out from the house, with Samuel and Ollie waving goodbye to Becky Sarah, who was standing on the porch. Claudette was inside the house with the twins. Cricket chased them as far as the gate, barking as if he were begging to go with them. But, like every time before, he gave up, and stood in the middle of the road, giving one last pitiful yelp, then turned and walked back toward the house where Becky Sarah was calling for him.

The morning was still young, and Becky enjoyed the ride through the hills. She loved the way the fog rolled in around the tall mountains. It looked like rolls of cotton squeezed down into the valleys, with the tree tops barely piercing through. They had started early so they would make it to her father's house before the wedding. Sarah, Mollie and Carter had gone on ahead when Tom, Pearly Mae and little Thomas Clark had moved to Tennessee.

Sarah was staying with Becky's sister Emma till the wedding. There had been so many changes lately that Becky's heart seemed as if it couldn't take it all in. Jeff admitted that he was certainly going to miss Tom, who had become his best friend and also his best worker in the church. Tom was often called upon to take care of the church for Jeff when he was called out for revival; Tom had always been available, and faithful.

Rufus Rutherford was also showing all the signs of being called to preach the Gospel, and Jeff was praying that God would call him, and that Rufus would obey. Dr. and Mrs. Parks had now become two of the most loved and respected members of the community. Saving the life of a white man, and helping carry him eight miles out of the woods, and nursing him back to health had cemented Dr. Parks' character firmly into the hearts of everyone. Both he and Carolyn were now accepted for who they were. Dr. Parks was no longer referred to as the *black* doctor; he was referred to as a *great* doctor. And God had answered their prayers. Carolyn was expecting their first child in November. Before Tom and Pearly left for Tennessee, Tom had given his land back to Jeff. Jeff, of course, didn't want to take it back, but Tom insisted that it be given to Samuel someday when he grew up. The new school teacher, Rachel Fowler, had married Harvey McAllister, and they had settled into the cabin behind the school house. The Flemmins' and the Rutherford's were all still active in church, never missing a Sunday unless they were sick.

The town of Bruceton Mills was very quiet as they passed through. The only sounds were an occasional dog barking or a rooster crowing. The Parks' mansion sat majestic and still, like a sentinel, overlooking the sleeping town. Becky wished that Carolyn and Joseph were going along with them, but since Carolyn was expecting, it was much too far for her to travel. Getting through the town and back onto the trail through the mountains, they journeyed, stopping just long enough to let the children eat and stretch their legs. It was such a beautiful sight. Wildflowers bloomed along the wagon trail. The sweet smell of honeysuckle filled the air. Becky's mind was filled with memories of all the good times she, Sarah and Pearly Mae had experienced. She sure was going to miss them all.

She remembered the time that she and Jeff had come this way when they first moved to West Virginia, and how far they had come since the day they pulled their wagon onto the Townsend Farm. Becky remembered how they had made camp and slept in the wagon until Jeff got their home built. Those were such precious moments that she would never forget. She smiled again as she remembered her first impression of the valley that they would later call home – "What a Heavenly place!" The children grew tired and fell asleep in the wagon as Becky and Jeff talked and laughed, sharing memories of their friends, some of whom had moved away, and others who had gone to Heaven. Arriving at the train station, the children awoke at the sound of the train whistle. This would be their first ride on a big locomotive. There were more tears, handshakes and goodbyes as Rufus helped them carry all the suitcases into the baggage car of the train.

The train hadn't yet picked up full speed as they passed the Church and the little cemetery. Becky could just see their dear friend Clark, with his flaming red hair and infectious laughter. Through tear-filled eyes she prayed that her father would make Sarah and the children as happy as Clark had. Jeff couldn't help but notice her tears as he also reflected upon the many good times that he and Clark had shared. So many bittersweet memories flooded his own heart as they rolled slowly past the Church and cemetery. He cleared his throat, trying not to appear as choked up as Becky, but still unable to conceal the sadness in his voice, he spoke, "I sure will miss Tom. The place won't be the same without him around."

"Not going to be the same with Sarah, Pearly Mae and the children gone either," Becky replied. "I sure do wish things didn't have to change, but we will just have to get used to it," Jeff added. He reached over and took Becky's hand, and trying to shift the conversation in a different direction, he asked, "Honey, are you going to be alright with the wedding and all, I mean with your father marrying your best friend?"

Becky knew that he was just trying to steer her thoughts away from the cemetery and all the sad memories surrounding it. She smiled her knowing little smile and leaned against his shoulder, replying, "Well, it's still gonna be sad knowing that Mother is gone, but father needs someone to love and comfort him, and so does Sarah, and I can't think of a better match than the two of them."

At precisely 10:00 p.m. Friday night, they arrived at the train station in Cleveland Tennessee. Daniel Ray was there with the wagon to take them on to his house. Samuel and Ollie pretended to be hiding behind Jeff and Becky as Daniel pretended to be searching for them, asking, "Now just where are them grand young'uns of mine?"

The two children immediately jumped out from behind Jeff and Becky as if they wanted to surprise their grandfather. He pretended to be totally surprised, grabbing them both up in his arms, hugging and kissing them. He could barely hold back a tear as he observed, "My! My! How you two have grown!" He started to shake hands with Jeff, but was given a big bear hug instead. He helped Jeff load all the suitcases into the wagon, and they headed for his house, about a mile from the station.

Becky's heart nearly skipped a beat as the old home place came in sight. She half expected her mother to come running out with her arms open to welcome them, but she knew better. Sarah came out with a big smile on her face, overjoyed to see them, hugging Becky so tight that she thought she would stop breathing. After a late supper the children soon fell asleep. Jeff, Becky and her father sat on the big long porch talking and laughing. Jeff, wanting to give Becky and her father some time alone to talk about the wedding and other things, gave her a kiss and said goodnight. They talked far into the night. Her father told her that no one would, or could ever take the place of her mother. He held his daughter close as they both cried, silently recalling all the wonderful memories they had shared while her mother was alive. In the wee hours of the morning they both went to bed. Jeff awoke as Becky lay down beside him. He reached over and hugged her close to him. "Feel better?" he asked. "Yes I do, thank you sweetheart."

The next morning was charged with excitement, with friends, family and total strangers coming and going. Becky's sisters and brothers all came by to see her, Jeff and the children. They laughed and talked about the great times they had while growing up, and all the mischief they somehow managed to get into. The time flew by all too quickly, and all too soon, it was time to go to the church.

Becky's father was very nervous. So nervous, in fact, that Becky had to help him with his tie. Jeff was quite amused at all the commotion. Samuel and Ollie were all over the place. Even after Becky got them dressed for the wedding she still could not keep up with them. She just prayed that they would at least keep their clothes clean.

They all loaded into the wagon and headed out to the Copper Springs Baptist Church. When they arrived Becky went into the back room to see Sarah. There she was, in a beautiful, long, silk sky blue dress with pearl buttons all down the front. Her hair was pinned up on top of her head in curls. A beautiful blue ribbon, intertwined with her hair, hung down the back. Becky had never seen her friend look so beautiful. Sarah's smile said all that needed to be said. She was radiant with joy. They hugged each other and nearly burst into tears. They both knew that they would not be seeing each other very often any more. But they would always have their memories of Bruceton Mills, and all the wonderful adventures they had shared together. Becky gave Sarah a final kiss, and took her seat.

The church was filled with family and friends. The music started. Mollie walked in, wearing a beautiful white long lace dress, carrying a basket filled with rose petals which she scattered down the aisle as she slowly made her way to the front. Jeff, Becky's father and Tom (the best man) walked out from the back, taking their places on the right of the pulpit. The pianist glanced toward the door as Carter Puckett and Sarah stepped over the threshold. She started playing the wedding march. All eyes turned to the front door where the bride was entering on the arm of her handsome son Carter, who was now as tall as his mother. Becky noticed he looked just like his father Clark, red hair and all. Slowly they approached the front. Jeff asked, "Who gives this woman to be wed to this man?" Carter replied, "Mollie and I."

Saturday, June 3rd, 1876. Copper Springs Baptist Church, Cleveland Tennessee

It had been thirty years since Tom left Cleveland Tennessee, and now he had come full circle. He had left a bitter young man, disillusioned and disappointed with life itself. And now he had returned, older, wiser, more mature, and having a settled peace in his soul. He was now a loving husband and father, and the Pastor of a thriving Baptist Church in a thriving city. Having come here with the high recommendation of Reverend Jeff Townsend had made Tom's acceptance much easier, because Jeff's name and reputation were well-known and highly-respected wherever he went. But once the folks around Cleveland got to know Tom themselves, and had heard him preach the Gospel, his own name and reputation were soon well-established upon their own merit. There was something in Tom that transcended the color of his skin. He was a kind and gentle person, easy to get to know, and transparent. And the Holy Spirit bore witness to his calling through numerous conversions, both inside and outside the Church itself.

Mary and Avery Tillotson had not seen or heard from their son in thirty years. They had no idea where he was, or what he was doing. Tom had often wondered if his parents were still married, or even still alive. Early on the morning of June 3rd, 1876, sitting on the front porch of her home, Mary picked up the newspaper. As she turned slowly from page to page, she spotted an article that caught her eye. It was a wedding announcement. It read…

>Wedding at Copper Springs Baptist Church.
>Daniel Ray Davis, widower and deacon
>of Copper Springs Baptist Church
>announces his upcoming wedding to Sarah Puckett of
>Bruceton Mills West Virginia,
>home of the notable Rev. Jeff Townsend,
>Who will be performing the ceremony.
>The Pastor of the Church,
>Rev. Thomas A. Tillotson, along with
>the congregation, cordially invites any
>and all friends and relatives
>of the Davis and Puckett families to attend.
>The wedding will take place
>on Saturday evening, June 3rd, at 6:30 p.m.,
>with the reception in the basement of the Church.

Mary's heart leaped into her throat as she read the name again – Rev. Thomas A. Tillotson! It couldn't be possible! Her own son, a minister and pastor!? It was probably just a coincidence, someone else with the same name! Her heart pounded wildly as she bolted into the house, showing the announcement to her husband Avery. Avery read the announcement and sat bolt upright, his own heart racing. He glanced from the paper to Mary, and back to the paper again. He could barely speak as he began to get all choked up.

"Mary, he gasped, do you think it's possible? Could this be our son Tom?"

"There's only one way to find out Avery, she quickly replied. The wedding is this evening at 6:30, and we are going."

The Church was nearly filled to capacity when Mary and Avery arrived. They managed to find a place to sit on the back pew, next to the aisle. They didn't see Tom anywhere. As the ceremony proceeded, Tom's back was turned, so that they still could not see who he was. But once the ceremony was over, and Tom turned toward them, Mary knew immediately that it was her son. She elbowed Avery in the side, exclaiming, "Avery, Oh Avery, it's Tom, it's our son Tom." She forgot all about the ceremony and the protocol. She ran past Daniel Ray and Sarah on their way out, running toward Tom, nearly running over everyone who got in her way, screaming, "Tom, my son, Oh Tom, it's really you. It's me Tom, your Mother Mary!"

Avery had now caught up to Mary, and was sobbing tears of joy. He tried to speak, but the words just would not come. Hearing the voice of his Mother, and seeing her running toward him, Tom nearly collapsed. No words were needed as she threw her arms around him, soaking his shirt collar with her tears. They were both too choked up with sheer joy to say a word. They held onto each other as if their very lives depended upon it, kissing each other's cheeks and sobbing.

By now a sizeable crowd of church members and the wedding party itself had crowded around, not knowing what was happening there in the aisle. When Tom and his parents had regained enough composure to speak, Jeff and Becky had now joined them there in the aisle. Tom managed to choke back the tears of joy as he proudly announced to Jeff and Becky, "Becky! Jeff! Allow me to introduce you to my parents, Mary, and Avery Thomas Tillotson.

Mama, Papa, meet my lovely wife Pearly Mae, and your grandson Thomas Clark, and two of the very best friends we have ever known, Becky and Jeff Townsend from Bruceton Mills, West Virginia."

After a lot of pictures were taken, and the reception was under way, Tom stood up and announced to the whole crowd, "Folks, I can hardly find the words to express my gratefulness for all that the Lord Jesus Christ has done for me, even this very day. Not only are we gathered here to celebrate the wedding of two of the finest people I've ever known, but we can now also celebrate a reunion. I have found my parents, whom I haven't seen for thirty years."

Tom then asked his Mother and Father to stand. As they stood, he introduced them to the whole crowd. Everyone in the reception hall stood and cheered both the newly married couple and the re-united family. As Tom looked out over the crowd, slowly identifying each member of the Church, and recollecting how each one had come to be a member of the Church, his heart swelled with such gratitude to a loving God who chose to use someone like himself to be their Pastor. He silently looked at Jeff and Becky, recalling the circumstances under which they had met ten years ago. He looked into the happy eyes of his Mother and Father, seeing the pure joy that shined in their faces, making him simply forget about whatever grief he may have caused them by leaving the way he did. He saw the sparkle of love in the eyes of his wife and child, remembering how easily he had fallen in love with Pearly Mae so long ago. He caught a glimpse of the deep love and contentment in the eyes of Sarah and Daniel Ray, and recalled that night when Clark was murdered in the woods, and the deep sorrow that had pierced Sarah's heart upon learning of her husband's death.

And then there were Jeff and Becky Townsend, two people who, more than any others, had been such a profound and positive influence upon his own life. He didn't want to even think of where he might be right now if God hadn't somehow placed these two in his life. In them he had seen the brightest example of Christian faith and love that he had ever known. He watched with pride as the folks from the Church met and greeted total strangers, making new friends instantly. He couldn't help but notice the joyful atmosphere of this occasion. It was as if God Himself was looking down from Heaven upon this gathering, and was smiling His approval.

Knowing where he had come from, where he had been, and where he was going, Tom smiled toward Heaven, breathing a deep breath of pure satisfaction and contentment. His heart drifted slowly back to the many times when he and Pearly would walk across the field to Jeff's place, and sit on the front porch with Jeff and Becky, just enjoying a peaceful afternoon of good conversation and fellowship. Now he understood what Becky had meant, and how she had felt when she would vividly describe the places where she and Jeff had made so many pleasant memories. He and Pearly Mae now had a few of those pleasant memories of their own, memories the two of them had made in their own Heavenly places.

The End